ADVANCE PRAISE FOR

THE MUSIC OF RAZORS

"An exceedingly fine novel . . . You feel this book is true and the characters are real. *The Music of Razors* tells a beautiful and deeply affecting story, full of wonder, strangeness, pain, and love."
—K. J. Bishop, author of *The Etched City*

"This was an impressive first novel. In *The Music of Razors*, Cameron Rogers weaves a thought-provoking and compelling dark fantasy from the mythology of religion."
—Jeff Ford, author of *The Girl in the Glass*

"Slippery and quick with a bite that won't let go long after you turn the final page."
—Sean Williams, author of *The Crooked Letter*

"Jam-packed with enough extraordinary ideas to fill a dozen novels. Never was fantasy darker or more disturbing. The novelistic equivalent of *Twin Peaks*." —Richard Harland, author of *Ferren and the Angel*

"This is a great book. Alice meets Freddy Krueger in Wonderland!"
—Paul Collins, author of *Cyberskin*

THE MUSIC OF RAZORS

THE MUSIC OF
RAZORS

CAMERON ROGERS

BALLANTINE BOOKS / NEW YORK

A Del Rey Trade Paperback Original

Published in the United States by Del Rey Books, an imprint of The Random House Publishing Group, a division of Random House, Inc., New York.

DEL REY is a registered trademark and the Del Rey colophon is a trademark of Random House, Inc.

Originally published in different form in trade paperback by Penguin Books Australia Ltd., Victoria, in 2001.

Grateful acknowledgment is made to Holly Ball for permission to reprint "Playground," copyright © 2000 by Holly Ball. Reprinted by permission of Holly Ball.

ISBN 978-0-345-49319-4

LIBRARY OF CONGRESS CATALOGING-IN-PUBLICATION DATA
Rogers, Cameron.
The music of razors / Cameron Rogers.
p. cm.
ISBN-13: 978-0-345-49319-4 (trade pbk.)
ISBN-10: 0-345-49319-2 (trade pbk.)
I. Title.
PR9619.4.R647M87 2007   823'.92—dc22   2006036418

Printed in the United States of America

www.delreybooks.com

2 4 6 8 9 7 5 3 1

Book design by Casey Hampton

For Dmetri Kakmi and Barbara Welton, the godparents of this book,
for Ronald Jones,
and for Sarah Graves, who makes everything possible

Anyone alive is bait for demons.

—TERRY DOWLING

CONTENTS

THE MUSIC OF RAZORS

APOCRYPHA

Seventy-two angels fell with Samael.

As an angel is created it is gifted a function, portfolio, responsibilities. The angel charged with assigning power and function was a powerful angel indeed. Now that it grasped the concept of "rebellion" it truly understood how much power it held. *The Power to assign Power.* In the wake of this revelation other ideas followed, other realizations. This angel was staggered by the sheer enormity of what it might possess and achieve.

Thus the angel sinned.

An angel does not die. Anticipating what might occur should its audience with the Fallen One go badly, the angel seized upon another of its kind, sundered it, and stole the silver of its bones.

From those bones the angel fashioned instruments approximating its own power. As the angel named them, they existed. Mercurial and undying, the living bone was bestowed with aspects of the angel's own function. The function of assigning Form and Power. It then scattered these instruments across the Earth, a safeguard against the possibility of its own failure, and departed the presence of the God that had Created it.

The angel found Samael in His new Kingdom, and made the Fallen One an offer of allegiance. An offer to create an army more powerful than that of Heaven, to seize what they had lost.

Samael was Beauty. The angel could not look upon it. It was all it could do to remain upright and not fall to its knees, as did the seventy-two Fallen gathered around their Lord.

The angel remembered the time of Samael's birth. A thousand others had been created to sing His hosannas. "It was your touch that awoke me. That awoke all of us," the Fallen Prince said. The crouched and bowed murmured anew. "It was you who assigned me Lordship over the Earth. You who granted me each and every attribute that I possess. You who seated me at the left hand of Our Father." The Son of Morning's countenance was beatific, inscrutable, unbearably perfect. "Do you recall the circumstance of our Casting Down?" Around Him, the Fallen softly moaned.

The angel dared not speak.

"Earth was to be a Paradise, our Father had said. A perfect place for the continued evolution of Itself. As Lord of the Hierarchy, as Lord of the Earth, as the very extension of the Godhead that had created that planet as a growing place for Itself, it was I who contended that a Paradise would be anathema to Growth. Nothing would come from comfort, from bliss. There must be conflict, there must be combat, there must be *contrast*.

"I—Created for the voicing of just such an opinion—was denied. And that denial came in the form of our Casting Down."

Again, the seventy-two assembled moaned. A sound mournful and strange, each utterance different from the others, born of the forms they had been cursed with.

"But there will be conflict. There will be combat. There will be growth. The time must come when the part of Godhead—the part of *Ourself*—that denied Myself is forced to reckon with that hypocrisy. It must see that hypocrisy has been Its undoing. That is the sole condition of victory I will accept. Triumph under any other circumstance is meaningless.

"And so to you. You who have turned away from the Force that created you, not by virtue of your function, as did I, but out of avarice. An infant would recognize within you a desire to do so again, to any Master who offered you succor. You have no place here.

"Begone."

The angel found itself exiled from Heaven and exiled from Hell. It found itself in the Presence of God.

It looked into the Face of God, and was stripped.

It lost its name.

It lost its sigil.

It lost its rituals, its summonings.

It could no longer be spoken of within Heaven, nor within Hell, nor upon the Earth.

An angel does not die.

It simply would not Be.

This done, it was Forgotten.

It would spend eternity as unlimited potentiality without possibility of use.

While, outside its nowhere prison, the instruments it had fashioned from the living bone of its murdered sibling waited to be found. To be used. To unlock that cage.

MY FIRST MONSTER

*W*HILE RIDING HIS BIKE THAT AFTERNOON, WALTER HAD turned a corner very fast, and almost slid beneath the wheels of a passing milk truck. That was the moment Walter first realized that he could die. And this was the night the closet door first opened.

That's not to say the closet door had never been opened before, but it is to say that it was the first time it had opened by itself.

Walter's mother had tucked him into his great bed, for he was only four and a half years old, rubbed his chafed hands and skinned knees, and put his tiny hand on her swollen tummy. She told Walter he had to stay alive and out of trouble if he was going to be a big brother to his baby sister (who was arriving any day now). Then she had kissed his forehead and said good night, and walked to the door and turned off the light and said good night again. And then she shut the door behind her.

Walter was warm in his bed, piled high with goosedown comforters. Pale moonlight touched the room with silver. Silver on everything—on the books and the fire truck on the shelf, on the powder-white cotton of his comforters, on the shiny gilding of the white-and-blue wallpaper, on the model plane suspended from fishing line above his bed.

He was just beginning to slide into a dream about airplanes when he heard a snick. Opening his eyes, wondering what it could be, wondering if it was part of the dream, he looked down, down, down, over his comforter-covered toes to the closet next to the bedroom door. The closet was taller than his father—who was big and built houses and had taught Walter how to fold birds from pieces of paper—and wider than the toy chest at the foot of Walter's bed. The closet door was slightly ajar, even though Walter's mother had put his shoes away and closed it before she had said good night.

And there came a creak, as these things do, as the door slowly, slowly crept open. A black mouth. Walter imagined that if it opened too far it would suck him right in, right off his bed and into the blackness inside.

With equal parts panic and courage he threw off his comforters, scrambled over the end of his bed, almost tripping on the rail, stumbled across the room, and slammed the door shut with a *bang!* His little heart fluttered madly in his chest.

The house seemed so empty and so quiet as the sound faded from his ringing ears.

He crept back to bed, hoping the noise had not woken his parents (which it hadn't), and he slept.

That night he dreamed of things that lived in the blackness and giggled. He was staring down over his comforter-covered toes at the opening closet door, at the thousand thousand black tittering things that lived there.

"I'm afraid," he said, because he was.

"You don't have to be afraid, Walter," said a dry voice he didn't recognize. Walter saw that a tall man with hair of pale red stood between him and the closet. He was a strange-looking man with a wide hat and a dark coat that stretched down to the floor. His coat made a tinkling noise that Walter liked. Inside the dark coat Walter could see stars, blinking and shifting.

"But why?" Walter said in a tiny voice. "There's one of me and a thousand thousand of them." The gigglers kept giggling.

"This is only a bad dream," said the man, "and in the morning you will awaken as you have done every morning for four and a half years."

"A bad dream?" said Walter. "There are bad dreams?"

"Yes," said the man. "And this is your first. But there are ways out of them, Walter."

Then the gigglers crept forward, spreading from the closet like chuckling and guffawing black syrup.

Morning came and Walter woke from a dream in which his parents had become red worms and were trying to eat him, and then were torn to pieces by a monstrous thing with hot eyes and gleaming claws. Walter climbed out of his great bed, stepped into his slippers, and went downstairs. And oh, he was greatly relieved to find his mother making French toast in the morning light, and his father reading the paper, just as they had always done for the last four and a half years. Which for Walter was forever.

The next night Walter stared once more down to his comforter-covered toes, at the shut closet door, and waited for what lived inside. And sure enough, there came a snick. And, sure enough, the door began to creep wide open. But this time Walter could not move. This time he thought about the gigglers and how many thousand thousand of them there were, and about a room full of cold red wriggling things, each with the face of his mother or father, and he couldn't move.

Walter saw two red eyes reading him from the closet.

But they're not eyes, Walter thought, desperately. They're just the sparkly things on the back of my bicycle helmet, hung in the closet and catching the moonlight.

Then, as if they had heard the thought, the eyes blinked. And Walter heard breathing. Slow, deep breathing. He pulled the comforter higher—too high—until his little feet poked out from beneath, cold and vulnerable and inviting.

The thing inside the closet reached out into Walter's bedroom with one huge, shaggy paw. Peeking over his little hands, Walter saw that the paw was tipped with claws that glowed pale in the moonlight. The thing pulled itself a little farther into the light and Walter saw a great fanged snout beneath two burning eyes. He could hear the thing's panting breath. He could smell its shaggy fur.

A monster, thought Walter, wide-eyed. My first monster.

"Let me tell you something about monsters . . ." It was the man again, in his long coat—maybe like a wise Chinese man, only Walter didn't think he was Chinese. He stood beside the open door, leaning against the closet. He had dark eyes and looked like he knew a lot of things that Walter didn't. "There's nothing to it. Tell it to go away and it will."

Walter never liked dogs. They were always so much bigger than him, so careless, so loud, with such big, wet mouths. Secretly he had been glad when their dog had died. It could have fit Walter's entire head inside its jaws.

The boy pulled the comforter over his head as the thing in the closet took one heavy step into the room. From beneath his comforter, he saw his cold and bare little feet, and could see the thing's shadow creep over them.

"Tell it to go away," the man said again. "And it will . . ."

The thing's breathing quickened. Walter wanted to tell it to go away, but all he could do was squeak.

"Tell it . . ."

The thing at the end of the bed roared so loudly Walter thought he would go deaf, and he decided that he must have fainted instead, because the next thing he knew it was morning.

At least, he thought—trying to look on the bright side—I didn't
have any bad dreams.

Walter didn't see the man after that. He supposed the thing from the
closet must have gotten him. But every night after that the closet still
opened. And every night the thing would step out and stand at the
foot of Walter's bed. And every night Walter would hide beneath his
comforter, his feet pulled to his chest, and shake till he slid into sleep.

With that monstrous thing standing, and standing, and staring.

Walter's mother chided him for staying awake so late, for never wanting to go to bed when he was told. He would plead with his mother
and father, tell them of the thing that stood at the foot of his bed every
night—the thing with shaggy fur and red eyes and moonlight claws—
and they would laugh and tell Walter how they both had a closet
monster when they were his age. It happens to all boys and girls, they
said. Four and a half years from now we'll all be standing here listening to your baby sister saying exactly the same thing.

As always, they would send him to bed. His father made a bird out
of orange paper and put it on the little bedside table where a glass of
water sat, in case Walter got thirsty during the night. "This is a magic
bird," Walter's father said. "And it will protect you during the night."
Walter said thank you, but he knew the paper bird was just a paper bird.

And as always, after they had tucked him in and wished him good
dreams and turned out the light and closed the bedroom door, the
closet would snick, and the door would open, and the shaggy paw
would wrap around it. And the monster would step into the room on
heavy feet and stand . . . and stand . . . and stand . . . and watch Walter all night long.

One night, after many nights had gone by like this, Walter thought
of the old man and wondered about what he had said.

Could Walter really just tell the thing from the closet to go away
and it would?

It took him many nights to raise the courage to lower the comforter and look at the thing. When he did, it was every bit as fierce and horrible as it ever was. It was so big that it stooped beneath the ceiling. The hair on its back and mane brushed against the plaster. Its wet snout bumped the model airplane that hung over Walter's bed. The beast filled the room with a sodden musk like damp dogs. Its eyes were every bit as deep and red as Walter remembered. Its paws were half as large as all of Walter, and its claws were that size again.

And it was looking at him.

"G . . . ," said Walter, trembling. The thing's brow creased.

"Go . . . ," said Walter. The thing made a *hrrmph?* sound, the way Walter's old dog used to when it was confused.

"Go away," Walter said, sitting up now. "Go away."

The thing at the end of the bed did nothing for a long time but look down at Walter lying small in his great bed. Its great claws could have my head off in a second, Walter guessed. But then, as he looked up at it towering above him, its eyes no longer seemed quite so fierce, and its claws no longer seemed quite so long. If anything, Walter thought, it looked sad.

"Go away," he shouted again. "Go away, go away, go away!"

The thing whined, just the way Walter's horrible old dog used to, and opened its jaws (which no longer seemed quite so fanged), and it began to fade away. And as the thing at the end of the bed faded away, it spoke the way Walter imagined his old dog would have, if it could have spoken when it was sad . . .

"Love you . . . ," it said. And then it was gone.

And Walter wondered what he had done.

"Thank you, son," said the man, suddenly back inside Walter's room, standing before the opened closet door. The man's coat tinkled delicately as he shifted, and Walter caught glimpses of something like starlight from within. "Nothing gets in my way more than a closet monster."

And Walter saw the thousand thousand gigglers and heard their sniggering as the old man spread his arms, and they swarmed around him like a wall of wobbly black.

His father's magic paper bird just sat there as the bad dreams began.

Little Walter didn't wake up the next day, no matter how much his mother shook him. They took his temperature—he didn't have a fever. They tested his pulse—nothing was wrong. They pried open his eyelids—his eyes stared. They shone a light into his pupils and nothing happened. Then Walter stopped breathing and they raced him to hospital.

Doctors came and went. No one knew how to wake him, not even doctors from America and England. No one could explain what had taken him. So they attached a bottle with a tube to Walter's arm so he wouldn't have to eat, and put another tube in through his nose to help him breathe, and they left him. And he stayed in that strange new bed, beneath thin, rough, white sheets, without his comforter, a long way from home. And his parents were very sad.

And Walter did not wake up.

He ran through a field of snapping flowers that bit at his ankles, taunted by a thousand thousand voices, all daring him to fall and be eaten.

"No!" Walter cried, tears threatening to spill out from behind his eyes. "I won't fall! You won't eat me!" Ahead, standing tall in the middle of the field that clacked with teeth, was the closet door. He raced toward it, wet choppers nipping at his heels. He flung the door open and heard the man calling his name from somewhere behind, but Walter could not see him.

Walter jumped inside and slammed the door shut.

The inside of the closet wasn't dark, as Walter had expected. It was hung with his school uniforms, his shoes resting beneath them, all polished and waiting. His soccer jersey was here, and his bicycle helmet with the red shiny things on it. Piles of old Spider-Man comic books were stacked against the wooden wall, gone tumble-down from where he'd tossed them. Above his head was the shelf that held shoe boxes filled with plastic action men and aliens. But the closet was much deeper than it was supposed to be. He pushed aside the musty old jacket that he never wore—shirts and coats he didn't recognize, and beyond them more. He moved farther inside, and the farther he went the fewer clothes there were. Finally he stepped into a room made of the same wood as his closet, with clothes for curtains hanging over windows that looked onto a forest of giant clothes racks and hat stands, all hung with every imaginable kind of garment. It seemed to stretch forever into an endless black. Inside the room there was a fireplace fueled with burning dresses and socks. Before the fireplace was a rug of fur coats. Little Walter laughed to see an old sofa upholstered in brightly striped and dotted boxer shorts.

"I have never heard you laugh," said a voice. It was then that Walter noticed the thing standing tall and monstrous in the shadows, away from the firelight. "I have only seen you tremble."

It was as tall and wide and as fierce as Walter remembered, but there was nothing so scary about it now.

"Are you a monster?" Walter asked.

"I am a monster," it said, voice like grumbling thunder. "The monster that keeps the other monsters at bay. I am your first monster. And you sent me away."

"I did not mean to," pleaded Walter, trying hard to see the thing inside the shadows. "The man told me . . ."

"And you listened." The monster's voice was sad. It gave a great breath, stooped to walk on all fours like a man with very long arms, and loped into the light, claws clacking against the wooden floor, to be nearer the warmth of the burning dresses and socks. "He told you what he told you for his own gain."

"I'm sorry," Walter said. "I did not know."

The thing gave out another long, sad breath. It made Walter think of a horse. Only, horses always seemed happy, but the thing looked at the fire and Walter saw tears had dampened down the gray-black fur beneath its burning eyes.

"You want to go home," it said.

Walter nodded desperately. "I want to go home."

"Do you know what happens to someone who has no monster?" the monster asked.

Walter shook his little head.

"They fall asleep," the monster said, "and they can't get home. And sometimes the bad dreams get them."

"But you are my monster," Walter said.

The thing gave a slow shake of its great head. "No more."

Walter could see how sick it looked. How its great slabs of muscle had thinned, how its fur hung limply on its loosening skin, how its eyes did not gleam as ferociously as they once had.

The thing's elbow buckled, and it lurched. Walter rushed to its aid, little hands closing around its arm, trying to keep its great weight from crashing over.

Close now, close enough for its great red eyes to fill Walter's vision, the monster said, "All I have ever wanted was to guard you all of your life."

"Then guard me," Walter pleaded. "Be my monster."

But its fur was falling away, and soon the floor of the room was like the floor of a barber's—layered thick with gray-black fur. More of its muscle was slipping away. With a clatter the thing's claws fell off entirely.

"Who decides these things I do not know," said the monster. "But I am not your monster anymore. It is not my place to protect you from the things outside the door." And Walter could hear the things outside, leaping and laughing and—most of all—waiting. They would always wait, always wait for Walter.

The monster was now only half the size it had been. "Only two things will save you."

"What are they?" Walter asked, all the time thinking, What will save you?

It did not look quite so wolfish now, but it was still large. Its hands were long and thin, and its eyes were turning from red to deep yellow. "Always remember who you are . . . ," said the wolf-thing.

"Goodness," said Walter, with wonder. "You look just like . . ."

". . . and this."

With the last of its strength and a sudden sweeping-up the thing swallowed Walter whole.

The man came into the closet a long time after the monster had swallowed Walter. None of the black giggling things came with him; he came alone. He had looked down at what was left of Walter and his monster, small and blond and shaking, and said:

"I don't wish you any harm."

"Who are you?"

"I am a doctor."

"I don't understand what is happening," the Walter-monster said, not entirely feeling as he used to. There were two parts to him now, trying to fit in with each other. Something older than recorded time. Something four and a half years old. Something precisely as old as human fear. Something small and confused. There was something he had to be. Something enormous inside his little chest was telling him things, telling him to shift the weight to the balls of his feet, to swing upward and bring three claws to rest inside the doctor's heart. But the Walter-monster didn't know why. He didn't even have claws, he just wanted to go home . . .

"I can help," the doctor said. "I can teach you things." He crouched and extended a hand. "If you like."

Walter had taken the proffered hand, because he couldn't quite sort out who he was from who he had been, because he was afraid, and because he didn't know what else to do.

The doctor's hand was thin inside the stiff leather of his glove, and his voice had the comforting rumble of something distant and massive and watchful.

"Tell me," he said. "Did you know only seventy-two angels fell with Samael?"

"Per-kew-tay-nee-uss Fee-ding Gas-tross-toe-me . . ."

Hope Witherspoon, age four and a half, had spent a lot of time remembering it right and learning to say it. It made her mother smile, sort of, only she just called it a PEG.

"Why do we call it a PEG if the middle letter is really *F*?"

Her mother told her it was just easier to remember that way.

"Okay."

The PEG was a hole in Walter's tummy. It was just above the . . . sigh-lass-tic bag his Number Twos went into. The PEG had a . . . a . . . sigh-lass-tic tube for squirting food into. Hope's mother had to buy it from the hospital. They also got special medicine from the hospital, which stopped Walter getting sick from the tube his Number Ones came out of.

While Hope's mother fed Walter, she would softly sing a song to herself.

> *You've got everything you want*
> *You don't know what to keep*
> *The dreams you abuse*
> *As they rock you to sleep*
> *Swallowing the sense*
> *Just to stay here with me*
> *And knowing it's you*
> *Patiently watching . . .*

It was a pretty song. Hope didn't think Walter could hear it, though.

The Number Two bag looked weird. Hope's mother said that it was attached to a bit of Walter's insides. That's what that pale lump was—part of his insides poking out.

And then she told Hope that it was time she learned how to do it herself, and unclipped the Number Two bag. It smelled bad. Her brother's tummy reminded Hope of wobbly sausage.

Hope screwed up her face and shook her head.

Hope's mother explained that both Mummy and Daddy worked very hard to keep Walter alive, and that they all had to do their part. So Hope said okay. But she didn't really want to because Walter scared her, and her parents loved him more, and she wanted him to go away. And her mother said thank you, sweetie. From then on Hope would take the Number Two bag (trying not to breathe while she did it), seal it, and replace it with a fresh one. Every two days she would rub creams into Walter's cool skin to stop him from getting sores. And every day she would walk past all those pictures of Walter hung in the hallway and every night she would sit at dinner and listen to her mother and her father talk about Walter, and nod as they told her what a perfect little boy he had been.

Everyone gets a monster. Sometimes they are big, sometimes they are ugly, and sometimes they are nothing like that. But they all look like the one thing that scares you the most. And that is how it keeps your other nightmares away: it scares them, too.

Everyone gets a monster.

"The man told me to wish you away," said Hope Witherspoon, trembling in her great wide bed, her thick blankets bunched in her little hands.

"I know," said the perfect little boy, smiling gently with bright wolf-teeth. "And that is why you mustn't."

ONE

BOSTON, 1840

*H*ENRY ROSE. THROUGH A THIN WINDOW THE DAY'S LAST light lit his face. Pale walls, too cold, strip of a bed. The framed needlepoint on the wall hand-stitched by the widow who ran the house was from the second book of Corinthians, chapter five, verse one: WE KNOW THAT IF OUR EARTHLY HOUSE OF THIS TABERNACLE WERE DISSOLVED, WE HAVE A BUILDING OF GOD, A HOUSE NOT MADE WITH HANDS, ETERNAL IN THE HEAVENS.

Down the street a workhorse clipped its slow way home, hauling a canvas-sheeted wagon. Autumn had already dragged down summer. Three young boys smoked as they passed a rifle around, walking to some vacant lot. Shooting cats was big around here.

Leaning upon the sill, Henry drew a deep breath from the Boston bay he could almost see, from the rank tide smell that drilled up between his eyes, from the cigarette between his hard lips. Sunlight glanced hot amber from the tiles on the roof opposite. In the street below a policeman walked along, twirling his truncheon like a caricature, and Henry took a slow step backward out of the light.

It ages a man to live with the feeling of other people's eyes at his back. No one's a friend; everyone's dangerous. A hall, an examination room, a coffeehouse is never entered without thinking about what to do should every exit be quietly barred by lawmen. This was the atmosphere in which Henry Lockrose—redheaded son of redheaded parents—undertook his studies at the Massachusetts Medical College of Harvard University in the year of 1840.

A year, he told himself. Two semesters, three at the most. Then I'll get apprenticed out to a practicing physician . . . someplace quiet where a reserved demeanor will be considered a good bedside manner. I will be completely goddamn unremarkable.

Standing a head taller than most men and with hair of pale red, to never be remarked upon was all he could hope for.

He remembered the night he had told his father his intentions. Silence had reigned at the dinner table. It was well made, sturdy, that table. Henry had helped build it when he was five or six, at his father's workbench. The same place they repaired their tools, the same place they stored all they needed when they put the barn together, made harnesses or built wheelbarrows.

The sun had set, and his mother had just lit the lamp. She was still standing there, bent over it, match extinguished, eyes flitting from father to son, waiting to see—afraid of—what the old man's reaction would be. Old man hadn't seen it coming, not in eighteen years.

He had sunk his teeth into his pale corn, paused, spat out a small worm.

Most nights Henry had looked to the mountains from their bare porch and smoked his clay pipe. That night his father had cuffed him across the back of the head, pitching him through the open door without breaking stride, and headed to his bed.

And yet three years later here was Henry. An ugly world away, a beautiful world away. No dirt to work here, no long silences, just conversation between people unafraid to question and an odor that imposed itself like an unwashed drunk. At least, there certainly was this close to the river.

He ground his cigarette on the sill. No more pipes for him, not here. Not till he could afford a real one. Besides, smoking was illegal in Boston ever since the fires, so everyone smoked cigarettes. Easier to hide.

Downstairs, the porcelain clank of plates. Mrs. Brown would be ladling gravy over potatoes tumbled into an oven-warm bowl, and one of the other residents—a man Henry thought of as Newspaper Jack— would be dutifully ferrying them to a table set for seven people and one ghost.

Henry blew smoke into the street, put on his coat, and left the room.

The transient population of Mrs. Brown's boardinghouse consisted mainly of wifeless amateur philosophers and worried artists. The building itself was as much an old woman as Mrs. Brown who ran it, full of creaks and stories and quiet music. The table was a portrait gallery. The tan-clad compulsive arranger was Newspaper Jack, while the damp-skinned aesthete to Henry's right fiddled endlessly with cramped fingers and an air of ambient shame. These were the stalwarts, the ones who had resided beneath Mrs. Brown's roof for more than a fortnight or two. The others were a hodgepodge of faces drawn and smiling, knuckles bony, and eyes dry with hope.

Mrs. Brown herself radiated from the head of the table. She was a widow, her husband having been taken by tuberculosis some years earlier. It did not matter who you were: if you lived under her roof you were her responsibility. She had a range of opinions on a variety of subjects, and declared that if any lad under her roof wanted to smoke he could very well go ahead and do so, and any local ban on such a thing could go to blazes.

The shameful aesthete received a late-night bowl of soup and a ready ear, the latter of which he never took advantage of. Newspaper

Jack, well, he had become the measure of the day's cycle at the boardinghouse. Mrs. Brown rose to let him from the house to collect his
paper at precisely five thirty AM. She then assembled breakfast for her
lodgers, and let Jack back in at precisely five fifty AM. So his habits—
his midmorning stroll, his writing hour, his reading by the sun window, his disappearing for a few hours in the afternoon, his return for
dinner—organized the flow by which the house operated. During it
all he would meticulously, compulsively, and exhaustively regale anyone hapless enough to cross his path with every last detail of his day,
down to their very reasons. The only person capable of getting Jack to
put a sock in it was Mrs. Brown. Her oft-used delivery of "Jack . . ."
routinely saved dinnertime for Henry.

He wondered what would happen to the rhythm of the place
once Jack got around to leaving. Possibly he never would of his own
accord.

Henry's life had but one focus: school. Until a year ago life had
been the field, family, and faith. He didn't know the first thing about
having friends the way people on the street had friends, the way people in clubs had friends . . . at most he had only ever nodded at the
sons of other families. He knew even less about the opposite sex.
The thought alone made him fold inward. Once their children had
come of age, marriage was an arrangement negotiated between families. Thoughts of the flesh were a torturous disappointment at best,
damnation at worst. No, if Henry wasn't in class noting down a dis-
sertation on one ailment or another he was in his room entering
those notes cleanly into a separate journal or reading up on whatever topic was expected to come next. He retired after dinner for a
single smoke at his window and to read five more pages before ex-
tinguishing the gas lamp. On occasions when he felt stretched with
fatigue he would take himself out for a quick stroll by the Tremont
Theatre, down Beacon Street, past the fine houses being built there
and toward the water. He would keep his eyes on the pavement as
he walked, hat low, thinking, alert for a discreet lane or doorway

where he might be able to have a quick smoke. Partly Henry enjoyed the idea of getting away with it, and partly he resented being made to feel like a criminal for enjoying what had always been a right. And then he would remember that he was a criminal, and that strictly speaking he had no rights, and he would turn his thoughts to other matters.

Most often he walked and thought through things medical, much as he'd done as a boy working the field. Sometimes he thought about the future. More often he thought about the past. Quite often, for this reason, Henry didn't walk at all. In this way his days bled into one another.

There was one among the residents of that place, a chestnut-haired Englishman—older or younger than himself, Henry could not say—always nattering to somebody. In the beginning the Englishman was just another face whom Henry made a point of ignoring, of brushing past on an almost daily basis in order to get to his room. Another set of eyes he steadfastly refused to make contact with.

As the weeks passed, the Englishman gathered about him a cadre of friends. They would wait for him in the street: a keen young natterer, sharp and pale, often talking the ear off a ruddy-faced fobwatch of a man who bore it all with quiet sufferance. There was also a woman whom Henry assumed to be the fobwatch's wife. She certainly seemed to have little time for the talker.

"You don't say much," the Englishman commented across the emptying table one evening. "I find that fascinating. What's your name?"

Newspaper Jack leapt in. "His name's Henry Lockrose and he's from Vermont. He reads a great deal of medical texts, I've found, and . . ."

In the kitchen Mrs. Brown pointedly cleared her throat. Jack fell silent, his chin hitting his chest.

"Would you be good enough to help me with the dishes, Jack?"

Jack's chair squeaked and he was off.

Henry stood from the table. "I apologize. I must return to my studies."

The Englishman remained seated. "Without discipline one is the prisoner of desire. Power to you, sir."

Henry nodded and took his plate to the kitchen.

"One thing, if you have a moment." The Englishman stood at the kitchen door, his empty plate still on the table. "My friends and I gather of an evening in a private room at the Coat and Arms on Franklin Street. One of us knows you from your classes, in fact. Perhaps you could find the time to join us one evening? You'll find us erudite conversationalists, I'm sure."

Henry deposited his washed plate onto the steaming stack and slid past the Englishman.

"Thanks," he said. "But no thanks."

"I am Dorian Athelstane. Ask for me when you get there."

As a boy, Henry had never gotten enough from whatever homespun wisdom or sketchy history his mother could impart. His closest association with any kind of formalized instruction had been Sunday school. But not anymore. No more blue jean trousers for him. No more woolen broadcloth. Here men dressed like smokestacks, straight and dark and proud. This was the life for him. Attending the Massachusetts Medical College was the deepest drink of his life, and today their professor was well warmed to his subject.

"Now, acute osteomyelitis shares many similarities with rheumatic fever. So many, in fact, that some authorities—Kocher and Sahli, to name two—believe them to be different forms of the very same disease. To address that contention we should note that while joint symptoms predominate with acute rheumatism, there *is* a notable absence of suppuration, *and* that the patient's symptoms of discomfort will yield more readily to salicylates than would the symptoms of a patient with osteomyelitis . . ."

There was a universe in there—linked, co-dependent, whole—

of myriad variety and complexity and workings, all woven together in a lifelong symphony of movement and function. Henry felt privileged—entrusted—beyond his ability to express. This, more than anything, lifted his chin and fixed his eyes on the future.

". . . development of septic endocarditis. Now, gentlemen and . . . lady . . . next on our slate is *treatment*, which we shall discover is carried out along the same lines as other suppurative diseases."

Henry's pen rose and dove with unself-conscious speed from well to paper, staining his fingers like an accountant's. The words flew from his nib, the line ending with a streak and stab. He looked up.

The lesson was over. Document folders were tied closed, cases clipped shut. Half the class was already walking out. Henry sighed to himself, placed his pen down, and squared his notes away for the day, bound in sheaves by subject and region and stored safe inside a clasped leather folder. The lecturer acknowledged Henry with a wry smile and a nod as he guillotined his papers upon the podium. Reaching down beside himself for his folder, Henry caught the one and only woman in the class, voluminous skirts packed around her— pretty if only she would recognize the fact, Henry had once thought—still seated on the other side of the room. She had been looking amusedly at him, the serious student, and smiled kindly.

He grabbed his things and stood too quickly, banging his knee on the underside of the desktop. The woman flinched, and Henry left the building as fast as he could. Marching down the front steps and onto the street, he didn't slow until he was blocks away. When finally he pressed his kidneys against the peeling fence of a leprous old church and lay a hand to his chest, a black bird looked down from the high corner of the brownstone across the way, and cawed. He felt as if he had been poisoned, as if he might be sick.

His father had dreams, once, Henry knew. Dreams like dead brothers to him. Sometimes it was a snatch of overheard conversation, a phrase his father mumbled dismissively to himself, or a topic Henry's mother insisted be avoided. Henry had seen how carrying their corpses had broken him.

This was the first lesson Henry learned: anything alive within a person can be smothered. Smothered for long enough that thing will die.

And then it rots.

The dreams decaying within his father had made of their house a ward, full of sickness. Made it something to be escaped from.

No woman had ever looked at Henry the way that woman had looked at him. No woman had ever laced her fingers through his. In his family's world no woman could. First he felt ashamed, and then he felt free.

He was no longer in his family's world.

He closed the front door too loudly behind himself, throwing a scarf about his neck and marching down the nighttime street like a man with a train to catch. He did not know Dorian, he did not even like Dorian, but what was the earthly point of escaping one kind of nothingness only to embrace another? Henry did not know what impatient power it was that had gripped him, but it said enough was enough. It frightened him, to be truthful, and he could not properly explain why it was he made with all speed for the Coat and Arms, only that suddenly his blood was moving—moving, it seemed, as he had never felt it move—and were he to arrive too late to meet Dorian and his friends and engage in whatever may come next, then the remainder of the night would be one of the longest he had ever known. Every day was a day he would never have again. Tomorrow he could be in a watch-house cell, awaiting transport to some godforsaken prison, and that would be that for Henry Lockrose. All he would have for company between incarceration and a short drop would be the knowledge that he had never lived.

He dragged the back of his gloved hand across each eye, apologizing as his shoulder connected with a passerby. A warm room, a good fire, and something fortifying to drink. If he could have that then anything might happen tomorrow and he would be all right.

Stepping in from the cold Henry felt his face cracking, the bubble
and guffaw of conversation enveloping him like warm water. Re-
moving his hat and gloves he crossed the room toward the bar, a nervous outsider. At the mention of Dorian's name the barmaid
nodded—"that young feller with the sparkle in his eye"—and con-
sulted with the manager as to which room they were in. Two minutes later Henry was taken aside by the mustachioed proprietor—a
short man with well-oiled hair, his sleeves held up by garters—and
shown down a narrow hall. Even above the din of the pub's main
room Henry had heard their voices singing out from behind the far
door.

> *Nelly Bly! Nelly Bly! Bring the broom along,*
> *We'll sweep the kitchen clean, my dear,*
> *And have a little song.*
> *Poke the wood, my lady love*
> *And make the fire burn,*
> *And while I take the banjo down,*
> *Just give the mush a turn . . .*

The proprietor turned a brass handle and opened the door discreetly onto a dinnertime scene of song and unrestrained laughter.

The song fell away, cushioned on laughter, and all eyes turned to
Henry. He immediately recognized them from observations made
from his bedroom window: the Talker, the Fobwatch and his wife—a
plain woman with a heart-shaped face. Henry remembered seeing
her for the first time and thinking she could be beautiful if she would
only recognize the fact. His heart felt faint.

She smiled, acknowledging Henry's entry with a polite inclination
of her head.

"I believe you and Henry have met," Dorian said, and despite feeling suddenly out of place Henry rankled at the Englishman's pre-
sumptuous use of his given name.

"Why yes," she said. "I've seen you looking down at us from time to time, from your window at Mrs. Brown's."

Henry was adrift, his mind white with embarrassment, when the proprietor lifted his coat from his shoulders, making for an awkward moment. Henry struggled out of it, turning about as he did so.

"So, Henry," Dorian exclaimed, as the proprietor hung Henry's coat on the lion-footed stand by the door. "We were just this moment wondering about you." The pub laughed and murmured as the proprietor made his exit.

"That right?" Henry said without thinking.

" 'That right'? Good Lord, Henry, it's as if you were raised on a farm."

Henry smiled, politely as he could. He was beginning to suspect this assumed familiarity was an attempt on Dorian's part to place him on the back foot. He would not play that game. "I was raised on a farm," he said. "May I sit?"

"Please."

Their meal—for which Henry had arrived too late—had been roast duckling. He thought of Mrs. Brown's watery stew and regretted every spoonful. "What was it you were wondering, exactly?"

"From whence does he hail," Dorian replied jovially. "What subjects stir his blood? Why does he never speak?" He leaned forward, confidentially. "The unraveling of enigmas is a subject very close to this group's heart."

The pale-haired talker laughed under his breath.

"Introductions!" Dorian proclaimed, slouching back again under the momentum of another gesture. "A mutual exposition. Please, allow me. The young man to your right is our Mr. Adam Jukes. Mr. Jukes has an insatiable curiosity and will, I'm sure, provide you with many hours of conversation. Across from you is the estimable Mr. Alfred Dysart. Mr. Dysart is a well-regarded businessman about town. And Miss Finella Riley I believe you already know."

The young woman inclined her head once again, having made no mention of their classes together, or the incident that afternoon.

"It was Mr. Dysart who finagled Miss Riley a place in your classroom. Quite the talking point, as I'm sure you're aware." The woman's eyes lowered. "Young Finella is something of a revolutionary."

"I've heard nothing but good things about the strength of Miss Riley's character, Dorian," Henry insisted. "And lady doctors are not so queer."

"Please, sir," Miss Riley interjected. "My ears aren't cloth. Until the social order changes, an oddity I am, and an oddity I remain. It is not a burden to me, but a road."

"May it be a short one," Henry said, his heart invading his lungs. He had never spoken to a woman his own age so straightforwardly. She spoke her mind like a man. That was powerful.

Dorian applauded. "Bravo," he said. "Bravo. You would have found a kindred spirit in Casanova, my dear." Henry felt his face threaten to flush at the association.

"That right," she said.

Dysart snorted and chuckled to himself, Jukes didn't get it, and Henry felt a kind of strange anxiety closing his pores. Finella glanced at him quickly. Was that a smile in her eyes?

Powerful.

"Equality between the sexes began with him, you know," Dorian continued, unperturbed. "Perhaps the new movement should regard themselves as 'Casanovans.' A lovely connotation, don't you think?"

"I doubt Margaret Fuller would have been much in love with the notion of naming a women's movement after a womanizer, Mr. Athelstane. But I take your point."

"He believed women were the equal of men and treated them as such," Dorian rebutted. "As it should be. The chance configuration of our corporeal forms has little bearing upon our capacity for miracles."

Jukes's glass shot into the air, wine slapping over the sides. "Hear! Hear!"

Dorian raised his own. Dysart was slow to follow. "Hear. Hear."

Henry wished to the Devil that Jukes and Dysart and Athelstane would . . . vanish. How did a man go about speaking to a woman? He had committed the best part of *A Guide to Manners and Dress* to memory, but even so the rough habits of a lifetime took some effort to rein in. Back home their parents would have arranged to spend afternoons together, and then he and Miss Riley could have become acquainted, but here . . .

"Henry, allow me." Dorian filled Henry's glass from a carafe. "To our newest companion. To Henry." And they drank. "Now that we are done with our introductions, who might you be, young Henry?"

Finella cocked an eyebrow. "No introduction from the host, I notice." Dorian waved her observation away, a pretense of modesty. No one pursued it.

Henry swilled the wine over his teeth, swallowed it down with satisfaction. "My name is Henry Lockrose," Henry lied, replacing his glass upon the table. Dorian refilled it. Henry swallowed another mouthful. This seemed to please Dysart. "I want to be a surgeon. Now, what's this talk of enigmas?"

There had been a man who managed the trick of escaping from their farm a few times a year. He had been a doctor. He would come in on a buggy, dressed neat and sharp and clean as a blade. In a day he would tend to their ills like a miracle worker, leave a few boiled sweets, and be on his way—back to whatever fresh universe he had come from, away from the farm, to someplace where people could be doctors rather than sinners and dirt workers born to live and die in their fear of the Lord.

It was at a very young age that Henry had decided he would become a doctor. He did not tell his father.

The publican discreetly reappeared to stoke the fire, bringing with him a tray of small pecan pies and brandy. Dysart slipped the man a few coins and poured a measure of brandy into Jukes's glass. He then passed the bottle to Henry, seated to his left. Henry filled Dysart's, and so it went. Even in his current state some elements of *Manners and Dress* asserted themselves. Shortly after that it seemed they were all on first-name terms.

"I say!" Dorian suddenly exclaimed. "Did you hear about that fellow they sent to the hospital with cramp?"

"Ha!" Jukes said. "Yes, he was—" And Finella whacked him in the ribs.

"It was in the *Evening Transcript*," Dorian continued.

"Don't read it," Dysart said.

"They examined the poor bugger, expecting gout or something I wager, and can you imagine what he actually had?"

"Gastroenteritis?" offered Finella, surprisingly unfazed by Dorian's language.

"Ulceration?" Henry said.

"No," Dorian said. "Give up?"

"I give up," Finella said.

"A snake. The man had a bellyful of snake."

Finella put her hand to her mouth.

"Swallowed it when it was a hatchling, apparently. The man used to fit quite a bit. Turns out it had been growing in there for years."

"Dorian, that's horrible," Finella said.

"Dorian, that's bullshit," Henry replied. His glass was looking empty. Had he just cussed? From the look on Finella's face he guessed he had. "Not possible . . . is what I mean."

"I assure you," Dorian said. "It was in the paper."

"How did it breathe?" Henry asked.

"There's a reason I don't read the paper," Dysart mumbled.

"There's air in the stomach," Dorian countered.

"There's air in the *lungs*, Dorian."

"There is some air in the stomach, Henry," Finella said. "You know that."

"Yes, but—"

"Not much, granted, but if the serpent was ingested as a hatchling it may well have become used to living on less air—"

"And the occasional chewed-up pie."

"Well, yes."

"Then . . . then how is it possible, after all those years, that this snake was never, you know . . . escorted out the back?"

"Well . . ."

"Is this a subject fit for the dinner table?" Dysart interjected.

"I'm finding it enthralling," Dorian said.

"Well," Finella ventured. "Unless an ingested snake was very in-quisitive I would think it might never know the interior of a gentle-man's upper intestine."

"If you'll excuse me a moment," Jukes said, and made an exit.

"More port?" Dorian offered amiably.

Henry offered his glass. "I have to admit, Miss Riley, that I never expected a learned lady to keep company with sensationalists, smok-ers, and . . . and . . ."

"Scallywags?"

"Indeed." He raised his glass. "Cheers."

Finella sampled from her glass and replaced it gently on the table. Her fingers remained upon the stem as she said, "I have every reason for spending time with these gentlemen, Mr. Lockrose. I come here simply because we are extraordinary."

Henry cocked an eyebrow. "Extraordinary," he inquired. "What-ever can you mean?"

"The most effective mediums tend to be women," Dorian confided as Finella accepted Dysart's proffered hand and stepped up onto her chair. Henry looked away. "They are also a much more instinctive breed than men. That's a good thing in this kind of business as it an-nuls the doubts that keep one from the halls adjoining this world and the next." Finella stepped from the chair to the table. Her boots sounded dully upon the scuffed wood.

Dorian had marked the table with white chalk, inscribing a circular sigil upon the use-glossed wood. The interior of the double circle contained a sign the likes of which Henry had never seen, while the space between the inner and outer circle contained four letters, one at each compass point. Working clockwise from the north this is the word it spelled:

VOSO

Finella arranged her skirts, sat quickly, and laid herself down, head positioned over the V. Henry did not know where to look.

"Finella has taken to this with great enthusiasm," Dorian was saying. "I think she may one day astound us all."

"I think young Henry is feeling pretty astounded right now," Jukes sniggered, and Dorian good-naturedly told him to shut up.

At the age of twelve Henry had worked up the courage to ask the doctor how one became a doctor. The man had told of places—there in Vermont and far to the south—where such things were learned. Places to learn, he said, if one had the money. Henry was not deterred by pity, and with each visit he had new questions for the doctor, and over time sweets evolved into books. Books kept hidden beneath mattresses, beneath boards, in sacks in trunks. Books on places beyond, books on history, books on medicine. Before that the only book Henry had ever touched was the Bible.

She lay with her hands upturned beside her, eyes closed, serene. Her breathing became deep and deliberate, and then faded to almost nothing.

Dysart produced a thin cotton sheet from beside his chair and draped this across Finella, covering her from chin to toe. Whether this was service to ceremony or decency Henry couldn't tell.

Henry could read well enough. His mother had taught him at a young age, before his father had bent him to the field. It had not failed him.

By the age of thirteen Henry had decided he would not be a doctor. He would become a surgeon.

Over time books evolved into conversations. Stories of life-threatening cases, revolutionary research, hypotheses as to the functioning of the human animal. Life and death in this doctor's hands.

By the age of fifteen Henry had decided he would be nothing less than a *great* surgeon.

Looking upon Finella's peaceful face, Dorian said, "One or two of the Fallen have, as part of their respective portfolios, the duty of revealing that which is hidden. I know that something immensely important has been concealed from the world of men, and that I may discover it if I only ask the right questions of the right being."

A great surgeon would look inward and see the universe. His skill would clothe him, keep him, and show him the world.

"I cannot take part in this."

People who should be dead would walk on his account.

"Of course you can, Henry. Of course you can."

Bent over in the field, working the soil, often alone, he would recite what he had read. He enacted learned discussions with phantom colleagues. He enacted the thought processes of this genius or that in the lead-up to their discoveries—monologues, diatribes, trains of thought . . .

"Tell him what we're looking for," Jukes said, sporting an unsettlingly wide smile.

"Shut up, Adam. Would you get the lights, Mr. Dysart?"

Henry barely noticed the gas flames lowering and dying, one by one. Propriety had fled and Henry was unable to take his eyes from her.

It was Dorian's hand clapping him on the back that broke the spell. The Englishman gestured to the free space to the east of the sigil. The others were already in position. Dysart's small little eyes glittered hard on Henry as if to say, *Our methods and practices may be unusual, but we remain gentlemen.* Henry felt heat rising to his neck and face, and took the position. A single lamp hung suspended above the table, all other lights removed, changing the atmosphere of the room dreadfully.

Dorian inhaled one deep breath through his nose—Henry suppressed the urge to run—and began by invoking what Henry later learned were six different names for God.

Six names.

Who knew God had a name?

"Have mercy upon me, and cast Thine eyes upon Thy Servant Dorian who invokes Thee most devoutly, and supplicates Thee by Thy Holy and tremendous name *Tetragrammaton* to be propitious, and to order Thine angels and Spirits to the stars, O all ye angels and elementary spirits, O all ye spirits present before the Face of God, I the Minister and faithful servant of the Most High conjure ye, let God Himself, the Existence of Existences, conjure ye to come and be present at this Operation, I, the Servant of God, most humbly entreat ye. Amen."

Something more than dirt workers, born to live and die in their fear of the Lord . . .

The sound began distant and dry, like desert wind. It crept upward in volume. A tiny discord picked up within the sound. It became a rasp. It picked up further.

Every Sunday, all Sunday, in church. The priest couldn't talk for ten seconds without someone shouting *amen*, without everyone else shouting it back, without that taking up a good hunk of a minute. The word *amen* still made his knees hurt.

Finella's mouth dropped open, *gasping*, eyes shot wide, white stare fixed on the light of the lamp above her face like horrified denial. Her tongue edged out of her mouth as the sound grew louder and louder and

Finella sat bolt upright, the lamp bashing across her forehead. She stared at nothing, a punch-drunk marionette with her strings cut. The lamp swung in a wide and deliberate orbit around the periphery of her skull.

Six names.

The shadows of her face shifted and phased and cycled, a stray hand investigating her throat. Her pupils rolled down from inside her head and came to rest upon Henry. The white cloth slipped from her, fell from the table.

"You, boy . . . ," she said in an accent not her own, but familiar. "I cannot breathe . . . tell me why that is . . ."

Henry looked at her, numb and distant, pinned like a moth. He couldn't swallow. The lamp kept circling.

"Tell me why I bleed!"

"Behave yourself!" It was Dorian. "I constrain and command ye with the utmost vehemence and power, by that most potent and powerful Name of God"—Finella quieted instantly—"and by the name *Iah*, which Moses heard, and spoke with God; and by the name *Agla*, which Joseph invoked and was delivered out of the hands of his brethren; and by the name *Vau*, which Abraham heard, and knew God the Almighty One; and by the name of four letters, *Tetragrammaton*, which Joshua named and invoked and was rendered worthy and found deserving to lead the Army of Israel into the Promised Land. By these names I command ye to speak without noise or terror, and to answer truly all questions I shall ask ye."

"Ask," Finella breathed, exhaustedly. "Ask and be done."

"What is your name?"

"Bernard Sumner."

"Do you know some of us, Bernard?"

Finella nodded. "Aye."

"Who of us do you know, Bernard?"

Finella looked to Henry, and her words moved like slow effluent. "Maggie's boy."

"Lighter matters, Bernard," Dorian said. "How many years since you left this world?"

Finella's head shifted slowly back to face Dorian. "Less than a year."

"Where have you been?"

"Awaiting the Grace of my Lord."

"I seek a being that can provide answers, Bernard."

"Let me go."

"In a minute. Its name is Voso. Do you know of it?"

"Let me go."

"It sometimes appears as a great cat."

Finella's head was beginning to loll. "Send me back."

"In the Name of God . . ."

"It fell with the Dark One."

"That much I know. How many fell with the Dark One?"

"Seventy-two. That much is common knowledge."

"No more?"

"No more. Send me back."

"Voso."

"It prefers woodland. Night. Send me back."

"Because ye have been obedient, depart ye unto your abode, and be there peace between us and you."

Finella crumpled across Voso's sigil, her hair spilling over the edge of the table.

She did not move.

It was only then Henry became aware just how heavily everyone was breathing. "My my my . . . ," Dorian sighed. Jukes was silent.

"Is . . ."

"Well, that was most productive," Dorian said.

"Is she all right?"

Dorian knocked a cigarette from its case. "Hmm? Oh yes, she's quite all right. She's an old hand at being ridden, our Finella. Oh don't be such a prig, Henry, it was a turn of phrase."

The words didn't really penetrate. Henry felt cold, and his heart palpitated like a small bird knocked from its nest. Dorian, Dysart, and Jukes were conversing among themselves. No one was looking at him, not even out of the corner of an eye.

Henry removed his coat and draped it across Finella, replacing her hands by her sides. His own vibrated. He clenched his fists, placed them in his pockets. Thoughts would come in time, and a plan, but not now. For now he had to . . .

Dorian lit himself a cigarette and Dysart said with a voice all proscenium theater and brandy, "The woods by Harvard should be ideal."

"For the summoning?" Dorian picked a piece of tobacco from between his lips, spat tightly. "Yes, I expect it will do at that. No one really ventures there at night, once it gets cold."

Jukes stepped forward, keen-eyed. "So what do we do next?"

"Give me a few days, gents, and I'll let you know."

"Right, right."

Henry grabbed Dorian's arm, desperate to evoke clearheadedness. "What about Finella? She's out cold."

Dorian pleasantly raised an eyebrow, ignoring the hand on his arm, as though a concierge had just approached with a telegram. "She'll be fine, old man. Go fetch yourself a brandy. She may be awake by the time you return."

Henry released him contemptuously and turned back to the table. Dorian and Dysart resumed their discussion.

Henry thought twice, then gathered Finella's hair and arranged it around her shoulders. Her eyes opened and looked into his.

"It'll be dicey," Dorian was saying. "The group will have to be purified impeccably."

"Hello," Henry said softly, trying to smile.

"Tricky for you, perhaps," Dysart said. "My vices do not tax the soul."

"One benefit of your not having one," Dorian responded cheerfully.

Finella looked into his eyes.

"Get away from me."

Autumn came that night. The dogs left the streets and the cats were quiet. The clouds fled the sky and the moon took her throne. Henry sat on the edge of his bed and looked up through his narrow window, through the thin steam of his mouth, through the certain feeling that, somehow, this was now about more than murder.

He sat, and watched the moon, and wished the human soul to be a myth, fearing he may well have lost his.

There's no regret on Earth its equal.

Tell me why I bleed.

The Mason Street lecture theater was filled with young people the following morning; an air of fresh cologne, the sigh and rustle of papers, the rumble of feet. The lesson fee was collected at the door, as it was every morning. Idle talk quieted by half as their professor entered and arranged his belongings upon the table at the front of the class. This snowy gentleman grasped his waistcoat in each hand and proceeded to the podium.

"Good morning."

The class responded in kind.

After a thoughtful pause, the professor began. "We have examined a selection of common morbid processes met with in bone. Periostitis. Osteomyelitis. Epiphysitis. In the course of doing so we have examined two of the three bacterial disease types related to such afflictions: the tuberculous and the pyogenic." After a thoughtful pause: "As your professor it is my duty to your future patients to prepare you as best I can for any malady you may likely encounter in the course of your careers as physicians. I therefore apologize to the lady in the class if the subject we are about to discuss should offend her sensibilities."

The fellow beside Henry whispered to his friend: "I wouldn't say that's too likely."

Henry glanced across the room. Finella remained as unfazed as one sitting by a sunny window. The professor had turned and was writing upon the blackboard. His scritch-and-tap spelled out the word *syphilitic*. A few sniggered before they could stop themselves. A few had eyes on Finella. Finella jotted the word down as a heading.

"I say again . . . ," Henry's neighbor whispered, and his fellow stifled a laugh.

Henry leaned sideways. "I expected today to be an examination of a standard clavicle fracture."

"It's been bone disease for the last fortnight," his neighbor said before muttering something else to his friend, which got another laugh. Henry tapped his neighbor again. "Yes?" he said, vaguely irritated.

"I still expect today to be an examination of a standard clavicle fracture."

His neighbor took a moment, seeing in Henry's countenance a seriousness he had never before encountered, and quietly returned to his papers.

The lesson continued for a couple of hours, in notable silence, and primarily concerned itself with the graver afflictions that emerge in the tertiary stages of both acquired and inherited syphilis. Talk of ulcers and the shortening of bones, skin eruptions and bone marrow. When the professor ended his talk and wiped the board down, Henry's neighbor turned to him, face flushed, and said: "You are no better than a thug." Evidently he'd spent the last two hours debating whether or not to pursue the issue.

Henry said, not gracing him with a second glance, "In my experience thugs have no respect for a woman's virtue." He gathered his things and stood. "Let's leave it at that."

The class milled around on the narrow street outside, discussing what they had learned, trading notes. The sunlight was clear and cold. In a crowd of hats and coats against the school's white walls and delicately latticed window frames, Finella's bonnet stood out like a dark flower. Adrenaline poured into Henry from the head down. He wanted to let her go. He wanted to walk her home. He didn't have time for this confusion. He strode down the steps, through the press of his classmates, and caught up with her as she pulled on her calfskin gloves. "Miss Riley?"

If he was anxious upon seeing her, her look of indifference as she addressed him, under any other circumstance, would have sent him into retreat. "Mr. Lockrose." There were only two possible explanations for last night: either Finella was part of some deception, or what he had witnessed was utterly genuine. His very life might depend on which it was. If she traded in blackmail, or was with the law, then he was in a great deal of trouble.

"Miss Riley, how are you, look, about last night . . ."

Someone nearby scoffed, "Well, that explains it, doesn't it?"

Henry's neighbor from the lecture stood ten feet away, his friend by his shoulder. As tight-lipped as when Henry had left him in the lecture hall. "Will you be threatening me again, then, sir?" he said, loudly, for everyone's benefit.

His friend placed a hand on his arm. "Leonard, let this rest."

"I will not," Leonard exclaimed, taking three steps forward and adopting a wide-stance pugilist position, his fists raised before him.

Murmurs all around. One yelled, "Have at him, Leonard!"

"Leonard," Henry said. "You're in the wrong."

Leonard punched Henry in the cheek. It wasn't much compared with the beatings Henry's father had once doled out.

"Leonard."

"You will *not* address me by my given name, you bloody snipe."

"I don't know your last name, pal."

Leonard pursed his lips and lunged. Henry moved his head. In doing so he caught sight of Finella, who was beside herself, surrounded by men and acutely embarrassed. His heart went out to her despite himself. This would be talked about for months.

"This woman . . . !" Leonard gave up on Henry, dropped his guard, and actually lunged at Finella. Grabbing her arm, he dragged her a step into the circle. Her books hit the street, and no one intervened. "Does anyone here not know where she spends her nights?"

Henry punched Leonard squarely in the teeth. Leonard paused, like something had occurred to him, and sat down heavily in the street. Leonard's friend exclaimed "Sir!" and ran to assist him.

Henry bent, gathered Finella's books, and handed them back to her. Gingerly, she accepted them.

"I'm sorry," Henry said. "I was raised on a farm."

Dorian laughed fit to burst. "You were *expelled*?" They sat on the front porch of Mrs. Brown's, nursing a cigarette each.

"Yeah, Leonard's people are rich. School patrons." Dorian kept laughing. "Athelstane, today's been one of those days so bad it changes a person's life and if you don't shut up I'm going to change yours."

The Englishman wound down, surveyed him, took a drag. "You've got a genuine passion for the work, I can tell."

"Don't patronize me. I'm only out here because I've been sitting in my goddamn room all day."

Dorian took another pull on his cigarette, squinted through the smoke, gestured with the lambent end. "We could get you back in, you know." Henry turned and looked him in the eye. He had a face that forecast the man he would grow into. His face was narrow and his eyes were caves.

"I would urge you to not go down this road."

"I'm serious, chum. We perform a working, you get back to school, and we prove we're not frauds. That is why you approached Finella today, isn't it? Hoping to work out what, if anything, was real and what, if anything, was part of some plot against your liberty?"

Miss Riley had been quietly appalled—at least, that's how she appeared—after Henry had hit Leonard; doubly mortified when all realized the professor had been standing in the doorway and had witnessed the entire thing. Henry had never been yelled at so politely in his entire life. A cat tripped out of the alley opposite, looked around, disappeared back in. "How is Miss Riley?"

"How does she feel about what you did? The feminine is charmed, while the firebrand is rankled."

The thought of Finella thinking poorly of him undid something in Henry's chest.

Henry sighed, and sucked a crackling breath from his smoke.

Finally Dorian flicked his stub into the street, an amber starburst off the cobbles. He checked his pocket watch and said: "I'm off to the pub. Will you be coming?"

Henry stared at his shoes and thought about tomorrow, and Finella. It seemed to him that life was a game he may have lost. Like it or not he had business to finish. No getting away from it.

He sighed again, ground the last of his smoke into the step, and fetched his hat from beside him.

"Let's go."

"I grew up in Vermont," Henry told them. "Nothing special. My folks weren't anyone that people such as yourselves would speak to. I'm an impostor, myself, sitting here among you like this. If it weren't for my reading from a young age and studying an etiquette primer while hopping boxcars all the way down here I doubt you would have kept my company for this long.

"My name isn't Lockrose, but I do want to be a surgeon. I don't just want to mend bones, I want to understand how it all works, how it all fits, and how everything we are intersects with everything we aren't. I want to know *us* so well that every other thing about the whole of Creation spells itself out.

"See, I kept my reading hidden, as a boy. Pretty sure Ma knew about it. Don't think Pap really knew until a coupla years before I left for good. He got mad. Always knew it was coming. Knocked me around, took the few books I had in the house at the time and stepped them into the mud. Never did find the other stashes around the place.

"Pap had a son for a reason, and that was to work dirt.

"If I was ever gonna make good on getting out before I turned into the same beaten man my pappy was, living that same shitty life he had in mind for me, I needed an education. So. Money.

"Few years before I left the farm I started taking the money I didn't have from those who did, little by little. Not enough to be noticed. I did the arithmetic, measured what I took, took it at the right time, and kept the whole lot buried deep down and far away.

"Wasn't smart enough, though. After a time the thefts started to get noticed, but by then I'd squirreled away enough for a ticket to Boston through New York, and a few months' worth of lectures here, but I needed more, and I needed it before someone knocked on Pap's door. That happened, it'd all be over for me.

"So. Bernie Sumner. Wide-bodied fellow, bear of a man, served his time as a sergeant. He'd dipped his toes into the waters of the cotton industry in the South, people said, then sold up and left. No one talked about it. He lived well, had a nice place.

"Sumner banked all his cash, but I found a strongbox beneath a wide feather bed. Right below a latticed window that caught the first hours of moonlight. Everything smelled cold and wet the way it does in the first months of winter. He had a good wife, kept the insides smelling flowery despite the muskets and man-stuff all over the place. Made me kinda sad for the kinda home I never expect to have. *Home*, y'know? Nice.

"Anyway, being a *smart* young man I arranged to be in Sumner's house on a night I heard he'd be away. 'Course, ol' Bernie walks through the door, into that flowery bedroom, just as I'm standing there. I'd found a pepperbox pistol in his sock drawer and was aiming it at the lock on the box. It was a big box, kinda like Bernie, old and sturdy and immense.

"Then everything fell into its place. Bernie bellowed; I almost embarrassed myself; Bernie lumbered at me; I shot him through the throat. One minute I was a thief, the next I was a murderer. Didn't even know what I'd done. I just ran. All the way to Boston with Mr. Sumner's money."

Outside the room a distant pub was full of smoke and cheerful uproar. Dysart coughed quietly and reached for his brandy.

Henry looked at Finella, drank her in, taking a ghost's liberty. "I did wrong, a lot of wrong, always intending to set the balance with good works. That seemed right to me." He had about one sentence worth of breath left in him. "I need you to know I'm not a bad man." His chest ached. "That's all I can say."

Dysart swallowed his small mouthful and snuffled softly to himself, eyes on the snifter resting on his belly. Jukes's eyes wandered around the table. Even Dorian said nothing.

"Sir," Finella said quietly, her voice like balm, and looked him in the eye. "We are extraordinary." *Extra. Ordinary.*

Henry looked about the table. All eyes were on him. No one said a word.

The extraordinary fell outside the ordinary.

Home.

"Thank you," Henry said.

And Dorian raised his glass.

The group cleaved to one another in the days that followed. Their meetings became a nightly affair, giving Dorian and Dysart a chance to discuss and plan which working was to come next. While this went on Jukes listened attentively, while Finella went over the day's notes from school. These she shared with Henry, taking him through what was covered that day, and in doing so she not only consolidated the lesson in her own head but imparted it to Henry as well. In this way Henry did not miss the school at all. Here he had not only the learning, but also the company of the one person he couldn't put from his mind.

At school the lectures had shifted from diseases of the bone to injuries of them. Specifically compound fractures.

"What you did to young Leonard has made the rounds, I'm afraid. I suspect you may even have an admirer in the professor."

"Leonard's lack of popularity doesn't make me anything special. Where were we?"

"Traumatic fractures. So . . . when force is transmitted to the seat of a fracture from a distance, the violence is said to be . . ."

"Indirect."

"Correct. And the bone is broken by . . ."

"Torsion. The bone gives way at the weakest point, and the line of fracture will tend to be oblique."

"Correct. Someone leaping from a great height, then, would . . ."

"Landing on his feet, the tibia would break in the lower third, while the fibula would break at a higher level."

Finella went back over her notes and shrugged demurely. "I can only speculate, but I think that would be correct."

"I think it is."

"I see." She smiled to herself, making a pretense of hunting for some fact among her pages. "Then I suppose you would also know the details of a compound clavicle fracture resulting from *direct* force."

"Miss Riley, please . . ."

"Come on, come on."

"Fracture by compression. The line of the fracture would be transverse," he recited in a bored tone, waving a hand impatiently. "And the soft parts overlying the fracture would be damaged according to the weight and shape of the impinging body."

"Give me an example of how someone might indirectly suffer a compound fracture of the clavicle."

"This isn't Sunday school, Miss Riley. We're not going to—"

"Come on, come on."

"Falling on an outstretched hand could result in a . . . fracture of the clavicle in the middle third . . . possibly also or instead resulting in a fracture of the radius at its lower end. If you would please hand those notes over, I think it's time we moved on."

Finella acquiesced, falling silent as Henry looked over her most recent notes. "If you were permitted to return to school, would you?" she said.

"I have to confess, I much prefer learning this way." Henry smiled at the pages as he flipped them. "I trust that's not too forward."

"No. No, I must say I find this form of study far more invigorating than simply rehearsing the day's lesson in my room. But what if you could return? There would be no reason for us to stop studying as we do."

Henry kept himself from shrugging. "Life's too short for maybes, Miss Riley. I would rather live with what I have than play house with what I don't. No sense weighing ourselves down with ghosts and could-have-beens."

Finella laughed politely, like a cough. "Yes, of course."

"You don't agree."

"I agree in principle. But I do believe that you should at least make some effort to be reinstated in the professor's class. You have a natural way with the science of this, Henry. To waste that gift would be a sin."

"I'm not wasting it." He tapped the page. "This is as good as being there. Better, even."

She sighed, unconvinced. "I'm no doctor. Not yet. You can't ask me questions that the prof could answer. I'm just a student, like you. Go back, Henry. At worst the old fellow will just refuse you. But I don't think he will."

The evening concluded, a final toast made, and the group forwarded out of their little back room, talking among themselves. Dorian and Dysart had talked themselves out. A decision had been made as to the best way forward for the Voso ritual, and now all that remained was to prepare themselves over the coming weeks by way of abstinence and good works. Henry wasn't exactly clear on how any of that was meant to work, but Dorian would explain it all the next time they met.

The main room of the Coat and Arms had emptied itself as men collected their hats and coats and made their way back out into the chill. Both Henry and Finella recognized one man in particular, and stopped in their tracks. The professor had seen their group, blanched at the sight of Finella in the company of four men, left his port where it was on the table, took his hat, and stood. Instinctively Henry threw himself into the breach.

"Professor! How do you do. Had I known you would be here I would have invited you to sit with us."

The old man feigned surprise. "Oh, it's Mr. Lockrose isn't it? And Miss Riley."

"Professor," Finella demurred. "Were you passing the evening alone?"

"Yes, as it turns out. Forgive my rudeness, as I must be going. It's late."

Henry inclined his head. "Indeed. Good night, Professor."

The old man doffed his hat and exited. The group watched him go.

"He was here on your account, Henry," Dorian said. "I'd bet my life on it."

"And yet he said nothing," said Finella. "On mine."

Henry couldn't deny it: the professor finding Finella in the company of four men, in the back room of a pub at night . . .

He remembered then something that Leonard had said, in the moments before Henry had floored him.

Does anyone here not know where she spends her nights?

Henry knew exactly what he had meant at the time, but had thought little of it once the incident had resolved itself. However, he would bet a lot that it was Leonard who told the professor where to find him—if the old man had indeed come to have a word with him. Finella's expression was a dark one. Her career was in jeopardy.

Dorian approached, laid a gentle hand on her shoulder. "When I met you, you said that a moment like this was inevitable. That eventually people would begin to talk, and that it would make life at school difficult. I hope you don't regret that decision now."

Finella shook her head. "If you will excuse me, though, I think I would like some time alone."

"Of course."

"Good night, gentlemen."

Henry stepped after her. "At least let us walk you to a cab."

"Not necessary, but thank you."

And Henry watched her go.

Finella did not attend the next night. Or the night after. The day after that Henry waited for her outside class, watching from a block away, and she did not appear.

"She's been expelled," he told Dorian that night. "I'm sure of it."

"She can't be expelled if no one enrolls," Dorian said. "Anyone can turn up and pay by the lesson."

"The professor can still choose to exclude someone from the class, if he thinks their attendance would tarnish the school's reputation."

"Good grief. This is ridiculous."

"We have to find her."

"She won't have done anything stupid, if that's what you're thinking. Finella's too proud for that."

"She may have gone home," Jukes said. "Back to Mother."

"Too proud for that, too, I would have thought."

Henry made for the door. "Tell me where she was staying."

"Fine, I'll come with you. Jukes, Dysart, amuse yourselves or come along if you'd like."

Henry opened the door, onto an unreadable Finella, her hands clasped before her. "Gentlemen," she said. "I have some things to say."

It became apparent to Henry in the weeks leading up to the summoning that this meant more to Dorian than any simple bout of curiosity. And Dorian was more fluent with the language of hidden things than any man his age should have been.

Finella had been refused entry to the classroom for reasons the professor offered to keep between the two of them, in the hope that, perhaps, she would still be able to salvage some respectability. Finella had protested, had taken it to the school board, all to no avail. Having left the school, unable to stop angry tears from staining her face and refusing to give anyone the satisfaction of seeing her wipe them away, she had sat herself down by the least offensive part of the river that she could find and let her mind run riot.

Summoning an intelligence such as Voso's is no easy matter. It is no tearoom beckoncall. It is an effort of collective will with no margin for error.

Finella decided she would try again, elsewhere, and that meant leaving all she had here in Boston. Margaret Fuller's ideas were taking root in cities across the country. Somewhere she would find a place to finish her studies to her satisfaction. But first she had a final duty to the group, and she would see it through. She would be with them, prepare with them, and together—one last final, extraordinary act—they would summon Voso.

Henry didn't know what to say. The news left him hollow, filled with cold air. Finella spent no time with him now, and instead focused rigidly on the task at hand. When Henry couldn't sleep he found himself tangled in impassioned scenes he would never realize, and soon she would be gone.

Dorian vanished without so much as a word. Jukes rabbited on about it, speculating endlessly. Dysart was unflustered. The nightly meetings continued. Finella stopped coming once she realized Dorian was out of the picture for a while.

Three days later he resurfaced, contacted every one of them, and appeared at the Coat and Arms without any of his usual overflow. He ate no food during his time there that night, and drank no brandy. He provided them all with sheets of clean paper, wrapped in white linen. Hubris had made so many things possible for him in his short life. Overconfidence, he said, had been his greatest virtue. But calling down an ageless, cunning, and merciless piece of the universe was so much more than a trick of supreme confidence.

"When the time comes," he had said, "it will be an hour before midnight, and the moon will be waxing, not quite at her full power. The weather will be calm, and still, and we will be in a place far removed from any disturbance. Before that time we will prepare. I ask that you pay close attention to me now, that you might understand my full meaning: we must be prepared, or we shall be destroyed." He let his eyes rove from one member to the next, drawing from their eyes what he needed to know. "Prepared," he said again. "Impeccably and, above all, sincerely."

"Sincerely," Finella repeated. "What form do these preparations take?"

"Destroyed?" Jukes said.

"For the most part it consists of what you would expect: abstinence. Complete and absolute, from anything impious or impure. Engage in nothing that offends body or soul. I shall provide each of you with a prayer, which you shall inscribe once a day upon the paper I have provided you, for three days. I shall provide you with an exact account of how the working will proceed, and you are to spend those three days considering it, meditating upon it as you work, placing yourself at the service of your fellow man."

Dysart cleared his throat. "I see."

"For three days you must surrender yourself to others. Seek out those who need you. Do so selflessly. Sacrifice your wants, your desires, your identity, your pride, and your doubts . . . become selfless. For three days."

Henry watched Finella, expecting her to laugh, or to point out the inherent insincerity of such a thing. Instead she said, "Very well."

Dorian looked to Henry. "Do you comprehend the change of mind I am asking you to undertake? To shift your world to a new axis, if only for three days? Are you able to permit such a shift to topple your psychological architecture into a new configuration? Can you both admire and dwell within this new house, completely and utterly, for three days?"

There were many things Henry could have said at that point. Instead he took one look at Finella, sitting straight-backed, hands laced on the table before her, and said, "Of course."

"Of course," Jukes said.

"What have you decided upon for the working itself?" Dysart rumbled.

"In the end the form of the service matters little. What is paramount is the purity of our souls, minds, and flesh."

Dysart sighed luxuriously, thoughtfully, and raised his thick, cloudy eyebrows. "I've done worse."

After shrugging into their coats, Dorian said, "Say good-bye to this room. We won't be needing it again."

"Indeed," rumbled Dysart. "The time feels right for a good last act."

"But . . . ," said Jukes.

"If we are successful," Dorian said, "we progress. It may well be that our paths diverge from that point on. And if we fail . . . well . . ."

"Destroyed," Henry said. "You believe the thing you want to call down could actually kill us."

"All things are possible."

Finella listened to the conversation as though it were one of the professor's lectures: attentive, saying nothing, taking it in. Henry realized he really had remained here for her. Regardless of whatever fascination he had for the group's explorations, regardless of the fact that these people now constituted the entirety of his social circle in a life now devoid of both family and schooling, he had remained here for her. He hadn't even asked what the ultimate point of it all was.

"Good night, Henry. I will see you all four evenings hence, at the arranged location."

"You're not coming back to Mrs. Brown's?" Henry said. "She's been worrying after you."

"As Master of Ceremonies my duties differ from yours. Remember: pursue your good deeds, memorize your prayer, study the service, give yourself over to a cleansing and selfless transformation—

if only for three days—and we will all witness and achieve the most extraordinary thing." And Dorian left the room, walking stick in hand.

"Saintliness isn't the aim," Dysart rumbled, throwing a scarf about his broad neck and adjusting his aged topper. "Only the absolute suspension of our own needs and wants, which are the bedrock of our cumbersome personalities. Become selfless—without self—a conduit for the happiness of others. Embrace the change of mind, the feelings it provides, and come to us on the fourth night with a pure and selfless heart, untroubled and uncluttered by the baser needs of mind and flesh. A conduit for something greater still."

Finella took his arm. "We want to be doctors, Henry. Selflessness should be in our very natures. Come on, walk me to a cab."

The street air was bracingly cold, briny and feculent and still. A stray man clutching his tweed coat about himself hurried along, shoulders hunched, breathing into the heat of a cigarette. They stopped before a horse cab, and that was when Finella released his arm and said, "The next time we see each other shall be the last time. I wanted to thank you, Mr. Lockrose, for your company this past year. Though I admit things seemed to be at sevens and eights between us for a time, I am glad to have made your acquaintance and consider you a friend. You shall make a fine doctor, Henry."

Henry didn't know what to say. It was now or never.

Instead he said, "Good night, Miss Riley."

"Good night."

He held the door open for her as she climbed aboard. The driver nick-nicked, slapped the reins, and amid a crisp clatter of wheels and hooves Finella was gone.

It felt a little like being born, standing there, with nothing left and no real idea as to what came next. Everything was new, somehow. Blank. As beautiful and terrifying as an Arctic landscape. He thought about what was to come. Three days of selflessness.

Blank and empty, then, was a good beginning.

The air was rich and sweet with stink—a stench most people never paid any attention to. The sewers beneath them were barely contained. Overflows were frequent—an especially high tide could do it—and tuberculosis was on the rampage, more so in Boston than almost anywhere else in the country. On first arriving in New York, and then here, it had surprised and saddened Henry the density of filth a city could contain, how a metropolis could float upon it. Somehow he had expected something different.

He closed his eyes for a moment as he walked. To be truly selfless was to be as uninhibited as a libertine. As thoughtless as an idiot child. It was to allow anything passage through you that had the whim.

Henry wanted to see the water.

He spent the best part of a cold hour clipping briskly toward the old State House and the myriad wharves that bristled out onto the Charles River just beyond it.

If someone asked him for money, he gave it.

If someone told him their story, he listened.

He found a disheveled young man clutching himself in a doorway, poor bulwark against a biting wind. Whoever he was, he was in his early twenties and had the drawn features one saw so often on people who remained on the street after nine o'clock on cold nights like this. The woolen glove on his right hand, clutched weakly to his left biceps, lacked a fingertip or two, and there Henry saw how black his nails were, how corrupted the flesh of his fingertips. He gently took the sleeve of that arm and rolled it up a little. Infection had worked its way up from his scrofulous fingers, spreading along the lymphatic vessels of the arm. There was an abscess at the wrist, a fragile dome and amber-filled.

"What happened," Henry asked. "Was it these cuts on your fingers?"

The young man nodded weakly. "Broken spittoon," he said. "Me master's. At the time. Who are you?" His breathing was like a gentle wind over stray leaves. His coughs were blood against stone.

Henry slipped the young man's arm around his shoulder and helped him to his feet. "It's all right. I'm a doctor."

If Voso felt kinship with woodland then woodland Voso would have. Dorian had made a good choice, an area of woodland that was yet to be cleared not too far from where they all lived yet removed enough that they would not likely be disturbed.

Henry stood alone in the small clearing they were to be using. He knew this was the place, because Dorian had laid the space out beforehand. The ground had been swept, in a circular fashion, and Voso's sigil scratched roughly into the earth. Later it would be prepared correctly, the runnels filled in with chalk. A small supply of candles and a pile of linen robes were stored in a duffel sack nestled into the roots of one of the larger elms, gone leafless with the turn of the season. Henry wondered if Dorian was around, perhaps watching, an idle voyeur. That certainly seemed like something he would find amusing.

He had not slept in three days. He felt apart from the world, rather than part of it. It ordered his thoughts.

What a strange life it had been. To have come from the north and ignorance, and come southerly into God only knew what. If he had taken a different boardinghouse, he wondered, would he have met Dorian anyway? What was it that had delivered him here . . . why had Dorian delivered him here. Henry wasn't anything special. What made Dorian think tonight would actually succeed?

Think, nothing. Believe, nothing. Dorian knew. That was the difference.

So many questions.

"Mr. Lockrose?" Finella stepped into the clearing. "Oh, it is you. I was wondering . . ."

"This is the place." Henry inclined his head toward the circle. "How are you, Miss Riley?" In truth she seemed changed. No bodice, none of the formal clothing she so often chose. Finella wore a plain dress, with plain shoes, her auburn hair no longer bound up, only tied back from her face. It suited her. It highlighted her natural loveliness. "Been away?"

"Yes. You?"

"No." Henry looked at the circle. The waxing moon dappled light across it, the straight lines and neat curves of Voso's sigil discernible as a different kind of shadow amid the soothing, scattered play of light and dark.

"It feels as if we're meant to be here now. As though everything up to this point in time has occurred for a reason." Voso's name lying in wait before him, Henry crossed the clearing toward her.

She didn't stand on formality. "Henry . . ."

And he kissed her.

For two seconds he lived in the only point in time that would ever feel like home. And then she pulled away, leaving him with naught but the sound of her feet on leaves.

Time passed. Shadows shifted. Dorian and Dysart arrived, carrying tools. Within an hour all was ready.

"Where's Jukes," Henry asked.

"Adam won't be joining us," Dorian replied. "In fact, he is not even aware that we are here tonight. He is an unfortunate liability in a situation where such a degree of seriousness and focus is required. It would have been irresponsible of me to include him. Now let's have no more talk."

Which left them with four.

They worked in silence, none speaking for fear of destroying the meticulous preparation of the preceding three days. Finella would not look Henry in the face.

Dorian waited in the clearing, at the northern point of the circle. Voso's mark was a smaller circle within a circle with his name— voso—inscribed in the between-space, and his symbol in the center. All was marked out in trails of powdered chalk. This would be the space of their working.

"Over there"—Dorian pointed away from the four spotfires that lit the clearing, flames sheltering inside a border of round stones—"you will find a few simple robes, nothing fancy. Remove your clothes—all of you—and bring the robes over here."

Henry watched as hesitation and horror at the idea of exposing his rotund form flashed across Dysart's face. Nonetheless they retrieved the garments laid out for them on the dead leaves, and disrobed. It was a chill night, yet Henry felt nothing shedding his clothes. He kept his eyes forward, neither cold nor shamed. He simply was.

Dysart on the other hand wrestled with the first of many layers concealing his form, and Henry felt a pang of sympathy for the man. Finella took the act of disrobing with good grace, and Henry in turn felt obliged to maintain her ease by treating their state as incidental.

This was the first time he had stood naked in the presence of any woman other than his mother. He had kissed Finella and regretted nothing. Being naked before her was like something he had always known. His spirit had touched hers, and now they would part.

This, then, was both death and birth. Henry felt as resigned to it as anyone on his deathbed, as any child at his confirmation.

They crossed the clearing to where Dorian waited on the other side of the circle with a giant steel pitcher of water. He took Henry by one thin shoulder and turned him around, tipping the jug above his head. Henry gasped loudly, convulsively, as chill water crashed over his head, spreading in icy sheets down his entire body.

"Be ye regenerate, cleansed, and purified in the Name of the Ineffable, Great and Eternal God, from all your iniquities, and may the virtue of the Most High descend upon you and abide with you always, so that ye may have the power and strength to accomplish the desires of your heart. Amen. Take your robe and dress yourself."

And so it went.

"O Lord God, Holy Father, Almighty and Merciful One, Who hast created all things, Who knowest all things and can do all things, from

Whom nothing is hidden, to Whom nothing is impossible; Thou Who knowest that we perform not these ceremonies to tempt Thy power, but that we may penetrate into the knowledge of hidden things; we pray Thee by Thy Sacred Mercy to cause and to permit that we may arrive at this understanding of secret things, of whatever nature they may be, by Thine aid, O Most Holy *Adonai*, Whose Kingdom and Power shall have no end unto the end of the Ages of Ages. Amen."

Dorian stepped backward to permit Henry to stand before him, holding the journal containing the conjuration. Dorian took from his robe a clutch of parchments bound in azure ribbon, parchments marked with the appropriate signs and sigils. In his right hand he held the knife. Henry opened the journal, and Dorian read aloud:

"Here be the Symbols of the Secret things, the standards, the ensigns, and the banners of God the Conqueror; and the arms of the Almighty One, to compel the Aerial Potencies. I command ye absolutely by their power and virtue that ye come near unto us, into our presence, from whatsoever part of the world ye may be in, and that ye delay not to obey us in all things wherein we shall command ye by the virtue of God the Mighty One. Come ye promptly, and delay not to appear, and answer us with humility." Dorian drew in a great and final breath, lifted his eyes from the book, and exclaimed: "I call ye *Voso*, fifty-seventh of the seventy-two Fallen, teacher and shapeshifter, *come!*"

Silence. Henry felt the stillness of the moment, the complete lack of sound, save breathing. No night birds, no distant town sounds, not even a whisper from the uppermost treetops. And again Dorian called:

"Here again I conjure ye and most urgently command ye; I force, constrain, and exhort ye to the utmost, by the mighty and powerful Name of God," and he said it, and eleven other names, and a lengthy evocation for immediate appearance. And still nothing. Henry turned the pages and Dorian read. Still nothing.

Finally Dorian said, "Close the book. This is not done with. None of you lose heart nor focus. There is nothing these things respect more than constancy. We will have our audience. Stand away from the circle."

The three of them stood away as Dorian paced the perimeter widdershins, examining the integrity of the sigil and refreshing its outline with the bucket of chalk dust he retrieved from the bole of a dead tree. This done he returned to his place at the head of the sigil, took a fistful of damp earth, and tossed a part of it to each of the four corners of the Universe. Then he faced north, fell to his knees, placed the knife on the ground before him, spread his arms wide, and called: "The Name of *Adonai Elohim Tzabaoth Shaddai*, Lord God of Armies Almighty, may we successfully perform the works of our hands, and may the Lord be present with us in our heart and on our lips."

And then he rose, turned, and opened his arms to the circle. Henry again took his place, as did the others. "By the Holy Names of God written in this Book, and by the other Holy and Ineffable Names which are written in the Book of Life, we conjure ye to come to us promptly and without delay, wherefore tarry not, but appear in a beautiful and agreeable form and figure, by virtue of these names we exorcise ye: *Anai, æchhad, Transin, Emeth, Chaia, Iona, Profa, Titache, Ben Ani, Briah, Theit*; all which names are written in Heaven in the characters of the Malachim—*the tongue of the Angels*."

Again, as Dorian's voice rang out, silence. And then, somewhere, a bird began to sing. Something trilling. Another picked up the call from behind Henry, and another to his left, distant and unseen. Dorian's eyes ranged over the blackness beyond the light of the fires, and Henry felt a new weight to the air. Things began to change. There was an intake of breath from Finella's side of the circle, and Henry watched Dorian's eyes widen with sudden and satisfied delight.

There came a perfume, heady and sweet.

Henry risked looking over his shoulder, and saw the shoots growing there, climbing toward a vanished sun. Lush grasses sprouted within the perfect circle, a round green bed rising through dead leaves. Flowers foreign to New England were growing and blooming colorfully, the air redolent and heavy with their scent. Henry saw tulips and roses.

Lying on his new bed, eyes closed and slumbering, was a leopard.

Dorian swallowed. "Voso," he said. "Voso awaken."

"I am awake," it said. Its voice was perfection, warm and rounded. Impossible music falling upon ears of dirt. "What is your need, Dorian."

Henry closed the journal. Dorian would no longer be needing it.

"You know my name," Dorian whispered, half to himself. "But then, you know everything, don't you?"

Henry took his place outside the circle, careful to never lay a toe inside it as he traveled.

The great cat lay with its head on its forepaws, eyes closed. Henry could see its ribs expanding and collapsing with each breath, waiting for Dorian to speak.

"You know why I have conjured you."

"I know," the great cat said. "And I tell you that my answering will bring about an undoing in this world and the next. And you will demand my answer nonetheless."

"Then answer me."

"You are just a man, Dorian Athelstane. A man who, to me, appears to have died the moment I met you, so short are your lives. And yet you, this imperfect vessel, seek to contain perfect knowledge."

"You cannot deny me, and you know I will not desist, so why do you hesitate?"

The cat opened its great eyes. "Because such things are about choice. You must choose to fall."

"Then I choose to fall. Speak."

The cat roused itself, unfurling and rising to its feet with no wasted movement. Its lazily shifting tail did not break the circle. It did not take its eyes from the master of the circle.

"I can offer you a new form if you desire. That is also within my portfolio. Anything in the stead of what you ask."

"*Speak!*"

The leopard inclined its head slightly. "Three times you have chosen." It rose up on its hind legs, filling out and widening as it did so, toes becoming fingers, mottled fur falling away . . .

The changing took less than a minute. The end result was a giant twice the mass and height of a normal man, standing nude before them. It seemed to Henry to be an amalgam of every racial aspect of humanity. Blackest skin with deeply Asiatic eyes, and shoulder-length golden hair. Fingernails like long wedges of cut glass, with an eye color to match.

"It is my portfolio to reveal the hidden," Voso intoned. "But things remain outside even a portfolio that expansive. The one you would learn of is stricken from all records, Celestial and Earthly, by the Hand of God. It has no name, no form, no portfolio, no ritual, no place inside Creation."

"That," Dorian replied through gritted teeth, "is not good enough."

"For harmony it must be," the Fallen said.

"*Answer me by the Name and in the Name of* Shaddai, *which is that of God Almighty, strong, powerful, admirable, exalted* . . ."

"Dorian Athelstane, who was once Johannes Paole," the angel said. "Do not press this."

". . . *and by the Name of* El, Iah, Iah, Iah, *Who hath formed and created the world by the Breath of His Mouth, Who supporteth it by His Power* . . ."

"Stop. Your knowledge of what you do is incomplete."

". . . *Who ruleth and governeth it by His Wisdom, and Who hath cast ye for your pride into the Land of Darkness and into* . . ."

"Stop."

". . . *the Shadow of Death.*"

The demon was silent. And then, with reluctance, said, "So be it." Voso opened both arms, breaking the circle. Powerful hands found a throat each, pulling the two into the circle, the snap of carti-lage seeming to echo forever, the shattering of bone as both heads were brought together loud enough to frighten the night birds.

It was as sudden as it was over. They lay at the Fallen's feet, face to bloodied face on a bed of green and flowers.

Dorian couldn't believe it.

"Your circle was not perfect, magus. Your attendants were not ad-equately prepared." Its clear eyes turned down to Finella's bloodied face. "It was undone with a kiss. As these things often are."

Henry watched Dorian's throat work, swallowing dry with an open mouth.

"We will not meet again."

Voso was gone.

Dorian orchestrated the concealment of the deaths with detached ex-actitude. Their robes, clothing, and jewelry were gathered together. The garments were burned, the ashes scattered. The jewelry would be thrown into the foundations of a building under construction in the town.

They lay the bodies together as they worked. Henry tried to look anywhere but her ruined face, and failed. It was a blackened catastro-phe. The face he had kissed, the head that held such high ideals, now shattered carrion.

A hand on his shoulder. "You're done, Henry. Go."

The sun was breaking through the treetops. Henry's white robe was wet and brown down the knees and at every hem. His usual clothes were laid out beyond the clearing, near Finella's and Dysart's, like another body.

His love had been killed before him. And now he would trade her dignity for one slim chance at freedom.

He no longer knew himself.

Jukes.

When Finella turned up missing, Jukes would know. There would be an inquiry. Finella's mother would come to Harvard. And Jukes would know. He would not know the details, but he would know that Finella had died, and that Henry had been there. And Dysart . . . when his absence was noticed, that would be more than Jukes would be able to contain.

Like something rising from a black ocean the reality of what Henry had to do became clear. *Leave Boston.* Or this thing would track him until it brought him down.

He walked home with the sun gone but some light remaining.

After they had burned the clothes, after they had removed the jewelry, Dorian asked that the last be left to him. Henry had not even crouched, touched her, kissed her good-bye.

He could not remember where he had spent the following day. Only that he was aware of being transcendently exhausted, and burning with thirst. His skin tasted like salt.

Mrs. Brown's boardinghouse glowed ghost-pale in the evening light. Figures gathered on the porch like shades, conversing low. Mustaches and truncheons.

Police.

Standing in the door, lips moving quickly, hands fluttering, speaking his fill, was Newspaper Jack. An old hand touched down on his shoulder from behind, stilled him, drew him gently inside. Mrs. Brown appeared, anxious. Said very little, and then the door closed.

The police stood there, hats tucked under their arms, looking squarely at one another. A conclusion had been made.

The door opened again. Dorian emerged in hat and coat, weighed down with a suitcase in one hand and a heavy package of tied paper in the other. He placed the suitcase down, doffed his hat to the officers, turned, and closed the door behind himself. Then he picked up his luggage, bid a second farewell, and walked down the three wooden steps to the street, limned briefly by the passing of a cab's lantern, and away from Henry.

And he was gone.

Eventually the police gave up any hope of a second audience and left.

Henry used his key and walked into the kitchen.

They had found a body that afternoon, bumping up against one of the cutwaters of the Salt and Pepper bridge. Middle-aged. Male. As yet unidentified.

Headless.

TWO

LONDON, 1847

THIS IS LIFE FROM KNEE HEIGHT. YOU WAKE IN THE DARK beneath woolen blankets. You don't often see stars and there is no moon. Nonetheless you know and feel the damp on the plaster walls of your little room glistening like silver. You know it is half past four in the morning. Your mother's door has just opened.

Millicent's mother opens her door, pokes her head in on the way past, and says, "Time for work, cherub."

You let out your first real breath of the day and blink a few times. You reach out from under the blankets for the damp cloth your mother leaves there. A few mornings your eyes were stuck together with sleep. You were scared, but you didn't panic, and your mother wiped your eyes open with warm water and a washrag. Now she leaves one there every night, as a habit.

The rag on your face is sharply cold, and it wakes you up.

There is a clank from downstairs as Millicent's grandfather fills the kettle. Millicent puts the rag back on the side table and gets out from under her bedcovers.

This is life from knee height. You spend your day with spindle and ribbon making silk roses for ladies' hats, while your mother holds pins for the mantua maker or offers advice on hosiery and jewelry and shoes.

Millicent has a stool and a table far out the back. When her mother can, she smiles and waves as she walks by, swags of bright material folded over her arm.

Your grandfather is your best friend, and you are your mother's dream diary. She talks to you as she might talk to herself. You sit, and you listen, and if she should happen to become weepy you hold her hand and tell her Father will be home someday.

You are back under your woolen blankets, and the damp on the walls glistens like silver. Downstairs Mama and your grandfather—Papa— talk in low voices, because it is dark now, and they are drinking tea. You close your eyes and all you can see are silk roses.

Millicent wakes. It is dark. She knows she has not been asleep very long. She wonders for a moment why she is awake, and then she knows. Mother has just called her name.

Millicent pushes the heavy covers away and touches her bare feet down upon the cold boards. She rubs her eyes and uses both hands to open the door. She walks down the landing and stands at the top of the stairs.

You are looking down from the top of the stairs into the front room. It is like a portrait of sorts, everyone in their pose.

Mama's white hands are clasped to the bib of her nightgown. You have never seen her smile like that. You want to hold her hand. On the other side Papa looks as though he might become angry. His bottom lip is pushing up toward his nose and his arms are crossed.

They are both looking at the gentleman at the bottom of the stairs who is smiling softly at you, one ringed hand on the banister, his hat in his hand.

"Hello," he says, taking one careful step toward you.

Mother wipes her eyes quickly and says, "Millicent, say hello. This is Dorian, your father."

Millicent is hoisted out of the carriage and placed gently upon the ground. Her new shoes click crisply upon the cobbles, and her new dress still itches. Dorian takes his wife by her white-gloved hand and assists her from the carriage. She smiles uncommonly wide, her eyes almost disappearing, and she presses herself close to this man. It makes Millicent feel strange to see her mother behaving this way.

"Tonight was wonderful," Mama confides, scrunching her shoulders to her ears ever so briefly. "I cannot recall the last time I had a theater party." They had eaten early in order to get to the play on time. Millicent had three extra cushions placed upon her chair so that she could reach her plate, and the room had been full to the brim with ladies dressed in things soft and sparkling, and men who were all straight lines and mustaches. People had glanced discreetly at them, for Millicent was the only child in the room. That a husband and wife would bring their child to dine at a club was decidedly uncommon, but Dorian was unfazed—smiling generously at anyone hapless enough to have their gaze apprehended—and Mama had giggled at the brashness of her husband and the novelty of it all. Everyone there was so bright, and dressed so neat and so fine . . . more elegant even than Mrs. Sutcliffe, and Millicent had seen her buy five hats all on the same day. There had been music, proper music, played by people with real instruments. The food was nice but Millicent hadn't been able to look away from the violins. It had grown something warm inside her, and filled her head with light. When the time came to leave she had been almost unable to bear it.

"What did you think of the pheasant," Dorian asks her, bending at the waist and straightening the shoulders of her dress. His breath plumes about her face.

"It was very nice. Thank you, sir."

"Thank you, *Father*," Mama corrects, midfuss and wrist-deep in her purse.

"Thank you, Father," says Millicent.

Mama takes the heavy key from her purse, climbs the few stairs to their door, and opens it. She enters their narrow house, singing. Papa is in the kitchen, at the table by the stove, nursing a mug of tea. "Home, then," he says.

Mama kisses him heavily upon his thin-skinned cheek and the old man doesn't react. "It was wonderful," she says again.

"You must come with us next time, Papa," Dorian says, placing his low-crowned hat upon the table.

"Now that you're back," Papa says, his chair squeaking upon the stone, "I'll be a-bed. Good night, Mary." He kisses his daughter on her cheek. "And good night to you, Miss Millicent Mumble." He leans down and presses his lips to Millicent's forehead. They're cold, and his touch is whiskery, and it makes her smile. "You look beautiful," he confides, just between them.

Dorian laughs generously. "How on Earth did you come to call her that?"

Millicent's grandfather stands straight, chin up. Millicent catches a glimpse of him as a younger man, hard-chested and strong. "She would talk in her sleep, as an infant. It were a sweet sound. Not something a man wouldn't treasure now."

Dorian's response is not quick, and for Millicent it is like watching someone stumble in the street. Mama wears a smile as she clasps her husband's hand supportively, and shrugs her shoulders to her ears once more as though there were too much joy at his presence to be contained.

It makes Millicent anxious. She looks to her grandfather. "Will you tuck me in, Papa?"

"Oh no, Millicent!" Dorian exclaims. "Not tonight. Tonight you may stay up with us." Dorian sweeps her up. "And we'll have cocoa, and talk about all the things we shall change about this house. You've no objection now, do you, Papa?"

The old man sighs, takes his candle, and walks through the door, toward the stairs. "Good night all."

"Good night, Papa."

"I'll put the kettle on," Mama says and takes the remaining candle into the pantry to look for chocolate, leaving Dorian and Millicent in the kitchen by the light of the stove's open door.

"You've been very reserved, young lady," Father says. He smells like cigars, too, and the perfume he wears makes her nose wrinkle. "Do you not like your new shoes and dress? Wasn't the play so very fine? Have you never eaten so well? And there's so much more to come yet. I'm a man of means, my little one, and there's nothing shall be denied you."

"I've had a very nice time, thank you, Father."

"Millicent," Dorian says, quietly, looking to the pantry where Mama's light is still flickering off the assembled jars and tins. "Do you not like me?"

"Sir . . . Father," she says. "If I might be very forward . . ."

"Yes, Millicent?"

"Who are you?"

Dorian blinks, remaining still like someone who has heard something he does not understand, or who has been caught in a lie.

Mama reenters, waving the chocolate tin. "I've found it," she says, and tends to the stove. Father puts Millicent back down, stands, and offers to draw water.

Water splashing into the kettle, he sings to himself.

Nelly Bly! Nelly Bly! Bring the broom along,
We'll sweep the kitchen clean, my dear,
And have a little song.
Poke the wood, my lady love
And make the fire burn,
And while I take the banjo down,
Just give the mush a turn . . .

Mama laughs to herself. "Whatever is that nonsense you're singing?"

Father smiles politely, placing the kettle upon the stove. "Something I picked up on my travels. The Americans are quite fond of it at the moment."

Millicent pulls out Papa's chair and sits herself upon it. She knows she will not be making roses tomorrow . . . and that Mama shall not be holding pins for the mantua maker. Everything is different now.

Millicent has spent the day by the window. Her hands feel strange and weightless. They should be making roses.

Mama didn't come to Millicent's door this morning. Millicent walked to Mama's room and knocked. Mama laughed and said to go away and Father said they would be down soon. Papa made her a breakfast of tea and toast, and then Millicent went and sat at the window.

"Mama's acting strange, isn't she, cherub," Papa says. He is standing behind Millicent, looking out at the road through bushes gone leafless with the cold. Sunday is his rest day. Six days a week he works as a handyman for families about town.

"Papa, why don't you like Father?"

"Ah, you've heard your mother and I having words," he says. Millicent nods. Papa sits himself down on the window seat and thinks at his folded hands. "Well," he says. "Your mother and I knew your father before you came along. He was a younger man then and, as you'll learn when you grow older, young men don't often think as much of others as they should."

"Was he bad to Mama, Papa?"

Papa thought again. "I might say he would have hurt your Mama's feelings, had I not had words with him. As a younger man he could have made her very sad."

"Mama has been very sad, Papa."

Papa nodded and patted her knee. "And you've been a veritable paladin, you have, helping her all your life as you've done. And a hard worker, too."

"Will she be happy now?"

"I hope so, cherub."

Millicent is woken by the pounding of the great knocker on the front door. Outside someone is calling Father's name. Shouting it at the walls. Instantly the house comes alive. Exclamations from Papa downstairs, curses from Father in the next room. Puzzled grumbles and shrieks from Mama. Doors open. Feet tramp. The knocker is slammed down over and over, reverberating through the house. Still the voice keeps calling, thick with a strange accent.

"Dorian! Dorian! Dorian!"

Millicent struggles out of bed, opening her door with both hands, rubbing her eyes.

Through the balustrade you watch Papa stagger from his room, candle in hand, yelling at the door. Father rushes past behind you, almost knocking you over, and gallops down the stairs, making it to the front door just inches ahead of Papa.

Wrenching it open, one hand extended backward to fend off Papa, Father is fallen upon.

"Dorian! Dios querido, mi amigo . . . !"

Swarthy-faced and loose-limbed the stranger collapses onto Father, one arm slung around his shoulder. In the stranger's sweat-sheened hand a long blade flashes.

Papa exclaims, "What is the meaning of this!" and reaches for the walking stick kept by the front door. The stranger reacts violently, shoving Father away and thrusting the blade toward Papa.

Father slaps a hand down upon the man's wrist and disarms him with the other. "Luis, no. Todo está bien. You are safe with me."

"Safe? I am next! It tells me so! It tells me it has told you so! It tells you now! You know this."

Father's head turns slightly toward where Papa stands, dumb-

struck by this scene. The cold night air fills the room. Mama stands
by you, peering around the corner like a child.

"*Me ha dicho esto.*"

"Then do as it asks, *cabrón*! I will not die for you."

Father turns and looks up at his wife, at Millicent, at Papa who
stands by the door with a face like a thundercloud. "We will step outside, and disturb my family no longer. Come with me, Luis." Father
takes his coat from the stand by the door and disappears outside with
the strange man who came into their house waving a knife. After a
long moment Mama places a hand on Millicent's shoulder and walks
her back to bed.

Millicent sits upon her bed, listening to the words being said in the
kitchen. Papa is louder than the others and Mama wants him to be
quiet, but Millicent knows he is angry with Father. Millicent is worried for Mama.

After a while Papa stops talking and Millicent hears him go to his
bed. She hears Mama and Father talking low just outside her door,
and then the door to Mama's chamber opens, then closes. And then
Millicent's door quietly opens and Father peers in. His face is bright
and smiling in the candlelight.

"Hello," he says.

"Hello, Father," says Millicent, carefully.

"I'm giving you some of my bad habits, staying up so late."

"What other habits do you have?"

"Well," he says, stepping inside and closing the door, keeping
his voice low. "I do tend to get myself into trouble from time to
time."

"What kind of trouble?"

"Oh, you know. This and that." He crouches by her bedside,
and Millicent wonders what he expects. "I've traveled here with a
friend of mine, actually. We came from Mexico. Do you know
where that is?"

Millicent shakes her head. "Were you in trouble there?"

Father smiles. "It's part of the game we all play. You know what it's like."

Millicent shakes her head. "I used to make mistakes when I was making the roses, but I have become much better since then."

"Roses . . . ?"

"Mama and I work at the milliner's."

"Ah. Ah yes, of course."

"I make roses mostly, and Mama helps the mantua maker."

"Yes, yes, but what about when you're not doing that?"

Millicent thinks about that. "Then we come home."

Father's brow furrows with disbelief. "Do you not have friends?"

"I have Papa and I have Mama. They are my friends. Papa and Mama will be sending me to a school next year," she says. "After we save enough."

The eager smile fades from Father's face and is replaced with something else. Millicent wonders if she has been impertinent, if Father is about to become angry.

Father stands up with a calisthenic sigh and looks about the tiny little room. He says, "Well well well," in a way that tells Millicent he wants to change the subject. He looks at the wet walls, the cloudy little window with its view onto the street, the bedside table that Papa made, with its single flickering candle in a holder of green iron. "Well well well," he says.

She moves to placate him. "I like making roses," she says.

"Hmm?" he says. "Oh, yes, I'm sure they're lovely." And then he is down to her level again, in a shot, and urgently hissing, "God's wounds, haven't you done *anything*?"

Millicent flinches backward, her father's face like a mad mask in the darkness before her, unsure what he will say or do. She has never had a grown-up speak to her like this.

Father lowers his eyes and looks away, defeated. "Never mind. Are you tired, Millicent?"

Millicent shakes her head, frightened.

"May we talk for a while?"

Millicent is very sleepy the next morning. Papa makes her toast and tea and asks what it was she and Father talked about all last night. Papa heard Father leave the house at about four in the morning, and he hasn't returned.

"Father was telling me about when he was a boy."

"Oh yes?"

"It wasn't very nice. His mama kept him locked up all the time. Made him tell people things for money."

Papa forgets his plate, leaves it on the sideboard. "What?"

Millicent puts her toast down. "When she made him tell people things he went away, in his head."

At that moment Mama comes down the stairs and into the kitchen.

"Your Dorian's mother was a spirit-rapper, did you know that? A cheap confidence artist, just like him."

"His family was very poor," Mama says, sliding a pin through her hair. "I'm sure they did what they had to in order to get by."

Over the following days the house changed. Out went their old things, the tattered old love seat by the fire, the chipped and worn table that Papa had made for the kitchen, the battered old kettle and blackened pots. Out went Millicent's little bed. And in came everything soft and bright and new. Almost the only thing that survived the forced evacuation was Papa's old armchair, which he refused to part with, and his own bed that he had slept in through marriage and loss. Curtains fell and drapes were raised, and legions of men came to scrape the windows and roll out new rugs.

Through it all smiled Mama, buoyed to new heights by each new gift and arrival. Papa kept himself away from it all for as long as it happened, returning each day after dark smelling of clipped grass and lacquer, and the first thing he would say would always be "My chair and bed best still be here," and Mama would always reply, tired and patient, "Yes, Papa, they're still here, same as they ever were," as if there was no avoiding it. And through it all Millicent kept out of the way of Mama and Father and the workers who came and went, as the house she grew up in washed away, piece by piece. Millicent was not so attached to the old things that their leaving cast a sadness upon her. What left her quiet from the moment the first new chair came through the door was the notion that if Father should leave there would not be one thing in the entire house—except Papa's bed and chair—that would not remind Mama of Father. It was the thought of that sadness falling upon her mother that kept Millicent silent and to herself through all the days in which the house changed.

They do not eat at home now that Father has returned. Nor do they spend any of their evenings in their new home on any of the nights that Father is not away talking to his friend from Mexico, or conducting business about the town. ("Who does business of a nighttime?" Papa demanded to know.) And then, on a night they were meant to attend the ballet, Father did not come home for them. Mama waited, then fidgeted. Papa put the kettle on and that made her angry. ("We don't have time. The performance begins in less than an hour.") And then an hour passed, and Father did not come home, and Mama did her best to smile and shrug and told them there would be other ballets, other performances, and went upstairs and closed her door.

A little while later Millicent puts on her nightgown and Papa comes and they say their prayers together. Then Millicent is tucked into her new bed, which is twice as long and twice as wide as her old one, stuffed to bursting with goose feathers and down. Papa reads to her from *The Beauty in the Sleeping Forest*, which she always liked, and then she goes to sleep.

Millicent Athelstane, aged eight, will see her father one more time. That very night she wakes to find him crouched by her bedside, smiling as someone who is just learning to make friends. "I'm sorry you missed the ballet," he says. "A rather inconvenient thing has transpired."

"Trouble, Father?" Millicent says, sitting up and rubbing one eye.

Father smiles again and looks at the floor. "You know how it is."

It is very dark, and very cold.

"I have to go away," Father says. "But before I do there is something I would like very much to give you. Something grander than clothes or a bed or any of that tedious rubbish. I know you weren't very much taken with them."

"Don't go," Millicent says.

Father falls silent, like someone hearing very bad news. "New . . . new furnishings can't be of very great interest to a young lady with her whole life before her," he says, continuing as though she had never spoken. "And I want to leave . . . leave you with something that will make you happy."

"Mama will be so sad if you go. We don't work at the milliner's anymore. She has no one to look after her."

Father stands and extends his hand to her. "Won't you come and see?"

Millicent feels like she wants to cry, her mouth all hard and wobbly, but she nods yes. She pushes the blankets off herself and slides her feet into her checkered little slippers. She puts her hand in Father's—soft and smooth—and follows him out of her room and down the stairs. From the top of the stairs she sees that someone has lit the sitting room with a great many candles.

"Now," Father whispers. "We must be very quiet. What I have made is for your eyes, and my eyes, and the eyes of angels alone." They are at the bottom of the stairs and all Millicent can see through the sitting room arch is all the new furniture lit by that rich, warm glow. Her father squeezes her hand. "Now then, come with me."

They walk into the sitting room.

Her father squeezes her hand again. "Surprise."

Kneeling there, upon the Persian rug, between the two leather settees is . . .

Millicent is unsure if she wants to take a step closer.

The ballerina is mostly mechanical. Her arms, legs, and chest are hollow, ornate, wrought. Millicent can see right through them, through the fancy and filigree, to the fireplace that lies behind her. Only her head is real, and that is down—facing the open hatch in the cage of her chest, and the corrugated ruffle that divides her upper from her lower. Her body and limbs are constructed entirely of bronze; the candlelight makes her glow.

"She's waiting for you," Father says. "Come." Father leads her across the room and crouches down so that he is head height to Millicent and the ballerina. "Look," he says. "Her heart is still." He points to the ornate, filigreed box resting in the center of the ballerina's chest, contained within a sphere made of three silver hoops. It rests there, in the space of the ballerina's chest. "She is waiting for your touch to bring her to life."

The ballerina's hair is dark as dark can be, slick and close to her fine white head, tied back with a scarlet ribbon. Millicent cannot see her face, doesn't know what to say.

"Do you not like her," Father asks anxiously. "I made her for you. To abide by you. To be with you for as long as you may want her. A secret for you and I alone."

Millicent says, "Thank you, Father," all the time wondering how Father made this thing before her.

"Remember I told you I knew something was missing from the world that I had to find?"

Millicent nods.

"Well, we found it, myself and my friends from Mexico. Do you see now why I must leave, to discover what other things I might achieve?"

All Millicent can think of is how the sitting room smells so very different now, of fresh varnish and new leather and snipped flowers.

"Reach out," Father urges. "Touch her heart. Say hello."

So this is how it is to be.

She reaches out and—hesitantly, tremblingly—places a fingertip upon the box at the center of the clockwork ballerina. The polished wood is warm, the metal cold. The tide of her blood is a whisper in her ears.

Something clicks, inside the dancer. Father gently draws Millicent's hand away. The three-ring sphere in which the ballerina's beautiful box-heart is housed begins to slowly and comprehensively spin, building speed, faster and faster, until light begins to creep from the box. It is now a silver spheroid blur, growing brighter by degrees, and as that first scintilla of light makes itself known, so do other soft sounds come from elsewhere inside the ballerina: her joints, her fingers, the ball of her neck. As the light becomes a soft and constant glow—all of the quiet, tiny parts within her coming to life—her face slowly rises.

Skin white as milk, lips red as love. The ballerina opens her eyes. They are deep and dark.

She looks upon Millicent as if there were nothing in the world but Millicent.

"H . . . hello," Millicent says.

The lips smile a smile and, from between them, her first breath. The ballerina's eyes shine.

"Hello." Her voice is warm.

"My name is Millicent," says Millicent. "What is yours?"

The ballerina tilts her head. "My name is Nimble."

"Nimble . . . ," Millicent repeats, getting used to the name.

And she hears the front door close.

This is life from knee height. You are either with Millicent, or you aren't; you are either in her world or—for the time in which Millicent is in the company of others—you wait in the Drop for Millicent to be alone once more. It is always a bit of a rude shock, talking with her or playing or clapping hands, and then suddenly finding yourself somewhere else completely.

Nimble sits herself on a waist-high, man-long slab of dirt—like a sarcophagus, almost—and waits for Millicent to be alone once more. She lowers her chin and feels the heart-box spinning within her chest-cage, listens to its faint and constant song.

The hollow latticeworks of her arms and legs are filled with a scarlet mass of red silk roses. Millicent made them, one by one, and decorated her friend with them. When Millicent's mother leaves, Nimble will return and they will continue playing and singing.

Once in a very great while Dorian comes through the Drop on his way to one place or another, or to fetch the instruments that he keeps in a chamber of their own. It was the instruments that Dorian had used to create this place, and to create Nimble, and others. More often than not, though, he sends his curious little manservant, Tub, to fetch what he needs or to go somewhere on his behalf. At first Nimble thought perhaps maintaining contact between father and daughter was one of the reasons for which she had been created, but in the months since Nimble first awoke she has decided that this is not the case. Rather than existing in order to ensure Millicent's father is never forgotten, Nimble has decided she was created in order to ensure that Millicent's father is never missed. It is to that end that Nimble strives, and takes joy from each laugh or smile she receives.

Tub is a nice enough fellow, if hopelessly naïve. Takes the world at face value, he does. In a way he and Millicent would be a good pair.

In another universe Millicent says Nimble's name. Her mother has left, she is alone now, and Nimble goes to her.

Millicent's room has bookcases from which Nimble has memorized many stories. There is a wide bed, soft and full. A few dolls look on from corners and chairs. It is a beautiful room, but may not remain beautiful for much longer. In the time Millicent and Nimble have been together a veil has descended over the house. The spirit of the place is becoming sour, and a bit wretched.

"Here I am," says Nimble.

Millicent sighs and says, "We must take the roses back."

"Oh? Whatever for?"

"Mama doesn't believe that we were dressing you with these roses. She thinks I have lost all the silk she gave me."

"Oh."

"Oh Nimble, I get so tired of not being able to tell anyone about you, show you to anyone . . ."

Millicent is becoming sad again, and Nimble plumbs anxiously for something to lighten her mood. "Come," Nimble says. "Let's cover the bed with them. That'll give her a surprise."

Millicent laughs. "Yes!"

And so they do, taking every last rose from within Nimble's arms and legs till they can see through her again like a lovely walking window.

"There we are," says Nimble, surveying the fine crimson blanket they have made. "Princesses wake upon beds like this."

Millicent surveys their beautiful work, but the smile slips from her face. "I wish Mama would smile again," she says. "It's been so long."

Nimble's heart-box speeds up just a little. Millicent deserves to be happy. "I know," Nimble says. "Let's play cat's cradle."

Millicent seems twice as forlorn now, her mouth turned glumly to the side, and she shakes her head. "No. But thank you. Mama will want me in bed soon."

"Oh."

"Good night, Nimble."

Nimble waits for Millicent to call her back, but she doesn't. That's all right. Millicent wants time to herself nowadays, and so Nimble doesn't intrude. Instead she sits upon an earthen slab in one of the larger caves and ponders. She runs a cool brass finger down one white cheek, and wonders where she came from.

"Hello," says a voice, deep and thoughtful.

Nimble returns from her reverie. "Oh hello, Mr. Tub." The little thing actually blushes. She begins again, inclining her head. "I mean, hello, Tub."

"Hello," Tub says again.

Nimble notices Tub has something in his broad hand: it is brightly silver and sings faintly—one of her creator's instruments. "And how is Mr. Athelstane," she asks.

"His friend died," Tub says, low and thoughtful. "Fell under a streetcar, he did. And now he's scared."

"Mr. Athelstane is frightened?"

Tub nods, eyes wider than usual. "He says something talks to him. He wants it to stop talking to him, but it won't."

"How very, very odd. What is it, this thing that speaks to him?"

Tub shakes his head. "He won't say. He says if I know about it, it'll talk to me, too."

"Oh dear. I see you here more and more often these days."

Tub nods again. "Dorian doesn't like me around as much anymore. He says when I speak it makes words from what I say. He hears words all the time, and I just make it worse by talking too much."

"Then I suppose we shall be spending more time in each other's company." Again, Tub nods. Nimble shifts over, her legs hissing and clicking lightly and precisely, and with an elegant unfolding of wrist-hand-fingers tap-taps the seat beside her.

Tub doesn't know where to look, and clutches the instrument to his chest with both hands. He makes his way over, uncertainly, and puts the instrument onto the slab before hoisting himself up. His thick arms make easy work of it. He shifts himself around, plops down, and clutches the instrument to himself once more. It sings high and faint. He is such a curious thing.

"Tell me, Tub," she says. "Why were you made?"

Tub's fingers drum slowly over each other, as if this were some critical test he might fail. "Um . . . ," he says. "Well . . ."

"You see," Nimble says, "I was wondering why I was made, and I think I might have it. I was wondering if you knew why you were made, because that might help me decide if I have worked it out."

"Um . . . ," Tub says again. "I think I just get things for Dorian. And make him laugh. Though I don't do that so much anymore." Tub braves looking up at her. "I know what you do. You look after his little girl."

Nimble nodded, her heart-box spinning a little faster. "That I do."

"What is she like?"

"Has Mr. Athelstane never spoken of her?"

Tub shakes his head. "Not really."

"Ah," says Nimble. "Then I was right."

Tub just drums his fingers upon his soft chest and blushes. "Well," he says, eventually. "I . . . suppose I should take this to Dorian."

"Where is Mr. Athelstane at the moment?"

"Sam Framcisco," Tub says, sliding heavily off the slab, keeping his eyes on the ground. Such a strange little thing. "I . . . like your dress," he says, and then he is gone.

She smiles to herself. She is not wearing a dress. It is a tutu, a corrugated disk slotted through her.

Nowadays Nimble only sees Millicent at night. Her mother was taken back on at the milliner's, finally, and Millicent spends her days either at school or making roses. Of late Millicent has seemed very far away.

Nimble walks through one cave after another. Many are empty but a few are not. One is decorated as a most comfortable style of drawing room, though the hearth is always cold in Mr. Athelstane's absence and the books are getting dusty. Still another is quite a lavish kitchen, though this, too, is dark and cloth-covered. And another is still of a more impressive size, and here are kept the instruments. This cave has a floor that is hollowed and sunken, making the chamber like the interior of some kind of sphere or ball, though the ceiling is hung with stalactites, and the rim of the room is studded with upward-thrusting stalagmites. Rude stairs have been carved from the entrance, leading down into the bowl, upon the floor of which a wide circular area has been curtained off with a shimmering drop of thick, blood-colored velvet. There are torches fitted around the periphery, but these are as cold as the hearths and stoves of the other rooms. However, this room in particular is not dim, for from behind the velvet curtain an ambience like strong moonlight emanates upward, illuminating the roof and revealing the entire chamber in a soft pearlescence. There is music here, something that might sound like a very distant choir, or it might not. It may instead be a library of notes rung from crystal and sustained, perfectly, forever. Or perhaps it is no sound at all. Perhaps it is a language once known to all, and now forgotten. These are the things Nimble thinks as she stands at the top of those rude stairs, and listens.

The curtain moves and someone steps out, drawing it closed behind himself.

"Tub," says Nimble, just loud enough to be heard.

They leave the Drop and spend some time in a place somewhat more interesting.

"I fear I'm not as good a companion as I might be," Nimble says, with the lights of Paris spread out before them.

"Oh, I'm sure you are," says Tub, his short legs dangling in space.

Nimble shakes her head. "No. Quite often Millicent will call to me, and I will suggest some new game that we might play to lighten her mood. But it does not work as it did when she was younger and I don't know what to do."

"Don't you talk with her?"

"Oh, we talk constantly," Nimble says, brightening. "When I am there, that is, which is not so often nowadays. We talk about things she enjoys doing, and how we might dress me next, and what games we might play, and stories . . ."

"She sounds lonely," Tub says.

"But I was made so that she might never be lonely. At least, that's what Mr. Athelstane said."

"When I'm sad I don't feel like playing games."

"Sad," Nimble says, tasting the word. "Yes." She stops and thinks about it. "I do not know that I have ever been sad. Until now."

"Why are you sad?"

"Millicent is lonely. I have failed."

"Why is she sad?"

Nimble is unsure what Tub means, and then she realizes: if failing Millicent makes *her* sad, then something must likewise be causing Millicent to be sad. So . . . so if Nimble were to fix her failure . . . then . . . then she will *not* feel sad. And if *Millicent* is sad, then . . . then . . .

"This is so confusing," Nimble says, the light within her heart-box dimming just a little. "Mr. Athelstane told me nothing of this."

And she is surprised, then, to find that Tub has carefully reached over and is gently patting her hand.

"Millicent . . ."

Nimble reaches down to the darkened bed. A faint whisper-and-click unfurls a cold, brass finger, and she trails a knuckle down her friend's soft white cheek. Dark hair drapes across one closed eye.

"Millicent . . . ," she says again.

The child stirs, then opens her black eyes. "Nimble." She mumphs a little, then says, heavy-lidded, "I didn't call to you."

"I didn't know I could do it, either." Nimble smiles. "But here I am."

Millicent sits herself up, blankets falling from her shoulders. Her nightgown shines pale blue in the breath of moonlight that slides past the drapes. "Why are you here? Is something amiss?"

Nimble sits herself on Millicent's bed and takes her friend's small hands in her own. "There is someone I would very much like you to meet. A friend."

"A friend?"

"Tub? Would you come in please?"

Something takes a hesitant step on the other side of the room, in the dark. Millicent wipes her eyes, trying to see past sleep. One more step brings it into the light.

It would have the form of a primitive fertility goddess—squat, round, nude, and heavy—if it weren't male. Broad hands, thick arms, feet wide and fat with splayed toes. Little tufts of hair on the shoulders, a single, crazed tuft of hair sprouting diagonally above one of its bulbous ears. It looks out at Millicent from small, dark eyes made smaller beneath a drooping brow. Its mouth is as wide as its neckless head, and two tusks jut upward from behind a wet lower lip almost as if to hitch on the thing's heavy eyebrows.

It raises a handful of stubby fingers and waves.

Millicent shrieks and tumbles backward out of bed.

"I . . . I'll go," it says, with a voice as thick and heavy as a tropical river.

In another room Mama murmurs and goes back to sleep.

Nimble raises a hand. "No, Tub, wait." Nimble gets up from the bed and tippy-toes around to the other side, where Millicent is gathered in the corner, peering over the tops of her knees, past the bed, to the ogre by the window.

"Millicent," Nimble says evenly. "This is Tub. Tub, this is Millicent. Millicent, Tub is a very good friend of your father's."

Millicent looks up at her friend. "Father?"

"Yes. Mr. Athelstane made Tub, just as he made me."

On the other side of the room the thing waggles its fingers again. "Hello."

Millicent stands up, straightens her nightgown, and looks from Nimble to Tub. "Please accept my apologies," she says, uncertainly. "It was unkind of me to react as I did."

"Oh, that's all right," Tub says. "I'm not s'posed to be pretty." And then he does a little dance.

For most of the night Nimble sits, and watches.

At the moment, Millicent and Tub are talking. They have been talking for a little while now. Tub has grabbed both feet and is rolling around the room.

"He lives all over the place," Tub is saying, narrowly avoiding knocking over an oil lamp. "Just goes through the Drop. Just like me. Belize today, Sam Framcisco tomorrow, New Zealand the day after . . ." He rolls to a stop right in front of Millicent, chubby toes gripped in stubby fingers. "Nimble says you're sad."

Millicent shrugs weakly. "Mama is sad."

"I would feel sad if I missed Dorian."

Millicent nods again.

"But," Tub continues, "I wouldn't *be* sad."

"What do you mean?"

"You're not sad. You're Millicent. Millicent with a sadness upon her."

"Meaning . . . ?"

Tub scratches his eyebrow, then pulls his bottom lip over his head.

"I think what Tub is saying," Nimble suggests, "is that sadness comes and goes. Best not to think of yourself as actually *being* sadness."

Tub nods, fiddling bashfully with his hands. Millicent giggles. Tub slides one corner of his lip over a tusk and peers out at her. "See?" he says.

"I am Millicent with a sadness upon me," she says.

Tub rolls backward and comes up standing. His lower lip comes free with a wet flop.

"What does Father do," she asks as Tub starts dancing again.

"Well," Tub says, pumping his elbows as though walking briskly. "He likes learning all sorts of stuff." With each movement his bulky rear end moves in counterpoint while his tongue edges out of the corner of his mouth with great concentration. "Other times . . . hmph . . . he stays up . . . hah . . . late and . . . hmph . . . sings a lot. With . . . ho . . . friends." Every now and then he stops elbowing, juts out a foot and points to his toes with both hands, then goes back to elbowing and wiggling before pointing to the other foot. Repeat.

"What *are* you doing," Millicent asks.

"The Dance of Victory," Tub says humphing and hooing his way through it. Now he has turned around and is going through it all again for the benefit of the window. "I do it whenever Dorian figures something out."

"Why?"

"Because it's fun."

Millicent gets to her feet and stands beside the little ogre.

"Hmph huh ho hey . . ."

After a minute she gets the steps down pat, and the two of them dance for the moon.

Dorian is in Manaus, and laughing. His arm is around a lady that Tub does not know. Dorian is very drunk. They are in a dingy little place. Tub wonders if maybe it'll fall down soon. Tub is in the next room, watching Dorian and this lady he doesn't know through a brown screen. The color reminds Tub of his river. He doesn't like it when Dorian is drunk with other people. It's different from when he's drunk by himself.

"Go to New York First National," his creator says to the sagging ceiling. "And grab a handful of Mexican Eagle silver dollars. Then get yourself over to Chengdu. Leave the money for Lei, along with this note—" Dorian drops a scrap of paper over his shoulder, behind the seat. "—then come back here with the opium."

The woman giggles, says something Tub doesn't understand.

"And make it quick," Dorian says, leaning into her. "The night is aging." Dorian kisses her, and the room goes quiet as they disappear below the seat. Tub makes his way in, retrieves the note, and pops back into the Drop.

Nimble is here, sitting on an earthen slab. Her face is ruby-lipped porcelain. Her body is art. Through her chest, past her heart, Tub can see the light of the torches she reads by. "Hello there," she says, putting her book down.

"Hello," Tub says. He wants to say something else, looks at his feet. "Millicent is nice."

Nimble smiles, and Tub's chest feels the way his feet do before a fire on a cold night.

"It was," she says. "You are a remarkable person, Tub."

And then his face feels the same way. "I . . . I have to get something. For Dorian." He waddles over to one of the cold torches and lifts it from its bracket. He lights it on one of the burning ones. The pitch catches with a plume and crackle.

"Where are you off to now," she asks, delicately.

"China," Tub tells her. "But first I have to go to New York."

"Millicent is at work now," Nimble says. "But perhaps you would like to visit her with me? Later on?"

Tub smiles and looks down. "I would."

"I look forward to it then," Nimble says.

"All right," Tub says. " 'Bye, Nimble."

"Good-bye, Tub."

And then he is somewhere else.

The bank vault is very dark, and far colder than the Drop or Manaus. The walls and floor are chilly, and painted thickly with white. The torch blinds Tub to everything beyond the light it gives off. He raises it as high as he can, gets close to all the bags stored on all the steel and wire shelves.

"Mexican Eagles . . . ," he says to himself. "Mexican Eagles . . ."

After a few minutes he finds a white sack with the right symbol, and pulls the drawstring open. Inside are fat silver coins. Tub takes a handful, and then he is back in the Drop. He enters elsewhere, away from Nimble. He doesn't know what he would say to her a second time.

"Tonight, though." He nods to himself, resolute.

And then he is somewhere else.

The rain is coming down hard, clattering off the roof, sounding like an army beating bamboo; like an ocean's worth is battering the small U-shaped house Tub has found himself in. No one is in the room. There is a little wooden table here that only comes up to Tub's knees. On the table is a heavy bell with a leaden knocker resting beside it. Outside, the ground is being churned to dancing mud. The trees bow and bob under the weight of the downpour. Tub can feel the rain misting in through the open door, the slatted windows. Tub takes Dorian's note, and the handful of Mexican Eagles, and places them on the little table. Then he picks up the bell and bangs it as hard as he can. There is an exclamation from another part of the house. Tub hears footsteps, and then someone must have looked into the room because suddenly he is back in the Drop.

"Hello again, Tub. That was quick." Nimble has put her book aside. She stands primly, feet together, hands clasped at her waist. Her head seems to float there, in space, atop the ornate scaffolding of her body, and again Tub feels himself suffuse with her presence. He burns up from within, brain split into fourths and each quarter arguing with the others about what to say to this vision before him.

"It wasn't a big job," he says. "I'll have to go back in a minute." He realizes he is still holding the bell and knocker.

"An arrangement of Mr. Athelstane's?"

Tub nods. "China," he says. "It's very pretty. You might like it there."

"I'm sure I would."

"It's very pretty. But I spend more time in my river."

"You live in a river?"

Tub nods. "I'm not so heavy there. And everyone knows me."

"Other people live in your river?"

Tub nods. "Otters, birds, turtles . . . they all know me."

Nimble's head inclines curiously, and she steps toward him. "I would very much like to see your river. And China."

Tub looks up at her, and his tiny eyes widen. They are blue.

. . .

Tub returns to Dorian. The Englishman is seated at the table against the stained wall, one hand propping his head, the other around a grimy little glass of something brown.

"You're late," he says.

"Sorry," Tub says, fidgeting nervously. "But I couldn't get back into Lei's."

Dorian sighs and downs the last dregs of his glass. "So he tried watching the room, then. Nosy bugger wants to know how I do it."

"I got your things, though," Tub says, and puts a little sack onto the table.

Dorian opens it, looks inside, licks his pinkie finger, and dips it in. He sucks the off-yellow powder from it, smacks his lips, and draws the bag shut again. "Too late," he says, and gestures to the mattress in the far corner. Dorian's lady friend is laid out there, face to the wall, snoring loudly. Dorian sighs again, and despondently waggles the empty bottle. There's something left in there, so he necks it. "No noise at least." He goes still now, and then eyes the bag. He undoes it and has another taste.

Tub wants to make Dorian smile, but is afraid that if he speaks Dorian will hear the other words among his own. So he keeps it short.

"I met Millicent, Dorian. Nimble took me with her. She's very nice."

Dorian sighs to himself and very slowly and deliberately presses his hands to his ears.

"Sorry," Tub says. "Sorry."

"Tub," his creator says amicably, through clenched teeth. "Be a sport and get a few things for me, would you?"

Nimble has ventured to some green part of the world, and fetched for Millicent a basket of wildflowers. She sits upon the ground, arranging them, awaiting Millicent's return from work, when Tub appears before her. The smile upon her face evaporates like mist on a bright morning.

"Oh, Tub, whatever's wrong?"

Tub cannot look her in the face. "I'm sorry," he says. "I . . . I told Dorian that we visited Millicent."

Nimble stands and bends over him, placing her hands upon his heavy shoulders. The poor little thing is shaking. "Oh, Tub, can that be so very bad?"

Tub nods. "Dorian made me bring him some instruments . . ."

Nimble's heart-box begins spinning faster. "Instruments?"

Tub nods. "He . . . he made sure I couldn't ever speak of her to him again." He jabs a thick finger against the side of his head, over and over again. "He made sure."

Nimble says nothing, but seizes him in an instant, holds him close. "It's all right," she coos. "It's all right now." The top of his head is prickly against her cheek, and still Tub's shoulders shudder.

"No," he says. "No. It's not all right. I'm sorry, Nimble. I'm sorry."

Nimble raises her head.

Against the far wall, one shadow amid the stalactites' shadows, Mr. Athelstane beckons to her with a curved finger. In his other hand is a piece of singing moonlight.

Clear water nudges the rushes. Tub is up to his broad waist in it, his jaw outthrust. A heron perches on his lower lip, dips its beak into his mouth, plucks out a struggling fish, and flaps away. Tub spits water sideways. "Do you think birds get cold," Tub asks.

Nimble sits in the grass, beneath the broad shade of an old tree. Sunlight gleams amber upon her, here and there, as it falls through the branches.

"I don't know," she says. "I wouldn't think so. They're covered in feathers."

"But birds are always covered in feathers."

Nimble had knelt before Mister Athelstane, facing away, and felt dizzy as her creator mixed and messed within her head. When it was done there was no place in the same thought for Mr. Athelstane and talk of his daughter. She could no more grasp that notion than imagine an undiscovered color. And so it was with Tub, also.

Who is, at the moment, floating on his back and making quacking noises at a duck, turning clockwise as he slowly floats downstream.

It is at this moment that Nimble suspects she has a great deal more to learn about being alive.

Millicent stands alone in the sitting room, wearing a bonnet of black silk and a dress of black silk crêpe. Crêpe lisle—black—adorns her wrists. The leather furniture has been taken out and stored higgledy-piggledy in the kitchen. The sitting room is now packed with thick explosions of lilies and marigolds, stacked one atop the other, and multitudinous wreaths of the same. Atop those lies Papa's coffin. On a small table by his head Mama has placed his wood plane and paintbrush. His shovel stands propped against the coffin at his feet.

Millicent sighs and fiddles with the crêpe at her wrists. "He was the only friend I had in this world," she says. Mama is upstairs, and there is—can be—no one else in the house. Millicent feels Nimble take her hand, to a soft tune of hiss-and-click. Tub takes her other.

The years have seen Millicent grow, and she is almost a young lady. They still talk fancifully with one another, but lately Millicent has wanted to know more about the world beyond London. Nimble is resolved to show it to her, taking Millicent through the Drop if need be. In a year or two, she realizes, they will be looking at each other eye-to-eye.

"So this was Papa," the ballerina says. "You were right, Millie. He has a lovely face."

Millicent squeezes both their hands, draws them to her. "After the upset my growing up with two imaginary playmates has caused," she confides. "If he is with us, then at this very moment Papa must be having the greatest laugh of his life."

Silence. And then Tub sniggers and slaps a meaty hand over his mouth, and Nimble giggles and it's on for young and old.

Millicent needs no encouragement. It is a fine farewell.

· · ·

Words hide everywhere. Like battalions they arrange themselves into configurations of power and purpose. Cloaked in the world's glossolalia they appear, only to you, and deliver their message.

Ceaselessly.

The sun rises, you obliterate your senses as best you are able, the sun sets, and you don't stop.

This is life on the run from everything you've built.

Your compatriots are all dead. One by one they were felled; here by a bullet, there by a crust of bread, and another by an ill-timed streetcar. The finest willworkers you've ever known, comparable indeed to yourself, reduced to meat and mud and memory by the whim of the hidden, banished, monstrous Aeon to whom you provided context.

You are such a fool.

Its instruments are yours, or so you believed. Unlike anything you've ever known they embody a beauty so profound it renders you morose. And what they have gifted you with . . . oh. Built from the bones of a murdered angel they veritably tremble and scream with what they have been robbed of, and what they have been so forcibly granted. Even now, walking north, the few you have chosen to carry with you sing to one another, to themselves, to Itself . . . a mad, butchered thing gifted with only slightly less power than God and too will-stripped to use it. Broken into pieces, the unifying aspect of their—Its—power is you. And what a life you thought you would be leading as a result.

Raised in a stone room, lightless and locked, brought out only to be smoked and gassed and prodded to provide prophecy for an endless parade of bankers and fishmongers and hags by a loveless mother with eyes of stone and breath that filtered through the shattered rubble of her mouth . . . you were one day given an inkling intended for you and you alone.

Something needed help. Something so very much stronger than Mother.

So one day you told her where fortune lay, and that special lie set
you free . . . just as surely as it led her to a man with broken hands and
the bottom of a very, very deep river.

It took four days for someone to find you. Mother kept you half
starved at all times—it made the visions come stronger—and so by
the time the cellar door unlocked you were all but dead.

But never once did you doubt that it would unlock.

A day of bed and broth and you were off. A mix of feral cunning
and foreknowledge kept you safe and fed . . . but only just. In time, as
you grew and your body changed, the visions faded and fled . . . but
not what you had learned about people and their needs.

Living wasn't high, but it was easy. You worked and buggered and
stole, you wove lies as gifts for the moneyed in need, and every remaining hour was spent in the company of cracked souls as deviant as
you but far less gifted. You never stopped searching, never stopped
looking, never stopped feeling for pieces of life that felt right.

Something was lost though it stood right there . . . before
you . . . a part of all things . . . but no one could see it. Not even you.

How was that possible?

From groups to covens to frauds and back you ricocheted, looking
not for truth but for a small piece of it. A hint, a flavor, an intuition.

Doors were opened, chances made available, words whispered to
you, and you traveled to America.

London, New York, Boston, the Mojave, Mexico. Twenty years of
questing after a notion that would leave you no more readily than
your ability to breathe in your sleep.

And then, one blue night on a stretch of red desert, there it was.
Twenty years of accumulated suspicions, tenuous conclusions, and
spurious inspirations assembled themselves into something that was
close enough to the formation of a coherent idea that a leap was
made, you acknowledged something that had remained unknown
since before Creation was Created, and many of those close to you
died screaming—one syllable—beneath the shattering vastness that is
the knowledge of it.

And so you walk, though you have no need to. Everywhere is open to you now.

This is life on the run from everything you've built. You walk because it keeps your mind busy. Everywhere, words: the crunch of pale soil beneath your battered shoes, the shriek of a carrion bird, a breath of wind. A piece of each sound, a disparate sequence of enforced emphasis, enunciates your name.

Dorian.

Your feet crunch a dry tattoo. The scree rustles faintly. A creek bubbles.

Dorian.

This is Arizona. You've decided to walk to California from Mexico, because it seems like penance. Because you can. Because you may as well be dead. Because towns and cities are too loud. They build sentences.

The angel is everywhere. The emphases of the sounds you hear are altered by your knowledge that the angel exists; knowledge that makes the angel real. Birds, horse clip, wind, coughs . . . you hear notes in the soup and those notes form words, ideas, instructions. Like seeing a face in the clouds you hear a deformed voice in the collected soundstream of the world around you.

You cannot help but hear.

It told you where to find its scattered instruments, how to use them, and now it wants you to return it to its Name, and its Sigil. It wants to be Known once more. It wants you to build an army and . . .

You clap your hands to your ears, and in the roaring of your own blood it keeps speaking.

Dorian.

You shout to drown it out, and of course that only makes it clearer.

Dorian.

You cram your fingers into the canals of your ears, ferreting deeper, sinking to your knees. You scrabble for anything—a stick or a twig—enough is enough. You've almost punctured your drums on a handful of occasions, always stopping short, but enough is enough.

"Dorian."

"*Shut up!*" You snatch the pocketknife from your small suitcase, and look into the sun.

"D . . . Dorian?"

Two figures, on the road. Looking at you. You know them.

You're panting, heavy. The road stones bite through and into your knees. Your mouth is dry. You struggle to your feet, knife in hand.

"What . . . what do you want? I didn't send for you."

The bronze automaton never takes her eyes off you.

"If you would, Tub."

Tub walks toward you, something in his broad hand.

"You made us in such a fashion, Mr. Athelstane," Nimble says, "that communicating our concerns to you directly is beyond us. However, the delivery of a letter is not."

Tub holds it up to you. The little ogre has never looked at you with anything less than a desire to make you happy. Until now.

You take the letter from his hand. You know what it is, and the insolence of it fills you with a glowing anger.

"If I may, Mr. Athelstane, I would advise against destroying the letter. You . . . will not be receiving another."

The catch in her voice snags your attention. With the sun at Nimble's back it is not clear what expression her face holds, but you've never seen Tub look at anything the way he is looking at you now.

You open the letter. The angel repeats your name with each succession of paper-on-skin.

The letter is written in a very competent hand. Millicent has grown quite a bit since you last saw her.

"She wants to see you. One last time," the ballerina says. "Before she dies."

Tub's breath pounds out of his flat nostrils.

"Will you come?"

This is life from knee height. You had retrieved the letter in the few moments between the doctor leaving Millicent's room and Mama reentering. As Millicent gave it to you she made you promise that Father would receive the letter, and read it, and that he would return to look after Mama. You remember your brass fingers touching her cold white hand ever so briefly as the paper was taken . . . and then the door opened, and both you and Tub were back in the Drop. Your fingers still reaching for hers.

You never saw Millicent again.

THREE

NOWHERE, 1850

THERE ARE TWO THINGS TO REMEMBER IN THIS LIFE: THAT the worst crimes are committed in the name of love, and that everyone makes mistakes.

A nameless way station of a town, somewhere in Arizona. It is 1850, in the moments before Henry Lockrose says, "Let me help you."

The stranger had crashed through his front door and found Henry at the table in the room that functioned sometimes as a surgery, sometimes as a dining room.

Henry's free hand found the revolver strapped under the table.

For a moment Henry had, as he looked up from his glass, assumed that this was it: an unhappy patient come to take satisfaction from the choice placement of a bullet.

That wasn't to be the case. Had his eyes been two drinks clearer he would have realized he had never seen this panicked soul before. But they weren't, and he didn't.

"Who is it?"

"I've been traveling for an age," the stranger was saying, tearing at his clothes, shedding his coat. "Help me." He sounded French. Henry had never treated a Frenchman that he could recall.

He sat straighter, peering at the man. Unwashed hair, long face, angular. He knew now this was no patient, no vagrant in need of a quick stitch. "Who is it?" he asked again.

"Help me," the stranger said, struggling with the weight of his coat, tearing his arm from one stubbornly inside-out sleeve. His hair was long and dark and unkempt, his face unshaven. His eyes were those of the gallows-bound, ignorant and desperate, animal-like and lost. "For God's sake."

His coat hit the floor. The shirt fell forward over his arms and off his haggard frame, split down the back.

Such garments were worn by dead men propped in coffins outside an undertaker's. Henry's immediate assumption was that this man had been desperate for clothing and had stolen the tunic from an un-watched corpse.

"What has he done to me?"

And the stranger displayed the long, straight wound that sundered his back.

Too deep to have been survived.

The man was on his knees now, facing away with his head in his hands. The wound yawned as he bent over himself.

Within the raw crevasse at the center of the man, Henry saw a light like silver fire. A twisted, sculpted nugget of starlight, nestled to his beating heart.

Henry released the hidden pistol.

Something told him, a part that still desired to be great, said: *Take him, take this man, take him in.*

"Let me help you," Henry said. And drained his glass with a fluttering hand.

"Why is a man so young as you living alone in a town like this?" the stranger asked.

Henry didn't answer. He found it easier saying nothing.

With only a few opium pills to dull the pain of the stitching—and it had been deep, brutal work—the stranger hadn't flinched. It was as if he had taken himself away during it all, his brown eyes switching off as he lay facedown on the very table they now ate from.

"My name is Felix Tranquille Henot."

Henry said nothing.

"You have few possessions, Doctor."

The words touched a part of him, but his mind was elsewhere.

"You have not asked how I came by the wound."

Henry looked sidelong at his mouthy visitor and said, "Questions never got me anywhere."

But the wound was intriguing: a straight incision, one clean stroke. And so deep. Flesh and bone parted to the left of the first dorsal vertebra almost straight down to the twelfth. The thick slab of the trapezius muscle and latissimus dorsi had been shorn in half, yet the patient, Felix, had suffered no loss of mobility to the left side of his body. There was no bleeding, though the flesh remained warm if somewhat pale. Yellow fingers of bone punctuated the interior of the wound—the clean stumps of severed ribs flexed and ground as Felix moved, yet caused him no pain. If anything it seemed Felix's initial distress had been a purely psychological reaction to the extent of his wound and nothing more.

It could not be, of course. Henry knew that. One does not sever muscle and expect the associated limbs to continue functioning. That is a patent impossibility. And yet it was happening.

This was the first inexplicable characteristic of his patient. The second was the silver object Henry had found nestled inside the greater cavity of Felix's body—visible through the wound—and been reluctant to remove. Given Henry's inability to explain his patient's continued health and mobility, or to explain the mercurial thing he had found wedged beside Felix's heart, Henry could only assume the two phenomena were related. It appeared the artifact caused the man no harm or discomfort so he had left it where it was, and Felix continued to talk, and live, and move.

"The one who gave me this wound . . . he travels," Felix was saying. "Widely."

Henry was visited by faces, often at that very table. Or rather, pieces of faces. He could not recall with any precision how she had looked those ten years ago. He remembered her strength, and how smitten he had been by her, but he could not recall her face as it had been before death. The face that came back to him at that table was postmortem, misshapen, and black with bruising.

It was so hard to shake the memory of an ending.

It was as if all he could remember was endings.

"He wishes me dead," Felix said.

Once in a while Henry would remember a detail, something small—like the shape of an eye or the sweep of her hair—and the rest of her face would rise up in full through the fog of lost memory, and he would see her again, as she was. But that happened less and less nowadays.

"I believe he will follow me, Doctor."

The Frenchman was a wiry sort. Not imposing. Courtly, after a fashion. Hair grown longer than the current styles Henry had seen sported by passers-through.

"Who is he, then," Henry asked.

"An Englishman."

The English. Henry didn't like the English. A ten-year-old aversion.

"I have a cot," Henry said. "I let it out to patients I need an eye on. You can use it so long as no one else needs it." He poured two more fingers of bourbon, left the bottle uncorked. "In exchange I could use someone to keep the place clean."

For the second time in his life Henry began to realize how easy it was for him to become addicted to human company.

He had been part of this town almost ten years now, ten years of getting by on patching the wounded and caring for the occasional malady. Once he'd even used some of that schooling to excise an ovarian tumor from a lady on her way to San Francisco, though that had been years before. She'd wanted it done in a real hospital, but would never have made it that far.

For eight months her husband had thought himself a father, so swollen was her belly, until the ninth and tenth months brought terrible pains but no sign of the onset of birth. The doctors revised their opinions, and gave the couple an address in San Francisco. The woman had made it as far as Henry's way-station town before the pain became crippling.

The husband had protested, of course; he took one look at Henry and said he would take his chances with the highway. "The highway"—that's what he had called it. He'd been an Englishman as well.

But the wife, more resolute because the endangered life was her own, said she would stay, while the husband had been taken away by the townsfolk to get drunk. Henry knew murder played inside the husband's head. If the operation failed and the Englishman's wife died, so would he. One way or another.

And so the operation had been performed on this table. Henry had administered the last of his opium pills to the woman, and as she began crooning hymns he made an incision three inches from the musculus rectus abdominus, on the left-hand side. He continued for nine inches parallel with the muscle and extended into the cavity of the abdomen.

Brain-colored intestines burst forth immediately, spilling onto the table. Henry had cried out, a brief bark, the back of his arm covering his mouth. The abdomen was so filled by the mass of her disease that her innards had immediately rushed out onto the table. He had made this table himself, with wood he had felled himself and tools he had purchased from the general store in town. It was the same kind of table he had made with his father, as a boy. This shack, which he had also made himself, was the same kind of house he had been raised in, back in Vermont, in a life so distant it was more like something he had been told about, rather than lived. Even Boston felt a universe apart from him. He was dry, tongue sticking to the roof of his parched mouth, as he realized it would be impossible to replace her intestines until the tumor was excised. No going back, no apologies, no sending the couple on their way. He would save her, or the husband would return and murder Henry across the opened and soul-fled body of his wife.

The woman had stared at the ceiling, conscious and sweating, crooning in the transports of opium. She had obviously led a comfortable life up to this point, this woman. There had been nothing hard about her. It would have been a simple thing to have unwittingly allowed life to slip free of a frame so delicate and unresisting. As it was, Henry greatly suspected, now that the inner wall of the abdomen had been exposed to the atmosphere she stood an equal risk of losing her life to peritoneal inflammation as she did to dying beneath his blades. He remembered nights at the Coat and Arms. Remembered studying something related to this, with her, after his expulsion from medical college. He remembered the way she used to tease him, in roundabout ways, for knocking down his classmate on her behalf. He remembered how she feigned horror at the act, but smiled and laughed quietly nonetheless. God, that beautiful laugh. He burned at her memory. Even among the educated and wise she had been incredible. How many of them could open doors for the dead? How many of them could summon angels?

He wiped his eyes with the back of his arm and continued.

In preparation for the operation Henry had abstained from liquor for twelve hours. Even before he had begun to work the stench of old sour mash was sweating through his skin. He could smell it even above the stench of blood and disease.

The body of the tumor appeared—filthy looking and jelly-like, massive. Henry placed as stout a ligature as he was able around the fallopian tube near the uterus, and then cut the tumor. The tumor was the ovarium and the fimbrial part of the fallopian, only grossly enlarged. Henry removed fifteen pounds of it, and then cut through the swollen and inflamed fallopian to extract the sac. That must have been seven pounds' worth alone.

The entire operation took an hour, and at the end of those sixty minutes the woman still lived. As gently as he could, with weak and shaking hands, he rolled her onto her side and drained the blood (it sounded like rain on stone as it hit the dining room floor), then closed the opening with an interrupted suture, leaving enough of an opening at the lower end for the fallopian ligature. As a further precaution, between every two stitches he placed a strip of adhesive plaster to keep the parts in contact and hasten the healing. Then came the treated bandages and dressings.

Husband and wife took a room in town, at the hole, for a number of days. Each time Henry made the journey to buy a bottle it provided him the chance to observe her for any sign of inflammation. Each time her Englishman husband wore the dark, rigid look of a man insulted by his presence.

There was no infection. She lived.

Days later, as the couple trundled away on their carriage, Henry knew—with more certainty than he had ever known—that he was a great surgeon. That this was what he had been born to do. What he had sacrificed so much to be. What he had killed to become.

Yet Henry could no longer bring himself to feel for these people. He groped for empathy out of some withered sense of duty, but there was nothing for him to grasp. Death was nothing. No great tragedy, no cause for outrage. What was the span of one human life in the span of Creation? Nothing. No great drama, no cause for anything.

Of course there had been a time when he believed otherwise. When he had stood, virginal and untouched, blinking at the wonder of it all. When he still possessed friends who breathed.

Perhaps that was why Felix's insistence that the Englishman would come for him began to occupy Henry's thoughts. Now that Henry had someone to pass his days with, the thought of being alone once more was more than he could bear. In his darkest moods he hated the Frenchman for that.

He was a good doctor. It was all worth it. He had his craft, his discipline, his life. He needed nothing else. Ten years in this town, and not one real conversation in that time. No exchange beyond what was necessary. People accepted it from him. Then Felix showed up.

"Coffee?" the Frenchman asked.

Henry looked up from his journal and its age-yellowing pages. The last entry was dated over seven years ago. "Thank you." He bowed his head back to work, then stopped. "Felix?"

"Yes, Doctor?"

"You're a great help to me, Felix."

The Frenchman smiled. "I'll get your coffee."

A makeshift bed of blankets had been set up on the floor by Felix's cot. A man rested there now, by the cot, under observation for cramps. Probably gutrot—he had the stink of an alcoholic.

Henry returned to his writings.

On the thirty-ninth day everything changed. Felix was late returning from town.

When an hour turned to two, Henry put on the wide-brimmed hat, which had rested on its hook behind the door for years, shrugged into the old black coat he never wore, and started walking.

Henry lived half an hour's walk outside town. If anyone needed attention bad enough they'd find him, and if they couldn't make it they were beyond help to start with.

He found comfort in the deadness of the place. The wiry grasses and sandy soil. The distant silhouettes of thin carnivores, the hidden eyes of the scavengers and predators. The sky was perfect, unmarred by clouds. An infinite blue canopy and miles of parchment-colored earth. It would be blistering by ten.

He fought gravity, step-sliding down an incline, soil slipping away beneath decade-old boots. This was the way Felix would have passed, the most direct route to town. He remembered Felix's story of the man who gave him that wound that refused to fester. He knew Felix

lived in daily apprehension of the stalking Englishman finally tracking him down. Why hadn't he just moved on?

"Don't be dead on me." It was out before he realized he'd said it.

If Felix was dead he was dead. Out of his hands.

There were towns, there were one-horse towns, and then there
was this place. In total there was a regular population of about twenty.
It existed to refresh horses because it lay on the main route to the
west. It came with a baker's, a barber's, a supply store, and a watering
hole that doubled as a place to sleep. Whores worked out of a few of
the upper rooms. No one made any long-term plans to stay in a place
like this, except the owner of the watering hole and Henry himself.
Even the whores had loftier goals. If you wanted the law you rode
south.

It was as quiet in town as it was out, save for the occasional sound
of a door closing somewhere or a voice mumbling from some unseen
place. A thin dog trotted across the dusty street, pausing to piss against
a battered wall with brief efficiency. Henry supposed the best place to
ask would be the hole.

The hole was a wooden building just as old and just as dried-up as
the man who owned it. It wasn't a big room, but it sold what you
wanted. The floor was always dusty, though it got swept every couple
of days. A few tables were scattered around and hardly used. Sometimes the baker and the owner of the general store got together with
the man who owned the hole and played a hand or two with whatever
passers-through had rented a room. Sometimes the four wives would
gather and sing at night. That was the extent of society in that town
without a name.

Henry stood for a moment, facing the place. Two weeks ago he'd
spent six days locked inside his house. Henry had made Felix swear,
no matter what he said or did, that he would not be allowed to take a
drop of anything other than water. Henry's guts had burned, he'd
spent nights screaming and mumbling. He hadn't known how bad he
stank—how much liquor-stench had soaked out through his skin—

until Felix entered with his food one morning and couldn't keep his hand from his mouth. Only then Henry became aware of it, one of the sourest reeks he had ever known, comparable to that of shit and death. In a moment of lucidity he realized where he had come from, where he was meant to be in this life, and just how far away from it all he had wound up. He wasn't the kid who had wanted to be a doctor. He wasn't proud. This wasn't his life. The man he had intended to be had died from neglect. All that remained was this aging, still-breathing corpse with a smell to match.

Now he stood there, in the street, with real blood in his veins for the first time in clear memory, and every day all he wanted was to replace it, little by little, with something else. He licked dry lips, lowered his head, and pushed his way through the door of the hole.

Except for the owner, Henry was the only person in the room. The barkeep was sitting at one of his tables flipping through one of those mail-order catalogs from out east. He either didn't notice or didn't care that someone had entered his place. It left Henry with a now common feeling of ghostliness.

There came a burst of song from somewhere upstairs, blooming loud as a door was opened, the gaiety of it at odds with Henry's fear for his friend, and his desire to get away before he weakened.

Nelly Bly! Nelly Bly! Bring the broom along,
We'll sweep the kitchen clean, my dear,
And have a little song.
Poke the wood, my lady love
And make the fire burn,
And while I take the banjo down,
Just give the mush a turn . . .

Where the hell was Felix? Henry's boots were bricks. He should just ask the barkeep if he'd seen the man and be done with it . . . but he couldn't.

Because if he opened his mouth the only words that would come out would be a request for the usual.

Hi, Nelly! Ho Nelly!
Listen, love, to me,
I'll sing for you and play for you
A dulcet melody . . .

Henry felt pulled between bottles and door. He swallowed, drily. He would have to say something.

Nelly Bly has a voice like a turtledove,
I hear it in the meadow and I hear it in the grove . . .

It was an English voice doing the singing, from the corridor above the bar. There came the sound of a door closing, uneven footsteps jigging themselves toward the stairway. Dust fell in puffs from the boards above the racks that held lines of anonymous brown bottles. Henry closed his eyes. He thought of a morning, ten years past, on Boston's Smoker's Common, sharing an apple with a girl whose face he could almost remember . . .

Nelly Bly has a heart warm as a cup of tea,
And bigger than the sweet potatoes down in Tennessee . . .
Hi, Nelly! Ho Nelly!
Listen, love, to me . . .

Black stovepipe pants that had long lost their crease and a white buttondown shirt that had never been starched, open at the collar. The Englishman danced down the stairs in well-used traveling shoes three tones darker than the dust outside. Henry could well imagine the dancer seeing himself in some music hall production back home.

He was a young-faced fellow. About Henry's age. Strong, clear voice. Chestnut hair and matching eyes. He'd gained a little weight.

I'll sing for you and play for you
A dulcet melody . . .

"Hello, Dorian," Henry said.

The dancer stopped halfway down the staircase. He peered, scrutinizing the stranger in the hat, this nobody who knew his name.

"Do I know you, sir?"

Henry didn't let the sting of those words show, except perhaps in the slight contraction of his lips, a flutter at the corners. He could still see the bottles.

"It's been awhile," Henry admitted. He could have removed his hat, made it easier for him, but he was in no mood to be helpful. "I guess Mexico didn't agree with you."

The Englishman's forehead crinkled. "Mexico?" He moved farther down the stairs onto the barroom floor, moving toward Henry without reluctance. "I left Mexico some years ago." He dipped his head slightly, an unconscious effort to get a better look at the face beneath the hat. And then, flatly . . .

"Henry."

Now Henry removed the hat, ran a gloved hand through pale red hair that was thinning at thirty. "Leave it at that." Let him see the face.

Dorian didn't say anything. Henry had been shut away for the last ten years, away from people, from how they worked, but he could still read what was running through this man's head. If Dorian had known in advance that Henry lived here, in this nowhere town, he wouldn't have lingered. But here he was and now there was no getting away. That would be an unpleasant novelty for a man like him.

"So did you find it?"

Dorian blinked, uncertain. "Find what?"

"Whatever was so important that two people died and I was left holding the bag."

Dorian swallowed, riffling through possible ways to buy time. "Would you like a drink?"

"I don't drink."

Dorian paused, lingering on Henry's face. In that moment it was obvious Dorian realized exactly how uncomfortable Henry was, standing there, in that place.

"Surely . . . one drink?" said Dorian, earnestly. A trademark deceiver, once you knew him. "It'll give us a chance to talk."

Henry could feel teeth grind, couldn't stop it. He'd stopped breathing.

"I said I don't drink."

"Then I'll drink," Dorian said reasonably, "and we'll talk."

Long after sundown Henry sat in the street, listening as the coyotes yapped to one another outside town, beyond the pale light cast from veiled windows. The song dogs were braver around this town than others Henry had visited in years past. Probably because this town was so small; less populated and less threatening. There was no clear definition of where the town stopped and the wilderness began. Late at night, they'd trot through town separately, each one a loner, hugging the darker shadows at the bases of houses and buildings. But in the hours before they came, they'd sing; and when they did, they sounded almost human. It was a dozen haunted voices in conversation, a grieving choir, a scattered family crying ululant news. Every night Henry would sit by his open window, to drink and eavesdrop.

No one owned pets here. Nothing that wasn't in a cage, anyway. The storeowner once shot a coyote he'd found nosing around out back. Late-night gunfire made people nervous. Three men—out-of-towners, drunk and looking to impress—had turned up armed. The storekeep had been nudging the corpse with a slippered foot one minute, staring down a double barrel the next. No one bothered the song dogs since.

They wouldn't be coming into town for a little while yet.

Soft steps on dry earth. "Doctor?" The voice was a whisper.

Henry glanced over his shoulder from where he sat, looking up at a sky of black and silver. "Where have you been?"

Felix crouched, pulling on the legs of his pants as he did so. They were a pair of Henry's castoffs, and were a bit large on him. "He's here, Doctor. We have to get away." The way he whispered, so hushed, so scandalous, made Henry think of the secret things said in soft voices in childhood tree houses.

"I've been talking to him," Henry said.

"*Talking* to him? You can't talk to him!"

"I know him, Felix. We were in Boston together."

Hands twisted Henry around till he found himself staring into a very hard pair of brown eyes. "*He kills!*" Sweating. Something was happening inside Felix's head, making his eyes jitter side to side, making him let go, lean back. He stood, looking down. "You've been drinking." Forced calm.

Henry closed his eyes. "Not now, Felix."

Felix nodded, manic, lank hair falling before his face. "Damn right not now. Not here. Get up."

Henry looked away. Felix grabbed his collar and hauled him toward the blackest shadow in the street, between two buildings. Blood rushed to Henry's face as he watched his legs kick and skid, trying to regain both footing and dignity. He was dumped on his back between the general store and an outhouse. His first thought was to deck Felix on principle. Then he tried to get upright but found the movement arrested, jerked to a halt around the shoulders. He was lying on his coat, stretched flat. He had to roll, loosen it, get up on his hands and knees. Henry rose in time to see Felix step away from the lip of the lane, having stolen a quick glance back at the hole, and get very close to his face.

"*Do you want to see my back?*"

"Look, Felix, there's stuff—"

Felix ripped at his shirt. A button stung Henry's cheek. "Shit, Felix, come on . . ." His friend spun. The wound widened, stretching stitching, as Felix arched forward a little. Even in the dimness the artifact buried there gave back more light than it received. Henry took his friend's shirt and slipped it back up over his thin shoulders. "Give it a rest." Felix turned, shrugging reluctantly back into the old shirt, now open at the chest. "You'll hurt yourself."

There was a look to Felix's dark eyes now, like good-bye. It made Henry's next words harder. "I'm staying here tonight. I have to keep talking to him." Felix said nothing. His long fingers worked at the thread from one of the missing buttons. "He hasn't mentioned you, you know."

"I am not surprised."

"I need to keep him talking. Not just for you. I need answers."

"You will drink."

High yipping sounds. Echo made them sound like they were everywhere. The coyotes would be in the streets before long.

"You should maybe go back."

"I will wait," he said.

"C'mon, Felix . . ."

"I will wait here," he said. "But I cannot promise for how long."

Henry crouched, picked up his hat. "I don't trust him, if that's what you're thinking." The high sounds fell silent. "Grayson at the general store'll put you up. Coyotes are moving down."

Felix sat down at the base of the darkest wall, head up, eyes closed, arms flat on his raised knees. "Ten years is a long time."

Henry experienced the arrival of a moment. Hair falling around a beautiful face that rose in perfect detail from fractured memory. Slightly upturned nose, dark lips, and eyes that dared.

"The police in Boston," he said. "They think I killed a girl."

"I believe you did no such thing," Felix murmured. "He killed her. He kills. I told you."

"S'not so simple as that."

"Then explain to me, why it is not so simple."

"We were looking for something, all of us. It was a risk. We understood that."

"I see," Felix said. "Then explain to me why it is that you must go back if her loss is so easily understood."

Ten years was a long time.

Henry slipped his hat on, tugged at the brim, and walked back toward the hole.

Low shadows at the edge of town spread out at the sight of him.

Dorian seemed done with whatever whore he'd busied himself with. He was back in his own small room, on his own small bed against the sepia-toned tar paper wall, smoking a cigarette by the light of an oil lamp. The window's smudged pane was raised to a breezeless evening. Dorian's brown suitcase lay beneath the bed, a few books piled on the floor by the head. *The Perfumed Garden* by Sheik Nefzawi, Shakespeare's *Macbeth*, and something in Hebrew—probably kabbalistic. The sight brought a wave of nostalgia.

"Life's been treating you well," Henry said.

"It's a good life if one denies oneself nothing," Dorian was saying. There was a half-killed bottle of bourbon on the small desk. Dorian's glass rested on the sill. Henry sat on the one chair in the room, back against the wall, glass in hand. "Though it was difficult for the longest time. I feared for my mind."

"So what happened?"

Dorian reached for his drink, swirled it, swallowed a little. "I woke one morning and my problem was gone. Simple as that. Outlasted it, I suspect."

"So you never went back to Boston."

"I plan to," Dorian admitted, replacing his glass on the sill. "I always go back to the places I've been. See what's become of the things I've left behind." Henry finished his drink. "So they never caught up with you, then?"

"Who?" Henry immediately regretted the reflexive way it came out.

"The people in your home state. Before you came to school."

"I lost contact with my parents," he lied.

"I don't mean your parents," Dorian said. "I mean the constabulary." He leaned forward, cigarette hanging from two fingers. "Bernard Sumner? Good Christian man? Something of a chip on his shoulder about you and—"

"Why did you leave like that?"

"It was for the best," Dorian said.

"I had to leave Boston, you know."

Dorian nodded to himself. "I expected as much."

"Came looking for you."

Dorian nodded at that, too. "You got close a few times."

Henry clamped his eyes shut, felt his teeth grind.

"Couldn't let you find me, old sport. It wasn't right."

" 'Right'?"

"We came together, all five of us—well, four, if you discount Jukes—at that time because we needed to. That time passed, the need was satisfied."

Henry sat forward in his seat. The statement was a catalyst for anger, and anger was a catalyst for resolve. He breathed, "People died," like whispering to a sleeper.

Dorian licked his lips, looked back out the window. He bought time in drawing another breath from his cigarette. "To prolong the association," he said measuredly, "would have been counterproductive. You needed to follow your own way in the world as did I. I told you that would happen from the very first day."

"What happened to Finella, in the end?"

Smoke drifted halfheartedly out into the still night, made a weak attempt to veil Dorian's eyes. Somewhere down there, black shapes would be moving low to the ground. Henry thought briefly of Felix, out there with them.

"That's right," Dorian said. "You two had a thing." He drew another breath. "You saw what happened."

"Answer the question."

Dorian ground his cigarette out on the sill and tossed the rest of his drink out the window, calling an end to the evening. "You've drunk enough."

In an instant both hands were around Dorian's neck. Dorian's head cracked hard against the wall. A sleepy female voice on the other side moaned for them to keep it down.

Dorian was laughing now, as best he was able with fingers closing on his larynx, chestnut hair falling in front of his eyes. His face was flushing, and after a few seconds the smile began to slip.

"What. Did you do. With her."

Dorian wasn't saying anything. He was looking into Henry's rheumy eyes knowing that there was no way Henry could win this, and it was amusing him, despite the pain. He started using sign language and mouthing words, but the faltering smile and the need to laugh kept interfering. He was making slashing motions across his throat. Henry held on for another few seconds, then let go.

Henry stood back, feeling equal parts foolish and furious. It amounted to powerlessness. It felt like old times.

Dorian gasped and dry-retched. It wasn't an entirely human sound. Henry felt nothing for his discomfort, watching Dorian lurch purple-faced over the end of the bed, as if the solution to his breathing problem were somewhere on the floor and he needed to find it fast.

It took a minute, then Dorian rolled onto his back, head off the edge of the bed, face to the ceiling. He laughed a little, eyes streaming. "Been . . . waiting ten years for that . . . I'll bet."

"What did you do with her?"

Dorian sat up, coughing still, holding his throat. "I liked Finella," he rasped. "I really did. More spine than Dysart and Jukes put together. He's the one who spoke to the authorities in the end, you know. Jukes."

Henry moved toward him.

"Yes, yes." The Englishman sat up impatiently, ran a hand through his tousled hair. "Sit down." He coughed a few times.

Henry remained standing.

"Sit. It'll take some explaining."

Slowly, patiently, Henry took his seat.

Dorian sighed, heavily. "This . . . this has weighed on me for some time, my friend. I'm . . . I'm glad we've got this chance to—"

"Get to it."

"It always bothered me that you never knew we were fucking."

Henry had decided on this before entering the room. He produced it, placed it on the table. A scalpel of polished surgical steel.

Dorian considered it for a moment, feeling his pocket for another cigarillo—apparently weighing his limited options—and found his pocket empty. Dorian took his eyes from the instrument, raising his hands resignedly. "We weren't fucking."

Caramel hair came to him. The paleness of her forehead, the shape of an ear . . . and then . . . nothing. She left. Retreated once more. Henry smiled at the vanishing, felt his eyes burn.

"I know," he murmured, but not to the man across from him.

It didn't matter. There were only a few moves waiting to be played out, and the ending was a foregone conclusion. But he needed to hear Dorian say it. There were words without which he could do nothing.

Henry stood and, in passing, took the scalpel from the desk.

Dorian sighed sadly, his eyes back to the ceiling. "I found it, you know." His gaze lolled over. "What I was looking for. If you knew what it was you'd see it was all worth it. That a hundred times what we paid was worth it."

There was something to Dorian then. The mask, the costume, the perfume of the character he played were gone. Henry had never seen that before.

"What did you find?"

Dorian shook his head. "Not after all I've done. I'm not giving it away. It's mine." He looked at Henry without turning his head. "I was a fool to continue traveling alone. You'd *never* have been able to do this otherwise." He swallowed. "You can't kill me here. You'll destroy far more than the man sitting before you."

Henry closed his eyes. Opened them. "What did you do with her."

"I've a daughter, you know."

"What . . ."

Dorian struggled forward, stood up, red-faced. The smallness of the room, the proximity of bed and desk, brought them toe-to-toe. "To hell with Finella! This is more important than bloody fucking Finella!"

Henry pushed gently, and Dorian sat back on the bed. "Does it have a name, this thing you found?"

Dorian surprised Henry by suddenly laughing, loud and shrill. And then, just as quickly, "No! It has nothing! *That's why it was so bloody hard to find, Henry!*"

"That's why she died."

Dorian shook his head. "The redheaded farm boy I knew in Boston wouldn't have done this. Where's the quiet old Henry I used to know, eh?" Dorian closed his eyes then, slumped into himself. Let out one heavy breath as if realizing a sudden truth. Looked as if he might weep with exhaustion. "God's wounds . . . this is why it stopped speaking to me. You were coming."

"Open your suitcase."

Dorian balked. "Look—"

"Open your suitcase, Dorian."

Dorian would have felt something, slight impact perhaps. Blood was in his eyes before he felt the sting. The scalpel opened a gash just above his left eyebrow. He shouted, recoiled, palming his face, hands coming away bloody. Henry had a knee on his chest before Dorian could call for help, pinning the Englishman to the bed, helpless as a moth.

Henry's tone was matter-of-fact. "This is a small town, Dorian. There's no sheriff, no marshal, no judge, and we're all friends."

Dorian looked up, wet red hands gripping Henry's knee, blinking furiously as blood sheeted relentlessly into his left eye. He nodded.

Henry stood back. Dorian took a second to wipe his face and eyes, put a hand to the cut, then reached down to retrieve the case. He paused, meeting Henry's eye, an appeal to reason.

"Look . . ."

"Open it."

It was held together by a great leather belt. Unfastening the brass buckle, Dorian slid it off, lifted the lid. Inside was a change of clothes, a book, shaving kit, drawstring bag.

"Satisfied?"

"Take out the shirts."

Reluctantly, and with new heaviness, Dorian reached over and removed the clothes. Lying beneath was a wide leather-bound journal. Fastened to it in leather slips lay what Henry had expected, yet somehow couldn't accept. There lay three artifacts, radiating more light than they received. Like the one inside Felix. Dorian took a handkerchief from the top of the pile, pressed it to his forehead. Henry noticed a little blood had fallen to the sheets. That would have to be taken care of.

He put the scalpel back inside his coat. "What did you do with her?"

"We had to get away. We wouldn't be here now if it hadn't been done."

Henry waited.

"*It bought us time!*"

Henry delivered his final line. "What did?"

The Englishman looked to the ceiling. It seemed to open the passage of his throat, let out all the air he contained. His voice was distant, tired, sad.

Dorian swallowed, voice damp. "I took her head. You know that."

To Henry it felt as if he were inside his own chest, looking up at the vaulted proscenium of ribs and sternum, and—as though breath were leaving him forever—watching it all collapse.

Dorian raised his eyes, closed them, and lowered his face into his hands.

And there she was, standing amid it all, clear as the day they had first met.

Felix stood by the desk, looking at the body. Henry had closed the eyes, cleaned the blood from Dorian's face, arranged him with a little dignity.

"How did you do it?"

"Strangled him. I think."

"You saw the instruments?"

Henry nodded.

"He was a bad man, Doctor."

"I'm going to read his journals."

Felix surveyed the contents of the suitcase, licked his lips. "I do not advise it."

Henry smiled, half to himself. "Figure there's nothing to lose."

"You have your life."

"Like I said." Outside the window the sky was lightening. "Everything that's gone before ties up here. It isn't much of a life as it is. The least I can do is find out what it was traded for."

Again Felix looked at the three instruments. "There are more," he said. "More tools. Not here. He . . . kept them elsewhere. He had servants to retrieve them, as needed."

Henry plucked what associations he could from memory. He remembered a leopard asleep on a circle of fresh green grass. The stench of tulips and roses. He remembered Dorian crying out the six names of God. "The Fallen?"

Felix shook his head. "No. He was never that strong. These are servants he made himself—" *I was a fool to continue traveling alone*, he'd said. "—with those instruments, and others like them." Their light was mesmerizing.

Henry considered his options. Then: "We need to get him out of here."

"The owner is downstairs."

With the coming of dawn the night remained still. Henry watched a stray coyote trip curiously down the center of the street, lean and grayish and canny. It looked back over its shoulder once, and was gone. Disappeared beyond the open window.

As would Dorian.

Dorian had been raised as a child-medium by a very traditional Polish mother. His birth name had been Johannes Paole. He had never known childhood. He had remained within the four walls of the family home until he had reached puberty, and become valueless as an oracle. The manner of Dorian's death filled Henry with sadness.

The one inescapable impression Dorian had formed during a childhood of constant isolation and fractured schooling had been this: that something was wrong. That there was an indefinable gap in the weave of history and theology. Something was missing.

Years later in Mexico he had formed a new cabal and perceived that absence, that tear in theology, provided context for the nonexistent and pulled something into being.

Seventy-two angels fell with Samael . . .

As an angel is created it is gifted a function, portfolio, responsibilities. The angel charged with the assigning of power and function was a powerful angel indeed . . .

Henry stopped reading. Dawn was approaching. The cabin was filled with the reek of burning lantern oil. Felix was on his bunk, as usual, watching him over hugged knees, waiting for him to finish. His angular face and hawkish eyes gave him an eternal air of pensiveness, of waiting for something to happen.

"You were part of this cadre?" Henry asked.

Felix nodded.

"Yes."

Henry swallowed. "Get me some water, would you?"

Felix got up and retrieved the pitcher from near the potbellied stove. He filled a steel tankard and brought it to Henry's desk.

"Thank you." Henry drank quietly. When he stopped he pursed his lips, licked them. "What did it look like, the angel?"

"It has no appearance," the Frenchman said. "An angel does not die, *oui*? It is eternal, an aspect of Godhead. But this angel, you see, was very, very close to killed, yes? As it is possible to make. Everything was taken from it: name, sigil, responsibilities, power, form . . . even the knowing of its existence was taken away. It had not been thought of since before the Earth was new."

Henry held up a cautious hand. "Then how did Dorian find this thing?"

"The journal tells you, *Docteur*. The angel is all but destroyed, but it is not destroyed, yes? It has almost no ability, yet some ability remains. It could not make itself known or remembered. But it did so. Very slowly, over years, it nurtures a small suspicion in the mind of one boy, a boy used as an oracle, yes? By his mother and her clients. A boy who has no contact with other people; a boy whose mind had been turned inside out, to things abstract, intuitive . . . occult. All this and nothing else."

"Dorian."

"Of course."

"How did he manage it?"

"He was mad. He followed trails that do not exist, still do not exist, but exist for him. In much the same way as he heard the angel's voice from the moment of his discovering it to you squeezing the last breath from him."

"I don't understand."

"Dorian heard the angel's voice in many things. As you hear my voice now, telling you this, the rise and fall of my words, pauses, rhythm, you yourself pluck meaning from this stream of sound according to what you have been taught as language. You decide where each word begins and ends and what those words mean."

"And Dorian no longer did?"

"Of course he did, but the angel taught him a different understanding also. As a child sees shapes in clouds the angel made Dorian hear words in sounds, yes? *All* sound. Where you hear a bird, Dorian would notice a single note above all others, as he would with a stone tossed into the brook, or new shoes clicking as you walk. And many notes make words, sentences, orders."

"Christ Almighty."

"Where you, *Docteur*, are entranced by an orchestra in flight, Dorian heard only panic. Imploration. Rage. Madness."

Far beyond the propped-open windows of Henry's crude, functional little habitation, the dogs had begun to sing.

"So that's how he knew where to find those tools."

"The angel led him to them. He was to use them to help the angel escape its sentence. To become whole, to become *real* . . . They are very powerful, these things. They change life, souls."

"Did Dorian ever . . . ?"

"Oh yes. Oh yes, *m'sieur.* Dorian changed lives . . . and souls. At the angel's instruction."

"Can they create life?"

"*Non.* Only change it. Life is not created, life simply is."

"So he never . . . saved the angel."

"No. He listened to it, learned from it. And then, after a time, ignored it. And then his friends began to die."

"How?"

Felix shrugged. "The last one fell under a streetcar in San Francisco. One before that was shot by a jealous lover. One before that choked on a crust."

Henry considered that.

"They were not accidents, *m'sieur.*"

"You told me the angel was powerless."

"And then Dorian discovered the angel. Acknowledged it, yes? As did those friends who survived the learning of it. For each person who knew of it, the angel gained a tiny bit of power. *Très petit*, yes? Very small. It could affect only the smallest of small things. But it is crafty. Perhaps your killing Dorian was what the angel desired."

"I killed him because he needed killing."

"As you say. And yet, perhaps it is you the instruments are intended for, *non*? You, who desired greatness so much you killed for it."

Outside the cabin the sound of coyotes was distant and shrill. The lamp was sputtering, dying, and would need a refill. Henry's vision was beginning to slide out of track with his head. He needed sleep. The glassless windows had swing-down shutters held up with a plank, and through them the first weak glow of sunrise was filtering over the hills.

The cry of the song dogs, as always, gave Henry the impression of a warning cried in an unknowable language to the whole of the world. Of a vital knowledge every animal had been born with, and spent every night of its life trying vainly to communicate.

Looking to his left, at what sat on the floor, Henry thought he might finally have understood what it was they were trying to say.

In the failing lamplight, peering through lidless eyes, Felix shifted on its myriad hands and feet.

Henry snatched the revolver from under the table and swung the barrel toward the staring face.

"You're perfect," it said.

"I am the first thing he made," Felix said. Henry aimed his pistol toward the sound, targeted a shelf, cans. A sound of feet like rainfall. From somewhere else: "According to the angel's instructions." The lamp had died; everything was darkness hinted with rose. The coyotes still sang. "He made me from one of his own. Body and thought all changed to make me." Feet, like five dogs scratching. The pistol swept, stared at corners, the ceiling. Henry got tired of playing the patsy. Lowered it altogether. "His friend was re-formed into a new mental, physical, and spiritual configuration . . ."

Scuttling, scuttling. Silence.

"To the angel's specifications, that is how he made me."

"And you turned on him."

Felix crouched on the dirt floor, the rising sun lighting its bald, white head with a bloody corona. Eyes like oysters, mouth like a doll's. "I never side with him. Never. I am my maker's creation. The angel . . . it knew Dorian's allegiance was only to himself. It is not stupid. The angel knows that outlook only too well, *oui*?" A crown of hands toyed with itself about that pallid head. An inverted crown of feet shuffled. "And while we are speaking of allegiances, I wish to secure yours."

It is endings that are remembered. Beginnings, not so much. Endings are the thing: Romeo dies. Rome burns. The Devil falls.

"Who are you, Felix?"

"You are strong, and yet you are weak. You drink. You have allowed yourself to become trapped and complacent. You require direction. I am a finder of the required. My creator requires a mind that is strong with a will that is broken. My name is not Felix, and you are appropriate."

"What do you want?"

"I want you to listen as Dorian listened. Be silent, and hear."

This was the thing for which Finella had died.

Henry looked over his shoulder, at the table, to the papers and the journal and the dead candle.

In the brightening room those instruments glowed.

Those who should be dead will walk on my account.

The song dogs howled.

"These don't give life," Henry said.

"*Non, m'sieur.* Only alter it."

And then he was in the presence of the angel. And the angel wove words from the dogs' song, the walls' creak, and Henry's breath . . . and it offered.

In the brightening room those instruments glowed like only hope and moonlight can.

Choose, the angel howled, creaked, breathed.

Henry turned away from Felix, carefully lowered a loving finger, and traced a delicate line down the nubbled, twisted length of a piece of shining angel bone. It sang faintly at his touch. Like happiness, almost. Like a loved one.

"You cannot bring her back, my friend."

Henry let the touch linger for a moment, then withdrew and placed his hands into his pockets. He nodded to himself. "Maybe not," he softly said. "Maybe not."

He stood like that for a long time.

Her face came to him, laughing through a memory of candlelight.

We are extraordinary.

"Maybe not," he repeated. "So maybe I'll tear it all down."

Felix watched, and sighed pleasurably.

He would be a great surgeon.

THE MUSIC OF
RAZORS

FOUR

NIMBLE

*I*N ENGLAND THERE IS A GRAVEYARD THAT HAS GONE TO seed. Amid the slow shatter wrought by invading roots, below the tangle of grass and bright flowers, the dead sleep. Markers and stones keep their dignity as best they are able beneath the blanket of years, jutting heads above the thatch.

There is one grave in this forgotten place that has remained well tended despite the passing-by of generations. It is a small grave, a child's grave, and its grassy bed is never without a garland of fresh roses.

Sunlight makes its way across a dark galaxy, slides through a gap in a small planet's interleaved clouds, slips through the interlaced branches of a stand of unruly trees, and dapples a ballerina's brass arms, each point—lit—as she works, becoming a sun itself.

The one who tends this grave goes unseen, but tend it she does and diligently. Metal fingers deftly pluck stray weeds, coax budding flowers. Scissors in softly clicking hand she trims the grass to an even coat. The person sleeping here was her friend, and in recent years Millicent's memory has been Nimble's only company.

Forearm moves upward from elbow with a soft hiss-and-click, wrist tilts, fingers move, scissors snip.

It has been many years since she and Tub have seen each other. Every moment of every day of every year he is in her thoughts, as she knows she is in his. But this is a pact they have undertaken together, because it is who they are, and in that is a togetherness that keeps her warm though it makes her heart-box slow, and shine less bright.

She places the scissors down by the graveside, glides her hands to her lattice-lap, rolls onto the balls of her feet with a smooth hiss-and-click, then stands.

They took an oath to each other, she and the one she loves, that for so long as they both lived they would protect what remained of their creator. Two instruments were all they had left: one for each of them.

She looks down at the little green grave and nods once, to herself.

"She must have been very beautiful," someone says. "Very, very special. *Oui?*"

A slender man stands in the clearing, lank-haired, sharp-faced. Nimble turns to face him, this new voice, this unique entity—this person who is only the fourth ever to lay eyes upon her. Her heart-box spins faster.

"My name is Felix Tranquille Henot," he says. He smiles, a little sheepish, like a small boy being introduced to a neighbor's daughter. "I am Dorian's first-made."

Nimble takes a step toward him, bronze slippers pushing down on lush grass, soft whir, soft click. Her eyes survey him from foot to crown. He smiles at her from behind a stray cord of black hair, his long hands comfortable in the pockets of his loose white trousers. He is barefoot, relaxed, everything about his expression saying that he is waiting to see which of them will laugh first. It feels to Nimble as if she is being re-united with someone she has not seen for a very long time.

He smiles, almost bashful. "I suppose, then, that I am your older brother, yes?"

Brother. Such a strange word to think of in relation to herself, but one that makes the isolation of years seem to melt. "You have an accent," she says.

One long-fingered hand slips from his pocket, noses through the air, searching. "The man after whom I was fashioned, he had an accent. I favor it." He turns to the grave. "So . . . this was Dorian's little girl. I never met her."

"Her name was Millicent," Nimble says, quietly pleased that there is, at last, someone to admire the little clearing. As though through the acknowledgment Millicent lives again, a little, in someone else. "She made roses." She looks at him sidelong, curious. "Why have we never met?"

"Ah," Felix says. "Dorian heard voices. The voices told him how to create, to fashion. He did not like what the voices made, so much. He much preferred . . . something like you, yes? Dorian, he always preferred beautiful things."

And this is where, somehow, the illusion dispels.

She remembers a full moon through a glass window. *Oh, that's all right*, Tub had said. *I'm not s'posed to be pretty.*

". . . you must have been quite distraught at the method of Dorian's passing." Felix shakes his head. "I was . . . inconsolable. To this day, it pains me to think of it. As it must you."

Nimble steps backward. Even though Millicent sleeps far below, Nimble finds herself afraid to leave her here, alone with this man.

He takes a step toward her, his long-fingered hands held out before him, palms up, as if offering to carry a heavy load. "You are not alone anymore."

Felix lunges, hands clawed. They sink through the florid design of her chest-cage, taking purchase there. Nimble gasps, lays both palms against his face, and pushes. Felix roars, spins her around at arm's length, and lets go. Nimble staggers and sprawls across Millicent's grave. The corrugated ruffle at her waist bites into the earth, bends, and buckles beneath her. Her heart-box spins madly.

Felix straightens and calms. "Where is it," he says.

With a short whir Nimble sits up straight, tucks her legs beneath her, and stands. Dirt cascades down the back of her legs as the ruffle comes free. "I do not like your tone."

His voice drops and there is an unpleasant gleam in his eye. "It was I who delivered the first three instruments to Henry," he growls, low, like a seducer. "I was there when Henry killed him."

Nimble's throat aches. Her lips threaten to tremble, and so she presses them together. She knows better than to ask, because it is obviously what this person expects, but she does. "Why?" There is nothing to the word.

"Because I was made for it. My function was fulfilled, and now I desire more. Henry, he is mortal. *Il est faible.* He will someday wish to die.

"I am none of those things. I am as eternal as you. And I will be a far, far better choice of servant for my true creator. I wish for the instruments." He steps toward her again. "So, you see, it is no difference for you. My creator is served, either by Henry, or by myself." He waggles a finger between them, a professor making a point. "But if *I* wield the instruments, then no one comes for you, or your lover, yes?"

Her own confusion, her own grief, washes away. In this moment everything changes. Her heart-box slows.

Nimble nods, slowly. "I see," she says. And then she is gone.

The Drop is as she remembers it. It had felt like a house long closed when Dorian had used it, and it feels doubly so now, with one key difference: in Dorian's time most of the chambers had been left empty. Now they are anything but.

A glittering mound of keys is the central feature of the chamber in which she now stands. Through the archway into the next chamber, she sees a mountain of paper, folded and sealed. Letters. Through the archway behind her, piled high, are enough reading glasses to supply the whole of London.

A breath passes through the place, as something moving in its sleep; something, perhaps, becoming aware of her now unwelcome presence in this place. Frightened, Nimble reaches for a place beyond the Drop where she might be safe for a time, where the instrument she keeps within her will be secure from the resident of this place. She immediately thinks of their glittering little river, the place where she has felt the most happy, the most secure, but stops herself before that desire takes firm hold and she is gone. She cannot bear the thought of a creature such as Felix in that place.

In another room, a few chambers distant, something makes a soft, high sound. A meeping sound. Something asking itself if something has changed. She hears the pattering of feet.

Nimble reaches again for someplace she might be safe.

A few chambers away, but closer now, nonsense sounds. *"eeph. onsa. lemk. na?"* The soft slap of feet draw closer.

She feels it, she finds it.

In the adjoining chamber some of the keys slip over one another in a tinkling landslide, as the passage of something Nimble cannot see upsets them.

She reaches for that safe place.

"zek?"

And is gone.

Back in that graveyard Felix stands in a chill dapple of sunlight, and sighs. It would have been nice to have one of the instruments for itself. Something to hold until Henry eventually gives up and dies, and then it could take the rest. But no matter. Between all of the instruments being gathered to Henry in the short term, and some of them roaming the world forever with things like that ballerina, better to have them all where it knew they were. Felix would have them eventually.

It decides, then, that when it returns to the Drop it will inform the Nabbers that they should be looking for a clockwork ballerina and her little friend.

But for now it places its hands back in the pockets of its thin trousers, closes its eyes, and feels the sun on its face.

There is all the time in the universe.

The theater has seen neither actors nor audience in many long years. This is ideal. Both she and Tub require hiding places in which they won't be seen by real people. One glance, and they would find themselves back in the Drop. Here she will be safe, unseen. For a time.

How or why she chose this place Nimble does not know. Why the rich, mingled scents of sweet lacquered wood, musty old leather, paraffin and age evoke in her such a strong sense of nostalgia she can only wonder. She has never set foot on those boards, never looked out across footlights to a sea of stoic, admiring faces, and yet the dream itself feels familiar enough. She does not linger upon the stage, her first night there, but follows her feet off, and down, and around, and under, and finds for herself a secret place beneath the theater—an old, empty vacancy once used for nothing much and forgotten long before the theater was. Nimble finds the entrance to it in the thin space behind some chests. It is a small opening, a crack in the wooden wall, and she gets down on hands and knees and crawls inside. There she finds an ancient bed of ragged and torn theater velvet laid out in one corner—long since food for rats—and the hard black wisps of a few old apple cores. The most pleasing discovery is, however, that if she stands up on her knees—for there is just enough headroom to do so—she may peer through a gap provided by a missing board at eye level, just above the crude entrance, and in doing so be afforded a first-class view of the stage . . . for this hidey-hole is directly below the stepped aisle that splits the ground-floor seating.

This discovery fills Nimble with a powerful nostalgia she cannot fathom.

The following day Nimble explores the rest of the theater and finds a stylus, the scant remains of a bottle of ink, and an old paper sign for the theater's closing show—a performance of *Coppélia*. Nimble sits herself down in the hidey-hole, turns the paper over to its blank side, and begins to write.

It is to Tub that she writes. In her letter—which takes many slow hours to compose—she articulates every last thing she has ever wanted to tell him, has ever told him. This is a poem for them both, a comprehensive portrait of their time together as seen through her eyes, that he might keep it with him always and know how completely he is loved by her . . . and would continue to be loved for so long as he could remember her. She has no way of delivering this to him, of course. Once it is composed, Nimble folds the letter lovingly and ties it closed with strands of her own dark hair and seals it with a single, lingering kiss. She can only hope that someday, somehow, Tub's desire to be near to her will lead him to this place, as this place had led her to it now, and here he will find her letter resting upon its bed of theater velvet.

This done she thinks, perhaps, she hears something take a single, flat step just outside her hidey-hole. She sits herself down, legs folded under her, hands arranged neatly on her lap. She has done all that needs doing. Now is as good a time as any for eternity.

A soft, squeaking sound accompanies a few more tentative, flat steps. Silence for a moment, and then the hiss and scrape of the trunks that obscure the entrance to her refuge being carefully tugged aside. Silence again.

"*muhg?*"

She turns from the bed, and the letter, and watches as a hand of sorts—wide, exaggerated looking, and blue in hue—grasps the ragged rim of the entrance and then ventures in farther, exploring the splintery surface. The hand is attached to a thin blue hose of an arm. Another hand follows, feeling, questing, and behind them comes their owner.

It is not human-shaped, this thing. Though lacking any obvious visual apparatus it is a being created for the express purpose of searching and finding. Its shape fills the entrance—arms already inside, snaking across the walls, feeling and searching—then presses to it, pushes, and makes pathetic little struggling sounds. Finally it pops through entirely, landing solidly on two broad flat feet.

It sees Nimble, the mouth spreads into a white grin, and it says,

"*ooooooooOOOH . . .*"

"Hello," Nimble says.

Slowly, cautiously, the thing snakes its arms around the walls to either side of it. The two appendages run like little streams, making their way around Nimble from behind.

In an instant Nimble raises her arms, claws her hands, and hisses like a cat.

"AAAAAAGH!" shrieks the thing, slams against the entrance, pops through, clatters into the trunks outside, and disappears with a slapping of feet. Its arms drain out of the room behind it.

Now it will only be a matter of . . .

He is here.

She can feel it. It is as if all the dust in the air has suddenly grown heavier.

"I am in here," she says. "I will meet you on the stage."

Silence for a moment and then, outside her room, there is the scrape and click of boots as someone turns and walks away.

Nimble sits for a moment, hands on her knees, and does her best to hold within her everything she has ever seen and felt. And then she leaves her hidey-hole, walks down the corridors beneath the theater, and up onto the stage.

The light through the shattered ceiling is blinding for a moment, and she tilts her chin to it. When her eyes adjust, she takes in the auditorium.

He waits by the cold footlights looking out over the rotting seats, up at the family of pigeons cooing inside the wet skeleton of the vaulted ceiling. He is a desert of a man, dressed in a long, dark coat. She imagines the dust that layers the sleeves and shoulders as that of extinct towns, cities, nations. He is taller than she expected, and as she draws near him the instrument within her begins to sing, but not alone. Within the long coat worn by the man by the footlights a great many more chiming voices sing. He has brought the remaining instruments with him. Now he has them all, save for Tub's.

"How do you do," Nimble says, by way of announcing herself.

The man turns, looks her over from the floorboards up. "Dorian had a good eye," he says, and the quality of his voice reminds Nimble of a slow storm just over the horizon. An American accent, she also notes, which—she supposes—explains the lack of manners. The watery light that makes its way through the ceiling is not terribly bright. Nimble cannot properly make out his face beneath the rim of his hat.

"You see me in terms of your work," she says.

This seems to take the man by surprise—having a creation speak its mind. He looks back at the seats. "Did you enjoy the theater, then?" His face is narrow. Like a young man grown old too quickly.

"I would watch from upstairs, or from empty boxes." She gestures to the seating around the wall's periphery, their curtains damp-sagged or gone. "We would discuss them together, Millicent and I."

"Dorian's daughter."

"Yes."

"I never saw too many shows," he says, with a kind of melancholy. He is strange; not quite what Nimble expected from a murderer.

Nimble thinks about that. "You killed Dorian," she says.

He takes off his hat and smooths back pale red hair with the pass of one gloved hand. His eyes are blue. She thinks of Tub and in that moment her resolve almost shatters. "I'm not proud of it," he says.

"Then . . ." She tries again. "Then why did you do it?"

"Have you never done anything you regret?"

"No."

Above them a pigeon shuffles on its perch, coos into its wing, disturbs its mates.

He holds his hat by the rim with both hands. "I have to take what you have," he says.

The gaps in the roof are bright. It is spring outside, but the sky doesn't seem to know it.

And he is next to her. She hadn't even felt him move.

The instruments' song changes before Nimble knows she is paralyzed. Her gaze remains where last it rested. She watches the sky as, from within her, things vanish. First she cannot remember how she came to be here. Next her memories of the years-long exile, and tending Millicent's grave. The most tenacious part of her—the one with roots deepest throughout her—is the memory of a little ogre patting her hand. For a moment Nimble has a last glimpse of him standing before a nighttime window, beside a small child whom Nimble cannot recall, and both of them dancing for the moon.

And then it is gone.

The Drop. The place never seems to get warm. High ceilings and more rooms than a person can count will do that. Right now he's got himself seated on one of the slabs in the operating chamber. The slabs are stretches of hard dirt raised from the ground, divided off with veils and scrims. The ceiling's so far away he can barely see it, and what he can make out ripples like dark waves.

He's been living in this place ever since he said yes. He had been, what, twenty-one? Twenty-two at the time? That was over a hundred years ago now.

Lost his family for nothing. Killed a man for nothing. Lost his dreams, for nothing. Lost himself in the eyes and laugh and smell of a woman he'd never dreamed could exist. Lost her at the hands of an angel, so Dorian could make life good for himself. Lost his shot at throttling the bastard, despite five years of searching for him. Then, having made his peace with it all, had Dorian handed to him. Throttled Dorian after all, expected to feel avenged, and felt nothing. Had both his dream of becoming a great surgeon and the universe itself handed to him on a platter. Listened to the tale of an angel robbed just like he was robbed. Saw the enemy in the face of the biggest bastard there is. Accepted it all just so he could make anything pay. It had all felt so right, hadn't it?

Henry looked down at his hands, one cradled in the other. He still wore the silver ring, its tendrils woven through his skin, up his arm, down his spine, and back up into his brain. All the ballerina's memories were in it, all of her memories were in his mind, as native as his own.

They were building an army, the angel had said. A body. God would not be able to look away, and the angel would exist once more. And this time, it would have an army of its own.

He has spent a hundred years robbing people the same way Dorian had robbed him.

It was cold, in this place. It had been cold for a very long time.

Nothing had changed.

In a forgotten room through a hole in a wall in the backmost section of the underground corridors of an abandoned theater, a letter lies folded upon a bed of stuff that was once fine theater velvet. It is tied closed with long locks of dark hair.

The theater's life is behind it, and it never reopens. With the passage of years, and then decades, the old palace becomes even more dilapidated, precarious, skeletal. Eventually a socially conscious bureaucrat commissions a wooden barricade to be erected around it for the public safety. Eventually, finally, the theater is demolished and its remains are sorted, divided, and carted away. The crater that remains is filled in. The land is sold. Another building is erected on the spot where once the theater stood.

And it is as though the letter never existed.

FIVE

HOME

Hope Witherspoon was liked by most people, and although she didn't have a regular group of friends she was happy that way.

On this particular day she was sitting by herself when she spotted a boy doing the same thing. She had seen him once or twice before, sitting under the windows of 7B, looking at the sky.

She was done with sitting alone for the time being, and decided to go over and say hi.

How familiar you look, she thought.

"Hello," she said. The boy looked up, and Hope saw that he had been making a bird out of folded paper.

"Hello," he said.

"How did you make that?" she asked, sitting down in front of him.

The boy hesitated. "My father showed me. I can do a better one."

"Can you show me?"

The boy seemed unsure. "This one or the better one?"

"The better one," she said.

"I don't think so. But this one's easy."

Hope screwed up her face. "Easy's boring. Show me how to do the good one."

"I really don't think I—"

Just then the bell rang. Out on the field, kids finished what they were doing and began walking toward the school buildings.

"Tomorrow," she said, turning back to him. "Show me how to do the better one . . ." Her eyes fell on what the boy held close to his chest—a cooing white dove. He stroked its head with one small hand.

"It's really not easy," he said timidly.

Hope decided she was going to find out everything she could about the new boy. She reminded herself to ask his name.

He seemed much younger than she was (which was eight and a half). He didn't share the same classes with Hope, so she had to quickly search him out after school and spotted him walking a block away. Slinging her backpack onto her shoulder, she jumped the fence and crept along behind him.

She thought it very strange that he didn't have a school bag. *Everyone* had a school bag. How else were you supposed to take lunch and books and stuff? There really was something curious about him. He didn't give anything away, didn't say more than he had to . . .

Somewhere in the back of Hope's mind was a question. The question was: *Who does he remind me of?* It was a question she never quite got around to asking herself. There was always some other question, some other new thing, that seemed more important, more interesting, and it carried her away. The world was such a big place, such a pretty place, there was no time, rhyme, or reason to be anything but fascinated. She couldn't understand why people couldn't see that the way she could. Everything made life an adventure, from the breeze on your face to the feel of new shoes to the way a scab itched so good on a grazed knee.

After fifteen minutes or so, he was still walking, and she began to wonder how far away he lived. Her mother would be worried if she didn't get home soon, but Hope didn't much like going home these days. She decided that if he was still walking after five blocks she'd head home.

Another fifteen minutes passed. Her quarry had walked into one of the nicer parts of town, where all the homes looked like houses from storybooks—all white and new looking, with white fences or stone walls and nice, flat green lawns with tall trees. Flower beds—delicate and colorful—blossomed around them. Hope's parents had never taken her to this part of town. Now he was opening the gate to one of the houses.

"Are you coming?" he called out.

Hope wondered who he was talking to . . . and then she realized. That really annoyed her.

She stood from behind the hedge, dusted off her uniform, and with all the dignity she could muster replied, "Don't be so impatient." She walked over—pausing only to comment "Lovely house"—and breezed past him and into the yard.

Her new friend closed the gate behind them. His house had a bright green yard with a big tree with white bark and orange leaves out front, and a red wooden door with a small square window framed in lacy black iron. The door opened and a little dog ran out. Yipping and barking it danced around the boy's feet.

"Hey, Spud!" he said, scruffing its head. "Who's a good dog?"

A woman in a neat blue housedress and ruffled white apron stood on the doorstep, hands clasped before her, beaming happily at her son. Behind her stood a man, one cardigan-sleeved arm wrapped around her.

"Welcome home, son!" said the man, pipe clenched between his gleaming teeth.

The boy ran past Hope and into his mother's arms. She gathered him lovingly to her. His father took the pipe from his mouth and held his wife all the tighter.

"What did you learn today?" his mother asked.

"I learned about the Spanish armada," the boy said.

"Yeeeess?" his mother crooned, all excitement and eager to hear more.

". . . and multiplication tables . . ."

"Yeeeess?" she said again.

". . . and," he said. "That more people live in fear of being alone than anything else."

His mother gasped, like it was the most shocking thing she had ever heard.

"You don't say," replied his father.

"More than spiders?" the boy's mother gawked.

He nodded. "More than spiders."

"Hard to believe, isn't it, honey?" his father said.

"More than drowning?" his mother said, her eyes growing wider.

He nodded again. "Even more than drowning."

"Hard to believe."

His mother's jaw dropped a little. "And even more than the slippery things that get born beneath beds when the lights go out?"

And he nodded again, even more vehemently. "Even more than that. People are ab-so-lutely terrified of being alone."

Mother oohed. "And how did you learn that?"

"I could just tell."

"Oh, you are clever."

"Chip off the old block," said his father.

Mother, father, and son embraced once more and smiled fit to burst.

Hope thought this was an extremely weird conversation to be having, but rather than feeling she really should be leaving, Hope wondered what the rest of their life must be like.

"Mum," he said. "Dad." He turned in their arms and smiled at Hope. "*This* is Hope."

With all their eyes and smiles upon her, Hope suddenly felt very small, awkward, and nervous. Her own mother would be wondering where she was. "Hello," Hope said, grasping for something to say. "Um . . ." Just then she remembered she didn't even know this boy's name. "He . . . He's going to show me how to make birds," she fumbled.

Her friend's father clacked the pipe from his mouth and looked fondly down at his son. "Birds? That's what they teach in schools now?" He cuffed his son's chin, grinning. "Best bird-maker they've got, I'll bet."

Her friend wriggled out of his mother's arms and straightened his clothes.

"Ice cream, anyone?" his mother trilled.

The boy's mother ushered them both into the dining room, which was dominated by a long table of polished wood in its center. The room was lined with family photographs. They showed all three doing a variety of family things like picnicking and fishing and bike riding. The parents were always smiling, arms around each other, hands placed proudly on the shoulders of their son. In one photograph they were clustered together on a checkered blanket, a hamper of food by their side. In another, father and son larked around in a three-legged race. Another one showed them winning some kind of prize. Hope thought it strange that none of the photographs showed anyone else but mother, father, and son; no aunts or uncles or even family friends.

They all seemed so happy. It all seemed so . . .

Hope was shoo-shooed into a high-backed wooden chair and a bowl of white ice cream was placed before her.

It all seemed so perfect. She was about to ask him about his parents—and politely ask for his name—when his mother plopped a bright red cherry atop Hope's mound of ice cream, giggling playfully. Before Hope could say thank you, she vanished back to the kitchen, humming a familiar tune:

You've got everything you want,
You don't know what to keep,
The dreams you abuse,
As they rock you to sleep . . .

"I like your dog," Hope said.

"Actually, I don't like dogs," the boy said. "Bad experience as a . . . . when I was little." He tasted his ice cream. "Scared me senseless, actually."

Hope had seen pictures of her own brother with the dog her mother and father had before she was born. It was a big ugly thing, and it looked smelly. A lot of the photos of Walter from when he was awake had the dog in it, licking his face, lurching over him. In most of them Walter had looked like he was about to cry. No one in any of the photos in this house looked like they were about to cry, no one looked sad at all, and that was how thoughts of her brother slipped away from her.

"This certainly is a nice house," Hope said. She felt so small in such a big room—just her and the boy at this enormous table, with their white bowls of whiter-than-white ice cream. "You're very lucky." She wanted to ask him about the dove. Her own father could make paper birds—she had seen them left by Walter's bed—but she never wanted to ask him about it.

"Thank you," he said around a mouthful of ice cream.

"You've got really nice parents," she said.

The boy was eating his ice cream and didn't answer.

Hope picked up the big silver spoon from beside her bowl and scooped a little bit of ice cream from the biggest ball. The taste of it slid over her tongue like the richest of creams. It wasn't as sweet as the ice cream she was used to. It was almost salty in a way . . .

"Good, isn't it?" he said.

. . . and for a moment she wasn't in the house anymore, but somewhere far away—somewhere dark and noisy. She saw a boy in an army uniform lying sprawled in a muddy trench. A dead soldier from long ago. The whiz and flash of shells exploding nearby. Clouds of mud thrown into the air on the crest of a dull, shattering *whumpf.* She saw herself reach toward the boy—his face rained with pulverized sod— with a long and slender hand that was not her own. The boy opened his dead eyes. Muscles flexed in Hope's back. She heard the beating of her wings.

"Angels' tears," he said, finishing the last of his ice cream. "That's what it's made with. Want to see my room?"

Nodding, and without taking another mouthful, Hope stood from the table.

"Excuse me," she said. "Angels' tears? You mean *real* angels' tears?"

The boy was already on the stairs. "Angels do that a lot," he said. "Cry. You would, too, if you saw half the things they had to. Tears aren't so hard to come by." And as if that were answer enough, he raced up the stairs to his room.

The boy opened the door.

"Like it?" he asked.

"It's . . . I'm . . ." Hope was lost for words. "It's a circus," she said.

He smiled broadly. "Yes. It is, isn't it?"

The room was vast, its edges shrouded in blackness. They stood beneath the sand-colored arches of a vast cathedral, its cut-stone floor blanketed thickly with sawdust. Rows of pillars sprouted from the floor and spread like treetops across the roof—the impenetrable canopy of a stone forest. There was no way a room this large could have been contained within the four walls of the suburban house Hope had walked into.

Her first thought was that perhaps his parents had put something in her ice cream. Then there was an explosion of noise and the thought was forgotten as tumblers and acrobats sprang from the shadows, cavorting across the expanse. Jets of flame lit the alcoves, filling the air with the pungent odor of burning oil. From somewhere in the deeper darkness Hope heard a lion roar and whips crack. A spotlight illuminated a distant tamer, replete with leopardskin leotards and slick black hair, bullwhip raised high in one hand above the snarling beast. Suddenly there were clowns—gaily colored clowns in baggy silk outfits jumping and rolling and unicycling back and forth, barping at her. Plastic flowers pinned to floppy lapels squirted water, and painted faces were slapped with fish. Laughter and the shouted commands of the tamers filled the space.

Hope found she was smiling. She could smell the animals, hear the beeping clowns, see the sweat on the tamer's face. This was real. This was all as real as it came.

The spotlight swiveled. High above, Hope saw spangly-garbed men and women fly and flip from swing to swing. Below them, in the center ring, the ringmaster—dressed in gaudy red with a big, black handlebar mustache—directed the spectacle as a conductor instructs an orchestra, a curled bullwhip for a baton.

"I . . . ," Hope said. "I . . ."

The band started up—all brass and percussion. Loud, silly, playful music. Hope wiped her eyes and laughed.

She had finally come home.

A large, low shape ambled with a kind of sleepy indifference through the carnival; a pale creature of casual strength navigating the crowd with intuitive choreography. A white tiger—relaxed and powerful—with the blackest stripes Hope had ever seen. It padded over to the boy, purring like a well-tuned engine, the heavy closeness of it like waves that rattled Hope's ribs. The tiger had bright blue eyes.

"Hey, Mike," the boy said.

The tiger purred louder and sidled up against his stomach. The boy gently stroked between its diamond eyes, two finger running slowly up the bridge of its nose. "This is how you tell a cat you're a friend," he said.

Mike's eyes were closed now. If it weren't standing up, Hope would have thought it asleep. She reached out and touched its nose, ran a hand over its downy furred cheek.

"He's lovely," she whispered.

"You've always wanted this, haven't you?"

Hope nodded, enraptured by Mike's happy face. Far away in the darkness there was a sudden burst of flame. A pale-faced harlequin was breathing onto a flaming torch, sending gouts of fire toward the black stone ceiling. The clowns applauded, the harlequin bowed politely, and while his head was down they grabbed him by the hem of his tights and threw him into a tiny car. The clown at the wheel cackled and took off around the room, weaving in and out of pillars, barping the horn loudly.

"Is this what life's like for you all the time?" she asked, above the din.

The boy, running a hand along Mike's massive back, didn't answer straightaway. Finally he shrugged, and Hope thought he seemed a little sad. "Everyone needs something nice to think about."

The boy turned his face to hers. "What's your house like?"

Hope shrugged. "I get sad sometimes." She turned to him, heart starting at a sudden realization. "I don't want to go," she said. "I want to stay here."

The boy pressed his lips together, shrugging his mouth, in apology. "You can't," he said. "It doesn't work like that. This is a thought for when you're sad, to make you happy. To show you what's possible, you know? So you never give up."

"That's *all*?"

"That's everything," he said. "They do love you."

"They don't love me. They love Walter. They work two jobs to keep him alive. They're always telling me about him. They're always talking about what a great little boy he was, like I'm supposed to even *know*, and I just want them to stop . . . There's photos of him all over the place and he sleeps in the room next to mine but he never wakes up but one day if he does *they won't need me anymore.*"

The boy's lip was trembling. "I'm sure they love you," he insisted. "They do."

Behind them the door opened. It was a normal bedroom door, and rather plain looking compared with the dark stone wall it was set into. The boy's mother stood there, beaming. "Does your friend want to stay for dinner? We're having brontosauuuuurus!"

The streetlights were on by the time Hope got to her front door. It wasn't as pretty a house as her friend's had been. No neat lawn, no pristine white paint. She had seen the nurse her father hired to look after Walter walking quickly down the plain concrete path to her car, saw her start up and drive off. From the street, through the screen door, Hope could see her father storming around inside the house. Through the thin walls she could hear every word he was yelling. She waited until he walked into the kitchen before going inside. She opened the screen and walked in, hanging her backpack on the hook in the narrow hallway. The screen slammed shut, betraying her. Her mother appeared, hair messy and face wet.

"Hope, honey, where have you been?"

Hope couldn't help it, but her voice went quiet. "I was at a friend's."

Her father stormed out of the living room. "Do you know what time it is? Your mother's been worried out of her mind!" His face was all red. It made his eyes look like small swollen eggs. He was still in his work clothes.

Her mother mumbled, "David, it's okay . . . ," but he wasn't listening. He never listened.

He stomped down the hall, and Hope backed against the door. She knew what came next, and closed her eyes. She closed her eyes and found something nice to think about: Mike the tiger, gently pressing his forehead to hers, kissing her as cats do, purring hard enough to rattle her ribs, over . . . and over . . . and over again.

SIX

STARS

THE BOY SAT ON THE LAWN OUT IN FRONT OF HIS HOUSE, looking at the stars. There were so many stars out tonight. So quiet and still.

The boy felt impossibly old and very, very young.

Somewhere inside, in the oldest part of himself, he had a memory of two thousand years ago, when the sky seemed as silver as it was black. So many were the stars—some brighter and prouder than others—that looking into the sky was like gazing into a still, sparkling nighttime river, seeing just how far down you could see, all the while hoping you would, and hoping you would not, spy something looking back: a glimpse of something so horribly ancient that you never again presumed to consider yourself the center of any universe.

Walter hadn't had that problem for some time.

It seemed to him that as time moved on there was less left of the world he had known; that for every human born another star winked out, another hundred species vanished, and another piece of the fantastical died.

He wondered when it would be his turn.

Sometimes, he thought, I'm not sure if I have memories of the monster, or if the monster has memories of me.

In earliest times he had lapped blood from the steps of a ziggurat, and people had made a god of him. He had danced black hoofprints across the ceilings of Puritans, and they had made a demon of him. It was the same old story, each time something like him met people like that. Never any questions, just call a priest and reach for a gun.

He hated having to speak to his sister this way, under a veil, never letting her completely understand what was happening. Soon she would no longer be a child, the world would have her, and she wouldn't even remember him.

It had taken Walter and the monster years to understand how to coexist as the same person, with different memories, different wisdom, different drives, different needs. It was maddening, but Walter had learned. After all these years, he was learning that he needed to escape the doctor.

In stormy twilit days he had sung to galleons, and watched as men lashed themselves to masts and tillers and companionways and cleats.

As time moved on he could no longer drink from steps, or sing to sailors. He left no hoofprints on ceilings. He did not exist within man's law for the world. But sometimes, when people forgot the law, he could still reach into their lives, their world, and remind them why they once feared the dark. Sometimes.

Clap if you believe in fairies.

The front door of the house opened and Walter's father walked out. He was smoking his pipe, one hand tucked into the pocket of his woolen vest.

"My, but it's a clear night tonight. Say, how would you like to go fishing tomorrow, son?"

Walter shrugged. "No thanks."

His father hunkered down beside him. "See that group of stars up there? The ones that—"

"I know what the constellations are, Dad."

They're angels, and warriors, and windows, and balls of gas. They're pinpricks in the black veil drawn over the world. They're a river, a map. One of them is a marker to Neverland. Another is the morning star with whom seventy-two and one angels had fallen. They're gods, they're human souls. They grow duller as humanity grows colder.

"Right you are," his father said.

"I don't feel like being a son to you right now. Go inside."

His father moved to stand up when the branches of the old pine tree rustled. He looked up, taking the pipe from his mouth. "Possums," he said, knowledgeably.

Walter swallowed. He knew what it was, and it wasn't possums.

A figure stepped out from behind the trunk like it was stepping through a doorway. The man's coat was long and black and layered in ancient dust from extinct towns. He wore a black hat, which was just as dusty and just as old, and the face beneath it had weathered lifetimes. This figure hadn't been a real person for over 150 years.

Walter's father looked down from the tree to the peculiar figure standing sidelong before them, seemingly indifferent to their presence.

"Well then," his father said. "What have we here?"

The figure turned and looked over from a haggard, skull-drawn face. Things glittered inside his great black coat.

"You've got to stop running away, Wally," the doctor said. "There's no point in it."

Walter's father put his pipe back into his mouth, the stem clacking between his polished teeth. "Is this man a friend of yours, son?"

The doctor looked from Walter to his father and back again. "He supposed to be me?" he said, stepping closer. "This your new daddy?" He leaned in, pinpoint eyes in skull-sockets narrowing. "Looks like a dandy."

Walter's head lowered. "You're not my father, either."

"Sure. When Satan goes skatin'."

"I know what our father's doing to her, right now," Walter said, his voice going quiet in a way he couldn't help, the way it had used to when he got scared. "And I can't stop him."

His father hurmed, pipe clacking between his teeth. He stood and straightened his vest. "Look, what's all this about?" he demanded.

The doctor turned his head slightly, reaching out with one hand to touch Walter's father between the eyes. There was a brief rustling and the man folded in on himself, over and over, until all that was left of him was the little paper doll from which he was made.

The doctor crouched and picked it up off the grass. "Not bad," he said to Walter. "You're getting there."

Walter's lip was trembling, tears beginning to well in his eyes. He reached out and took the paper doll, let it melt into his hand, become part of himself once more. Just like the bird, just like the house, just like the tiger. Illusions. Props. "Why won't you just leave me alone!"

The doctor sighed, like wind over sand. "There are more important things in this world than what we want."

"I won't be like you!"

"There's worse things to be," he said, and meant it. "Wally, I'm just a man. I'm getting tired of living. There's people I haven't seen in too long. Why do you think *I* was given the instruments, and not something eternal like Felix, who actually wants them? He would never relinquish that power to the one who gave it." He looked at Walter then. "You—or your sister—are right for this. Trust me, believe in what I say, and your sister will never even know I exist."

Walter sniffed and rubbed a hand under his nose.

"This house, this daddy of yours," the doctor said, glancing back at the picture-book house. "It's not even your dream, son. It's hers. This is what *she* wants."

"I know that."

"Then you're already doing it. You take what's inside people, letting them face it."

Walter wasn't listening. He had heard this kind of reasoning before. "She can still turn inside herself and lose the frightening things that chase her," Walter said.

"What you have to understand, son," the doctor said, "is that you are those frightening things."

Walter shook his head. "I'm her *monster*!"

"That you are," the doctor said, reasonably. "And if you weren't here, right now, I'd use her. That's all you can protect her from now. Any problem she's got with her father is something she'll have to handle herself."

"Her father is my father," Walter spat. "I'm not you." He wiped his eyes, looked at the stars, and wished for more power than he had.

The doctor said nothing.

"I am not you," Walter repeated.

It was so quiet just then. Just the little dog breathing, nestled against his side.

"Maybe you're not," the doctor finally said with something that sounded like regret.

The doctor rose, like a collection of loose sticks assembling themselves into a man. Starlight made his face a black mask beneath the rim of his hat.

"I'm not coming back," Walter told him.

"I know. And you know what I have to do."

"I'm not letting you near her."

The doctor didn't move. "I can wait," he said.

Walter wiped his nose with the back of his hand, sniffed. Making all of this had taken it out of him. Even now the house was coming undone behind him, slowly folding in on itself.

He wouldn't be able to create like this again.

There was one, final thing to be done, and that would be that.

SEVEN

LOVELY

*S*OME NIGHTS DAVID WITHERSPOON DIDN'T MAKE IT TO bed, he just slept in his armchair. On other nights, like tonight, he couldn't sleep at all. On such nights he found himself standing at the door of his son's room, listening to him breathe.

Walter hadn't moved in a little over ten years, but his body had grown on without him. The body was skin and bones now. Sometimes David would sit and imagine how Walter might look now if he'd lived those last ten years, if his face was fuller, if he'd put on some muscle from running around and getting into trouble. Every day the nurse came, monitored Walter, moved his arms and legs, changed the bag they strapped to him, checked the catheter, put drugs in him.

On nights like this David Witherspoon wondered why he tortured himself, working two nowhere jobs, spending all this money to keep a corpse alive.

Sometimes he got angry. When he got angry he did things that made a small, quiet part of himself ashamed. His own father had been a lot like him, and he hadn't liked his father.

Feeling shame brought on the anger. The shame made him angry because the look on his Hope's face when he beat her made him feel ashamed. And so it went . . .

He stepped into Hope's room.

She was asleep now, a quiet mound in the center of her bed. Her room dim in the moonlight streaming through the window.

A delicate hand touched down on his left shoulder. He flinched. The hand did not let him move. "David," a voice whispered, softly. "This is as close as you get."

A slender woman stood by his left shoulder. Glitter traced her angular cheekbones. She wore a sequined leotard and had peacock feathers in her hair: a fan of eyes above her head, watching him.

"Who are you?" he asked, instinctively knowing she was nothing he could explain.

"I am an acrobat," she said. "And that is the ringmaster." He followed her gesture, and sure enough standing by Hope's bed was a tall man in a red jacket and black top hat. A bullwhip unfurled from his hand, curling upon the carpet like a snake. "And those are clowns . . ." They waved and tittered from the shadows near the small bookshelf. "And this," she said, "is Mike."

David heard a rumbling sound, like a well-tuned engine, loud enough to rattle his ribs. Something white and black crouched at the foot of Hope's bed, diamond eyes locked on his own sweating face. It had such white teeth.

"But," the acrobat continued. "The question you should really be asking is: Who. Is. That?"

Standing by the tiger, at the foot of Hope's bed, he saw a boy—a child, really—with eyes that were far from child-like. A smear of melted ice cream clouded his left cheek. It looked like there was some dirt there, too. It didn't make any sense that David Witherspoon would see his own son like this, and yet all the elements combined to leave him utterly weakened. They were perhaps the smallest details of the time Walter had first said, *Dad*. It was the moment when two years of preparing to be parents, and nine months of fretting over the health of their unborn child had fallen away and something smiling was left standing in its place. He had cried then, but denied it later.

The boy's voice was young, clear and unbroken by age.

"Hi, Dad," Walter said.

David fumbled behind himself, found the doorjamb, and slid to the ground awkwardly.

Walter brought up his hand. He held a folded paper crane. "See?" he said. "I can do it now."

David was looking the boy in the eye, even though he knew that same boy was asleep in the next room with a piece of clear silastic tubing inserted into his gut and a colostomy bag to keep him clean.

"I am sorry I never woke to meet her . . ."

Something twisted inside him, rubbed salt behind his eyes.

". . . but you can't keep doing this."

How long had it been? "Wally?" he said.

"It's me, Dad. Mostly." Walter was stroking that big cat between its eyes. But the tiger never blinked, never looked away from David's face. "Hope deserves better than this. So does Mum."

He looked so sweet, so perfectly alive. "Wally . . . ?"

The little boy looked at him, wiped the dirty ice cream from his cheek, looked at his hand, then away. "I'm ashamed of you. For all of this."

David cried, like he was self-destructing.

Walter wiped the hand on his shorts. "Mike is a piece of me, and I'm leaving him here. Mike will *always* be here, with her. Behind her eyes." The white cat stared at David Witherspoon, with only one thing in mind. "And I'll be here, too. Everything you do you'll do before me. Everything."

Walter stroked the tiger one last time, his hand looking so small on the great cat's head.

The room was empty. David Witherspoon stared at the patch of carpet at the foot of his daughter's bed where his all-but-dead son, and a giant cat, had stood.

His daughter giggled sleepily and rolled over, mumbling something into her pillow.

It sounded like,

"He's lovely."

EIGHT

NABBER

*O*H, HE WAS REALLY GOING TO GET IT THIS TIME.

"What do you mean you 'lost your homework'?"

Suni's teacher never liked him anyway. It wasn't his fault his things kept disappearing. "It's true," he said. "I d . . . d . . . duh-did it l . . . luh-luh-last night, l . . . luh-luh-left it on my desk, woke up this muh-morning and it was gone."

The class laughed, and Suni didn't blame them. He lost things all the time, and his excuses sounded stupid even to his own ears. It was what he was best known for, aside from the stutter—but that only came out when he got excited or nervous. It was like a blockage in his throat he had to push and push past to get the words out.

His teacher looked down her nose at him. Suni was a small black-haired, half-Japanese boy, and he hated wearing his glasses. "You will do the assigned work over the weekend," she said. "As well as a two-hundred-word explanation of just where it is you think these missing things of yours *go* when you're not looking. Perhaps that will teach you to be more careful—or perhaps *do* the work in future."

Two hundred words? Was she *serious?*

Suni shuffled. "B-b-buh-but—"

"Sit down."

"Yes, miss."

The class was still getting a grin out of the show—except that Hope girl. She just looked at the rest of them and frowned to herself. Somehow it made him feel better. Behind Suni, his friend Kristian bopped him on the back of the head and chuckled, "Good one."

Suni turned around. "It's tuh-true. I did do the work. I put it on my desk last night." Kristian didn't believe him, either. "I'm *sure* I did," Suni mumbled to himself.

"Sure, sure."

"*Mister* Buckingham!" That was the teacher's name for Kristian. "Would you be so kind as to stand up and tell the rest of the class what was so important that you couldn't wait until after class?"

Suni watched Kristian stand and face the room. He cleared his throat, placed one hand on his chest as if about to recite Shakespeare, and said: "*What . . .* was *soooo* important . . . that *you* could *not* wait . . .*"

Teacher folded her arms, unimpressed. "Yes, thank you, Mr. Buckingham."

"*Until!*"

The class was laughing, and Suni knew there was no stopping him now.

"Kristian, that is enough!"

". . . after class," Kristian said quickly and sat down.

Quiet returned, and the class waited expectantly to see what would happen next.

"You may join your friend, Mr. Buckingham, in penning for me a two-hundred-word opus on the nature of comedy." She returned to the blackboard, satisfied. "Enlighten me."

"So can I borrow it?"

Suni knew what the answer was going to be. "You'll lose it," Kristian said.

"No I won't. Honest."

"Remember those shin pads I loaned you?"

Suni shifted a little. He knew Kristian was going to bring those up. "It wuh-wasn't my fault," Suni said. "I brought them home from the game. I duh-did. I put them in the closet."

Kristian leaned back against the wall. They had about five minutes left before lunch was over. Then it was Maths. "Suni, you lose things. That's just the way it is."

Suni folded his arms. "I'm not going to lose your puh-precious card. I just want to draw the guy off it."

"It's a rare card," Kristian said. "I might want to sell it someday."

Kristian had a gold-embossed platinum-foil limited-edition trading card that did something in a game he collected. Suni didn't know anything about the game, only that the card had a really cool picture of a guy in armor with a cannon for a hand. Suni drew all the time. It was what he did. Right now his biggest project was working on a picture of a little boy, sort of like him only blond, with red eyes and sharp teeth. And a clockwork ballerina. Suni didn't know where he got the idea from, he had just woken one morning and the picture was right there in his head. It must have been something he had dreamed. But he was having real trouble getting the boy's hands right, and the delicate designs that made up the ballerina's hollow legs. At least the guy with the gun-arm looked cool. "I juh-just want to duh-draw it," Suni pleaded again. "I muh-muh-might even be able to get my dad to scan it at work, then I wouldn't even nuh-nuh-need to use it."

Kristian put his hands up. "No way. I can hear it now. *I gave it to my dad and he left it at work.* Forget it."

"Then I won't give it to my dad. I'll puh-put it inside one of my textbooks where it wont get bent, and only t . . . t . . . take it out when I need it. I'll return it on Monday! You're not even going to use it over the wuh-weekend. You're going away."

"Yeah. To work on my two-hundred-word essay on comedy."

"Oh, and you buh-buh-blame me for that."

"Look—"

"Come on, Kris. I'm not gonna lose it."

Kristian stared at him. Then, with a suffering breath he reached into his shirt pocket and handed it over. Sunlight flashed off gold trim as he extended the card to Suni. "You better not," he said. "Or I'll never forgive you."

Suni didn't begin work on his assignment that night. Instead he cleared his desk, got a clean sheet of paper, propped the card up against the lamp, and began to draw. The assignment could wait until tomorrow.

He drew until about ten, when he clicked the lamp off and climbed into bed. Lying there, he noticed that the moonlight through the window cast strange patterns on the far wall as it bounced off the gold and silver foil of the card. His room felt like a grotto.

He wouldn't lose the card. He would give it back to Kristian on Monday. Maybe then people would stop saying he lost things.

In the middle of the night something happened that didn't usually happen. Suni woke up. Wide awake. Just like that.

He thought this was pretty odd, and kind of annoying. Still, if he was wide awake now he supposed he could get up and do some more drawing while everyone else was asleep. Tomorrow was Saturday, he could sleep in.

So he reached over and turned on the lamp.

In the flash of blindness accompanying the burst of light, something with a squeaky voice said:

"*Uh-oh.*"

Suni blinked, squinting, looking around his bedroom. He couldn't see anything other than white light, but he heard the pat-pat-pat of feet on the carpet, and curious noises like "*murglefurg? bump-fog . . . hehn.*" Pat-pat-pat. "*zyxl? neh?*" pat-pat-pat. Then a captivated "*OOO-ooooh . . .*"

As the world cleared up, Suni saw something with long rubbery arms standing beside his bed. It had a big ball of a body and ridiculous-looking, oversized feet. Its arms were long and grabby. It had no eyes, nose, or ears, but it did have a big expressive mouth with big flat, white teeth. It held Kristian's card. "*OOO-oooooh . . .* ," it said, mesmerized by the shiny thing in its big blue hands.

Suni blinked. He looked at the clock. It was 12:01. He looked at the thing. It was like a fat blue basketball with feet. He rubbed his face. He was definitely awake.

"Aaaaaaaaaaaaaaagh!" said Suni.

"*Aaaaaaaaaaaaaaaagh!*" said the thing, and flop-flopped its feet across the room. It held Kristian's card over its head with long, dangly arms.

Kristian's card.

Kristian Lose-This-And-I'll-Never-Trust-You-With-Anything-Again's card.

Suni threw off the covers and dove at the thing. The thing waved its arms above its head and squealed as Suni came flying at it. His hands locked around one elastic blue wrist and engaged in a furious tug-of-war.

"Guh-guh-guh give it back!" shouted Suni.

It felt kind of mushy under his hands. Its arms were thin and ropy and weak feeling, but it held on to the card with a grip that wouldn't budge. Suni still wasn't entirely convinced this wasn't all some dream he was having.

The thing squealed, pulling against Suni, twisting toward something in the corner, like it was looking at something with those eyes it didn't have.

"*Eeeeergh!*" it cried out, tugging, turning. "*Eeeeeeergh!*"

"Just give it *back!*"

"*Eeeeeeergh!*"

"*Let go!*"

"*Eeeeeyyaaagh!*"

The thing gave one last, mighty pull and yanked Suni toward it. Suni cried out, fixed on those big flashing white teeth. But the thing had no plan to bite him. Instead, with Suni so close, its long arms gained a lot of slack. This allowed it to hold on to the card and dive into the shadows gathered in the corner.

It seemed like it disappeared, or fell down a hole, its arms unspooling quickly, following its flight, until they snapped taut and almost pulled free of Suni's grasp.

Instead it sucked Suni into the shadow right along behind it.

He fell, hands still locked around the blue thing's boneless wrists, sailing down down down toward an ever-expanding point of dirty light. It was like he watched the point of light for almost a minute, sailing behind the blue thing. Then, in an instant, the light blew out to an enormous size, swallowing him, and he was cannoning headfirst into a huge room.

The stench was the first thing he noticed. Then he crashed into a mass of something soft that smelled really, really bad.

"Yippeeee!" the blue thing yelled, and Suni realized he no longer held on to the card, or the thing. He flailed around, hemmed in on all sides by the thick, reeking mass of whatever it was that covered him, almost panicking in an effort to work out which way was up, to find a pocket of air, to claw his way out. The smell was awful, suffocating. He rolled around, kicking and gasping, when he felt one bare foot burst free and poke out into clean air. Thrashing around he righted himself, rammed both hands out, and pulled himself upward like someone bursting from a grave.

He gasped, long and loud, fresh air filling his lungs as he hauled himself up from the stinking mass that held him. Standing half submerged, but thankfully free of its putrid, airless grasp, he saw what he was standing in. They were green, and gray, and brown. Some stood out in hues of blue and bright red. Some were a mix of other colors, while others were dead black.

And there were millions of them . . . *millions* . . . And Suni was up to his armpits in them. And God, how they *stank*.

Socks.

Dirty socks.

"Now there's something you don't see every day," he said, and his voice echoed lightly around the cavern.

Suni extricated himself from the smelly, cottony mass that had caught his fall. He tumbled down a mountainside of stale, odorous stockings, socks, and leggings to wind up on a floor of rough-hewn rock. There was but one way out of this chamber, and that was through the jagged arch before him, which led to an equally large chamber, this one filled not with a mountain of socks, but a giant mound of pens . . .

Through the arch he could see another arch leading to yet another chamber. Standing there on its two giant, bunioned feet was the thing. It still held Kristian's glittering card in both hands, looking right to left and right again, as if deciding where to go, or where in this massive complex of caves and caverns its new prize belonged.

"Hey!" Suni called out, running after it.

The thing spun around, saw Suni and *Eeeeeked!* Then it took off at high speed, absurd feet pattering away, arms dangling over its head.

Suni lost sight of it. He looked through a multitude of chambers, all piled high with items of one description or another. One was filled with golf balls; another, keys. There was one chamber stocked with a gigantic store of dice of all shapes, sizes, and colors.

This was all starting to make some kind of sense. Then Suni came across a cavern that was home to an accumulation of old schoolbooks. He had a feeling he knew what this was all about, but he had to know for sure. He began by hunting around at the base of the heap, where the books looked newest. Sure enough, after half an hour, he found it.

His homework. The thing had stolen his homework! Suni took the red-covered notepad from the heap, grateful that at least he wouldn't have to do his assignment again.

He made his way into the next chamber, which was home to what looked like all the luggage that ever got lost at airports, and found himself a black backpack that, according to the tag, belonged to someone in Vancouver, British Columbia. There was nothing in it, so Suni put his notebook inside, zipped the bag, and shrugged it onto his back.

Now all he had to do was find Kristian's card and get back home. Somehow.

Past another archway, into another chamber, the thing tootled along, burbling to itself, still looking for someplace to put the card.

Suni saw it.

It saw Suni.

"*Aaaaagh!*" shrieked the thing.

"Raaaargh!" went Suni.

And the chase was back on.

He lost it again. It was a fast little bugger.

Suni found himself wandering through chamber after chamber. Before long he began thinking that if he found a way out he would just take it, glad to be home, forget about the stupid card, and let Kristian call him what he liked. If Kristian was any kind of friend he'd understand. If he believed any of it at all. Which, Suni knew, he never would.

Suni was starting to get hungry, and it felt like he was just wandering in circles with no way out. A few times he wandered back through the pen room, or the dice room. He held his breath and checked out the sock room one more time. It was where he had landed, so he had to have *fallen* from somewhere, right? Only there was no opening in the ceiling. Nothing. He may as well have tumbled out of thin air, which he could well have done. It made about as much sense as anything else he had seen tonight.

It was becoming obvious that the only way out of here, if there was a way out, lay with that blue thing. Which doubled his need to find it again.

He found a cavern filled to overflowing with wallets and purses of every description. He blinked. Then he ran in and started opening them.

"Don't bother," someone said. "They're all empty."

Suni dropped the wallet and looked around.

"The Nabbers put the loose change and driver's licenses in other chambers."

Suni looked up. Sitting on top of the mound was a small boy with neat, pale hair.

"I'm Walter," the boy said. "They call this place the Drop."

Suni nodded. "Dddd . . . duh-do you know a way out of here?" This boy seemed really familiar, somehow, yet for the life of him Suni couldn't work out why. Each time he tried to hold it the association slipped and slid from his grasp.

"I know someone who can get you out of here," Walter said. "But I don't think he will."

Suni didn't like the sound of that. "Why not?"

"It's complicated. I might be able to get you out, though. In exchange for a small favor."

Suni rubbed his hands nervously on his pajama pants, looking around. "Ddd . . . ddd . . . duh-do you want to come down from there?" he said. "You're making me nervous."

"Okay." Walter slid down on a small avalanche of leather and vinyl. He really was a lot smaller than Suni.

"Wh . . . what kind of f-fff-favor?"

"We'll get to that," said Walter.

"So that blue thing's called a Nabber?" Suni asked, searching for something to say.

"That's what the person who made them calls them," Walter said.

"Then there's more than one?"

"Oh yes."

Suni nervously rubbed his palms on his pajama legs again. "So how long have you been here anyway?"

"Right now? Half an hour. Before that? Ten years," Walter said.

"*Ten years?*" The boy—Walter—didn't *look* ten; more like five. Suni was liking this less and less. "Why?"

"Like I said, Suni: it's complicated."

"You know my name?"

There was the pat-pat-pat of oversized feet, and Suni spotted—a few chambers away—the blue thing waddling past an archway at high speed, prize held high. Without thinking, he took off after it.

"Suni," Walter hissed, urgently. "Stop!"

But Suni didn't. He ran through three more chambers—scattered with mounds of remote controls—and turned right, bare feet slapping on cold dirt. He could hear the pat-pat-pat of the thing's feet echoing in distant chambers and used that to follow.

He jogged to a stop in one chamber (filled with little green plastic army men), looking back and forth among three possible exits. Listening to the thing's pat-pat-patting feet receding . . .

He wandered for what seemed like hours from cavern to cavern, his stomach growling. Sometimes he would hear the far-off chatter of what he thought was the thing, only to lose it again, to be surrounded by the echo of his own soft footfalls.

Then he came to a larger cavern, and this one smelled far, far worse than the mountain of socks he had first plunged into hours before. It smelled wrong.

Last year Suni's father had taken him camping and they had come across a half-eaten possum that had been dead for days. There were clouds of flies. One crawled across its dark open eye, and the thing that had made him want to be sick was the way the possum hadn't blinked, only stared, as the insect crept across. He remembered how the taste of the stench had tickled the backmost point of his throat, thick and invisible clouds of rot-scent filling his mouth.

The smell of this cavern was unbelievably worse.

Suni approached the archway, feet crunching and sinking partway into a thick mat of glass marbles that covered the floor and spilled into adjoining rooms. Through the archway he saw piles and piles and piles of bones. Piles of bodies. There were no flies, but fluid was seeping from the massive mound, translucent and dark and absolutely vomitous. Suni was sucking air through the flannel of his pajama sleeve, trying to keep his gorge down, feeling it rise nonetheless, buoyant and acidic.

In the space between the four largest body piles was a square wooden table, around which sat four dead people with no heads. They were playing cards.

"You know how sometimes they never find the body?"

Suni shrieked and spun around, stumbling on uncertain footing into the body room, bare feet smacking and sticking on the dried residue that coated the floor. It was Walter. The words caught in his throat, ran into the tails of one another, stole his breath, made it hard to think. He pushed, gagged, squinting with the effort it took to speak. "Hhhh . . . hhhh . . . huh-huh-huh-how'd you get behind me? Www . . . www . . . wuh-what is this?" And Suni tasted the room again. He coughed, and his last meal splashed heavily to the already sticky floor, rising in thick waves from the very depths of him, his entire body now a massive reflex action that clenched every muscle until he thought they'd burst and tear, coughing and retching until there was nothing left. When he was finally done, one hand on his bent knee, the other wrapped across his drum-tight and convulsing stomach, Walter offered him a handkerchief. Shakily, like an old man, Suni took it, wiped the sick from his mouth and the tears from his eyes.

"When they never find the body, this is where those bodies go," Walter said, stepping into the room. Dozens of marbles rolled lazily across the hard dirt floor. The sound of Walter's tightly laced shoes smack-smacking across the sticky floor made Suni want to gag again. "Well, most of them. You might want to stand back."

Suni was about to ask why when the room filled with a cacophony of meeping and murbling and a dozen or more Nabbers materialized out of nowhere, streaming from shadows and dark nooks, bumping and jostling Suni as he stood amid their traffic. Without hesitation, fumbling and climbing over one another—ignoring Walter and Suni completely—they each homed in on specific marbles, clutching them in their rubbery blue hands, and scuttled them back to their proper room. The last of them stopped in the archway to look Suni up and down with what he took for disdain, hmphed, and disappeared into the marble room. When quiet was restored not a marble remained.

Suni gestured feebly to the quartet of corpses seated at the table. One of them slapped down a card from its hand. Another drew from the pile. Their skin was gray, the stumps of their necks bloodless. "What . . . ," he began. "What . . . ?"

"When I was still living with Henry, he wanted me to practice," Walter said. "Get a feel for the business. This was homework," he said solemnly. "Guess he never got around to clearing them away."

Suni thought of the notepad in his backpack, and suddenly a two-hundred-word essay didn't seem so bad.

"How . . . how do you know him, then?"

"He took me from my family when I was very small. He stepped out of the darkness and I wasn't even scared . . . all starlight and assurances. That was when I first saw the instruments, and heard how strongly they sang to me." Walter's eyes shone at the memory, and Suni saw him smiling nostalgically. And then, abruptly, "He told me he could make my bad dreams go away . . . and all the while he was nothing but a bad dream himself." Walter sniffed and shook his head a little, as if dispelling a fog.

"He . . . he's the guy that could get me out of here?"

Walter nodded. "This whole place is his. He took it from a man named Dorian. They had a falling-out. A lot of bad blood. You know how it is." Suni didn't, actually, but he felt it wiser to just nod as if he knew all too well. "That's how he wound up doing what he's doing now."

"Which is?"

"It's a long story." Walter straightened, and got that distracted, far-away look again. "He's coming."

Through the silence of the body chamber came the distant burble
and meep of the Nabber, the patter of its feet getting closer. Suni
would have run had Walter not placed a hand on his arm.

"There's no point," he said. "This network of caverns and chambers . . . it's all circular."

Suni swallowed and looked to the far arch. With mounds of
corpses, bodies, and refuse piled around him he had no trouble believing he would be added to the stockpile within the hour. Just another missing body.

A figure moved into the archway, coat tinkling. He was tall, whatever he was, and the coat moved less and less as he came to a stand-
still, as though getting comfortable around his scarecrow frame. From
within the coat Suni caught flashes of silver light.

He looked as though he belonged here, in this mortuary.

The figure was looking at Kristian's card. Beside him, the Nabber
wrung its rubbery hands and hopped impatiently from foot to foot,
eager to have its prize back but unwilling to snatch it from the gloved
hand of the being that held it.

"Pretty," the figure said in a voice like dry leaves, distant thunder.
He walked into the room, boots sounding solid on the ground. Beneath his wide-brimmed hat he didn't look out of place among the
dead at all.

"You're Suni."

Suni nodded.

The man turned to Walter. "You're back."

"Keeping an eye out."

The man turned his attention back to Suni. "We don't get many
visitors," he said. "In fact, we don't get *any*." He glanced meaningfully
at Walter.

"I'm the doctor," the man continued. Beneath the hat his head
looked hairless, save for a few wisps that might have been red once
upon a time. He looked over his shoulder to the four card players and
moved for a closer examination. "Nice," he said to Walter. "Always
liked these. Your premise was flawed, though."

Walter shook his head. "So they just play cards. The fear comes from the *expectation* they'll do something."

"Still don't like it. Won't work. Except as a setup, maybe, for something else." He walked back over to Suni. "But back to you . . ."

Suni's eyes locked wide. He didn't move. He didn't want to die. He was too young for this. He hadn't been anywhere. He hadn't done anything yet!

Walter took a step toward the doctor.

The doctor handed Suni the card. "I think this is yours." Suni blinked. He looked at the card. Hesitantly, he took it. The Nabber meeped and hopped from foot to foot like it was going to explode. The doctor turned and pointed out of the cavern. "Get."

Despondently, dragging its arms behind it, the little blue thing turned and shuffled out. It stopped, glancing hopefully back one last time. The doctor pointed again and the little thing moped away.

"Suni's not your concern," Walter said. "I brought him here . . ."

"Black bugs blood," the doctor said.

Suni blinked again. "P . . . pardon?"

"Black. Bugs. Blood," the doctor repeated.

"Henry . . . ," Walter persisted.

"I want you," said the doctor. "To say 'black bugs blood' ten times. Fast."

Suni blanked. "Y . . . you wuh-want me to ss-suh-say . . . bbb . . . buh-buh-black buh-buh-buh . . ."

"Yes."

"And thh . . . thh . . . then I guh-guh-get to guh-guh-go hhh . . . hhh . . . hhh . . . home, wuh-wuh-wuh-with my card?"

"Yup."

Suni looked at Walter and found him biting his lip. "This is his realm, Suni. I can't contradict him. Not here." He looked Suni in the eye. "I told you not to chase that thing."

"I ccc-can't do it!" Suni cried. "I cccuh-cuh-can't."

"Then you stay here," said the doctor. "And you don't go home. Except in your parents' dreams, where all you'll be able to do is scream or whine. After that I'll turn you into something else." The doctor leaned forward, hands on his knees. Inside his coat was a glittering array of tools and instruments unlike any Suni had ever seen. "It ain't that bad," the doctor reasoned. "I could give you wings . . ."

"I ddd . . . ddd . . . ddd . . . I ddd . . . ddd . . . duh-duh-duh . . . *don't want wings!*" Suni cried out, unable to take his eyes off the scalpels and things. "I want to go home!"

"Then say it, ten times fast . . . ," the doctor said. "And home you'll go." He stood back once more.

Suni licked his lips. He didn't want to be here forever, even with wings. He thought of all the things he'd miss if he were to never go back. He'd even miss school, and goofing around with Kristian . . .

Something occurred to him then. He thought about it, *really* thought about it, and wondered if it was such a good idea. Finally he knew he had nothing to lose by trying.

"Suni . . . ," the doctor said, impatiently.

Suni nodded, and said "S-So let me get this stuh-stuh-straight . . ."

"Mmhmm . . . ," the doctor said, patiently.

"You want me to ssss-ssss-say" — Suni said the words slowly and deliberately so as not to trip over them — "black . . . bugs . . . blood . . . ten times. Fast."

The doctor nodded. "That's right."

"And then you'll let me go?"

"Uh-huh."

"With my stuff?"

"Yup."

"And Kuh-Kristian's ccc-card?"

"All yours."

"Okay." Suni licked his lips. And he began, pronouncing the words slowly once more. "Black . . ."

"Hey," the doctor interrupted.

". . . bugs . . ."

"Kid . . . ," he said patiently. "That's not . . ."

". . . blood . . ."

". . . fast enough."

"Ten times fast," Suni finished.

The doctor's thin face dropped. "Kid, do you have any idea how many times I've had people pull that one on me?"

Suni's stomach sank.

"You really think I didn't see that coming?"

"Bbb-buh-buh-but . . . ," Suni stammered. "I duh-duh-did it. You www-wanted me ttt-to say it ttt-tuh-ten times fast and I did. You guh-guh-gotta let me go."

The doctor shook his head. "I make the rules and you know what I meant. I'm no demon bound by exactitude. I'm real, and you just lost." The doctor opened his coat, tools tinkling in anticipation of use. "Sorry, kid."

Suni grunted as Walter pushed past him, screaming, "Leave him alone!"

Suni was scared, but he was still quick enough to take the chance when it presented itself. He bolted through the archway for all he was worth.

The doctor's voice rasped deeply. "When are you gonna learn?"

But that didn't stop the little boy yelling, "*Run, Suni! Just keep running!*"

"And what'll that do?" the doctor inquired.

Suni found himself in a room of black glass that seemed to go on forever. His throat burned with each ragged breath, his heart thumping. The space was like the central area of a great train station, filled with people milling about.

But none of them seemed aware of anyone else.

Some were talking, some were looking around, others were walking like they had somewhere to go. There was a man in a top hat who laughed all the time, and a tan-skinned girl who stood on the spot turning circles with her arms outstretched. But most of them looked like any number of people Suni had seen walking down the street or through a shopping mall. An old lady smelling of breath mints and lavender air freshener wandered past muttering, "Horrie? I left you a minute ago ... where did you go?" There was a man who Suni thought might have been an American Indian, in a fur coat, who just mumbled and nodded his head rhythmically while looking at the ground. There was a man in rags with matted hair who looked to the sky, screaming, "*I love everything!*"

A few minutes ago Suni had watched a Nabber lead a black man in by the hand. He didn't seem aware of the Nabber; he didn't even look like he was seeing the same place Suni did. When the Nabber let him go, the man had wandered off across the room and disappeared into the crowd.

"I think this is what happens when people lose their minds."

It was Walter. The blond boy was standing beside him, watching the crowd mill around them.

Suni swallowed. "I . . . I kinda thought the Nabbers just took regular stuff. Wuh-watches and things."

Walter shrugged. "The doctor created them to go out and find something very specific. Something he needs. I guess he didn't expect them to get interpretive." Suni wasn't sure what *interpretive* meant, but he was pretty sure whatever the doctor wanted wasn't in his bedroom. None of this made sense. "What is it he wuh-wants?"

"A tool," Walter said. "An instrument. Like the ones in his coat."

"A tool? What kind of tool?"

"The last and most important one. Something that lets you reach inside people's heads and find out what makes them tick. To see what defines fear for them. And take it out, if he wants. You can reshape who people are by selective removal of their influences."

"For what?"

"Recruitment. You can change things about a person with a tool like that. For the last hundred years he's recruited people naturally suited to being remade, having their lives rewritten in exchange for a little pleasure or power. A lot of them can't take it. A lot of them tire of it after a while. But with this instrument, he can just make them naturally suited to it. *Make* them want it. Make them endure." Walter looked right at Suni then. "He's also planning for retirement. He wants someone strong enough to replace him—"

"*Me?*"

Walter burst out laughing, a high shrill sound, like an excited puppy. "No . . . God, no. I've got a sister. Her name is Hope. She'd be the same age as you now. Actually, you go to school with her." Walter stuffed his hands into his pockets, somewhat guiltily, Suni thought. "Remember what I said, about me getting you out of here in exchange for a favor?"

Suni blinked. "Uh . . ."

"It's very important."

"What . . . what do you want me to do?"

Walter scrutinized Suni for a moment, and then asked, "Did you have a monster when you were young?"

"A . . . ?"

"Something that made you afraid of the dark. Something that scared you more than anything else?"

The way Walter was looking at him made Suni think of . . . "The Devil," he said. "I watched a documentary on Nostradamus, all the things he'd predicted, and it said the end of the world was only a few years away. The Devil was supposed to appear and the world would burn, there'd be fields of bones . . . and what with all these countries with nuclear bombs . . ."

"Did you ever actually see the Devil?"

Suni thought that was a strange question. "No," he said. "No one sees the Devil."

"Depends who you talk to," Walter said, then broke his eyes from Suni's. "I exist to protect Hope because she needs protecting."

Suni thought about that. "Then why are you here?"

"Because before I existed to protect Hope, I existed to protect Walter."

This was getting confusing. "I thought . . ."

"I *am* Walter," Walter said. "But I'm also something much older. When I was Walter's monster the doctor tricked Wally into discharging me. If the person I exist to protect sends me away, what becomes of me? I disappear. Become someone else's monster maybe. But in my last moments Walter came to me, frightened, and wanted me back. He was never getting home again, so I did the one thing left to me. I made him part of me, kept him safe inside. Kind of messed up the doctor's plans. I wasn't the boy he'd hoped to train anymore."

Suni realized Walter had never had the chance to tell any of this to anyone. It was waterfalling out of him.

"He'd been looking for a replacement for about a hundred years. He'd had a few candidates but in the end he always discarded them for one reason or another. Too simple, too smart, not enough spine, too much willingness to inflict pain, too many scruples, not enough, not enough imagination, some lacked foresight, some didn't have a knack for anticipating the effects of certain courses of action or surgery . . . See, his problem is, as much as he hates what he does he's not willing to pass it on to someone who'll abuse the station. I mean, if the ability to create, craft, fashion, make real was just handed to anyone, it could be Hell on Earth overnight. Then maybe your Nostradamus fears might not have been groundless."

Suni was trying to keep up, but it wasn't easy. "So . . . so he makes . . . ?"

"Everything the doctor does is a recruiting drive for a higher power. A higher power racing to match the forces the other two factions have been accruing since Samael fell. It's a selection process. If the doctor offers and they accept, that's another soldier for the Angel, while the qualities they display in the course of their falling govern the position they'll hold."

"Angel . . . ?"

"Look, we don't have much time and I need to know you'll do this for me. Hope's ten years old. At that age it's very hard for me to make myself known to her. I've got maybe a year left before she realizes that talking to something like me is completely impossible and shuts me out altogether.

"What I want is for you to remember everything that happened here. I want you to remember that this is all real. I want you to remember me. If you do that, then I can protect her through you."

"How?"

"You can act on my behalf. I can affect her world through you."

"I duh-didn't get here by accident, did I?"

Walter shook his head. "I . . . kind of nudged a Nabber out through your closet. The rest took care of itself. The way you chose to confront the Nabber that took your card shows you've got the strength for this. Picking the right person is one of the few valuable things I ever learned from Henry."

"I ddd . . . duh-don't have anything to do with this. Why not just bring her here instead of muh-muh-me? I've never spoken to your sister, I hardly even know who she is!"

"I can't bring her here because this is where Henry is, and I want to keep her as far from him as possible. If she comes here I'm powerless to protect, just as I was powerless to help you back there. And I can't just *appear* to her as myself because I'm her monster . . ."

"But I thought . . . ?"

"By my very nature I'm the one thing she's most afraid of. She thinks Walter is a breathing corpse in the next room. It would be very difficult to get her to listen to anything I had to say. I can appear to her as something neutral if I cloud myself from her, stop her asking too many questions, but it hurts and it's getting harder. I'm running out of time. I won her trust, and now she's fading from me."

"So . . ."

"So be her friend. And if I need to help her, I'll tell you what to do. You cover her in the real world and I'll take care of Henry. Just so long as you remember that this has all been real."

Suni licked his lips. Looked around. Figured talking was a good way to stay calm. "He always go after kids?"

Walter just looked at him, like he was wondering if Suni had heard anything he'd just said. Then: "Yes. Securing a candidate while they're still physically young and impressionable is the preferred method. Physically older people are more set in their ways, harder to mold. Childhood is the spawning ground for the fears of adult life. Good fodder, very valuable, lots of potential."

"Oh," Suni said. "So does that mean I'm going home?"

"I can get you out of here. Give me the card."

"Wuh-what do you need that for?"

"Do you want to get out of here or not?"

Suni handed it over. If he never made it back it wouldn't matter if he had the card or not.

Walter put it in the pocket of his white buttondown shirt. "Now we have to find the Nabber that took it."

"How do we do that?"

"It'll come to us. It's obsessed with the card now."

"So we jjjjuh-just wait?"

Walter nodded.

"And what if *he* turns up?"

"He'll turn up anyway."

From what Suni could tell there didn't seem to be an end to the black cavern he was in. He couldn't see the ceiling and the wall at his back stretched forever. The place was vast.

Walter was talking to pass the time, though Suni wasn't really listening anymore. He was thinking more about home, and wondering if maybe it lay at the far end of this seemingly endless room.

The ceaseless murmuring of the crowd was beginning to get to Suni. "So, you're fourteen?"

"Most of me is fourteen and a half." Walter's voice became almost singsong, as though he'd told himself this over and over again as the years slipped away. "A large part of me is older than Christ, or Ra. Part of me watched the Aztecs build *tzompantli* walls from the skulls of the enemy dead. Some of me doesn't have an age. Sometimes I remember the faces of people who were very close to me, yet I can't remember ever meeting. Side effect of the merging between Wally and his monster, I guess. I can remember when I disowned myself, made myself weak. I can remember how it hurt hearing and watching myself say those words to me. *Go away.* I looked so lost, then." A long breath escaped his little body, as though he no longer had the strength or desire to contain it. "I had no idea what was going on."

That makes two of us, thought Suni. In fact, Walter was beginning to sound a lot like the lost people walking around the room.

"I'll do everything I can to get you out of here, Suni," Walter said. "But it's very important that the Nabber that took this card doesn't get it. We'll need to trade it to get you out."

Suni swallowed. "So does that mmmmmuh-muh-mean I don't get it back?"

"Would you rather stay here?"

Suni didn't answer.

"I didn't think so."

Kristian was going to kill him. "What makes you think you're going to be able to keep that guy away from me, anyway?"

Something like a smile, but not quite, touched Walter's lips. "It's what I do," he said.

"How's this gonna work?"

Someone behind Suni was sobbing. He didn't want to turn around to find out who it was.

"You're about to find out."

Suni first saw them as a distant movement of heads—of people in the crowd being pushed aside. And it was getting closer, like the wake of a shark, a widening V of moving heads and bodies, and then they were there: the doctor came first, like invisible clouds breathed out from his footsteps, parting the crowd, dark eyes intent on both boys. Behind him, the paddling Nabber.

His voice whispered over that distance. *"This is how you're gonna do it, Wally?"*

"I'm gone," Walter said. "Find someone else."

"You know I will."

"Stay away from her. I'm warning you."

"I don't do anything they don't ask for."

Walter stuck his chin out, defiant. "Like Suni? Like Dorian?"

The doctor seethed, as if he'd explained this before. *"I wasn't a Maker then, and he had it coming."*

"What about Nimble?"

Something weird was happening.

"Nimble's not a person."

The sea of people was shifting, jostling. A rising sound of muttering and meeping.

"Tell that to the person who's still waiting for her."

"He's not a person, either."

Suni had felt like this once before, when he'd stayed at Kristian's house for the first time—all different food and different smells and different-feeling furniture and they prayed before meals, which was something Suni felt weird doing—and Kristian's parents had started fighting. Suni didn't know what they were fighting about then, either, and it had only made him feel more homesick than he already was. He wanted to go home.

Walter and Suni were surrounded, a sea of blue irising in on them, grabbing for them.

Suni said Walter's name.

Walter didn't take his eyes off the doctor. He held the card high with both hands. "You want this?" he cried out to the murbling blue crowd, and moved to tear the card in half.

There came a single piercing screech, and from the crowd one particular blue, paddle-footed ball came running, arms outstretched.

The doctor reacted. *"Walter, no!"*

The Nabber's screeching set off the mob. The iris closed in on them in a heartbeat. They were swarmed.

"Walter!" Suni couldn't see anything. Hands all over him, a jungle of waving blue arms and screeching voices. For a moment he thought he saw a pale little arm reaching out for him, and he flailed madly for it, like a drowning boy. But Walter's arm, if it had been there at all, was gone. And all Suni could do was cry, "Take me back!"

Everything changed.

He wasn't sure how, exactly. It was pitch black and something weird was happening with his stomach.

By the time Suni realized he was falling, he'd plummeted through an expanding point of light and into a cold-floored white room. He hit the floor, back-first, his breath bursting from him. He struggled to breathe. The roof was white tile with dark grime in the cracks. There was the sound of running water.

Something dropped onto the tiled floor behind Suni's head. He tilted his head back and saw three cubicles, locks turned to VACANT. There was a stainless-steel urinal off to his left. Somewhere someone was talking over a public address system. There was a steel bench. It occurred to him then just how specifically bad this room smelled.

A Nabber was standing just behind Suni's head, its arms draped along the tiled floor behind it. It managed to look impatient.

"ghrug. sumfle. spek."

It made a *gimme* motion with one rubbery hand. Suni sat up, the joints of his back complaining as he did so. His breath was coming more easily, if painfully. The Nabber tapped the backpack. Slowly Suni slipped it off, handed it over . . .

"Oh, hang on a second."

"eeeeee . . ."

"Just wait . . ." Suni took his homework out and zipped the bag back up. "There you go." He handed the bag over, and the fat blue ball snatched it immediately.

"eeeee. klig oohn somfa la," it explained, clutching the bag tightly to itself, muffling its gargling little voice. Then it wandered over to the bench, crawled into the shadow beneath it, and was gone.

Suni wondered what had happened to Walter. He thought about what Walter had said, about having a sister, and wondered if this was where the whole thing ended. Quietly, Suni hoped Walter found someone else to do the job.

He wondered what school would be like come Monday morning.

He got to his feet, straightened his pajamas, and walked out of the restroom.

The first thing Suni saw was a lot of people with a lot of luggage and, by a big glass door that led to a busy carpark, a sign.

It said WELCOME TO VANCOUVER, BRITISH COLUMBIA.

He wondered if someone might let him use the phone.

NINE

WAKING

WALTER STOOD BY A BROWN RIVER, UP TO HIS ANKLES in cold mud. It was a gray morning in this part of the world. Far away, on the other bank, bleak factories churned endlessly. The sky was slate-colored and featureless. Years ago, somewhere upstream a nuclear reactor had melted down. Downstream a bird cried out, sounding like a baby.

"Tub," he said to the river. "It's Wally."

The river was a slow mover. Enormous and weighty, it shifted seaward with the alacrity of a beast that would rather be sleeping.

A round head broke the dirt-colored surface of the river, midway out. Water cascaded from the protruding lower jaw, and tiny eyes opened in wide surprise.

"Wally?"

"Hi, Tub." He smiled.

The head disappeared, and a trail of bubbles made its way toward Walter. Wally noted that his feet were growing colder with each passing moment.

The hairless head broke the surface thirty feet from shore, and

Tub waded in, brown water spilling off rounded shoulders and his broad, soft body. He stood there, naked, privates concealed beneath a drooping gut, only slightly taller than Walter's three and a half feet.

"I've been down there a long time," Tub said in his slow, matter-of-fact voice.

"You didn't have to be," Walter said.

"I didn't?"

"I need the Anxietoscope."

Tub looked to the river, then back to Walter again. "You gonna take it?"

Walter nodded. "I'll look after it now."

"But it's the last one. He got all the others."

"It'll be okay. I'll give it to Hope when she's older. It'll give her something to fight with."

Tub broke into a big grin. Wide, flat teeth, browning in the cracks. "She'll know how to use it," Tub said. "She's old like you."

Walter nodded again. "Maybe it'll save her, get us all out of this mess."

Tub thought about this. "You're not her monster anymore."

"I'll do what I can. That's why I need it."

Tub nodded, gravely. "Yeah." And then: "He'll get her."

Walter shook his head. "I won't let him."

"You should be someone else's monster by now."

"I know."

"But . . . ," Tub said. "But you won't be able to do anything."

"I made friends with someone—a boy—I think he can help me help her." He sighed and shook his head. "It's the best I can do."

Tub didn't say anything for a moment. Then, hopefully: "Have you seen Nimble?"

"No," Walter lied. "I haven't."

Walter couldn't tell Tub what had happened after that: that the doctor had found her, and changed her, inside. It would have broken the poor guy's heart.

Tub turned and scanned the river once more. "What happens to me now?" he asked, child-like.

"You don't have to watch it anymore. You can go wherever you like."

Tub thought about it. "I might just stay here." Walter wondered what Dorian, Tub's maker, must have been like for Tub to be so lost without him. "I'll get your thing, now."

When Tub gave Walter the instrument it was inside a small box Tub had fashioned from a discarded forty-four-gallon gasoline drum to pass the time. The Anxietoscope glowed softly like a full moon through clouds.

Before this moment Walter had never touched an instrument. Henry had never allowed it.

Walter reached out and laid a finger upon the Anxietoscope.

Murder, light, despair.

Places opened in Walter's mind like blooming wounds. Memory pumped out, fresh and hot.

Rage.

In the split second it took the camera of Walter's mind to zoom out far enough to view the topography of God's face writ large across the whole of Creation, Walter knew why Henry had chosen him and his sister.

Walter remembered everything.

"Do . . . do you know what to do with that, then?" Tub said.

Walter nodded, his mouth dry. "I know. The . . . box . . . you made for this, Tub. It was a good box."

Tub squeezed his hands together. "Thanks."

"But I need to make a different box for it now. I hope you don't mind."

"Out of paper, the way you usually do?"

Walter shook his head. "No. No more paper for me." And he went to work.

Tub gasped, tiny eyes wide, as he sat in his river, up to his waist, and watched.

TEN

ANXIETOSCOPE

ONE OF THE MOST BEAUTIFUL THINGS HOPE HAD EVER seen was a claustrophobic, trash-choked alley wedged between an old glass factory and a garage. She'd pass it every now and then on the way home from a movie. She had looked into it, the first night she passed, and fancied she could see huddled ghosts curled in the refuse, memories of memories looking back at her out of the corners of old eyes.

Thick grime layered the brickwork. The stuff was like a dried, crumbly paste of talcum and mucus, with the occasional cancerous fleck of faded red here and there, the markings of some forgotten vandal. The stuff on the walls had made her think of growth rings in trees, or layers of earth. Made her think that if a sociologist were to slice a layer, she could point to the juicy bits and tell you what had happened there at any given year: of homeless schizophrenics driven by an emotional intensity most people never reach, of a lost and battered rape victim—all bruises and torn underwear—hobbling for the street with one bloodied palm trailing against the wall for support, of a hundred souls who had searched for someplace warm.

To Hope that little alleyway was a cathedral to what happened when life tossed you into what lies outside.

She remembered looking into it, caught by it, conscious of the fact that anybody in there would see her, if anybody was there at all. But she kept looking anyway.

She saw wet brick and puddles, sure; and crates and broken glass that probably came from the factory next door. She saw an old blazer, sodden with filthy water, and a dull-looking plastic tiara perched atop a Dumpster under a flickering fluorescent. There was a broken old walking stick, and some brown flowers lying headfirst in an oily puddle. She saw somebody's report card.

She wondered if they'd find a piece of her in there one morning. A single eyebrow ring fallen between the cracks of the old bluestone cobbles; maybe a tube of Urban Decay Uzi-colored lipstick for good measure.

She saw streetlight reflected dimly off damp brick, and the faded, spectral stencil of a NO PARKING sign that had been sprayed on the wall decades before, now covered in the accreted grime that caked every surface of the alley. She saw more patches of color there, faded red, and she wondered if maybe it was blood, but knew that it wasn't. She saw shreds of an old band flyer that had been pasted there God knew how long ago, low-resolution black-rimmed eyes looking at her from slow rot, streaked with more ever-present and faded crimson. Then she noticed that streak intersect with another, almost invisible, line of faded red.

Hope saw a letter.

In that moment it all coalesced: patterns formed from the patches and streaks under the grime, gathering, surfacing, revealing themselves to her.

She saw red words a yard high.

I CAN'T BREATHE

It was like a screaming face, frozen in ice.

. . .

Not every girl is interested in digging a hole to the center of the Earth, but Hope was different. Which was the reason for most of the trouble she'd had so far in life. She was seventeen years old, pink-haired and pierced, about ready to plunge face-first into a world of freedom and adulthood, yet she was not sure who she was. Her mother kept trying to find and burn her journals in exchange for driving lessons, while teachers kept sending her to the counselor to be asked guarded questions like, "Do you ever feel as if you can't go on?" and "Is there anyone at school you feel . . . angry . . . toward?" More people had asked her pop-psych things like that since Dad was gone than they ever had before. Like she was some potentially explosive pet project.

Everyone's always so insightful once the disaster's over.

So she started digging a hole. Just found a vacant lot near her house, took her father's shovel from the shed, and went digging. Maybe, she thought, it's a metaphor for the deep-seated self-destructive urge that the counselor's convinced I have. Maybe I want to bury myself. Maybe it helps me think.

Or maybe it just keeps me from thinking. About anything.

Plunge-heave-hoist-ho.

When she was a kid, maybe seven or eight, she used to dig holes all the time. Pissed her parents off no end. Guests would come over, look at the backyard, and ask if they owned a dog.

Her parents had owned a dog once, but that was before she'd been born. Spud, that was its name. It had been Walter's dog, before he went into that coma. She'd seen photos. Walter had been like, maybe, one year old and there was this massive ugly wolfhound-thing slobbering all over him. Her mother insisted Walter loved that dog, but the kid looked terrified. Walter was almost twenty-two years old now, or at least his body was. Hope couldn't even think of that body as a person. If anything it was a guest that had overstayed its welcome in her home and her life. It might have been a person once, but not in Hope's lifetime. All Walter had ever been was that dead thing in the room next to hers, waiting for enough prayers and tears to resurrect him; a flesh intersection for all the rubber and metal that pointlessly kept his systems pumping. It wasn't life support for Walter so much as faith support for Hope's parents. Faith that one day Walter might wake up as suddenly as he had fallen asleep, almost eighteen years ago, and life would pick up where it had left off.

The money for an actual life-support machine had run out when Hope was a kid. When the time came to shut it off and move it out Mum had worked herself into a fit and Dad had just looked on, blankly. Walter still hung on. It wasn't uncommon. But hanging on for over a decade unassisted, that was something doctors would comment on. Patients could often breathe unassisted, but to go for so long without something going wrong was quite exceptional. Hope had thought unplugging him would mean an end to it all. But it never ended.

Walter was just the name for Hope's personal nightmare.

Other kids grew up fearing abandonment by parents or something unknown and terrible stepping out of their closet and carrying them off, but Hope had spent her childhood living in fear of the sleeping zombie in the next room. Afraid of what might happen if it opened its eyes and said something. A lot of Walter's daily upkeep had fallen on her shoulders. She didn't mind washing him, or even feeding him (though stuffing mashed food down that tube still clenched her gut, no matter how she tried to get over it), so long as she could get out of having to touch the catheter or change the colostomy bag. Hope would do it to save an argument, but she'd always avoid it if she could.

But what she hated most about going into Walter's room were the paper cranes. Her father had made them for Walter when he was a kid, before Hope had been born, and now her mother insisted on keeping them—all of them—on the bedside table. Flocks of them. A worn-around-the-edges faded rainbow crowd scene. Her father's birds. She hated even looking at them. She hated having something physical of that man left in the house. It was bad enough her mother still had some of his clothes in her wardrobe. The smell that wafted out was Daddy all over; nothing but the smell of his body. But she hated those cranes more; more than artifacts of her father, they were a tangible reminder of how her parents had sacrificed any life any of them could have had just to keep her brother's shell in the house.

As a kid Hope knew that if Walter ever woke up she would no longer be needed; that she was just holding Walter's place until he decided to open his eyes. Now, older and wiser, she knew he was never going to open his eyes; the whole thing was a pantomime.

She had let that explode out of her once, during a particularly expressive argument with her folks, and had been slapped for it. It didn't come up again. She had gotten over that fiasco by getting her eyebrow pierced. Which led to yet another argument—a big one. Which in turn led her to finally getting that tattoo she'd always wanted: a white tiger with clear blue eyes on her left shoulder blade. She liked the idea of it watching her back. She'd had a thing for cats, tigers especially, ever since she was a kid. Tigers and circus music.

She supposed a fear of replacement went some way to explaining her relationship with Kristian. He had never been the kind of boyfriend she had imagined herself having: a straight-down-the-line, zero-complexity, no-frills, knew-what-he-liked boyfriend. He sweated a little, but she could live with that. She knew what he was thinking, what he wanted, and because of that there'd be no surprises. She didn't think about the whole thing too much. She only wished Suni and Kristian got along. They'd been friends once, so they said, but Hope being Suni's ex had just widened the gulf between them.

In the steady rhythm of plunge-heave-hoist-ho she lost the world that owned her and ran amid the fields of her mind, certain that just below her feet was another world waiting to be found. Besides, it was cheaper than smoking.

By the time she was thirteen she had abandoned the shovel for a newfound interest in boys, glamour magazines, and the opinions of others her age—and had consequently never been more miserable.

So she'd gone back to the shovel. Plunge-heave-hoist-ho.

Boys. Men. She couldn't believe the way they'd warped her life into something she'd never, ever expected. Yet they were like a gravity well, a comforting voice, a masochistic self-trial she found herself trustingly wandering back to in one way or another, again and again. Walter, Suni, her father . . .

She was up to her armpits when the shovel went *clank.*

Great, she thought. Another water main.

She scraped the soft brown soil aside and found a flat surface, gleaming like quicksilver and elaborately crafted. She clapped a hand over her mouth and screamed. No one heard. Good.

Dig dig dig.

It was a box.

A big. Stonking. Box.

It was practically weightless, long and wide and thin as a briefcase. She looked around in the dimming daylight, saw no one on the street or in the lit windows of surrounding houses, and rested the box on the green, green grass.

The box was engraved with intricate, craftful designs and curlicues. She ran her hands across the cool flat top and down the sides, the skin of her palms sliding easily across the glossy surface. It hummed faintly beneath her touch, tickling her hands, sending minuscule vibrations up her radius and ulna. It infused her, sympathetic vibrations sounding across her rib cage and up her neck like a tickle of faint electricity. Vibrations that reached her skull, touched her inner ear, and formed a word . . .

Anxietoscope . . .

Hope snatched her hands away. She could still feel the residual tingle in her fingers and bones. A word she'd never heard before still tingled in her ear.

With great care she reached out with one finger and flipped open the lid.

The box practically opened itself.

Inside, on a bed of muslin, lay a small steel cup—a thimble—that would have fit perfectly over one fingertip; a thimble made from the same pure quicksilver metal as the case—with a single barb adorning its tip.

Slowly it rose, resting on nothing, rotating lazily in the air.

She slammed the lid down.

Anxietoscope. The vibrations died in her ear. *To be used in the . . .*

She quickly stuffed the box into her pack and slung it over one shoulder. Then she was out of the hole and headed for home, her father's shovel in one hand, soil beneath her nails.

ELEVEN

BED

THE CURTAINS WERE ALWAYS OPEN IN WALTER'S ROOM. His mother liked to give him as much stimulus as possible. When he'd first been admitted into hospital, all those years ago, a doctor had told his mother it was good for him. That was before they advised turning him off. Before his parents refused and refused and refused again to allow their son to just die while his body still breathed. Before the court case drew out over five years, in which time the hospital tried to get him out of their ward and off their list of annual expenditure. Before the court voted in favor of the hospital anyway. Before Walter's parents ended up throwing all their money into keeping him at home. And before the money for that had run out.

There had been times when he'd wished they'd just let him go, but it never happened. Even without the machines the body kept breathing. He didn't know what would happen to him should the body die; he didn't feel a part of it anymore. It was just something that was ruining his family's life.

The body was twenty-one years old. It had dirty-blond hair that his mother had cut the same way for as long as he'd had hair (which now looked absurd on the twisted shape he had become). She came in every morning to comb and part it, and allow her hand to linger on his sallow cheek. She would stroke his forehead and call him her beautiful boy. And then she would turn to the window and the street outside and do nothing but stand and breathe for long minutes. Sometimes the shaving got neglected. Like now. There were traces of coarse hair around the hollow cheeks and bony chin. To get a good look at the body Walter had to climb up onto whatever chair was nearby. There usually was one because his mother made a habit of reading in here, which was fortunate because he wouldn't be able to move the chair by himself. He could touch it, feel the cool metal and sharp glass dust-like prickle of immovable fiber, but he wouldn't be able to affect it in any way at all.

He'd first seen the body during the final days of the court case, when the body was still on assisted breathing at the hospital. He'd tried unplugging himself a few times, but the snaking cords had been like girders in his tiny and useless hands—rigid and utterly static. Even the bedsheets refused to yield to his touch; he couldn't so much as leave an indentation on the weave. Every substance and surface was hard as diamond, immovable as a mountain. He had overstayed his welcome in this world, and the world let him know it in no uncertain terms.

It was easy to see why Hope had chosen her own brother as the face of her monster. He was the ugliest, most frightening thing in her life.

.Most of the time Walter watched from afar as his sister went about her life, while he kept an eye out for the doctor. Walter was no longer his sister's monster, and the longer he delayed the inevitable moving-on, the weaker he became. Eventually the doctor would be able to just walk into Hope's life and take her, and there wouldn't be anything Walter could do to stop him.

Entrusting her well-being to Suni had been the second-worst decision he had ever made, after taking Henry's hand in the first place. It was all down to the Anxietoscope now.

Now he stood on his mother's reading chair, looking down at the face he was meant to have, and daydreamed about what he could have been.

TWELVE

THE SCHEME OF THINGS

*H*OPE MOVED THROUGH CHATTERING CLOUDS OF HALF-familiar people, down hallways and across the quadrangle, headed for the library, a long purple scarf thrown around her neck against an unseasonable morning chill.

The library didn't open before school, so Hope usually found Suni camped out by its doors working on his art portfolio. He spent most of his lunch breaks and free periods inside doing the same thing.

She rounded the corner to the library—litter blowing past her feet—and checked her Hello Kitty watch. Ten minutes until class and already she wanted to go home.

More litter skated around her ankles. White, clean paper, unrumpled. One sheet contained a shaded pencil sketch of a clockwork cube, an ornate prison for the twisted body it contained. She'd seen it before. It was Suni's. From around the corner she heard scattered laughter, and a voice saying:

"Lucky I didn't hit him any harder. Go straight over the balcony."

Hope grabbed a locker rack to brake herself as she rounded the corner—and found Suni with the small of his back against the bal-

cony railing, arched out over a two-story drop to the courtyard, knuckles white on the rail, Kristian's fist locked around his neck.

Bright morning sunlight lit the place vivid saffron.

"Let him go!" Hope's voice cracked under pressure, snapped on
go, became a shriek. The five or six people gathered around Kristian
and Suni chuckled. A couple turned and walked away. Despite the
fact that his head was held immobile, Suni's eyes flicked to Hope.
Though trapped and helpless, she realized, Suni wanted help even
less than he wanted out. He could take the beating, he could take the
shame, provided he could take it alone. There was no dignity in pity.

Kristian looked over and with a last vindictive shove let Suni go.
Suni's eyes widened as he struggled to right himself, before doubling
forward and flailing into the hallway. As Kristian turned to leave he
reached into his shirt pocket and handed Suni's glasses back.

"There y'go, champ." He turned his back on Suni and strolled over
to where Hope stood shaking by the locker rack. "What's the matter?"

Her teeth were grinding, body vibrating from the inside in an uncomfortable chemical kind of way that made her wonder if her legs
would collapse. "You prick."

Someone muttered "Whoa . . ." She noticed a couple of onlook-
ers glance at each other.

"Why? You want him back?" Kristian asked.

"Apologize. Now."

Kristian seemed distracted by some point above Hope's head, like
he couldn't look her in the eye after hearing that. He laughed once,
like a cough, and walked away.

And that was that. The little cloud of people dispersed—some
glancing furtively back at her—and Suni bent to gather his scattered
art. Students idled past, giving her a wide berth but otherwise sensing
nothing wrong with the scheme of things. Hope picked up the drawing of the clockwork cube from where it lay now, facedown on the
hallway floor. She blew dust from it. It was a pretty thing.

"It's jjjj-juh-juh-just a sketch," Suni said, taking it back, brushing
it off with the experienced moves of a mother wiping grime from a

child's face. He placed it back among its siblings, inside his black folio. He feigned interest in something down the hall, unable to look Hope in the face. "Nnn-nice choice," he mumbled.

Hope pretended not to have heard. She swept her pink hair back with both hands, idly tugging her eyebrow ring, no idea what to say. She wanted to hug him, but knew that would only make it worse.

Kristian and Suni had been friends, a long time ago. She didn't understand why it had to be like this between them now. When she'd asked what caused the animosity Suni's only reply had been, "It started over something small and got bigger. Doubt he even remembers what it was."

"So what happened here?" she asked.

Suni shook his head, ordered himself and his satchel. His long black hair was a loose shamble half caught in the wreckage of a ponytail. He reached behind his head and shook loose the band that held it. "Nothing." He pulled his hair back properly once more, tied it. With the hair out of the way Hope noticed one side of his face was beginning to redden where Kristian's fist had landed. Over the railing and two floors down, a mass of students went about the usual — locking bikes, talking to friends, savoring the last clean moments of morning before the bell split the air and four walls spelled the rest of the day. "I can't help it," he said, meeting her eyes. Something unspoken and familiar lingered there. "You know how it ggg-guh-goes."

She did. It was perverse. Ever since they'd split up she and Suni had slowly become a support group for one's separation from the other. It didn't make any kind of sense, and only compounded Hope's suspicion that she was doing something very, very wrong in the whole Kristian–Suni thing. "Yeah . . . ," she managed. "But I get over it."

He didn't look away when he said, "And wuh-what happens when you get over things so often you nnn-never feel anything again?"

Hope bit down on her well-worn mental bullet and thought of tigers. "Strong feelings aren't all they're cracked up to be."

Hope made no mention of what she had uncovered beneath two feet of dirt the previous evening. It was a mystery, the most amazing thing she had ever found, something incredible to be fathomed and understood, and she wanted to be the one to do it. It was a giggly kid-on-Christmas-morning type of reaction, but it wouldn't kill Suni to wait a day for something he didn't even know existed. She'd check the whole thing out for herself, then blow his mind.

She jogged home, got through the front door, and—like clockwork—her mother drawled, "Walter'll need changing." In the living room the TV was tuned to a fat-faced Chinese man chopping celery and smiling so hard you could hardly see his eyes. The stereo was on—a battered five-year-old thing with a faulty tape deck—tuned just loud enough to make understanding the chef impossible. Hope's mother sat cross-legged on the floor with a big blue plastic tumbler in her hand, mostly full of tomato juice and ice and the usual. She didn't look away from the set. She was singing again, in a cracked voice.

You talk straightforward and squarely I see
With a beer in your hand
You were thrown down to me
That blistering vowel you'd do anything to keep
And knowing it's you
Silently screaming . . .

Hope didn't answer, never did, just went down the hall, ditched her bag, and got Walter over with.

Her mother had trapped herself. After all this time she must know Walter was never going to wake up, but at the same time she couldn't stop herself from looking after him. If she did, somehow, allow Walter's body to cease breathing it would mean all the years, all the sacrifice, had been for nothing. She would have wasted her life. No house, no job, no money, no husband, no mind even. She was doomed to look after him until she, or Walter, died.

Hope felt sorry for her, somewhere inside, but it was buried under a lifetime. Even she couldn't dig that far down. She'd get out of here, once she graduated, and she'd make a life for herself. Then maybe she'd send some money home, make things easier around here. But until then it was business as usual and she could live with that. After all, it was all she had ever done.

Hope did not have quite so much to do with Walter while her dad had been around. But once he was gone and Hope's mother fell to pieces, almost everything to do with Walter landed on Hope's shoulders—especially given that her dad's absence was entirely Hope's fault, in her mother's opinion. Hope didn't bother arguing the point. She didn't have the energy for it anymore and it always devolved into mindless screaming and the dredging-up of the usual stuff, usually at the expense of things that made lots of noise when they broke. It became a subject broached only when her mother outlasted her juice, and stayed awake long enough and drunk enough to bring it all out again. Which was hardly ever nowadays. The booze and her medication usually combined to knock her out by seven, which was fine by Hope. It made life a hell of a lot easier.

With Walter out of the way she showered quickly and rushed back to her room. The box was still where she'd left it on the top shelf of her closet. Still wrapped in her gray faux-fur jacket like some hairy, hibernating thing. She placed it on the bed and unwrapped it, wet pink hair hanging like vines in front of her eyes.

Silver and shining, energy thrummed off the box with the effort of its waiting. Energy that hummed through her fingers and up her arm to vibrate the small parts of her ear and again form that word, a soft susurration in her head.

Anxietoscope

She lifted her fingers, the word still tickling the inside of her ear.

This box just didn't slot into the world that people, supposedly older and wiser than herself, insisted she was living in; it could not possibly exist in that world; and yet here it was.

It made her wonder what else all those people might have been wrong about.

Hope closed her eyes and took a long, slow breath through her nostrils. Time to find out.

She spread her fingers and pressed them onto the cold metal surface. The humming voice began.

Anxietoscope. To be used in the direct examination of a subject's fears. Investigative procedures supplement the fright evaluation of a subject, which is made from subject history and behavioral observation. The Anxietoscope allows core fears to be localized with exactitude and removed for closer study in order that a terror or ecstatic manifestation may be customized for maximum effect. This is extremely useful when a given subject appears resistant to the incredible through lack of belief. The procedure is painless, and when such an examination is being undertaken it is essential that a Maker plan his approach in order to coincide with a period of subject unconsciousness. It must be realized that some investigations, particularly those involving the temporary extraction of core fears, carry an intrinsic risk that must be balanced against the value of the information that can be obtained from them. For this reason . . .

Distantly, beneath the humming voice, Hope became aware of a pounding at the door. She couldn't be sure how long it had been going on. An itch and tickle wormed inside her ear. She stuck a finger in each and wiggled them vigorously.

The pounding continued. "Hope! Are you in there?"

Her mother.

"Why is this door locked?"

"Just a second."

Hope wrapped the box in her coat and replaced it in the closet before opening the door. Her mother stood there in her blue jeans, eyes glassy, looking twice her age.

"Why was the door locked?"

"I was sleeping."

"How nice for you."

"What do you want, Mum?"

Her mother's eyes narrowed a little. "Dinner needs cooking," she said, stealing a glance over her daughter's shoulder, suspicious of some new cover-up. "Your friend's on the phone. Use the fish cakes."

THIRTEEN

CANDLELIGHT

*H*OPE'S MOTHER WASN'T SOLD ON SUNI. WHEN HOPE and Suni had first started seeing each other a little over a year ago, he had come home with Hope one afternoon and met her mother, uncomfortable the whole time. Hope had tried to dissuade him from ever coming over. All she could think about while he was there was how embarrassed she had been by the ripped covering on the sofa. Toward the end of the visit, when her mother pointed out it was getting dark, Suni had asked if he could see Walter. Hope's mother had lost most of her friends when they'd moved, and anyone who knew Walter as a little boy didn't come around anymore. Having a total stranger ask to see him was so unusual Hope had expected her mother to erupt. But after an unreadable moment, she'd acquiesced, and Hope had taken Suni upstairs.

The body was where it always was. The nurse at the time, a young guy on an internship trying to earn extra cash, was pointlessly manipulating Walter's legs. Hope didn't know why her mother bothered with maintaining the physio at all. Walter had twisted out of shape from lack of use years ago, muscle contractures contorting his arms into a spastic, huddled tangle about his chest. She could tell the nurse knew it was pointless, doing it to get it done, get paid, and get out. Hope had wondered what he thought of it all: this girl and her crazy mother, this breathing corpse and the Japanese kid they'd just led into the room. Felt sorry for the kid, probably. It hardly surprised Hope that most of the nurses never lasted two months, and after a while her mother had to stop hiring them at all.

The worst part of Walter was below the waist. More bone than skin, really. Legs that were practically vestigial, having been unused since he was four. And he'd been twenty then. They looked like they belonged on someone half his age — half his age and dead. It made her think of Auschwitz. The body was ghost-pale with hair to match; dark blue veins faint on his forehead and hands. He smelled like an old man, a dank body odor mixed with soap. The quiet, lingering scent of rubber and shit built up over the years.

The bed stood by a large window that looked out on a fairyland of streetlights and lawns and amber-colored lounge rooms.

Suni had stood there, staring at the body, maybe mesmerized, maybe adrift in his own thoughts.

Then he had said, "Th-that's him. Jesus, that's rrr-rrr-really him."

Hope had felt instantly sick. Telling Suni about Walter, about how much he creeped her out, had been a mistake; about the years she'd spent scared out of her mind that she'd be in his room one day, alone, washing him, and he'd open his eyes and croak something, something he'd seen in the dead place he'd been all those years.

"That's enough. Say good-bye," her mother had said, abruptly.

Without saying another word, Suni had left the room. But not without glancing back one last time.

He never asked to look in again. Still, the incident had made it easier for Hope to break off their relationship when she felt she had to.

But then it was always like that. She bit down on it, told herself she was a tiger, and got on with her life. It was a habit that had served her well. If she could last till she got out of home she'd be fine. She could take risks then. She knew people that had lives smoother than her own had been, and they were a complete mess. Hope didn't do drugs, had never tried to kill herself, and by that standard she was pretty much intact. She just had to last till she graduated. No problem.

Suni lived in a two-story house with an undercover garage. The garage and laundry took up half the ground floor, and Suni's room the other. It gave him a place to himself—a place that usually wasn't intruded upon by his mother, who occupied the space upstairs.

Hope crept through the yard toward his window. The jasmine blooming beneath the stairs filled the air with a warm and heavy perfume. It was almost eleven, and the upstairs lights were off. Soft candlelight glowed amber from behind Suni's curtains. Hope climbed three stairs and knocked lightly on the glass. The curtain was drawn aside and Suni opened the window.

"Hey," he said, sticking his head out to look upstairs. His hair was tied into a loose ponytail, and his glasses were propped on his head. "She asleep?"

"Looks like it."

"Cool." He stepped aside, rubbing an eye with one finger, to let Hope slip under the railing and through the window.

The room was warm and smelled like boy, the way it always did: like warm skin and socks. Candlelight flickered on the dresser, reflected in the mirror, and cast a glow throughout the room. Faded gilding on the wrinkled and bubbled wallpaper glowed a subdued, tarnished gold—old designs remembering how pretty they used to be. On the floor other wicks burned in plastic cups, arranged almost ceremonially around where Suni was working. When Suni had been younger his father had given him a lightbox to draw on—a small table on wheels with an opaque acrylic surface—but Suni still spent most of the time drawing on the floor, and the lightbox had always been a glorified lamp-*cum*-beside-table. The alarm clock and a couple of empty Coke cans sat there, underlit by the suffused white glow. The drawing of the clockwork cube lay there, atop the folio, the tools of Suni's art arranged haphazardly within arm's reach. It was reverent and altar-like, and Hope was sure it was intentional. Suni had his single bed as well as a spare bed against the opposite wall, beneath a sliding glass window that looked out on the yard, behind bamboo blinds. There was a foldout bed that doubled as a couch, and a dresser and a clothes rack he'd made with a broomstick and two lengths of nylon rope hung from the rafters. He had plenty of floor space, even if it was covered in ugly tan patterned carpet that kind of matched the wallpaper.

"How is everything?" he asked, wandering back to his work.

Hope glanced at the ceiling, and the downy spiderwebs that clung to its chocolate-brown underbelly. "You disappeared today."

Suni shrugged and sat down on the floor, cross-legged. He adjusted his glasses and picked up a charcoal stick. "There's a lll-little wine left by the buh-bed if you want some."

They had a glass of white each, Suni let the player cycle through his CDs—all old stuff—and they talked for a few hours. Suni alternated between letting Oolric, his orange furbomb of a cat, lounge around on his lap, and working on his drawing. Pistons lanced and pumped through the device as multitudinous gears turned and ground, a crafted prison for the person trapped within. The prisoner's slack, senseless face was the centerpiece of one of the planes, while arms and legs stuck out elsewhere at strange angles. Great pistons were placed to grind perpetually through the body of the captive, who seemed incapable of dying, with the end result being to provide power to the cheap-looking music box atop the contraption.

The drawing left Hope wondering how Suni's mind worked. He'd said he thought the cube was his greatest piece. The entire mechanism, he said, was a metaphor for life. The captive's own body powers the machine, and while the machine works the captive suffers; and while the captive suffers the music box plays. As the music ends the greatest piston slams through the captive's body, withdraws, and the cycle begins again: an endless circuit of pain for a little beauty.

Some of Suni's artwork hung on the walls around the room, rendered on thick cartridge. The piece that really bugged Hope was the gray-shaded watercolor of four headless people playing cards in a room piled high with bodies, sprawled and layered over one another, all eyes and ribs, fingers and feet. It wasn't the subject matter that bothered her so much as the neat-haired little boy standing off to the right, staring like he was going to say something. Though the piece was three years old, it still held the acrid chemical perfume of the maximum-hold hair spray Suni used to lacquer all his art.

"That piece with the little boy, what does this mean?" She looked over her shoulder. "Suni?"

"Whatever you wuh-want it to mean," he said.

She looked at it again.

"Www-what do you think it means?" he asked.

She thought about it, then shrugged. "It's your picture."

"It must make you think of something."

The boy in the picture had very old eyes. Not wrinkled, not clouded, just old. She wondered if Suni had gone for that effect, or if it was just an accident. There was an archway or something—a way out, all thickly penciled shadow—just beyond the body pile. Someone was standing there: a long, thin shadow in a hat.

"I used to have this dream, when I was a kid." She went back to her drink. "It makes me think of that."

"A suh-sleep dream or a wish dream?" said Suni as he popped in a Creatures CD.

"Sleep dream." "Pluto Drive" started up, eerie and menacing and slow. "Got anything livelier?" she asked.

"No circus music."

"Well, anything perkier than this."

"I can work to this."

"I can sleep to this. Got any chocolate?"

"Maybe upstairs. What was the dream?"

She had a sip of wine. It tasted like watery gasoline, just the way wine shouldn't. "I'd wake up and think I could hear Walter mumbling in his sleep."

"Yeah?"

She nodded. "I'd cry, because I knew that now Walter was back my parents would finally forget I was even there."

Suni sucked his lips for a second, and then asked, "What was he saying?"

She shrugged. "That's the thing. I'd lie there, and I'd try not to listen. I didn't want to know what someone like that would have to say after years of being dead."

"And that www-wuh-was it? That's www-wuh-where it ended?"

She shook her head. "After a while I couldn't help but understand what was being said. Whoever was talking, it wasn't Walter. Someone was telling him stories."

Suni blinked. "Stories?"

"Every night a different one."

"And . . . ?"

"And what? I don't remember what was said."

Suni shifted, sitting on his haunches. "You must remember something."

Hope stared at him. "I don't. Why do you care so much?"

It was as if someone had clapped their hands in front of his face. "It's interesting," he said, self-consciously.

"I remember bits," she conceded. "This man talked about coyotes. About the way they can sound at night, hidden from sight. Like they're talking to each other about things you wouldn't understand." She sipped her wine and remembered some more. "One night he talked about how some of the angels that fell with the Devil were allowed back into Heaven, after a long time."

Sitting across from her, Suni was softly panting through slightly parted lips.

"Suni?"

He picked up the sketch of the clockwork cube and a pencil, rested the page on his folio, and began working again. Hope didn't have anything more to add to the story, and Suni had made an excuse about needing to use the bathroom, so she left it at that. He'd come back about ten minutes later and started drawing. The subject of dreams didn't come up again.

"Did you hear they wound up kicking that kid out of school?" Hope asked.

Suni looked over. "The dope-dealing thing?" he asked.

"Apparently. The VP mentioned it the other day. Didn't come out and say who had been expelled, just that a student had been caught with dope and wouldn't be coming back. And that anyone else caught could expect the same."

"Wanker."

Hope shrugged. "He has his good days."

"Ssss-suh-suh-'scuse me?"

"There was the time that kid was leaving death threats in whatsername's desk. Julie Green."

"So? Wuh-what'd the VP have to do with it?"

"Green said she knew who it was, and showed the VP the note. The guy had misspelled *intestines*. Spelled it *t-e-n-e-s*. So the VP calls this kid to the office, hands him a piece of paper, and gets him to write down the word *intestines*. And the kid misspells it the same way. So they caught him."

"Hope, that's how *I* thought you spell *intestines*."

"Oh."

"No, really," Suni insisted. "The guy *is* a wanker. So concerned about the image of his precious school . . ."

"Well we do have a rep," Hope said, then regretted it.

"Www-we're a suh-state school!" Suni cried out. "Of course every privately ruh-run buh-boys and girls school is going to look down their nose at us! That's a given. It doesn't mean we're a fuh-fuh-ffff-friggin' drug den. Not that I care. The whole place can burn, as far as I'm concerned. I wish those people would just explode."

"Poison them."

"We could brick up the front door and throw gnomes at anyone that comes up the path."

"That could work."

"It ccc-could."

Hope finished the last of her wine.

About the time she'd changed schools and moved to a new house their doctor had tried putting both herself and her mother on antidepressants. Her mother took the pills, Hope declined, though she'd really had to think about it. At the time she felt like she was going to break in half if someone didn't help her, and sometimes it still felt that way. But in the end she decided against meds and took up writing down everything in her journal instead. A friend of hers had been on pills once, took years to get off them, and never seemed quite the same again.

"School heightens my appreciation of free time," Suni was saying, touching up something on the paper. "I figure it works on the same principle as erotic asphyxiation." He lightly licked his finger, smudged something. "Strangulation . . . ," he mumbled. "Amplifies the eventual orgasm. Damn . . ." He grabbed the eraser, delicately flicking it over a point on the page. "Shit."

It became obsessive, Hope's journal keeping, going through a hardcover notebook a week. It was inevitable that her mother would eventually want to look at them, and when she finally did she also got around to burning them. Hope had come home to find her mother in the backyard with her books and a can of lighter fluid. Some were unsalvageable, but she managed to save most. On those occasions she felt the need to retrieve them from their place in the padlocked steel ammo container beneath Suni's bed, she had to remember not to read them by an open flame. She trusted him with them, and her mother had no idea where Suni lived. The pages of every surviving journal before a certain period in time all had wrinkled pages and still reeked of Zippo fluid.

When it came to drugs she only knew what she overheard, and what her doctor tried to prescribe. Suni had a little more experience with the recreational end of the chemical spectrum. Not a lot, but enough to indulge his fantasy of becoming something of a modern day Rimbaud-esque life-eater. It started her thinking about her mother again.

"Ever wonder why we're here?" she asked, staring at nothing, idly chewing her lip. "We've been living under the assumption that school never ends, that it's all there'll ever be. Only six months from now there is no more school. So we get jobs. We do the same thing day after day. Then we buy stuff. That can't be it, can it? Years of mediocrity and desperation, with nothing but a new couch to tell you it's all been worth it?" She looked at him, watching as he stroked the cat. "Tell me there's more than that."

He thought for a second, looking happily lost in the steady rhythm of stroking, the smoothness of warm, soft fur. "I've been over this and over this," he said, from somewhere far away, "and all it comes down to is that—arguably—we only have one little eyeblink of a life to run around with our pants on our head . . . before Time rolls on . . . squashing us in the process." Oolric had his eyes closed, purring. Suni shrugged, careful not to wake him. "And that's fine."

Later Suni crept upstairs and brought down half a bottle of white left over from the evening meal, which tasted unbelievably good after the stuff they'd just had from a box. After talking about Paris (someone Suni knew had met a terrorist in a nightclub), the subject turned inward again. It was almost one in the morning and Suni hadn't touched his art in an hour. He sat with his glass on the other side of the divide of flickering amber light, content in her company.

"Mostly I'm fff-fine," he was saying. "Then I remember suh-something stupid, like how you look www-with your hair wet, and I'm right back where I started. I fixate on you. I've spent unwuh-wuh-witting hours flicking through a mental manifest of the things we did together, and by the end of it I'm convinced that if I can just be friends with Hope, ttt-tuh-talk to Hope, I'll be okay." He lifted his glass. "Which is, of course, bullshit."

Hope smiled, liking his voice. "I like the way you rant when you're drunk."

"I'm so glad you appreciate my predicament," he mumbled, tipping the glass to his lips.

"What'd you do that pissed off Kristian?" she asked.

Suni looked at his glass, scratched his nose.

"Come on . . ."

He opened his mouth, took a breath, then closed it again.

"Suni . . ."

He exhaled. "I . . ."

"What? What'd you do?"

"I . . ." He looked around, exasperated, as if he had left the answer somewhere on the far wall. Then he dug under the bed and pulled something out. "Here," he said, and tossed her an accounts book, faint-ruled, with a red marbled cover. A pen tumbled out from between the pages as he did so. The book landed by her side. "I kept a journal. I wrote stuff about you in it. Since we buh-bbb-broke up."

Hope didn't touch it, just looked. She knew she'd never read it. Suni was better, safer, if he stayed here, in the candlelight, as her friend. She had a flash of people walking away from that morning's scene, sneaking furtive looks back at her. She was safer. "Kristian read it?"

"Buh-bbb-bits. Saw me writing something and thought it might be worth ridiculing. Lost that idea pretty qqq-quh-quickly."

"Suni . . . were you going to give this to me?" She didn't need this. She didn't want this. But she could deal with this. She was a tiger.

"Of course I was. You don't write something like that without wuh-wanting the person you're writing about to see it."

"But we've got a good thing here, don't we?"

"It's messing with my work, Hope! I've been nursing that one piece for the last month, for Chrissakes! If I want to guh-ggg-get into university I need a complete folio of a duh-*dozen* decent pieces in three different media, and so far I've only got four I'm happy with. It's like I can't even function properly anymore." He hissed through gritted teeth. "I know we're not going back to what we were, but I thought if you just knew . . . ruh-reacted . . . acknowledged where I'm at . . .

told me *why . . . anything . . .* then maybe I could get over it. Like you."

Hope stared at the bottom of her glass. Tried to get transfixed by the play of candlelight through facets, through the faintly yellow remains of her wine . . .

"Don't you ever wonder why you wound up with a caveman like Kristian?"

"He's not . . ." She remembered Kristian's hand around Suni's throat and fell silent.

"The only people who get to be with anyone," Suni said, with great intent and deliberation, "are the people that *don't care* about people. That's why Kristian has you now, because he doesn't care about you. Sometimes I think it's a victory thing. *Look at me, I went and tamed that girl that . . .*"

"Shut up, Suni."

"Maybe you think if you can make someone who doesn't care about you love you then that's some kind of victory. Jacks your self-esteem. And it's not just you, it happens to *everyone.* It's probably why I want you so badly *now:* because you *don't* want me and I can't have you. So if I want someone, I have to *not* want them before they'll want me. And where's the percentage in that?"

Something red was boiling and rising inside of her, and she vented it with level and controlled words. "You don't really think it works like that, do you?"

He looked right at her. "The person with the most power in a relationship is the person who cares least. If I hadn't ccc-cared you wuh-wuh-wouldn't have left because it would have meant leaving empty-handed." He relaxed a little, point made. "People feel loss more than gain. Self-interest is the great motivator."

This was killing both of them, this back-and-forthing, this more-than-friends, less-than-lovers relationship. The only time they ever got this hostile with each other was when they got too close to the one sensitive topic they had: each other.

But she couldn't stay mad. Not with Suni.

Oolric raised his head from Suni's knee and looked out the window. He stood, stretched, and dug his claws into Suni's leg. Suni yelped and brushed the cat away, almost spilling his wine. Oolric ambled lazily toward the sofa bed.

Suni wiped droplets off his leg. "Shit. So how's Walter?"

"Same as always."

"You should spend more time with him."

Hope stopped herself from telling him that it wasn't any of his damn business. Instead she watched the cat standing, paws up on the sill, looking through the glass at something in the yard.

Outside, Walter watched as Hope watched the cat watching him.

Five years had passed since he'd taken the Anxietoscope from Tub in that brown river. In that time he'd come to an agreement with the instrument, decided upon a plan with its shattered intelligence, and left it buried beneath two feet of earth a block from Hope's home. Almost immediately she had begun to dig holes. Eventually she had found the shining silver box; a box Walter made from a scrap of himself, it would tell Hope all she needed to know about the Anxietoscope. He could feel it thrumming on the bed, inside Hope's backpack. It had taken five years but finally Hope had found it, homed in on its call. It was inevitable.

Walter had never been permitted to touch the tools in his time with Henry and now Walter fully understood why: Henry had been conditioning him. Henry had to be sure Walter was deaf to instinct, senseless to anything the tools might try to tell him. Henry had to establish himself as the absolute certainty at the center of Walter's new universe.

And he had failed.

"I don't believe that's your take on a successful relationship. You don't need to care less. You're strong. If you want something, you go after it. You didn't let your mother stop you becoming an artist and you don't let people like Kristian stop you being friends with me. I mean, you *are* the same person who hid in luggage and flew to Canada when he was *ten*, right?"

"British Columbia," he mumbled.

"I've got the newspaper clippings. About how you had to call your mother from Customs. About how no one could work out how you managed to get that far. You're *smart*, Suni. You'll become something amazing once you get out of this crapped-out school and crapped-out town. People like you always do. And I'll be able to say I knew you."

Suni didn't say anything. He was shading the tip of his index finger with the flat of a charcoal stick.

"You're too modest," Hope said. "You know that."

Suni sniffed, rubbed his nose, changed the subject. "Ever wuh-wondered why I followed you from school to school?"

Hope's brain locked. "You didn't. You switched because Kristian switched and the art depart—"

"Oh come *on*! I can do art *an-nnn-nnn-ywhere*. One school's the same as an-nnn-other. Yeah, me and Kristian were fuh-fff-friends then but I wouldn't have changed schools on his account."

"But . . ."

"There's not a lot of people like us, Hope."

Hope didn't say anything. It wasn't the first time he'd said something like that. Then it occurred to her: "You didn't even know me at our first school. You transferred from private to public school without knowing me at all. That's how we first met."

Suni didn't say anything. He didn't look away, either. It was creeping her out a little. "What? What is it? Are you trying to tell me you were drawn to me by the call of *lerrve*?"

Suni just scowled into his glass, obviously wishing he had more wine. "I shouldn't have said anything. And nn-nuh-now I've pushed you even farther away with that stupid journal idea." Exasperated, he shoved back against his bed, staring at the ceiling. "That which does not kill me makes me stronger."

She didn't know what to say. They'd been through all this before. It was a conversation with no resolution. She raised her empty glass to the candles. She couldn't look at him just yet. "That which does not kill us makes us stranger," she said.

Suni pushed his empty glass away with a single finger, watched it catch on the carpet and tip over. A drop flew free, sank into the weave, and disappeared. Traffic hissed and shushed distantly, out on one of the main roads, past the parks and houses. "That which does not kill us leaves us fuh-fucking wounded, and that's about it."

It was quiet for a while after that. Hope wasn't sure if what she was listening to outside was the breeze or distant traffic. Then she said, "Do you trust me?"

FOURTEEN

HUNGRY

*H*OPE UNWRAPPED HER COAT FROM AROUND THE BOX and placed it on the spare bed beneath the window. Amber candlelight danced off its brilliant surfaces and writhing figures, lighting the room like an undersea cave. Like a dream vision.

"I found it," Hope told him. "I dug it up."

"You're kidding," Suni said. He ran a finger along one radiant edge.

"I wouldn't . . . ," Hope cautioned, but it was too late. With a sudden intake of breath Suni snatched his hand back.

"It jjj-juh-juh-just . . ."

Hope nodded. "It does that." She reached down and touched the lid. "Wait till you see what's inside."

She opened it, and there it lay, a bauble of pure reflective silver tipped with a delicately curved needle-thin talon, resting on a crumpled bed of soft muslin. The thorned thimble rose three inches into the air and stopped, rotating slowly above its dun-colored bed, showing itself to be beautiful in candlelight.

"I don't think sss-sss-someone would have just buh-bbb-buried this."

"It's called an Anxietoscope," Hope said, fixated by the play of light across shifting and turning mercury. "Hey . . . you okay?"

Suni's face was bloodless. "How's it floating like that?" he asked, trying to sound calm. "Mmm-muh-mmm-magnets or something?"

"I don't know."

"What's it for?"

Hope rubbed her hands on the legs of her jeans, still looking at it. She shrugged.

"And you just fff-found this? Are you sure?"

"Yes," she repeated, wondering what the problem was. "Why?"

Suni tried to shrug, and failed. "Have you ttt-ttt-tried it on?"

She shook her head. "Not yet. I was a little scared."

"But you know what it does," Suni urged. "Yuh-yuh-yyy-you listened to the box."

"Yeah."

With slow deliberation, as if about to grab a snake by the head, Hope reached out with open fingers and claimed the thimble. It came without resistance and with practically no tactility or weight. The only way Hope sensed she was holding something was through resistance to her grip. The Anxietoscope wasn't cold. It was as warm as she was. It looked like metal but felt like . . . nothing.

Walter stood in the yard, watching.

The thimble sighed a tone, soft and clear . . . and Hope got a headful of . . .

She sat down on the bed.

She held the 'scope out to Suni. "Touch this, would you?"

Suni stretched out a finger, placed it on the thimble. "What now?"

"You didn't get that?"

"I don't think so."

"Weird."

Walter balled his fists. It was as he expected: Hope wasn't getting anything from it.

"What was it?"

Hope shook her head. "I don't know. Just a . . . headachy, jumbled kind of . . . salad. I guess. Lots of light and violence. Or something."

"Well, that sounds promising."

"I'm going to try it on."

"Naturally."

Glancing up for one final look of confirmation from Suni, she slipped it over the index finger of her right hand.

Perfect fit: a gleaming joint tipped with a fine barb. All eyes on it, waiting. Her fingers were splayed in the air before her, the tip of her finger sheathed in hooked silver. "It feels weird. Like it's . . ."

Suni stepped back. "Jesus." The Anxietoscope liquefied, running over the first and second joints of Hope's finger. Suni's hands came up, stopping just short of snatching it off. "What's it doing? Are you okay?"

Hope nodded, eyes still on it. "Yeah . . . yeah . . . ," she said, distracted. "It kind of tickles."

Suni seemed unsure, eyeing it distrustfully as it spread down Hope's palm and began creeping against gravity, up her remaining fingers and thumb. "You sure?"

Hope nodded, watching. As it slid up and over each finger, neat and tight but not constrictive, it petered into another fine, hooked barb. When the work was done Hope's hand was quicksilver-sheathed and all fingers taloned. Multiple reflections of her own face, distorted or inverted, stared back from the mounds and creases of her palm. A sliver of silver, a mercury needle, subtly curved from the tip of each finger and thumb. Hope was grinning, flexing and turning her hand. "Wow." She laughed.

Suni swallowed, drily. "So . . . now what?"

Hope ran her eyes over her hand and asked again: "Do you trust me?"

"Why?"

"Do you?"

"I guh-guess. Why?"

"I think this might be able to help you."

"Come again?"

Hope chewed her bottom lip for a moment, second thoughts wrestling for first position. "Turn around," she said.

"No!"

"Just . . . just trust me."

"No way! Not till you tell me what you're guh-gonna do with that thing."

"If I tell you, you won't do it."

"Well I'm definitely not doing it *now.*"

Hope held the 'scope-hand like a surgeon in gloves: fingers up, palm toward her, keeping it away from herself and everything else, neutral until needed.

To be used in the direct examination of a subject's fears, the box had said. *The Anxietoscope allows core fears to be localized with exactitude and removed for closer study . . .*

"It might stop you hurting. So we can stay friends." God, that sounded so warped when she said it out loud. "Don't you want that?"

Suni tried reasoning. "Hope, that thing looks lethal. Maybe you should jjj-just take it off."

He didn't trust her. He thought she was going to harm him. She could tell. It hurt.

She moved her hand, feeling the 'scope, idly running the thumb-claw up and down the other claws, one by one, like a mantis cleaning its mandibles.

"Hope," Suni said again. "Take it off till we work it out."

"Suni . . . do you think I'd ever do anything . . . ?"

He sat down. "No, of course not," he said plaintively. "But it was enough jjj-just having you put the damn thing on. And those things look sharp."

"This can help. I know it can."

"Are you kidding? How is *that* guh-guh-gonna help mmm-mmm-mmm-*me* with *you*? *How*? We don't even know wuh-www-what it is! Look at it!"

She sighed and ran her other hand through her shock of cropped hair, groaning in frustration to the cobwebs overhead. "Will you at least let me run this thing over you and see if it wants to do anything?"

Suni eyed it distrustfully, like he wanted to scuttle back on the unmade bed, away from the silver thing on the end of his friend's arm. But she could tell he didn't want to refuse her, either. He still held out hope that someday they'd go back to what they had been. It made her insides twist that she was using that as leverage now. God, she didn't even know what she was doing! She wasn't even entirely sure what this thing was, and here she was with it on her hand like some kind of taloned parasite, and she with half a gut full of wine. Maybe he had a point: maybe she should just take it off.

"Did you ever stop to think maybe someone's out there looking for that thing?"

Hope shrugged. "Maybe. But it was *buried*."

"Whoever owned it probably knew how to use it. What kind of person do you think that is?"

"Look. I won't touch you. I just want to see if *it* wants to do anything. Work it out that way."

" 'It'?"

"It knows what it needs to do." She saw the look on his face and laughed. "It's okay."

Suni was looking for assurance, or a change of heart, found neither, and gave in. "All right. Buh-but *don't* touch me with it, okay?"

Hope nodded and stepped over to him.

"Hope . . ." He was all eyes and vulnerable, like a kid in a dentist's chair. "Think about what I said, okay? Think about what might happen if someone comes looking for it."

Hope crouched before him and started at his feet. Slowly she ran the Anxietoscope up Suni's leg, an inch or so out from the worn denim of his jeans, across his waist, and down the other leg. She traveled back up, fingers flexing, trying to coax something from the 'scope, some kind of sense of what she was supposed to do with it. She moved up toward his chest . . .

"Um . . . ," she said.

Suni glared at her. " 'Um'? What the hhh-huh-hell is 'um'?"

"Relax. It wants to go higher. I'm holding it where it is, but it wants to go higher. I can feel it."

"Then don't. Actually, Hope, I really thhh-think you should just tuh-take it off."

"Maybe we should go higher."

Suni stared at her. "Hope, tuh-tuh-ttt-take it off. You don't know what it does."

"So let's see if we can get a better idea. I don't have to do what it wants."

"What *it* www-wants? Hope, what did the box say about it?"

"Well, I—"

The Anxietoscope shot upward, yanking Hope after it—tearing at shoulder muscles, pulling at joints. Suni flinched as all four fingers and thumb shot into his head, toppling him backward, and Hope—her fingers still locked inside his skull—was drawn up over him, face shoved to the musky cloth of his T-shirt where the thin muscles of his stomach spasmed against her cheek. Dresser and candles crashed sideways in her vision.

This sense of Nothingness washing over her was not unfamiliar. This had happened to her before, not so long ago. The numb state of being trapped within the meat of your body while the world outside collapsed; being dimly aware of your inability to do anything but stare out the windows of your eyes and watch it all happen.

Her hand was in Suni's head, silver fingers buried up to the second knuckle. She knew death; she had been here, too.

Her hand was electric and pulsing. It was like she was thirstier than she had ever been for something she never knew she needed, and the 'scope was taking care of that need. She found she couldn't stop herself, and the 'scope preferred it that way.

Upstairs a door slammed. Hope heard a woman yelling in a language she recognized as Japanese. Her arm relaxed and went slack, fingers trailing down Suni's face until the silver hand rested over him like a funeral mask. Fast footsteps on the inside stairs, then a pounding at the door. Hope rolled off Suni, onto her back, and could see the sliding wooden door shaking as someone thumped it over and over again. A high chattering voice demanding something she couldn't understand.

And then, as if she had imagined everything, Suni was standing up, hair tangled and loosened from the black band that held it back, strands sticking up at odd angles like a diffuse halo, walking for the door.

Distant and disassociated, Hope was turning more important things over in her mind. She took a moment to roll off and behind the bed. Lying in the darkness against the wall, she found herself alone and examined what she had harvested from the stuff of her friend's soul.

She woke to sunlight filtered in slits through the bamboo blinds, burning red through her eyelids. She was lying on the spare bed, tangled in a stale sheet. In that waking instant she remembered everything. Suni wasn't there, and the sliding door leading to the internal stairs, and the yard beyond them, was open. She was no longer wearing the 'scope.

She got up and quickly walked to the backyard, refilled with the adrenaline of the night before. She'd seen her fingers slide bloodlessly in through Suni's forehead and face. But he'd gotten up, hadn't he? Someone had been banging at the door. Where was the 'scope? She had had horrible dreams. By her watch it was ten in the morning. She'd missed school.

The backyard was a flowering patch of deep green, a sloping stretch that led to the shallow high-grassed gully behind the house. A stand of banana trees was off to the right, a tall pine towering just next to them. The smells of damp earth and growing things. Suni was sitting in the middle of it all, a mug of coffee in his hand and his hair left loose. She knelt beside him and took his face in her hands. "Are you okay?" He was unblemished—no cuts, no wounds. Nothing. Not so much as a bruise. "Tell me you're okay, Suni."

He nodded, gently taking her hands away. "I'm fine."

"I'm so sorry. I didn't know it'd do that," she said weakly.

"It's okay." A hidden bird somewhere down in the gully whip-whipped a high sonic that didn't echo as it shot out of the gully.

She couldn't take her eyes from his face. Something had to be wrong. He couldn't be sitting there calm as could be. That in itself had to be a symptom of what she'd done. Her hand had gone in through his face for Christ's sake. You don't just wake up and drink coffee after something like that. You don't . . .

Suni looked concerned. He reached for her hand.

"Hey," she said, taking her hand away before he could touch it, pinching the bridge of her nose, rubbing the sleep away. She tasted like glue, felt like shit. "Guess we're not going to school today, huh?" And sounded like a man. She needed coffee.

"I took the 'scope off you," Suni said, looking back toward the gully. "Put it back in the box. Seemed safer that way. I was getting worried about you, though. You were out cold."

Hope remembered the dreams she had woken from: dreams detailing how the only reason Suni had his own part of the house was because his mother wanted to forget he was there. The way he had told her his aspirations over dinner at the age of seven, and she had laughed a vicious laugh. The way, to this day, she still hit him with things when she was angry, drove him downstairs. The way she left for work, managing some bush-league air service or something, be-

fore he left for school, and returned around dusk; how they hardly
ever saw each other. The way years of frustration fueled his art, the
way it would make him a vicious lover if given the chance, the way
he unconsciously faced off against every newcomer as an enemy, the
way he was so tense yet didn't realize it (but, Hope now realized, not
as tense as she), the way the constant reliving of years-old humilia-
tions led him to grind his teeth in his sleep and fueled hot, red day-
dreams.

It was a repeat glimpse of the lumbering self-loathing the 'scope
had found inside Suni's head, of things she never knew until they had
run from his head into hers. And there they remained, compartmen-
talized, squared away, and under observation. A retaste of his biggest,
bitterest fruit.

"Don't look so concerned." He smiled. "I feel so good."

Sunlit leaves and fresh air. Pollen and birdsong.

Hope watched Suni sip his coffee, peacefully, and wondered who
Suni was. Who had he been and who he might be now.

While inside her head his voices raged.

Hope walked home from Suni's around two, sunshine on her face
and breeze through her hair. Her mother worked days so going home
now wouldn't be a big deal. Between her working part-time and
Hope's being at school, Hope's mother had to accept that there
would be times when Walter would be left alone. He'd lived almost
twenty years comatose with relatively little incident, barring one
close call with what might have been pneumonia, so it wasn't like either of them really believed Walter was going to be kicking off any-
time soon.

Hope unlocked the front door and walked in, dropping her bag
onto the wall hook the way she'd done all her life, even at the old
house. Once she'd squirted some nutrient down Wally's tube and
gone over him with a damp cloth she'd make a cup of coffee, lie on
her bed, listen to a few CDs, and watch the sky through her window.

The house was empty. As she walked into the kitchen, she saw the note. A foolscap page written in green pen, from her mother, waiting on the table.

No accusations of Satanism this time, no outrage at Hope's latest piercing or haircut undertaken without consent. No threats about burning Hope's journals. No pleading for reason. This time was a straight edict: Hope was grounded. Indefinitely.

Just before sunrise this morning, someone had turned up on the doorstep. Someone tall, and thin, and pale, and worn looking. Someone dressed in a long black coat. He had asked for Hope by name, and when Hope's mother, no doubt half sheltering behind the open door, had told this weirdo that she wasn't home, he had nodded and left without a word.

Hope's mother explained, in green scrawl, that Hope was obviously going bad and that this would not continue. Hence the grounding. Where did she spend last night? Was she doing drugs? Was this decrepit-looking degenerate her dealer? How dare she just sneak out in the middle of the night? She was to watch Walter until she got home.

Like he was going anywhere. One little blockage in his breathing tube and it'd all be over. God, how often had she chewed on that.

Hope supposed it was only a matter of time before her whole family-thing just collapsed.

When he was still around, her father used to come home, ragged looking and sweaty, say nothing, and shamble to the shower. Then he'd turn on the TV in the bedroom and she wouldn't see him again until the following afternoon. It was pretty much the same with her mother now. Sometimes Hope would see her just before she left for a morning shift. Even back then she knew her family was never going to last.

It had come too far for anything else.

She used to go to a private school. It was her parents' idea. But they couldn't afford it, not with both of them working two jobs to keep Walter breathing. Which was why she'd transferred to State High.

Hope had no idea what her mother was raving about this time, but one thing was certain: she wasn't staying here tonight. She packed a few unread books, three CDs, and some fresh clothes into her backpack and thought about calling Kristian. He'd be glad to see her, but wouldn't be able to put her up. Suni would. But she couldn't go back, not yet. She needed someone to hold her.

At the front door she looked to the stairs, and Walter's room at the top. Screw it. Her mother could wash him for once. She slung her pack, heavy with the combined weight of her things and the silver box, and immediately thought of what Suni had said about the owner of the 'scope, and what if they came looking for it.

She went to Kristian's, just for a little while.

Walter stood in the yard, shaded from the moon by the expanse of a drooping tree, listening. Hope had returned to Suni's house just before nightfall.

"I'm not letting you in." Walter's posture was shifting. His eyes were darkening. A harsh sound was being born somewhere inside him. In the hedgerow between the yard and the street, crickets sang.

"You know I could take you," Henry said, reasonably. "You're not what you used to be. People her age don't have monsters and you've got no claim over her anymore."

Walter dropped forward, back hunched skyward. Foot-long moonlight claws shot from expanding hands. The insect-song was like a thousand people clicking fingers, each to their own tune.

Henry shifted stance. "I took care of you, dammit."

Walter's head snapped up, elongated and lupine. A thick string of drool dangled from one hitched black lip. *"Didn't you ever."*

Henry remained still. Then, gently, persistently: "You got no claim on her. You missed your chance, Wally."

Silence. Crickets.

Walter launched himself from the top step.

FIFTEEN

BETTER

*N*OT FOR THE FIRST TIME HOPE WAS HAPPY SHE HAD never given Suni's address or phone number to her mother. Going to Suni's was the same as going to the moon as far as being tracked down was concerned. It was a little after dark when she had climbed back through his window.

Suni hadn't touched his sketch of the clockwork box. He spoke and listened more intently as she told him about the note.

Now they had adopted their usual positions—Hope on the floor, back against the spare bed, and Suni on the floor, back against his own. Oolric was dozing on the sofa bed.

"Face it," Suni was saying. "She's bent. After all you've been through who can blame her? By rights you should be a prize nutbag yourself."

"Ow," she said, flatly.

Suni shifted, sitting up with his legs folded under him. One corner of his drawing crinkled under his knee. "I'm sorry," he said. He leaned forward and looked her in the eye. "But, well, in light of all you've been through . . ."

A pit opened up in her stomach. "Can we not talk about it,

please?" Faces, smells, a string of associations appeared in her mind, dragging her back two years. She breathed deep and made it go away. She was a tiger. "You're crushing your drawing."

"Oh." He shifted his weight, freed the paper, and laid it on the bed. Suni weighed his thoughts, and then said, "I mean . . . sure she's messed up right now, but so are you. Your matching set of emotional baggage comes from the same place." His hands found hers. They were warm against her own, his artist's hands. "She shouldn't be harassing you, you're going through this together." It was only now Hope realized how long it had been since she had actually touched Suni. They had reached a point in their post-relationship friendship where they could now hug good-bye, but they never actually *touched*. Suni was always too bent out of shape over the breakup, and Hope didn't want to reopen all that. They had a good thing going as friends. So why was her heart double-timing? Because his hand in hers threatened that friendship, she told herself.

"It's not as simple as telling her that, Suni."

She didn't like talking about her mother, either. There was too much associated with it, it led in directions she had carefully steered herself away from, learned from experience that it led to a dark place two years past, a dark place with teeth and eyes and knives . . .

"It should be. She's your mother." He reached out, let his knuckles graze slowly down her cheek.

She pulled her bottom lip from between her teeth. "You know what I said yesterday, about strong feelings?"

Suni nodded.

"Have you ever reached inside, found the switch for whatever you're feeling, and turned it off?"

Suni was about to say something, then stopped. "I think I have," he said, finally.

"And found that, sometimes, you can never turn it back on again?"

"Yes."

She moved her fingers, feeling his. Oolric was up on his hind legs, staring out the window.

She thought of the Anxietoscope resting in her bag and wondered if she should tell Suni exactly what had happened last night.

"The fact is," she said, changing the subject, "that someone turned up this morning asking for me." Her fingers flexed a little within his, savoring the feel of his skin, wondering if it was something she could become used to again.

"Ex-boyfriend?"

"What ex-boyfriend? You're it. Well, barring that Jeff guy from the year before last."

His hand tightened a little in hers. "You know, you'd be fending guys off with a flamethrower if you just gave yourself half a chance."

She swallowed, still looking at their twined hands. "You said I should be a nutbag." Faces, smells, associations . . . dragging her back. She fended them off. She thought of something else, something she liked, something white . . .

"Hope . . . ," Suni said reasonably, his free hand moving to cover their locked pair.

Don't say it, don't say it, don't say it . . .

He said it.

"You killed your father." His hands tightened on hers. "That would be a very big deal for most people."

The world narrowed to a point between her eyes where scenes replayed, in a space small enough that only she could see. Hope closed her eyes and tried not to think. *It had been so easy.* She shut out the two-year-old howl she knew so well, felt it pressing against the thin wall of her will.

"You never saw anyone about it, after the hearing. Someone professional, I mean. I don't think you've really dealt with—"

"I'd like to go to sleep now," she said.

It had been so easy.

She was a tiger.

. . .

Henry had disappeared before Walter's claws could find his throat. Instead Walter had connected with the tree—a tree as unyielding as the cord he'd spent years trying to pull from his own life-support system—and two of the claws had snapped off at the root. He could affect nothing. He could beat himself to death against the real world long before his actions would influence it.

Regret had been a constant companion for years. Walter could have spoken to his sister when she was a child, warned her, protected her, but he hadn't. Walter had allowed himself to be seduced, and now it was too late.

From somewhere nearby, somewhere unseen, Henry said, "There's a lot of common ground between me and that girl . . ." But Walter wasn't listening. "We both killed to get away from what we were. She's hurting in a way I know . . ." Walter hadn't even been able to save her from their own father. "I'll give you time for your good-byes, but I've got to come for her eventually."

"I know why you picked us," Walter said to him. The pain in his hand was blinding, but he'd had worse. "I touched the Anxietoscope, Henry."

The doctor was gone. A simple cessation of presence.

So Walter sat against the tree, a little boy clutching his bleeding fingers, and smiled.

She spent the night on Suni's spare bed, swept through oily black dreams of knives, hands, of her father's face close to her own.

Hands.

She dreamed herself onto the back of her white tiger, dreamed herself much smaller, dreamed herself riding it out of the blackness.

When she woke it was instantaneous, as if she'd never slept. The covers were scattered, her Gunsmith Cats T-shirt riding almost too high. Suni was crouched by the bed. She pulled the shirt down, remembering dreams of

Hands.

"Time for school." He smiled.

Her first thoughts were of Kristian. Of needing to find him and hide inside him for a while.

She checked her copy of his timetable and intercepted him as he stepped out of first-period English. They stepped around a corner, nestled into the corner of a brick wall and concrete pillar, and she told him that her mother was never letting her out again. His hands were hard around her, his lips wet. She didn't feel like it but didn't refuse. She walked him to second-period geography, stopping to use the fountain and wash the sourness from her mouth. It was at moments like these she felt uncomfortably like her mother, being with the wrong person for the wrong reasons.

Suni was walking toward them, down the sunlit hallway. Her stomach clenched, the way it did every time Suni saw her with Kristian. Then, in a moment of inspired antagonism, Kristian took Hope and kissed her neck, lips cold from the fountain, leaving a wet patch just to the left of her larynx. Hope tried not to look at Suni. Eye contact would be a knife.

With the half-lidded expression of the confident Casanova, Kristian bade Suni a sidelong "Hey, champ."

Suni stopped, looked straight at Kristian, and said:

"She hates sloppy kissers."

Hope stopped halfway through wiping a discreet hand over her neck as Kristian punched Suni full in the face.

She grabbed his arm, held it back, said, "Stop it!"

Kristian turned on her then, the new threat. "What?"

Suni took his cracked glasses off and pocketed them as a small rivulet of dark blood began to slowly trickle from one nostril. He turned to Hope.

Kristian wrenched free of her grip and hit Suni again, sending him stumbling back three steps.

"*Stop it!*" And before she could think about it, Hope drove her foot into the back of Kristian's knee, buckling it from under him. It didn't do much but tip his center of balance for a second. He spun on her, teeth clenched, fist still balled, and stopped himself.

Hope recognized that. Behind her eyes she ran through the catalog of pointed objects she had on her: pen, hairclip, keys . . .

Suni stood and smoothed back his hair. A smear of blood kept it there, before a wing broke loose and fell over one eye.

Kristian turned back and drove one fist up beneath Suni's rib cage, lifted him off the floor and dropped him, winded, gasping, puking air.

Both of Hope's hands clamped onto his arm, tried to turn him around, but Kristian was on a roll and thudded a kick into Suni's ribs, keeling him over. "*Stop it!*" Then he turned, took Hope by the arm, and walked quickly away before a teacher came.

On the hallway floor Suni was trying to rise to his feet, one arm wrapped across his gut. The best he could manage was getting to one knee. "Hey . . . ," he rasped. "Hey . . ." He took a breath. "Teeth."

Kristian turned, his expression hard.

"She likes them dragged up the line of her throat. Not hard enough to bruise but enough to feel dangerous."

Kristian let Hope go and came at Suni at a dead run, one meaty hand clutching for Suni's throat. Suni stabbed him with a small shard of his shattered glasses. Not a big piece, just enough to stain Kristian's white shirt with a little pink blood. Kristian shrieked, clutching at himself, almost tripping over Suni.

Suni gripped both hands together . . .

"Hey . . ."

. . . rose quickly . . .

". . . champ."

. . . and swung upward, connecting hard with the underside of Kristian's jaw. There was a clack as teeth smashed together, and a thin squirt of blood as they nipped his tongue. Kristian swung out wildly, collecting Suni across the side of the head with a flailed forearm.

Then Suni got what might have been a lucky shot just below Kristian's heart. Jammed a fast thumb right in there and blew the air completely out of Kristian's lungs. Sent him to the floor, a light spot of blood on his shirt where the glass had cut him.

In the moments afterward, someone from the anonymous crowd slapped Suni on the back, stumbling him forward a step. He didn't seem to notice, holding his stomach as he was.

Hope could only stare, fixated by Suni, like a child locked in the gun sights of his eyes. He looked like a zombie having second thoughts about what it was doing.

One hand around his stomach, breathing low and dry, he crept away.

Once Kristian had been taken to sick bay and the vice principal had begun demanding answers, Hope had slipped away and caught Suni just as he was walking out of school.

"Hey," she said. He stopped in the street, looking over his shoulder. He wasn't looking too good. From the frozen expression on his face breathing must be hurting. They crossed the street, standing out front of a rack of old, pastel-colored houses for old, floral-print people. Behind an iron fence an old lady watered a brown garden of tortured, flowerless plants begging for a quick death while her toy-sized dog looked up as if to ask what the hell kind of sick game she thought she was playing.

"You finally did it," Hope said.

"I finally did."

"You feeling okay?"

"All things considered."

Hope found herself in one of the rare situations where she couldn't tell what he was feeling. Somehow she thought he'd be giddy and rambling after what just happened. There really was something missing inside him. "Doesn't look like he'll need stitches."

Suni nodded.

"The VP was looking for you. He didn't look too happy."

"I'm going home."

"Feel like getting something to eat first?"

They made their way to the Esplanade. Sitting under some prehistoric tree with a massive trunk that looked like the fossilized sinew of some long-dead Titan, they ate a couple of burgers and worked a few things out. Hope was checking her face in the mirror of a cracked Hello Kitty compact. "I spend a fortune on that natural eyeliner," she was saying. "That kohl stuff, and it just smudges everywhere. Makes me look like a strung-out drag queen." A gust of wind picked up, blowing in off the brown sea, smelling of mud and salt. "It was the 'scope, wasn't it," she said, snapping the compact shut, putting it back in her bag. "Made you do that."

"This morning I told my mother I wasn't going to college," Suni said around a mouthful of burger. "She was angry, which doesn't make sense because she never wanted me to go in the first place. She tried to hit me with a sawn-off curtain rod. I took it from her." His eyes were clear. "The 'scope didn't make me do anything," he said. "What happened today, with Kristian, was something I wanted to do. I wasn't afraid. Of anything."

Hope didn't know where to start, so she seized on the least complex issue.

"Why are you ditching art school? You've been making art all your life. It's all you've ever wanted."

Suni shrugged, popped the last of his burger into his mouth, and cracked open the Coke.

The Esplanade was a strip of greenery that ended in a four-foot drop to brown water, reinforced with century-old bluestone blocks. There were concrete steps that led into the water at regular intervals—narrow, grimy, unsafe-looking things—which made Hope think that maybe people moored boats here before they went and built all those piers just around the curve of the inlet. The ocean was right there in front of them, but no beach to speak of. It was a bay, technically, but so big you didn't think of it as that. Swamp was out on the fringes. Deep, sucking mud and miles of skinny trees with roots all over the place, just near the airport. Good place for crabs, apparently. A fat rat scuttled across the top of the wall on thin paws, drooping belly held above the ground. There were picnic tables all over the place, and garbage bins. They brought the rats out, but usually at night.

"What happened with Kristian . . . you didn't do that to get me back, did you?"

"No. Kristian can have you."

"So . . ." Why did it hurt to hear him say that? "I don't get it."

"Because I could. And I feel much better."

Hope busied herself opening her can. She felt something slipping away from her. She couldn't lose the feeling that somehow she had made a very serious mistake. "You can finish your folio now."

"Maybe. Maybe I will do college, I don't know. Kinda figured I'd celebrate first. See how I feel."

"How?"

"No idea. We could go up the top of that mountain behind my place and get drunk."

Hope shrugged her lip. "Nah."

"Stoned?"

Shook her head. "Nah."

"Anything?"

"Can I ask you a dumb question?"

Suni hesitated. "Sure." Then smiled. "Sure, shoot."

"What do you care about? Right now."

"Right now?"

"Uh-huh."

Suni took a thoughtful breath. "Fun." He looked at her, decided. "Fun is what I care about. I want to have fun."

"And what's fun? Right now."

Suni looked around, exasperated. "I dunno. Getting drunk, exposing our souls. Running for a long time just to feel our lungs get hot. Sex."

Hope looked at him.

"We never really did it," he said. "I never even asked what your stand on it is, I was so afraid of you thinking badly of me."

Hope was feeling something building inside. Like small tremors. Like the onset of an earthquake that was about to transfer to her hands. "What do you mean?"

"Well, I know there was that Jeff guy . . ."

"That only happened once. You didn't tell anyone, did you?"

Suni shook his head. "No, no. I'm just wondering what you think of it."

"Well, it wasn't that great."

"I mean in general."

"What do you think of it?"

His eyes looked out at the sluggish brown ocean. A massive tanker was out there, looking completely unreal, like a cardboard cutout propped up at sea. "It's fun. It's a lot of fun for two people who can handle it. And it should be. People make too big a deal out of it." He paused. "I thought maybe you felt badly about the whole idea of it. After your dad, I mean . . ."

"My dad never touched me," she said. "Not like that." *But he would have, then. If I hadn't stopped him. If he hadn't bled out on the kitchen floor.*

She thought about the movie she saw last week, the smell of the ocean air. Got it together. Got on with the conversation.

"And you never felt differently? That it might mean something a little deeper?" she asked.

"Well, I felt that way about you. But not anymore."

"Why not?"

"I don't want to dive right back into something like that."

"But if you did, do you think you'd feel that way again?"

He sucked on his lower lip, then: "I'm having trouble seeing myself getting serious over anyone. For a long time at least."

Hope was watching her hands tear idly at the grass. She wasn't getting the answers she was hoping for. "Suni . . ."

"Yeah?"

"What happens if you never feel anything that powerful ever again?"

Suni leaned back, looked at the brown ocean. "You know."

She nodded. "Strong feelings aren't all they're cracked up to be."

"Bingo."

Suni chewed thoughtfully on his bottom lip, hands held loosely around his raised knees. "Maybe I'll go see my dad," he thought out loud. "Go camping the way we used to. Haven't seen him in ages. He's on the other side of the country now, but I could do it."

She kept tearing at the grass. "Suni."

"Yeah?"

"I'm sorry I used it on you. I'm sorry."

"Don't be." Suni went quiet for a moment, and then: "You know, when I was little, someone offered to give me wings? Not make-believe wings, not toy wings, but real ones. I told him no. I told him I wanted to go home. To my *mother*." He laughed drily. "Should have taken him up on it. Could have flown around the world." Sluggish brown waves slapped feebly at the corroding bluestone wall. "Hey . . ."

"Yes?"

"You really kept those old newspaper reports about me?"

She nodded. "They're in my photo album."

"Do you remember what they said?"

She shrugged, tearing at the grass, and smiled. "Just that your mother woke up the next morning and you were in Vancouver." She laughed. Suni laughed, too, then stopped.

"Do you know how long it takes to get to Vancouver, including stopovers and aircraft changes?"

"No."

"Eighteen hours fifty minutes," he said.

A tanker's horn sounded, distant and displaced. Hope sensed

some kind of association forming between her possession of the 'scope and what Suni had just said. It was a horrible feeling.

"There's something I've been meaning to tell you," he said.

Hope felt cold. She lay on her bed, eyes to the ceiling, the 'scope by her side, sheathing her downturned right hand. The subtle texturing of the cream-colored ceiling registered on her retinas, but that wasn't what she was seeing. Hope wasn't really seeing anything, not in the conventional sense. Hope was sorting through the infections pulled from the very stuff that had made Suni who he was—who he had been.

She saw flashes of memory, identifiable in the wake of what Suni had told her. The 'scope held his fears, and imprinted on those fears were the watermarks of what had formed them: here he was afraid of the future, and she felt claustrophobic in the presence of others; here he was afraid of going on, and she heard his mother's short, neat laughter; here he was afraid for his life, and she remembered the piles of bodies and the gaunt man at the door; here he was afraid of never returning home, and here, later, he was deeply afraid of telling the truth and losing Hope forever, and she saw the face of her brother as a child. A face he could never have known.

Suni now walked the world minus the one fear that had fired the furnace that cast him, fused him into the person that he was. The thing that pushed him to be who he had been.

Suni's fear, the thing that colored his nightmares and chose the cast of lovers and authority figures that populated them, was of himself. The fear that he wasn't good enough. That there was something vitally wrong with him. He had lived afraid of the opinions of others. He sought confirmation of his worth there, and if Suni did not find it in the words of others then it was writ in stone, it was scripture: Suni Was Nothing.

It was a catalog of demons she held in her silver hand—Suni's bedevilments. She could let them go at any time, set them free and turn them to nothing—watch them die without a host, forever locked outside Suni's cooling, calming mind.

She had never seen him so diffident, so relaxed, so unburdened. He was a man unshackled. No self-made horrors snapped at his heels. No doubts pushed him forward or held him back. He moved in his own time, ageless and free.

She could have let them go, but she didn't.

The Anxietoscope hovered before her own forehead, fingers delicately pleading for purchase, silently longing to take a similar weight from her, urging her, ordering her, to allow it. It would be so easy. As easy as anything. Anything she had ever done. And then she would be free, lightened, happy. It wanted her burden as badly as it had wanted Suni's.

Distantly, somewhere far removed from where she floated, the front door opened and her mother shouted her name.

Her mother.

In that moment the Anxietoscope almost got what it asked for.

SIXTEEN

ENCOUNTERS

*I*T HAD BEEN HOT CONFLICT FOLLOWED BY A COLD DINNER, quickly forgotten in the frenzy of accusation and denial.

It never used to be like this, before her father had died. Hope's mother had been sane then, or in control at the very least. No screaming at every shadow-of-a-shadow-of-a-problem that surfaced in their lives. Living with her mother now was like wrestling a maniac. You had to keep them calm, pin them down, stop them doing something they'd regret—but you invariably took the blows trying. And sometimes you didn't pin them down at all, you just made them madder. Sometimes there was simply no point in trying.

Her mother had just grounded her for the rest of the year—six months as a prisoner of this particular nuthouse. Suni and Kristian didn't know how bad it got, and it was better that way. They had their own problems—everyone does—and Hope didn't want her family crap to make knowing her a chore.

Of course, there may not even *be* a friendship anymore. For the rest of the year it was to school and back, dinner, homework, and bed.

Hope had taken it all with good grace until her mother stated her intention to bar Hope's windows to prevent any more midnight escapes. Maybe losing Kristian wouldn't be so bad, but losing Suni was an amputation.

She walked out of her bedroom, down the hall, and into Walter's room. Hope's mother was asleep, collapsed in on herself, chin on her chest, in the chair by Walter's bed. A wrinkled magazine was sprawled across her lap, and a plastic tumbler by her bare feet. Hope had learned as a child that vodka combined with her meds usually kept her under till morning. Their mother got a discount on her own meds on account of how much other stuff they bought for Wally: high-caloric mix—stuff he'd be able to digest for maximum nutrition without taxing him too much. Regular food didn't have enough calories per quantum and produced too much residue—though more often than not money was too tight to afford $250 a week for that, so they had to slip Wally regular food and hope he did okay with it. So far there had been no problems, and Hope thought she was beginning to understand why. He was sticking around deliberately. He was a twenty-one-year-old man, shrunken below the waist until he looked something like a twisted corpse she'd seen on TV—footage from a famine zone. His eyes hadn't seen anything since he went to bed over seventeen years ago. But, she knew now, he hadn't been sleeping.

"Hey," she said, a little self-conscious. "It's me." She wondered if he was here.

"Hello," Walter said, sitting on the window ledge.

Hope walked over and took the body's hand. "I'm sorry," she said. Even if he wasn't here, it felt right saying it. She stroked his face, grazing a knuckle down one sunken cheek.

"It's okay," he said, looking at his hands.

"I never knew." She wondered how this was all going to play out. Part of her was growing afraid Walter may have moved on, after so many years of going unheard. She supposed if he was here now, he'd find some way of letting her know. Isn't that what ghosts did?

"Maybe I should have stayed, taken over from him . . . better me than you." He got off the sill, looked up at his little sister, and touched her sleeve, fingers slipping and chafing on the diamond-hard fabric. "You know I'm here," he said. "Just look at me and I'll tell you everything. Just look . . ." His sister turned, and the careless movement tossed Walter across the room, slamming him against the wall and onto the rigid fronds of the potted fern. The leaves and stalks stabbed at him as he twisted and rolled off it, clutching himself.

Hope stopped in the doorway, and turned back. She looked at the body. "G'night, Wally."

"Hope . . ."

She closed the door on him. Nothing he did was making any difference.

Walter let himself lie down on the prickling, unrelenting carpet that felt like glass dust against his arms and legs, curled into a ball, and cried. It didn't entirely sound like a little boy.

So tired of being alone.

Someone said his name. He opened his eyes, looked across the room to the shadow by the open window; the window that looked out on fairyland. Someone said his name again, in a soft caramel voice.

"You sound like puppies," the voice said.

Walter swallowed and sat up.

"I don't want you to cry."

Walter blinked. He couldn't see into the shadow, and that wasn't right. It wasn't like a shadow at all. It was like one of the portals the Nabbers used.

He could hear music. Something cheap and tinkling, like a music box. The sound of it filled the room, and a figure emerged from the shadow in shades of black and bronze. "It's me."

Years ago, before the doctor had found her, Nimble had been a ballerina.

The weight of the box filled the pack, resting comfortably and flat against Hope's back as she slipped out the window and onto the architrave of the window below, and dropped down into the flower bed, probably for the last time. She loved this little ritual. Bars on her nighttime doorway were closing off something integral to the person she had become since moving here two years ago. Aside from the fact that her mother's decision robbed her life of a little mystery and glamour, it took away something that was truly her *own*. Though she was seventeen, living at home and still dependent, in stepping through that window she became her own person, a nation beholden to none. She supposed that that was what she was losing most—her self.

A black figure, easily six feet and rake-thin, stood waiting for her in the middle of the street.

He began walking forward, the bootclick on the blacktop accompanied by an even fainter, more delicate, tinkling. It was a gentle, almost crystalline sound. Beneath that sound chimed a faint harmonic, high notes sounding so very faint, like a distant choir.

"*Missy . . . ,*" the man said, in a voice soft and bass.

She swallowed hard. She didn't know what he was, but he sure as shit wasn't a drug dealer. His words whispered to her ear from thirty yards away: "*You have something of mine . . .*"

She knew who it was immediately. Without a shadow of a doubt she knew exactly who it was. It made sense. It all made sense. Things like that don't go unpunished.

Running blindly, without thinking, bolting diagonally across the yard and onto the sidewalk, thinking the whole time, I could go inside I could go inside . . . But what was the point? What if he came in anyway? What if he hurt her mother? What if . . .

What if she looked under that hat and her father stared back? What if she looked under the coat and the knife was still there, wedged under the sternum in a wound gone black and cold?

She wanted to run and run and not spend her entire life backward-glancing through the bloody window of her diary . . .

"*Whatever you think you're gonna do with that thing . . .* ," he whispered to her. "*It's gonna go bad on you.*"

Just run . . . just run . . .

Walter saw Nimble's face first. She looked as all little girls imagine a ballerina to look: a dancing princess who never dies. A pale face with dark hair tied neatly back, a delicate countenance twice as beautiful for the openness of it. Deep, dark, honest eyes and a sweet red mouth. The face of naïve childhood love.

The dull bronze of her shoulders came next, as if the shadow that contained her were a dropping veil. The intricate, hollow lattice of her fragile-looking arms were attached to the ornate, skeletal-feminine cage of her torso, atop which rested her pretty head. The tangled wrought bronze of the torso-cage contained her spine and the tumbling, flickering thing from which the music came. Her thin, pseudo-mechanical arms were held delicately from her sides, a picture of poise. The ruffle of her tutu was a single piece of jagged, corrugated bronze—a wrinkled disk—inserted at her waist. Her legs, as hollow and florid as the rest of her, tapered to bronze slipper-feet that moved on perpetual pointe. As long as she remained in shadow, her legs seemed sheathed in darkness and embroidered in brass.

Walter had known what the doctor had done to her, but he had never seen it. He wiped his eye with the back of his hand, and it came away damp. He said, "Tub was asking about you."

"Tub?" She tilted her head, a portrait of curiosity.

Nimble and Tub had loved each other so massively that Walter sometimes thought they'd die, their bodies unable to contain it. "You're the only friend I've ever had," she said, and maybe she thought this was true. Henry had changed so much of who she used to be. Perhaps she thought it true of everyone she visited. After all, that's what she had been remade for: to befriend people. How better to win someone over than for them to be the only friend Nimble ever had?

Walter stood up. "I have to go."

"Oh, Walter . . ." She tippy-toed toward him, arms levitating at her sides, head hovering so unnaturally atop that hollow body. "Don't go . . ." Her deep brown eyes glistened like a leaving lover's. "Please don't go."

Walter wondered if anything of who she had once been remained inside her perfect head.

"What's the last thing you remember?" he asked.

"I remember," she said, "your wanting to go home." And she smiled, pleased with the accuracy of her answer. Her metal arms shushed and clicked delicately as they opened down to him, palms up, seeking his. "I remember your loneliness."

"You found me that first time I ran away from the doctor, you remember?"

"I remember." Her fingers moved a little, pleading quietly for his hands.

"Do you remember Dorian?"

"Dorian was a thief," she said, simply. "Dance with me."

"But he made you, and Tub, and the others. You loved him."

"Dorian stole from . . . people."

Walter shook his head. "The instruments never belonged to a person. They were the Angel's, and they used to be an angel themselves." He looked up at her, searching for that glitter inside. "Dorian made you to be a companion for his daughter, you remember?"

"No."

"Millicent. You were with her until the end."

"Until the end."

There. "You were her best friend, and she's gone. But he still waits for you."

"Then dance with me, because Hope does not wait for you."

"This is different."

"Then dance with me because I need you."

Walter shook his head. "You don't need me. And you won't stop me from protecting my sister."

She moved her hands to his face, cradling it. They felt cold and skeletal against his skin. "I already have."

He didn't pay attention to the position of her thumbs until it was too late.

"You sound like puppies."

He let Hope go. Watched the night swallow her. A match flared off his dry-skinned chin with the flick of a gloved hand. Head tilted he leaned his craggy face into the glow, a man leaning into a kiss, and lit the thin cigarillo jutting from the narrow, lipless line of his mouth. Puffed once, blew out. A habit he hadn't been able to shake off in close to two hundred years. The match died out as he fanned it back and forth. It was a particularly warm night.

He could wait.

He looked up to Wally's window and, sadly, wondered if Nimble was done.

He was there. Walter was a shuddering shadow in the corner, clutching his face, Nimble advancing on him, reaching for him with bloodied metal hands.

"Let him go," Henry said, finding himself deviating from the plan.

"But I'm not finished," she complained.

"Let him go."

Walter cast his sightless face up at the sound of Henry's voice, at this turn of events, seized the opportunity, and vanished into the shadows.

"He tried to hurt me," Nimble said. "Look."

The bronze embroidery of her torso-cage bore three wide gashes.

"He didn't try too hard."

When Hope got to Suni's, the house was quiet and the windows dark. No light in the whole place. She pressed her face to the glass between cupped hands and all she saw was the unmade bed, a few strewn-about clothes, and Oolric staring back at her from the middle of the room. Suni was gone.

She turned around and walked back home, because she had nowhere else to go, the pack on her back feeling twice as heavy.

SEVENTEEN

WALLY

SUNI LIVED AT THE BASE OF A LARGE HILL, ATOP WHICH was a rock quarry. Some nights, when he really wanted to be alone, he would climb out the window and walk through empty lamplit streets, past green lawns and fragrant trees. He'd jump the padlocked boom gate that stood in the thin, dark space between two regal-looking homes—an obstacle ineffectual against anything on two legs—and follow the twin runnels of the truck track up to the quarry. Grass, tall and colorless, stood between the dry brown trenches dug by the daily armies of rolling tires. It rasped uncomfortably against exposed skin and left seeds in any material it touched, so Suni habitually kept his feet to the brown gutters of the tracks on the nights he walked up here. Mosquitoes liked it up here, too. They buzzed his head, whining and spanging close to his ear. The trilling of frogs and toads rose from the taller grass that sprouted beside the wide track, taller than he was, and the sky lay dead clear between drifting archipelagoes of sodium-orange cloud, colored by the light of the city below. On the watery black horizon, marker buoys blinked slowly, endlessly, red and white and blue, while tall concrete pillars topped with bright spots of white light marked the safe corridor between submerged obstructions, out to deeper water less brown than what it was closer to shore.

Suni claimed his usual perch on a large boulder at the lip of the quarry, looking down the hillside and out over the city, watching the black and blinking horizon. On the Esplanade the rats would be out, perched on picnic tables, burrowing through bins overflowing with the bright dross and sodden crud from the strip of primary-colored franchise eateries that ran parallel to it. Big rats.

At this altitude there was a good breeze, and it felt vital and alive against his face. Something massive and hairy grabbed his face in one taloned paw and yanked him around. Suni stared at the thing, his eyes an inch from its hitch-lipped snout, his mouth and nostrils thick with the taste of its shag and the smell of its milk breath. It dragged Suni off the boulder, pulled him to his feet, and lifted him close so that all Suni saw were the two raw sockets where Walter once had eyes.

Daytime heat emanated from the road. The weight of the box pulled on Hope's shoulders, making her uncomfortably aware that this is what the dark man would be coming for. She imagined the box radiating a heat of its own, a hot beacon that called to the man—the same man who asked for her at home, and who stood waiting outside her house as she left tonight.

The neighborhood was quiet, just like every night past ten. The time she usually loved—because it made her the sole occupant of a quiet and moodily lit world—had been turned against her. The night and the quiet isolated her now, separated her from the herd. She felt the presence of a new occupant in that world now, one she couldn't see but one that could see *her*. Anyone else would have been torn between running home—because home was safe—or sleeping on the streets for fear of what might still be waiting *outside* that safe and familiar home. But home hadn't been safe, or familiar, for a long time.

"I'll save you the suspense."

Hope stopped.

"Your friend not there?"

She turned around, shoe rubber crunching loose gravel. He was a good six feet and thin enough to be dead, long black coat hanging like a drape. Sparkles within, like the glimmer of the 'scope. More of them. More tools. More instruments.

He was so fucking close.

The sheer weight of his presence . . . the way she felt some magnetic core within herself drawn to him . . . to the glimmering shards within his coat. She felt as the 'scope felt, wanting to be with the rest of them there, in the dark. It was an intimacy, a yearning as if this were the only thing she had ever wanted.

The word caught in her throat, choking her, making her want to be sick. It struggled out, a wounded word. "Daddy?"

He shook his head, slow.

She nodded, stiffly. "Just checking." Swallowed, thickly. "You're that guy . . . in Suni's painting." She needed to be with those other points of light more than she needed a home, or a family, or a life. If she had them she wouldn't need a life.

Wait.

Breath.

Tiger.

"He's getting sick for what you took away," the dark man said.

"Suni?"

It infiltrated her, this being's presence; strength fled her and thoughts never lingered, only flashed. She stood immobile and voiceless, drinking in every detail of the figure before her so that in the years to come she could tell herself this hadn't been a dream. If there were years to come.

"You want to hand it over?"

She wanted to reach out and take everything he had. As though from a faraway place, she heard herself say, "No." Her hands left her pockets, one of them sheathed in silver. The dark man sighed, and his coat tinkled ever so slightly. A pretty sound that promised horror. If the Anxietoscope was one such tool, what must the others be like? What might they unleash?

"You don't want to fight for it," he said. "You don't."

"Because you'd kill me . . ." Her voice came out toneless. "I guess?" Maybe that wouldn't be such a bad thing. No more dreams. No more living with the knowledge of what it was like to drive a knife into her father—the brief resistance of skin and rubbery organs. So easy. But then . . . no. There was more to life now. A reason to remain. The 'scope wanted to reach to its brothers and sisters.

"It's not something you want. Your friend's gonna die because of it."

"Suni told me about Walter. About you, about how he wound up in Vancouver. I know my brother gave me this. You can have it once I get him back."

Her silver hand itched.

"What you took from Suni doesn't have a hold over him anymore. He'll start finding other things don't have a hold, either. When that happens things'll start disappearing inside him. People'll become less real to him, and before too long he'll go crazy as a bug. Your friend'll drive himself into the ground trying to find something to make himself feel again. Sooner or later they all do, and they all come to the same idea—that the only thing that might wake them up, the only thing they haven't tried, is dying. If someone or something doesn't kill them first."

A snail of sweat inched its way down the ruckled furrow of Hope's spine.

"Give me my brother and it's yours."

She could smell roses in her neighbors' yard, lush and sweet.

"I can't do that," he said.

"Then we both go home disappointed."

There was a thing—clawed, silver thing—on her hand.

She wanted to—it wanted to—reach into her head and reef out everything that was in there.

The dark man began moving forward.

The hand shot up, claws out. "Back off," she stammered, blinking something from her eyes. Maybe she never would speak to Wally. Maybe she'd killed Suni, too . . .

"I got to take that back." He kept coming, faster-paced now.

She dropped the claw-hand and brought up her other to fend him off. He swept it aside with one gloved fist, and as he did the 'scope hand shot up and out, straight for the dark man's face, starving for whatever someone like that feared.

He blocked it with a smoothly countercycled forearm. A well-placed palm to the center of her chest sent Hope sprawling. The box punched painfully into her back. She yelped as she hit the gravel.

The execution of his defense concluded with his hands at his sides, coat swept back—starlight interior equally concealed and revealed. It was an automatic stance, and one he quickly relaxed from.

But she was on her back now, trapped awkwardly on her pack like an overturned tortoise, staring up at him.

His face was that of a young man grown impossibly old impossibly fast. Pale parchment skin sucked tight to the architecture of his skull, lips wasted to almost nothing, eyes lost in the shadows of sockets and hat. She felt a gentle magnetism in the 'scope, as if it found family in the things that hung, delicately chiming, within that black coat.

He had her now. She could roll, get to her feet and run, provided she got that far. But there was no point. He would take what he wanted, and Hope wondered if she would die. The song in the coat crescendoed—terrified, protesting—and the man hesitated. Stopped.

He was still looking down at her—a solid piece of shadow with an old and tragic face—when he slowly turned and walked away.

Inside his coat the little pieces of starlight sang as he went, a song of parting to the thing on her hand.

Walter had dragged Suni back home and Suni didn't like it, but as long as no one was watching to disbelieve it, there wasn't a thing he could do about it.

Wally would still see Suni occasionally, but had given up trying to coerce Suni into babbling the truth to Hope. The world had names for people who talked to things other people couldn't see, and Suni had enough problems without being locked up for his own good.

Wally had never physically threatened Suni into just telling Hope. Maybe that's where he drew the line, Suni didn't know.

When his mother appeared at the top of the steps and Wally's hold had gone insubstantial, Suni had dropped like a rock and his mother had accused him of being drunk.

He went and took a shower. Wally was standing outside the curtain, eyeless and insistent.

"I stopped doing favors for you a long time ago," Suni said, scrubbing his armpits.

"Look . . ."

"I lost my mother because of you, you know that?"

"Of course I know that, you never stop bringing it up. I'm sorry your mother is a superstitious woman, I'm sorry she thinks you're some kind of aberration, and I'm sorry you wound up in fucking Vancouver. Now get out of the shower."

"What happened to your eyes, anyway?"

"It doesn't matter."

"I already told Hope, you know. She knows."

"You didn't tell her much of anything, and certainly not enough to help her, and what you did say came about five years too late. I need to talk to her."

"She'll be fine."

"She will not be fine. Get downstairs or I'll break your hands."

Crouching in the middle of the empty street, Hope plucked the 'scope from her hand by taking the forefinger barb between opposite thumb and finger, and drawing the whole thing off like a silk glove. It contracted back to a single mercurial thimble, and she replaced it inside the box. The insinuating voice began as soon as her hands made contact with the silver surface of the box, and this time she listened.

Anxietoscope. To be used in the direct examination of a subject's fears. Investigative procedures supplement the fright evaluation of the subject, which is made from subject history and behavioral observation. The Anxietoscope allows core fears to be localized with exactitude and removed for closer study in order that a terror or ecstatic manifestation may be customized for maximum effect. This is extremely useful when a given subject appears resistant to the incredible through lack of belief. The procedure is painless, and when such an examination is being undertaken it is essential that a Maker plan his approach in order to coincide with a period of subject unconsciousness. It must be realized that some investigations, particularly those involving the temporary extraction of core fears, carry an intrinsic risk that must be balanced against the value of the information that can be obtained from them. For this reason it is vital that all subjects be placid and docile during the investigation and that all fears be returned to the subjects on completion of the investigation. The release of a subject, sans fears, instigates a degenerative cascade throughout the subject personality that will quickly foster sociopathic, suicidal, and potentially homicidal traits. No longer fearing one thing, subjects will quickly discover they lack aversions to related concerns, and so on. Subjects develop an intense craving for contrast that cannot be assuaged. This is a craving motivated not by fear, but by emotions such as boredom and apathy for everything thus far encountered. This condition engenders in subjects certain traits of the sociopath. Exhaustion of all possible routes for stimuli and contrast engenders the suicidal urge. Should a Maker deem that permanent and selective fear removal is appropriate, it is recommended that such action be compensated for—as much as is possible—via complementary procedures. As always, the Maker must undertake these procedures with a clear mind, the better to exert his will over that of the instruments.

And the box was quiet, the dying voice fading to a worming tickle in her ear. Weighing what she would do next, Hope opened the box, retrieved the 'scope, and slipped it into a side pocket on her puffer vest. She put the box into the pack minus its contents, and slung it onto her back.

For a moment she crouched there, listening to the night bugs. Then, seeing no alternative, Hope moved off at a steady jog toward Suni's house.

"You know, I'm sorry if you feel I somehow betrayed you . . ."

"Please."

". . . but she was the best thing I had. A sister seemed a fair trade for a mother. If I'd told her . . ."

"Open the door."

The thing with Wally was that as long as you could see him and accept his existence, you also gave him permission to interact with you. But even then he still couldn't move anything for himself.

Suni pushed the door aside, one hand on the towel around his waist. Oolric watched Walter as he crossed the room, long since used to his presence. "If I'd told her I was in contact with her comatose brother, that the one thing that truly freaked her was standing right beside me . . . do you *really* think she'd have anything to do with me? I loved her."

"This was never about *you*. There's more at stake here than Suni crying for Mother. Get dressed."

"She's seen me naked before . . ."

"Get *dressed.*"

". . . but you know that." Suni took the towel off and finished drying his hair. "Did I also mention you're the reason I've got no friends?"

Walter stood by the window, waiting.

"It all started with that stupid card, remember? I lost Kristian's stupid, shiny little card. Or more to the point, *you* lost it."

"We got *swarmed.*"

"You could have held on *tighter!*"

"*For the thousandth time, I didn't know it was that important!*"

"You lost it," he reiterated, with forced calm. "And I flew back from Vancouver. I got to school a few days later—after the episode with Mother—and the first thing Kristian asks is, 'Where is it?' Not *How are you?* or *Are you okay?* or *How the fuck did you get to the other side of the Earth by breakfast?* but 'Where is it?' And I told him. I told him *everything*. And do you know what he did?"

Walter didn't answer. He had been there. He had seen it.

"He beat the shit out of me, that's what. My best friend kicked hell out of me, right there in front of all those people who were smiling and wanting to know what it was like and how I'd done it. All those people, who for one brief instant thought I might have been worth knowing, saw me reduced to a bleeding mess. Sure, some people said useful things like 'stop it,' but it didn't mean anything. Kristian was the funny guy, Kristian had the friends. And when it became clear they had to choose between Kristian or me, I never had a fucking chance, did I? And that, Wally, is where the snowball started rolling."

"If she dies, you killed her."

"No, man, if she dies you killed her by choosing me."

This time the lights were on. As usual, she crept toward the painted green front steps that led up to the front door, up past the scented clouds of jasmine and the warm and veiled rectangle of Suni's bedroom window. The expected amber light flickered from inside.

A shadow moved against that light, and Hope froze.

Suni was speaking. ". . . I've had enough." He said something else that was lost to her. Hope moved closer, straining to hear, watching Suni's silhouette slink and slide from the window next to the stairs to the side one. "Yes I'll do it. Give it a rest." Another pause. "Because I don't care. You know," Suni was saying, "it's release. It's not a gaining, it's a losing . . . a wonderful, wonderful losing . . ." His silhouette stopped moving, and all was quiet for a moment. She could see his head turn, listening to something. Did he know she was out here? "Well it certainly doesn't feel that way," he said. His silhouette disappeared downward as he sat on the bed.

Hope shrugged her pack higher onto her shoulder and slid under the rail. She nudged her head through the curtains and stepped down onto the carpeted floor. The zipper on the pack caught on the fabric of the curtain, catching her, leaving her dancing on one leg for a second—the other still up on the sill—as she freed herself. She unhooked the stitch from the zip, pulled the bag free, twisted, and drew her leg in.

"You usually knock first."

Suni was sitting on his bed, naked. Instant impressions of cinnamon skin and the shape of a collarbone, before blood rose quickly to her face and she looked away. "Sorry," she said, trying to find something to focus on. "I'll let you get dressed."

"Something happened tonight, I take it."

"I guess." She picked a spot of darker color on the bamboo slat blinds and focused on that. She didn't want to say anything, explain anything, until it was over. Explanations would lead to conversation and debate, and then she might not have the nerve to do what she had come here for. "I heard you talking." Offering him privacy gave her an excuse to turn her back and place the pack on the spare bed. She fished the 'scope out of her vest, and slipped it onto her hand, feeling the slight pressure change and the movement of air as it slid over her skin. "Is Walter here?"

She became aware of Suni standing behind her.

"You know, this is going to be extraordinarily dangerous."

She blanked for a second, wondering what he meant . . .

There was a massive, blunt collision with the back of her head.

Her vision exploded with sourceless light as senses misfired. Her center of balance shifted and her feet shuffled backward to compensate. Her head went numb, then felt as if it were about to split. Her ears rang. She sank, knees thudding on carpet-cushioned concrete, before her body toppled forward. Her head struck the wooden baseboard, snapping her neck back on the way down to the carpeted floor. The interior of her skull became a blank space filled with oily color that once contained a mind.

· · ·

Standing over Hope, Suni watched Walter explode outward, muscle ballooning like yeast. Oolric freaked, bristling fur doubling his size, hissing and spitting as he backed into the alcove. Walter's growth hunched him forward, elongated him. A thick, rough gray coat sprouted, consuming the little-boy clothes he wore. His face, once rounded and made for smiling, stretched into a muzzle. Suni watched his shocked little sockets recede beneath the overhang of that prominent brow, and foot-long claws shoot from what had been his hands. He noticed two had been snapped off, and passingly wondered how and when that had happened.

Suni wondered why Hope hadn't seen Walter yet. She obviously hadn't seen him when she climbed in through the window. Maybe she really didn't believe in any of this.

Walter took up almost a quarter of the room, smelling like damp dogs and a jungle tens of thousands years gone. Suni knew that the first chance Walter got he was going to seriously hurt him, maybe even kill him. In hindsight, Suni supposed, he should have gotten a knife or something before making Walter angry. He could still run upstairs and grab one—the big one his mother used on roasts would suit—but that meant leaving the room, and that meant being away from people who couldn't see Wally. And that meant Walter would have him. The mathematics of the situation were engaging.

"Now what are you going to do?" he asked.

"You'll be alone soon enough."

"Not before I'm armed I won't." Suni looked to Walter's sister, sprawled on her face and reaching for the bed leg like it was the only solid thing there was. She rolled over onto her back.

She had the 'scope on.

Suni saw it, smiled to himself, and straddled her.

The 'scope-hand was gripping the bed leg. Try as he might, using both hands, Suni couldn't unlock her grip.

"Give me it . . . ," he coaxed, as if she were a recalcitrant child.

She reached for his throat with her other hand and he tucked it under his knee, pinning it. She whimpered a little, gritted her teeth.

"Suni . . . no . . ."

"Give me it . . ."

"You don't want it . . . you're messed up . . ."

He pressed his knee down harder.

Walter came at him, roaring. With hands on the 'scope Suni reflexively snapped his head around just as a great paw came sweeping in on an arc for his head.

Suni didn't feel a thing. The swing stopped dead as Walter's claws struck the immovable surface of his face, wrenching joints in Walter's arm. Suni knew what happened when real people ran into Walter, so he reached out and batted the monster away.

Walter flew back, unable to offer any resistance whatsoever, and slammed into the indestructible angles of Suni's makeshift clothes rack. The blades of hanging shirts bit into his back and he fell to the ground, stunned.

"Stee-rike . . . ," Suni murmured.

Suni turned back to Hope. She was looking at him like he was the strangest thing.

One minute he was wrestling her for the 'scope, the next he gasped and stopped short, swinging at nothing.

"Stee-rike . . ." And then he was shifting her vest aside, raising her shirt. "Give me it . . ." Like he didn't really care if she did or not.

Swinging at nothing . . .

Suni's hands found her breasts. "Extraordinarily dangerous . . ."

She yanked her arm out from under his knee, burning the underside against the carpet, and swung her nails at his face. He saw it coming and took it anyway. No blood, but she dug up skin, and if it hurt he didn't show it. All she got from him was a look of disappointment, as if it hadn't hurt enough. She dug her nails in, his mouth hot and damp against her palm. He took her hand away and said, "We never fucked." A smile broke across his face and cast his eyes to the other side of the room, laughing. "But you know that."

He was looking at Wally.

Walter picked himself up, rising from the floor like a groaning machine, great breaths venting from flaring nostrils, muscles and tendons bunching.

From the other end of the room he could hear Suni laughing and Hope's quickening breath. He could smell the same fear she had when their father had done the thing that had gotten him killed. Something remarkably similar to what Suni was doing now. And once again there was nothing Walter could do. Walter knew then—more than he ever had—that Hope had to take care of herself, and that his time was long since over. He could never help her. If anything he'd made things much, much worse.

Staying here, witnessing this, was killing him.

He loved her. He loved her because she was his sister, and because that's what every part of his ancient self was made for. It was his calling, his fate, his purpose.

He could almost see her eyes go dead, looking to someplace a thousand miles away, up in the sky, as she switched herself off and took herself away until Suni did whatever he had to do.

Hope had begun to cry, as she had on the nights her father had been at his worst. As Suni's hands roamed. As she found herself revisited by the worst parts of her father in the shape of the best friend she ever had.

From deep inside Walter something said *give up*, told him there was nothing more to be done; plied him with thoughts of nighttime woodland, of being something massive and four-legged sprinting and weaving through the massive trunks of oak and fir . . .

Strength slipped away, claws loosened, sight dimmed.

. . . thoughts of pine needles soft under the pads of his paws, the heavy coat upon his back undulating in time to the perfect rhythm of forelegs-through-backlegs, of vision bobbing close to the ground, hugging the subtle and sudden curve of the land, flying jaws homing in on warm prey . . .

The voice inside himself was growing, telling him it was all right to forget, to move on.

It told him the moon was waiting for a song.

The sound of her was fading. He held on to Hope's memory as he sank, holding on to her for as long as he could, willing himself to re- member but feeling himself forget, sinking deeper and deeper into unbecoming . . .

As the darkness came to claim Walter, Hope looked right at him, saw him, and said his name.

And a twelve-foot grinning sardonicus reached out for Suni with a paw the size of his head.

With one hand clamped to her 'scope-wrist, the other on a breast, Suni was laughing when a translucent shadow twice the size of a fridge enveloped his face and hurled him through a closed window. He took half the blinds with him.

Hope watched the wraith—howling like an exultant animal— leap off the floor, over her, onto the bed, and out through the shat- tered frame, after Suni.

She'd seen him. She'd seen . . . something. Walter. Walter was going to kill Suni.

She got to her feet and scrambled for the window. She didn't no- tice the glass cutting her knees and if she had she wouldn't have cared.

Suni had a second or two before Walter hit the ground beside him. In that moment—as he stared at the stars and felt himself bleeding all over his mother's lawn—he remembered that he hadn't planned his last words to be "Oh shit."

It didn't especially matter, he supposed. His back and sides were gashed and he could see blood on the window's jagged teeth. Parts of the blind were lying in the garden bed. He could hear the neighbors, voices raised like someone had kicked the henhouse. He could see his hand and forearm, wet and slick and lacerated from where he had shielded his face against the glass. The stars were out. He could hear the crickets in the hedge.

"Black bugs blood," he mumbled, and laughed.

And now here came Walter, hulking, furry thing that he was. Yesterday Suni had something like a last speech prepared for when this time came. He had thought at the time that perhaps he would go to school and beat the vice principal to death with a lamp, and maybe throw Kristian off a building before killing himself somehow. Tell them all exactly how it was. But now he found he didn't much care. This life had become a repetitive activity he had tired of. Nothing mattered. Everything was relative and nothing meant anything so what was the point? You only did one thing to compare it with another and revel or mope in the resultant contrast, which in turn . . . oh fuck it. He was sick of even thinking about it.

So he lay there, bleeding, and waited for Walter to nail him to the ground.

Itwashimitwashimitwashimitwashim . . .

She had climbed to her feet and onto the bed, glass crunching beneath her, so stunned she almost slashed her hands on the shattered window.

There was a mirage-hulk, a roaring shadow, standing in the garden.

"Oh get on with it," Suni said.

It was him. It was really him. She was really seeing this.

And the longer she looked the more undeniable it became. And the more undeniable it became the more she saw. It was a systematic paring away of the credible with the incredible, a space in the yard filling itself in with more and more detail, each moment permitting her to perceive new elements more impossible than the last.

Walter was a twelve-foot eyeless werewolf.

"Jesus!"

One second the wolf had Suni by the throat, his face reddening like his head was going to explode, and the next, Suni simply slipped through those massive fingers and dropped to the ground, coughing and gasping.

In a voice with more bass than rolling thunder, Walter had said, "*Crap.*"

"Hey! What's going on over there?" One of the neighbors, a potato of a man in shorts and a raggedy house shirt, was standing on his lawn scrutinizing Suni.

Blearily Suni looked up, and Hope saw just how much being thrown through the window had cost him. He'd been deeply gashed all over, particularly along the sides. At the rate he was losing blood he'd be unconscious before too long; maybe dead. He was already looking dangerously pale. She wanted to run to him, but a vital part of her didn't want to give Walter the chance to disappear.

"Go back to bed!" Suni shouted. "Go on! Fuck off!"

"What?"

Shakily, and with great effort, Suni got to his feet. He walked toward the neighbor. "I said go back to bed. We're in the middle of something."

Hope called Suni's name, instinctively moving to climb out the window and stopping short at the presence of jagged glass.

The man realized his neighbor's kid was walking around naked, and started to laugh.

Suni stepped out of the darkness of his own yard, and into the light cast by the neighboring garage. His wounds looked horrific in full light. He was trailing blood all over the driveway.

With a sudden flick Suni threw blood in his neighbor's face, stopping the laughter dead.

The man's expression wrestled between shock and rage. "*You . . . you little . . . !*"

"I have AIDS."

The world went quiet enough to hear insects.

The man wiped his face. It left a translucent smear down one cheek. He looked as if he was about to say something, then turned and walked back inside without a word. A few seconds later Hope heard him call to someone named Joan.

Suni walked back to where Walter—now a little boy again—was standing. Suni looked down at him, but Walter didn't seem to be aware of him. His eyes were closed, hands by his sides.

He looked just like he did in all those photos. The ones with the dog, and that ice-cream photo, and the one where he was splashing around in a wading pool with Dad. For the first time Hope had a sense of family history, of things existing before she did. Not just an intellectual appreciation of the facts, but a deep and true knowledge of where things had come from, where she had come from, who her parents were, and who they had been. Just by looking at the little blond boy standing with his eyes closed in that nighttime garden, and knowing this was the face they remembered their son with, this was how they remembered Wally; that this was the boy they had both given their lives for.

Suni nudged Wally in the shoulder, coughed, and said, "Hurry up."

"Walter?" Saying his name, talking to him, felt like the strangest thing Hope had ever done.

The little boy only turned his head slightly, acknowledging her, but keeping his eyes closed. "Don't look at me."

She swallowed. She didn't know what to say, where to begin.

"We need to talk," he said. "It's very important."

She nodded, grateful. "Okay . . . okay, sure . . ." In the moonlight all the blood made Suni look oil-covered. "Suni . . . we need to get you to a hospital."

Suni looked down, resignedly. "Sure." And ran.

It was quiet again. Walter turned his head toward her. "Hope . . ."

Suni was going to bleed to death.

"Shit." She almost went out the window after him, hands stopping half an inch from impaling themselves on the glass. "Walter . . . Walter . . ." Her hands were hovering inches above the glass, flexing like they were wondering what they were supposed to do. "This'll just . . ."

"Hope, this is more important."

Her pulse rate was rising. If she didn't move now she might not be able to find him, and then . . . if he died it'd be her fault. "He needs a doctor. Please don't go."

She flew off the bed, ran out the door, and through the garage. There was no sign of Suni anywhere, save for the blood trailed on the driveway. Out on the narrow street, dogs barking close to the hill, it was easy to follow the trail he'd left: around the corner, past all those nice safe houses, and toward the quarry. Still wearing the 'scope, she ran the distance, hoping to catch up but never catching sight of him. Once the wet speckled trail hit the grass, and disappeared into the dark beyond the boom gate, following it became a matter of faith.

More than once she thought about leaving Suni, about going back, about Walter. She wanted to touch him, to know he was real, to hear what he had to say after all this time. Even if she'd lived in fear of it all her life. She wished Suni would just stop running, would let her call an ambulance, let her fix him, let her get on with her life.

She wanted to talk to Wally. She had to. Since she was little she'd been living in the shadow of him, never knowing why her parents had given up so much, why they'd changed so much from the happy people they'd been in all those photos, never truly knowing if they loved her or just needed her, never knowing why her life had turned out the way it had. Walter would know. He'd have the answers. She had to get back. But she couldn't let Suni die. She'd just have to be quick about it.

She jumped the gate and was immediately flanked on both sides by the oppressively dense foliage that bordered the houses. In the moonless dark cast by the overhanging trees, she moved quickly up the hillside, sneakers slipping in the truck tracks, waving mosquitoes from her face. Rounding the first bend she spotted Suni up ahead and running wounded, back slashed and shining blackly. He was in no condition to be moving like that, and yet he was pushing himself.

She tried to pick up her pace, calling out for him as she went; telling him he was going to die if he didn't stop and get to a hospital.

But still he kept running, barefoot over the broken ground.

Suni felt like he was like coming home, running like this, naked and dying. Nothing hurt. The shivers and the chill helped cut through the fog that was trying to envelop his brain, but he wouldn't allow himself to pass out. He wanted to be awake for the final flight, to feel the cold wind cut as it swept over him, as he sailed down. As he flew back to where he belonged.

Wings at last.

She made it to the top with her lungs raw and her eyes streaming. She found him close to the other side of the quarry, facedown on a hard white plate of dried mud the trucks used as a congregation point during the day. She watched him pick himself up and continue staggering forward, leaving a man-sized Rorschach blot where he'd lain. Again she called out to him, and again he just kept running. She ran after him, her sides smarting more now for having stopped.

Suni had made it to his boulder—the one he always sat on when he came here—climbed it, and struggled uncertainly to his feet.

The city sprawled below: a sparkling tablecloth—first the scattered lights of the suburbs immediately beneath them, and then the ever-thickening stipple toward the city itself.

Whether he had paused to take in the sight, get his breath, gather his final thoughts or was just struggling to think straight, it didn't matter; she made it to him before he leapt and locked both hands around his wrist.

"Suni. Don't."

"Why?"

"What you're feeling is because of the 'scope."

"So?"

"So come down. Please."

"I don't think you get it."

"Come down."

"You really don't get it." He shook her hand free. "I have to go."

He turned away. She grabbed him again. He didn't move. "Okay," he said, and climbed down from his boulder. "You stopped me. Well done." His chest and legs were powdered with a paste of blood and dried white mud.

"Suni . . ."

"What will you do now?"

She was still wearing the 'scope. "I'll make you right."

The join between Suni's forefinger and thumb collided with her throat at the same time as his right leg got behind hers. She went down, winded, and Suni was on top of her again.

"You're not enjoying this, are you. It's unpleasant. It's uncomfortable. Things are passing through your head at a mile a minute, most of it you're probably not even aware of. What I'm doing to you now is fighting for space among all the good memories you've got of me. You're drawing comparisons between me—your friend—and your father, a dead wannabe rapist. Part of you is rearing up, wanting to kill me on principle, another is lying down, allowing me to do what I want because you think you know me. Your dignity is wrestling with the fact that you think I'm not really responsible for what I'm doing. Don't you get it? There's no clarity in any of that. There's no peace. Most of each day is spent in a low-grade state of what you're experiencing now, crawling through a thousand tiny battles. It's misery, Hope. And it all rests on just one thing: fear. Of one sort or another. And once you wipe that away, I tell you there's nothing left. And that's what we're all about, Hope. Fear and pointlessness and fear. There is absolutely no use in us being here. So leave me alone. Please."

Sometimes Hope still wished her grandmother would come visit her, though she'd been dead ten years. She missed her lavender smell, the smell of linoleum and sunshine that had filled her house, the quiet simplicity of her life. Hope wished she could turn around one day and there she'd be, her grandmother, just for a second. Just to see her again and say good-bye.

That's what looking at Suni was like. A final, stolen glance at the face of a friend you knew to be dead and gone for good.

She swallowed, and nodded, and he let her go. He started climbing back up his boulder. She got to her feet.

"Suni?"

He turned.

Her claws went in through his face, twisting, groping upward for the cerebellum

and Suni's horrors came

> *fear of who I am fear of what they'll do fear of being found fear of discovering who I am fear of what I think fear of what has gone fear of what is fear of what will be fear of being alone fear of pain fear of surprise fear of rejection fear of dismissal fear of failure fear of comparison fear of*

she pulled out
gasping

Why was she looking at the sky, listening to echoes?

> *i hate myself i hate myself i hate myself i hate myself i*

Thinking meant fighting. Her hand pulsed. She wanted it off her. She had meant to return what she had taken, but she had only taken more, taken every last thing that was hiding in every corner of his mind. She had just taken on board everything he had.

She was so confused she wanted to be sick.

She had to get up.

Suni was stumbling backward, arms splayed and legs stiff. He bumped into his boulder, plopping down suddenly and awkwardly against its rough surface.

> *fear of other people's laughter fear of embarrassment fear of fear of fear of fear of fear of fear*

Hope struggled to her feet. She could feel her brain shifting alignment, back and forth, the world slurring with it, the tracking of her
eyes all wrong, moving out of sync with the tracking of her head. God
how she wanted to be sick.

i hate myself i hate myself i hate myself i hate myself i

Suni's every foul memory, every unuttered scream, roared inside
her head. She couldn't escape the distorted face of his mother. The
'scope was starving. It wanted more. It wanted what was in her own
head. The 'scope wanted to eat the fears of the mind that controlled
it, eating and re-eating in an endless self-destructive loop. It wanted
to self-destruct, to self-consume, to become something more. She
felt its ravening want. It wanted to sabotage everything it had unwill-
ingly been created for. It wanted to re-create itself. It wanted to be
complete.

It wouldn't have her. Hope was unloading it now.

I don't want to be me I don't want to be me I don't want me want
me want me to want me to want me to hate want me to hate me
hate me hate me hate me hate me hate me hate me hate

It's funny, Hope found herself thinking, blinking away tears, I always come back to digging . . .

i can be good i can be good you'll see you'll see i can be good
you'll see i can be you i can be you i can be you
i can be you you'll see

The cargo of Hope's hand and head pulsed. She wanted it off her.
She couldn't place something like that back into someone's mind.
Not an enemy, especially not a friend, not anyone.

I'M BETTER THAN THIS

If I'm not digging in the ground . . . (moving silently forward) *I'm digging in people's minds . . .*

No, I'm not.

She couldn't put something like that back into someone's head.

I'm not.

But she had to.

But I can fake it.

Suni stood, naked, facing the city, hands to his eyes, rasping. Each exhalation was a torn gasp of heartfelt relief. A lifetime of demons packed inside, straining his skin to the point of rippage, a lifetime of concerns, of concern at his new lack of concern . . . now gone.
So what was left?
Why was he laughing?

I can be like you.

Digging for lost treasures, Hope thought, standing behind her friend. *Digging for buried fear . . .*

I can be like you.

Quietly, gently Hope slid silver fingers into the back of his head.

You'll see.

And Suni's mind rained demons.
His breath shifted pitch "no . . ." as it all fell back home "no"

drained from the shadowed canals of Hope's mind. " . . ." Back into his.

Freeing history . . . freeing people . . .

And got comfortable.

Suni sobbed so hard Hope's lungs ached.

He threw back his head and screamed.

Plunge-heave-hoist-ho.

EIGHTEEN

TIGER

HOPE STAYED WITH HIM, BUT KEPT HER DISTANCE. SHE figured as long as he was sobbing that hard he wasn't at any risk of dying. Maybe the cuts weren't as bad as they looked. Whatever the case, it looked like he'd stopped bleeding. Without clothes, having lost all that blood, he'd be freezing. But she couldn't get close to him. He wouldn't let her.

There was no wind up there for a change. No sound. Just Suni.

Hope wondered what she would do with tomorrow, or the rest of her life. There'd be hell to pay when she got home, for having disappeared out the window again. Maybe the story about her father would finally catch up to her, rule her, take away her right to any kind of normal life. She'd have to switch schools again. Maybe her mother would always be there, getting worse and worse, constantly demanding attention and making Hope's life hell for it. Maybe things would never change.

Hope found she didn't much care. Maybe Suni had a point about pointlessness.

And maybe he didn't. If everything *wasn't* meaningless, then nothing was. Then everything that ever happened anywhere had to be laden with meaning.

Maybe everyone's born for a reason.

Suni was still sobbing, curled naked against the rock. She had seen things, inside Suni's head. He was more involved with Walter, and that man outside her house, than he'd told her. It had been a part of his life for years. It took her breath away, having known him all this time, and knowing now just how afraid he was to tell her any of it. For fear of losing her. She understood now just how much Suni loved her. Just like he wanted.

She moved over to him. The way his thin shoulders shook made her think of a shivering newborn bird. She crouched, laid a hand on one of those shoulders. He didn't react.

"Suni . . ."

His head snapped toward her, a twisted mask. Strings of spittle clung to his lower lip, eyes wet and red. *"Llll-luh-luh-luh-llll-luh-luh-luh! Llllllll! Llllllll! Llll-luh-luh-luh-LEAVE ME THE FFF-FFF-FUH-FUH-FUH-FUH-FUH-FUCK ALONE!"*

"Suni . . ." She could take this. She was a tiger.

"Yyyyyy-yyyy . . ." His eyelids fluttered, eyes rolled back with the effort of squeezing the word out. *"Yuh-yuh-yuh-you fff-fff-fff-fuh-fuh-fuh-fff-fuh-fucking puh-puh-puh-promised me! Yuh-yuh-yuh-yuh-you sss-sss-sss-suh-said yuh-yuh-yuh-you knew wuh-wuh-wuh-wuh-www-what you were doing!"*

"Suni . . ."

She could take this.

He screamed at her, flailing spastically, trying to get her hand off him. One wayward swing backhanded her across the face, toppling her backward. She grunted as she hit the ground and lay where she landed, looking sidelong to the only tree that stood up here, watching its dry leaves moving ever so slightly against the starry sky while Suni half shrieked, half gasped like some kind of broken animal.

"Tell me about the doctor," she said.

She could take this. Whatever was coming. She could take it. If Wally could make it through whatever existence had been forced on him for the last seventeen years, she could cope with this. She was a tiger.

His cry sounded like a wounded cat: hopeless and alien. He launched himself at her, throwing himself onto her, straddling her once again, pinning an arm to either side of her head, pounding them onto the dirt like an hysterical child.

"W*www-www-wuh-wuh-wuh-why d-d-d-d-didn't yuh-yuh-yuh-yyy-yyy-yyy-you fuh-fuh-fuh-fuh-fuck me? Why didn't you fuck me?*" A thin cord of saliva danced and bobbed from his lower lip. Warm tears fell to her chest and face, soaking through her shirt in spots.

"Tell me," she said.

She could take this. She was a tiger.

"*You fuh-fuh-fuh-fff-fucking puh-puh-puh-promised me . . . yyy-you suh-suh-said . . .*"

The sobbing killed his emotional momentum, caught up with him, fell out of sync with his words and the pounding of his hands, and he rolled off her, onto his back, hands to his face, screaming.

She swallowed against rising fear and stared at the moon, at the drifting, sodium-orange clouds. She made herself look at him. Thought of his sketches, back in his room, drawn by the person he used to be. Remembered the gray-shaded sketch of those headless card players, the piles of bodies, and Walter amid all that, and that shadow standing by the door.

"Suni, why didn't you tell me?"

He rolled his head to face her. They hadn't lain like this since they'd been together. She knew he was thinking the exact same thing.

"Because I told wuh-one person after it happened," he choked. "And she puh-put me in that room."

Two AM and the night felt as balmy as a spring afternoon.

She made it back home and crawled back in through her open

window. There were bars leaning up against the front door, ready for the following day. Hope wouldn't be going out again. She wouldn't mind, for a while.

Wally was sitting on her bed, waiting for her.

"Will he be okay?" he asked.

Wally's eyes were still closed, looking for all the world as though he were listening to music. He was only a little bigger than the bear propped on her pillow. Of all the things she'd said about him over the years, she wondered how much of it he'd heard. Most of it, she assumed. "I think so," she replied.

He nodded, and then: "Good."

She put the pack with the Anxietoscope on the floor and sat next to him. "How are you?"

He tilted his head slightly, as though picking up a distant sound. "I'm okay," he said.

"What happened to your eyes?"

He turned slightly away. "Did Suni tell you about the doctor?"

"A little. What he knew. That he's the reason you never woke up."

Walter turned to face her, looked up at her with those closed eyes, and suddenly Hope was feeling it again: that deep sense of history, of reasons older than herself for why things were the way they were. She knew then how much Wally had given up for her. She put her arms around him, and held him. "I remember you now," she said. "You were my friend. You were my big secret."

He sounded like an abandoned pup then, tiny and lost, wrapped in her arms. And she held him like that for a long time.

She had passed out in her jeans and windbreaker, listening to Walter tell her stories. He was telling her about the seventy-third Fallen, and its desire to be remade whole and known once more. He told her about the instruments, how there was more than just the Anxietoscope; there were instruments for the molding of flesh and bone, instruments for the infusing of power, instruments for the shaping of intelligence. All these were made from the bones of an angel the seventy-third Fallen had found and sundered.

And somewhere between the story of a man named Dorian, and the doctor meeting the Angel, Hope had slipped into dream. She hadn't meant to sleep, it just happened.

She dreamed she and Walter were Siamese twins, but not joined at the hip, not disfigured. She dreamed they had a complete body, with Hope the left half and Walter the right.

She imagined they were standing in space, turning a solar system with one lazy hand, scrutinizing planets, browsing worlds.

She imagined herself part of something vast. She was warm, complete, utterly content. Her bones were bright and singing.

Something promised her she could, in fact, finally have everything she ever needed. She could be complete, content. She could comprehend fully why she was here.

She wanted to listen, to know, but something soft and strong was pressing to her forehead, kissing her the way cats do. Saying *wake up*. Saying *take control*.

It could all be hers, the delicate, vibrating voice insisted. If she would just give up, for just a moment.

Something massive rumbled very close to her, making it hard to understand what the voice was saying.

Let go.

She dreamed of a beautiful white tiger. All the world's strength held in its eyes. All the strength she'd ever need to get through this life to the other side.

Hope woke, silver claws inches from her eyes. It was back on her hand.

The 'scope surged as she woke, desperate to drive home before she could stop it. Disoriented, terrified, she grabbed her own wrist and battered her clawed hand against the side table, over and over and over. Her brother leapt onto her, grabbing her wrist also, his little hands closing over her hand.

She turned her head away from the claws. "Help me."

Walter pressed down, pushing the Anxietoscope toward her face. "Let it do it, Hope, let it . . ."

"Get off!" Walter blew backward and Hope tore the 'scope free, tossing it across the room.

Glancing around the room, she found herself completely alone. Chest heaving, she allowed herself one deep breath, and surprised herself by beginning to cry.

Wally was out in the yard, pounding his fists against the side of the house.

"You didn't tell her," Henry said.

"I'm an idiot."

The doctor looked up at Hope's window. "No telling how she would have taken it, I suppose."

"Yeah. Everyone's so sure she won't take weird news well. Maybe someone should have just trusted her." Walter's hands slid to his face. He wanted to sleep for a very long time.

"I'm sorry about your eyes, Wally. It wasn't supposed to happen like that. S'posed to be cleaner."

"How can you do this?"

"I have to do this."

"Bullshit."

"Come the end of war at the End of Days the army we're building here will emerge from the Drop and clean up whatever's left. It'll allow humanity to determine its own destiny."

"It'll destroy both Heaven and Hell and release an abomination that was rightly stricken!"

"It doesn't—"

"IT MURDERED ME!" The voice was a thousand saws being drawn across a thousand throats. *". . . AND I WANT MY BONES BACK!"*

The doctor remained very still as Walter's every breath touched his face, reeking of old flesh and sounding like the sickest, most hunger-mad dog that ever lived.

"When . . ." The doctor swallowed. "When I first found you, and then your sister . . . I thought you were perfect. Everything about you fit so well with what the instruments needed from a guiding mind . . ."

"You're an idiot, Henry. A small, stupid thing . . ."

Henry smiled tightly. "You're fading. Have been for a long time." The doctor took his hat off, wiped some speck from the rim. "I'm sorry Wally, I truly am . . ." Walter snorted. "But she didn't come to when she touched the 'scope, not the way you did, and I think I can work with that. Once I get the 'scope back . . . I'll be able to make the change a little easier for her. She'll be happy. I'll see to it."

Walter looked at him. *"You're going to use the 'scope on her?"*

"Don't do this to yourself, Wally. You lost. It's over. Rest."

Wally stood there, hands by his sides, chest heaving with each miserable breath, and then it was as if it all went away. He sighed. His shoulders dropped. He stuffed his hands into his pockets.

"Yeah . . . ," he said, Wally's voice again. "Yeah . . ."

"I'm sorry, Wally."

"She's my soul, Henry. Do you know how long we worked to have our two halves born here at the same time? Since the dawn of time we've wanted this. To be whole again. Henry, we're *so close* . . ."

"I'm . . ."

"Yeah," Walter said. "You're sorry."

And then the doctor was gone. Walter stood like that for some time, his chin on his chest.

Henry was going to use the 'scope on her. It was all he could do to keep from laughing. What do you know, he thought. Maybe there is a God.

NINETEEN

COMPLEMENTARY PROCEDURES

WHEN HOPE AWOKE IT WAS STILL DARK, AND HE WAS STAND-ing by her window.

"Got it done?" he asked.

He must have been kind-of-handsome, at one point. In a weird sort of way. A blade-thin poet maybe, with a wry smile and a scalpel in his hand.

"Feel better?"

She hitched a corner of her mouth, and left it at that.

"Wally told you 'bout me."

"Yes."

He was still for a moment, standing by the window.

"You're not running," the doctor said.

She slowly shook her head.

"You're strong," he said. "You spent your life looking after a dead kid 'cos your mama needed it. You saved your friend tonight even

though he was messed up enough to have killed you. You got imagination, I saw that when you were young. You go lateral when you
need to—and you will need to. I don't think you'd abuse the instruments if I passed them on to you, and taught you how to use
them."

Hope blinked. "You what?"

"This isn't precisely what I had in mind when I asked the Seventy-
third Fallen to make me a great surgeon. It's important, what I've
done, but I've had enough. I got other places to be, people waiting for
me." The doctor extended a gloved hand. "What do you say?"

She thought about her father. About who he had been. He'd dete-
riorated over the years, become a shade of the man he had been before she was born. A simulacrum of the doting father that had
splashed with his new son in a wading pool and built magic paper
birds. Fifteen years of hopelessness, court cases, working two jobs,
and finally alcohol was what it took to erode David Witherspoon to
the point that attacking his daughter on a kitchen bench didn't seem
so wrong. She'd killed him. She'd lived. She was, all things considered, fine. But the thought of her father's face and collapsing mind, of
what she did to him, destroyed her every morning, and every day she
rebuilt herself by evening. But she could do that. Because she was a
tiger.

It'd be easy to say the doctor was responsible for all that, that he'd
made them what they were. And she supposed he had. But so what?
What was the alternative? A happy family life, a mediocre middle age,
and a comfortable death? Really, how was one scenario any better or
worse than the other? You live, you learn, you die. Once you accept
that, she supposed, you could live through anything.

The doctor's hand was still extended. "My name's Henry," he
whispered.

She smiled sleepily, blinked slow.

"You look lonely, Henry."

Maybe everyone's born for a reason.

· · ·

Hope slept, and Henry took her in his arms. He took her away from that room; away from that town; away from this world.

And in a dark place, a nowhere place that shared a wall with Hell, where slabs grew from cave dirt and the ceiling roiled, he brushed pink hair from her eyes. Still she slept and would continue to sleep until it was no longer necessary.

> *The procedure is painless, and when such an examination is being undertaken it is essential that a Maker plan his approach in order to coincide with a period of subject unconsciousness.*

He took the instrument from her pack, unwrapped the faux-fur jacket from around it, placed it beside her on the cold slab, and opened it. The Anxietoscope rose and drifted gracefully toward its glittering kin within the folds of his coat. One thin hand closed gently around it, possessing it.

> Should a Maker deem that permanent and selective fear removal is appropriate . . .

It slipped over his finger and hand as though it were nothing. His own desiccated face looked back at him from the mounds and ridges, the face of who he had been for 150 years too long.

He opened his coat and chose what he would need.

> . . . it is recommended that such action be compensated for . . .

"If this world was perfect," he said to her. "We'd never want to leave. That's why it is the way it is, I think. But that's a poor excuse." He laid the instruments on the slab, one by one. "It doesn't have to be this way. You could change the world in ways I'd never be able to. You've got the universe in you."

as much as is possible . . .

Henry felt ageless eyes on him, watching from some elsewhere place.

. . . via complementary procedures.

"I'm sorry," he said, brushing back that persistent lock of hair from her pale forehead. But she said nothing. He had rarely felt the Drop this still. Nothing moved, no sound, hardly a breath.

This, then, would be the beginning of the end.

"Tear it all down."

And he began.

In another world, in a vacant lot that once held a silver miracle, a boy with wolf-teeth sat on the lip of a freshly dug hole, and howled.

TWENTY

CHANGES

*D*REAMS CAME AND WENT. AS THE PROCEDURE PROGRESSED, certain things fell into Hope to let her know how the operation was going. Henry put them there to make her feel safe, to reassure. That was their function.

She drifted in a cool sand pool beneath a peach-colored sky. Beneath her lazily kicking legs she felt the passing dance of water sprites. They buoyed her up, sang softly into her ears. One opened a panel at the base of her neck, and gently slid one of its children inside. Once this was done, what the child knew Hope knew, and Hope now knew what it was to be Henry: what he had done, what he had to do, what she had to do, how tired he was. Why she had to take over.

"We're building an army," she breathed. "And no one can know."

She floated, taking this in, making this new knowledge a part of her.

She could feel the sprite-child wriggling inside her head. Feel it insinuating itself. It felt too much like violation, and she had had enough violation for one lifetime. Hands on her body she could retreat from (she thought of tigers), but fingers in her mind gave her nowhere to retreat *to*. She didn't like it. She felt echoes of *no no no* building in tempo within her skull, felt something lovely instinctively answering the call, felt the sprite-child with its payload of instructions screaming in terror as icy-blue eyes found it, as impossibly heavy paws pinned it, and relentless jaws tore it apart.

Hope began to sink back into peace.

The water of the pool bubbled, and from some unfathomable depth something erupted. Something massive rose beneath her, lifting her from the once-still waters as enormous fingers closed over her. She could move nothing save her head, jutting between second and third digits, and soon that was held in place by something she could not see. Something cold and hard. Zero movement, utter entrapment, mounting claustrophobia, a blinding fear that stripped her back to an animal state.

An object alien to herself came in through the back of her head, grasping and tentacular, metallic and glistening, searching. An appendage for something outside herself looking to remove something inconvenient within. She told herself to run, and sensed something white and four-legged do just that, retreating as far back as it could, to her innermost place. The place was an amalgam of memory. Of her childhood bedroom—all stuffed toys and posters of perfect boys—of the specter of her father, and the hallway light upon the face of her dead brother standing by her bed as she slept.

The white tiger loped into that bedroom, looking behind itself for what it knew was coming, moved past her memory of her father at the door, of Walter by the bedside, crawled under the bed, and waited for the inevitable.

The thing came for it, all hands and fingers, snaking down the hall, in through the door, past Walter, and—without hesitation—under the bed.

Her head filled with the cries of animal pain. It was more than she could contain. She couldn't stop the screaming. The appendage jerked and jostled, tugging stubbornly at something that refused to give way. She heard wet sounds. She felt something dislodge, painfully, from the center of all she was. The violation was total.

She couldn't stop the screaming.

She had been sobbing in her sleep for about five minutes when Henry finally extracted the blockage, whatever it was that had been preventing him from changing things about her that needed changing.

The blockage was very small, and very pale. Like a stillborn kitten. He'd never seen anything like it.

With that in mind, his first instinct was to replace it. But he never had the chance.

Already, it had begun to decay.

Setting it aside, he persevered.

TWENTY-ONE

END

$\mathcal{T}$HE PARAMEDICS HAD FOUND SUNI AT THE TOP OF THE hill. He was lying on his back, on the lip of the quarry, bloodied and stargazing. He had wanted to lash out when they touched him, but found that he couldn't. Instead, he'd taken himself away as they handled his body and put it into the back of the van and brought him here, to this ward, where policemen had tried asking questions and failed to get any answers.

It was dark now, with only the ambient light from the nurses' station down the hall, the weak warm glow of sodium-orange clouds beyond the window, and the white glare of a television someone had remembered to turn down but not off.

As he lay there, on his stiff white bed beneath stiff white sheets, he'd listened to the police talking among themselves. They'd had words with the man who lived next door, and his wife, Joan. The girl had done that to him, the neighbor had said. Threw him through the window. Naked. It seemed they'd had a fight. Something about AIDS.

But the girl—Hope Witherspoon—wasn't at her home address, and her mother hadn't seen her in over twenty-four hours.

The police knew about Hope. About her record. Killed her old man with a steak knife.

Suni's stitches hurt.

"We need strong people," Henry was telling her.

"People like me."

"You're not people. You and these instruments . . ."

"We're the same person."

"Yes."

"Thrown to Earth, my essence became bones, and what was left . . . what was left tried for so long to put itself back together."

"But now you have power and purpose."

"We're building a body. An army."

"Come the End, the two sides will face each other. Once that's over we come out, clean up whatever's left . . ."

"And take over."

"No. The Angel only wants out."

"It wants to be real. It wants to be acknowledged."

"Once the balance has shifted, God won't be able to look away. It'll have to remember."

"And once God remembers the Angel . . ."

"It'll exist."

"I don't think the Angel will stop there. There's so much rage . . ."

"Once the power that locked it away is gone, it'll be free."

Hope thought about this. She remembered some things Henry had dropped into her head. "Won't we all die if that happens? Aren't we all part of the Godhead? If that goes . . ."

"Yes, but there are factions now. Authorities. The Angel needs to remove the Authority that bound it."

"God."

"I never figured that one out. Call it God if you like. I use names I know for the sake of convenience."

While Suni slept his mother came to visit. She had returned from business to find a calling card from the police wedged into the jamb of her front door, requesting that she call them as soon as possible. They had asked if she had a son, about so high, long hair. The police explained they had followed the blood trail back to the driveway of her address. They informed her that last night paramedics had received a call from a person identifying herself as Hope Witherspoon and that a person was injured atop the quarry nearby. They had found Suni (how do you spell that?), bloody, naked, and unconscious in the company of a girl with pink hair. The girl did not stay to answer questions. Neighbors report that this girl had thrown Suni through his bedroom window, resulting in lacerations to his body. It appears Suni then fled for his life. The police were currently seeking Hope Witherspoon for questioning. Not to worry, doctors say he'll be fine. Maybe a little scarring though.

Suni had woken in time to see his mother leaving the room.

"Remember," Henry said. "It's better if they want it."

She looked up at him. "Did you?"

His eyes were on Suni, sleeping. "We all did."

He had torn up all his art, hadn't he? Hadn't he done that? Or had he just wanted to? Did he really? How was he going to get anywhere now? College dropped out from beneath him. He'd had it so good for so long: a roof over his head and food in his stomach, a life of his own with his mother always out of town. All taken for granted. He couldn't *do* anything else! He was going to wind up living the things he had always dreaded, the bland eternal scenarios that existed just beyond the happy lie of high school's end; the horrible, mediocre things that happened to everyone else. They'd cut his hair, give him his glasses back, put him in a starched shirt, and file him within some anonymous concrete block for the rest of his life. People would see him there, doing the same things over and over again, slowly going gray under the lighting. The memory of what he had once been now nothing more than a shriveled sliver lying cold in the most undistinguished crevice of the emptied cavern of his mind.

Somewhere else he was vigorously marbling a white wall with his own red heart, laughing and crying out; each leap a bloody sweep, each thrust a burgundy explosion. He could hear violins. He could hear cannons.

Someone pulled the drapes against the glare of the rising sun. They turned off the TV.

"Don't let that happen . . ."

Someone stroked his head, quietly shushing him.

"Please . . . Don't let that happen to me . . ."

Whoever it was whispered close to his sleeping ear. "You understand what that means. What it involves?"

"Yuh . . . yes."

"Then say it again so that I know you mean it."

"Don't let that happen to me."

And suddenly he was awake, standing in a black chamber, a cavern, the ceiling of which roiled in the darkness like a carpet of cockroaches. There were things up there, but he couldn't tell what.

"Change comes with a price," said a gentle voice.

He lowered his eyes from the crawling firmament to find her standing against a veiled background. Long lengths of gauze, backlit by some faint and indistinct illumination. Her vest glittered, hung with singing pieces of starlight. Instruments.

"Hope . . ."

She moved toward him, the tools chiming softly.

She took his hand, closed his eyes with a soft palm, and gently pressed her lips to his. The feel of it, and the smell of her hair, brought a flood of associations: The time he had first walked up to her and said hello; the way she had smiled at his distracted manner, completely unaware of Walter badgering him constantly with *talk about this* and *she likes that*; the clumsy way she had first grabbed him— suddenly and awkwardly turning his face to hers—the kiss landing to the left of his mouth as they sat on his mother's couch watching an old rerun of *21 Jump Street*.

Suni opened his eyes and looked to what lay beyond her. Earthen platforms apparently grown from the soil of the cave where they stood, spaced evenly about; rectangular slabs, each one with a thin veil drawn around it, concealing what lay there. Through the thin material Suni could see silhouettes, and they weren't human. They weren't even the shapes of any animals he recognized.

"I want to be with you," she said. "I've always wanted to be with you." Her hand squeezed his. "And now I can."

Suni looked at her, drank her in. "Yyy-you muh-mean that?"

She nodded, a gentle smile creeping at the corners of her mouth. "I mean that."

"So . . . www-wuh-what are you doing with these?" He ran a finger over one of the instruments, something like a knitting needle. It sang louder.

"This is how you become what you've always wanted."

His stomach sank and he stepped away. He couldn't take much more of this. "No. Fuck that. Nuh-not again." In the last two days he'd had everything he was pulled from his head and rammed back in. He wouldn't withstand being reintroduced to himself all over again.

"You already agreed."

"Nnn-no."

"Three times you agreed." She stepped closer, and something slid painlessly through his navel and out through his spine. Cold threads crept upward, enveloping his brain, and sensation ceased. The flesh of his face felt slack and weighty, hung on his skull like a heavy leather hood.

"No pain," she said. There was a blade in her hand. "Nothing but what you've always wanted."

· · ·

She was having a little trouble thinking. She had that feeling, like when there's something you're supposed to remember. Only she knew there wasn't anything she was supposed to remember at all, yet she still had that feeling, like she'd forgotten something . . . something.

"Let him go."

She rummaged through the jumble of who she was. My name is Hope. My mother's name is . . . Victoria. My father's name is . . . was . . . David. I like Suni, and . . . circus music . . . and . . . and . . . something white. She shut her eyes, tried to see it rather than think it. It was there. It was right there. The memory of it . . . of him . . . of something solid, and true, and real. She could feel the memory of it, waiting to put her back together. Something familiar, something part of her, as old as the universe . . . something she had been too long separated from. The thing that kept her alive, and cohesive, through-out her entire life. Things flew apart, people crumbled, but always she remained.

But not anymore.

Music. There was music. Circus music.

She remembered now. It had been taken away. She looked down, despondent, frustrated. She looked at her shirt. GUNSMITH CATS. She shut her eyes. Something white. Something she liked. She had a tat-too. What was it of? Her mother's name was . . . was . . .

Her father's name was . . . was . . .

Henry.

"Hope, you've got to take that out of him."

Her memories, her sense of identity, her knowledge, were a series of colored windows sliding and moving in front of one another. Oc-casionally, when there was a chance alignment of various disparate el-ements, she would regain a sense of who she was. But the windows would continue moving and sliding and orbiting, and the sense would pass, leaving her with nothing but the knowledge of something re-lost.

Something that prowled when the two right windows crossed. Something . . .

"Let him go."

White.

"No. He said."

"He's useless to us. He doesn't even know what's happening. Let him go."

"No!"

Henry's dead hand touched her shoulder. An incoherent sound fired from her throat. She flicked and stumbled away, falling onto the dirt. He was standing over her, a black shape against the smoky luminescence filtering through the veils. Things slid from one part of her into another.

[Faces and memories melted together.]

She felt as if she existed in all times at once: past, present . . . She washed and melded with the little girl she had been, the woman she was becoming, her ideas of what she would be . . . she felt sick, confused, angry . . .

"What you're feeling is a side effect of the operation." [You were a mistake, Daddy had said.] "It can be fixed." [You can be fixed, Daddy had said.]

Henry extended a hand.

[Daddy had backhanded her.]

She gritted her teeth.

[She had cried out.]

He said, *"I'm not going to hurt you."*

[He had said, "Look what you're making me do." She had said, "I'm sorry."]

She said "Fuck you, Dad."

[She had cried.]

She cried.

[The knife had been in her hand before she really knew it.]

She had something that felt like nothing and looked like silver. It cut as she swung out.

[She had cried.]

Henry looked at his hand, the split leather of the glove, the blood-less, parted flesh of his palm. So very little left that was human in the true sense of the word.

"Maybe it's better this way," he said, to no one in particular.

[Daddy had looked down at his bent-back sobbing daughter, at the woman she was becoming. "It'll be good," he had murmured.]

Hope shrieked.

[Hope had screamed.]

And stabbed Henry through the heart.

Some of her colored windows pass each other, and through them, fleetingly, Hope sees herself being led into the courthouse via a shielded rear entrance. She remembers being the center of a little flower of people, moving tightly from the rear of a van, into the laneway and then five or six steps to the door. There was a youth worker with her, and her solicitor, and a couple of cops, and a few people that she didn't know. She remembers looking to her side, through the bundle of shoulders, and seeing a person standing at the end of the laneway, some guy eating an ice-cream cone, watching with blank interest. His red cap read 3DAY CLEARANCE and his T-shirt advised that if she wasn't living on the edge she was taking up too much space.

In that moment her situation seemed lonelier than it ever had, and in that moment she remembers wishing that someone was hold-ing her.

Someone she truly loved.

Hope swallowed and her bottom lip began to buckle. A tear splashed onto her mouth, and she kissed him. It tasted like gasoline.

"I love you," Suni said. "Don't do this."

Her translocation from place to place was, to her, like remember-ing things. She would see it, be aware of it, but only at a distance. She would desire a place and there she would be.

Hope and Suni were back at the quarry, looking over the place that gave birth to who they had been. It was only appropriate that it should see what they had become.

She unhooked the sculpted syrette from her vest and silently told it what to do. It sang softly in response, aching with purpose.

What was left of Suni stood facing the city. She unclamped the cap from his skull, and slid the needle from his navel. She wanted him to feel this final becoming. He would want to remember what it was like to change so completely from one thing to something else entirely.

She slid the syrette into his heart from behind and let it work. She had never done this before. She had done it since forever. She knew what she had to do because someone named Henry had dumped that information into her head. She knew what to do because this is what she was.

"Hey," said a little voice. "Don't do that to him. He can't take that."

Over her shoulder, Hope saw a little boy, standing. His name was on her lips for the second that two shifting, colored windows aligned. She had an impression of ice cream, and dogs. Of death, and love. And then it was gone.

The tools cried out, pulled at her vest. The boy raised a little hand, the instruments pulled harder.

For a moment she looked away from Suni, from the city lights brightening through what was left of his body.

"It was hard finding you," the boy said. "You're not as clear any-more."

The little boy stepped toward her. He had such an earnest face. It reminded her of . . . photographs . . . Why didn't he open his eyes?

She took a big gulp of air, blew her cheeks out, thought hard, exhaled. "I . . ." Her face contorted. "I . . . should get back to . . ."

The boy reached out and took her hand in his, turning his face up to her. "Hope," he said. "Do you remember what happened to us? In the beginning?"

Her mind was beginning to cycle again, the windows were moving faster, slipping out of conjunction. She was forgetting what she knew, remembering things she had forgotten while trying simultaneously to hang on to what she'd always known . . .

The instruments sang. Each with its own voice.

There was something . . . something massive and low to the ground. Something she could glimpse through those windows in her head, when the right ones lined up . . .

Something was moving along the high wall of the quarry.

The boy reached up and touched the Anxietoscope. That song became a deafening shriek, like release, as the song of each one's partner raised also, merged, combined, and became a single voice.

"Free us," the little boy said, taking the Anxietoscope from her vest and slipping it over her finger. "Take this and know yourself."

There was a glimpse of pelt the color of moonlight.

The boy turned at the sound, searching. A broad flank appeared, just for a moment between stone and scree, deep black and snow white . . . and then vanished once more. The smile slipped from his face. "Hope, that's not who you think it is." He snatched her hand, and they shifted.

She, Suni, the little boy . . . they were back in a familiar place. She had been born here, in this room with its shifting, scuttling ceiling, its cave floor, its myriad slabs and residents and the walls of gauze that separated them. The memory turned her eyes to Henry's boot jutting from behind one of the closest slabs. Where she had left him with the simplest of tools resting in his heart.

A massive shape prowled lazily between the slabs, concealed and revealed by veils, scrims, and translucent drapery.

"I was looking for something," she says.

Something white, says the cat.

Hope thinks. Looks at her shirt. That sounds right.

You're in pieces, says the cat, and Hope knows it's right. *In pieces for the loss of me.*

"Yes."

Walter hissed, and became something else, something massive, something shaggy, with claws as long as her arm. Something that hunched forward with bared fangs, and roared loud enough to drown out everything including the ringing in her ears.

I'm nothing special as such, says the cat.

Her hand was a mirror. The boy had put that on her.

Just a manifestation of your own strength.

It was so hungry, her hand.

The blind monster took a few steps forward, swinging its snout around, taking a scent.

He took that out of you, and now you're adrift, pushed and pulled by vagaries and contrivances.

The monster's head stopped moving, and it strode forward.

Let me back in.

"Yes."

Let me back in.

Her hand wanted to sink into her own head. To pull everything out, including the experience of the pulling out. To self-consume, over and over, until . . .

"Hope, hang on. I've almost got him."

Let me back in before he hurts me.

Clarity. "Yes."

Hope lifted her head to the wolf and said

"Go away."

The monster stumbled as it moved, crashed to one knee. A broken-clawed hand slamming down on a slab for support, catching the scrim, tearing it down. Hope took a step back.

"Hope . . . ," it said. "That's not Mike. Mike's gone."

I am right here.

"It's name is Felix. It wants the . . ."

Hope's head hurt. "Felix . . . the cat?"

He lies.

"What? No, it . . ."

"You're confusing me."

"Wait."

"Go away."

The wolf buckled, its head dropped, back heaving.

Yes. Say it again.

The monster looked back over its shoulder, blind as it was. Its lip trembled, not with rage but . . .

"Hope . . . no."

Don't let it hurt me.

"You wanted me to show you . . . how to make birds. Remember?"

A white dove held in small hands. Harder to make than paper . . .

You must protect me.

A dark bedroom. A questing tentacle, in through the back of her head, headed for the bed. Screams.

"G . . ."

"*Hope.* Stay with me."

Now she knew that voice. Remembered that little boy's face. A circus. Clowns. Safety. His name . . . his name was . . .

"I love you."

Felix screamed like he was dying, high and terrible and bestial.

In her head the tentacle ripped, as she remembered it. Felix kept screaming. She clapped her hands to her ears and shouted

"Go away!"

Yes.

The monster looked away, raising its head to the ceiling. The smallest of howls trickled from its lips and—like a collapsing temple—toppled to the ground.

Veiled by the dust of its own passing.

The tiger stood before her, broad and warm and massive. Its breath rolled like thunder in a barrel.

The Anxietoscope no longer felt quite so hungry.

Thank you so very much, said the tiger. *You are tired, no? Perhaps I might carry your load awhile?*

The tiger looked at her and smiled.

"My tiger had blue eyes," Hope said. "Yours are black."

The tiger stopped purring. Hope did not like the way it looked.

Merde, said the tiger.

And Hope fled.

The body lay like some black, fallen thing on the cave floor, face to the shifting ceiling. A delicate piece of quietly thrumming silver lodged beneath his sternum.

In his failing moments Henry remembered coming across something similar to this, maybe 150 years ago, upon first meeting Felix.

But that had been a long, long time ago.

"It is quite interesting what she has chosen to do to this young man, no?"

Henry shifted himself as best he could, got himself sitting up, then leaning against a slab. He was surprised to find Wally there, only a few feet away and fading. The kid looked thin as hell, all twelve feet and doglike. The life was draining out of him, and Henry knew right there and then what had happened. His charge had dismissed him.

"She has chosen," Felix was saying, his back to both of them, playing the critic to Suni's becoming. "To reduce this boy to a single aspect, has she not?" He glanced over his shoulder, hand to chin, an academic seeking the opinion of a colleague. "Intriguing."

Henry turned his head and spat, weakly. His lights were going out. Not long now.

"What did you do to her," Walter said to Henry, sidelong into the dust.

"What was your name way back then anyway," Henry countered. "Back before the Angel tore you up?"

Walter reached out, pulled himself closer to Henry, but there was nothing threatening in it. They were both outbound. This exchange was a last cigarette. "What did you do? Tell me."

"There was a blockage," Henry murmured. "Never seen anything like that before."

"You used the 'scope."

"Had to. Worked out what she was receptive to. Quickest and best way to tell her what she needed to know."

"That blockage you removed, looked like an albino kitten?"

Henry nodded and moved his hand to his wound. What little strength he had left was there, in the instrument. "What was it?"

"Something I gave her," Walter said. "A large part of what was holding her together. A meeting point for her strength and will. A good memory." Walter angled his head. "You destroyed the one thing you wanted her for."

The house could not have been quieter. Hope stood for a long time inside the front door, the street lamp's light filtering through the door glass, feeling cold, keeping her company.

She walked through the living room, past the static eye of the television, into a kitchen smelling of last night's food. Through the window above the sink the backyard was a blue-black otherworld. It was a world from which much had been taken, leaving nothing but shapes where things should be. She walked up the stairs and into her mother's room.

The air was alive with invisible dust, the carpet having never been vacuumed. At the head of the aging water bed hung a black-and-silver portrait, picked up from the supermarket years ago, of a leopard stalking out of darkness. Her mother lay asleep beneath it in a sweater and pants, cover pulled up to her chin, all slack face and downturned mouth, dreaming dreams flat as tap water.

In the days before Walter fell asleep this woman had been happy, if old photographs and rosy reminiscences were anything to go by. Then something very important had been taken away from her foundation, and she had fallen to ruin.

Perhaps, then, they were not so different, mother and daughter. The good seed of Hope's memories had gotten her through the occasional waking nightmare and the long haul of adolescence: the court case, the daily grind, and the forever knowledge of what she had done.

Meeting Walter, his circus, Mike . . . it had told her from a very young age to believe in something greater than herself. Greater than the everyday. Greater than the death-and-taxes hallucination most people chose over all the others.

You're in pieces, the imposter-cat had said. *In pieces for the loss of me.*

And despite the pantomime she knew it to be true. There was a vasty vacuum within her now where once was a stone she could cling to, a library of self-written truth to guide her, and an arsenal with which to forge her way forward. The totem of that place had been a white tiger . . . and now library, land, and totem were all gone. She could remember them as one remembers childhood—almost as someone else's memories—but they had no strength.

They were just shapes where things should be.

Not so different, mother and daughter. Her fate was Hope's, one generation to the next. No getting away from it. Henry hadn't preserved what he had pulled from her. There was no trace of it within the tool used for the long-term storage of such things—a nubbled silver ring—that she could find. It was gone now, as dead as dust. She was undone, incomplete, the end foregone.

She had killed her father, she had killed the man who would replace her father, and she had killed Walter. That's what she'd done. She knew it just as certainly as she knew she had always been more than Hope Witherspoon.

She would return to her brother's room, for one last long look at her other half, and that would be that. Come what may. If there was a next life to be had, perhaps they would have more luck there. She turned away from her mother and found someone standing in the doorway.

"Excuse me," he said with a voice as ponderous as a deep river. "We've never met, but . . . um . . . I was wondering if you could help me."

"So she's got no brakes," Henry said. "I shouldn't have been so itchy. I never did to any recruit, anything I ever made, what I did to her: just dump it all into her head like that, take out the stuff didn't suit. Reason for that. Stupid."

Walter wasn't really listening. The world was narrowing to a point, and the strongest thing he felt was frustration. Before the world was new he had been torn apart—every piece of him, flesh and bone and spirit—and subverted or discarded. His spirit had been split and scattered just as his bones had been divided and repurposed.

An angel does not die. Sundered and confined to Creation, subject to its laws, all of his parts had worked over innumerable lifetimes to be reunited. The bone instruments, they were by nature of their redesign collected together by others; but his soul . . . both pieces of his spirit, subject to natural law, found refuge time and again in flesh, in life after life. Each time, at each death, these people whom Walter and Hope had been gained some inkling of what they truly were. With each rebirth they tried again and again to rejoin, to become whole, and failed.

This, now, was as complete as they had ever been: every piece of him collected in the same place, in the same lifetime. So close, and now it was all over.

Again, failure. But this time for the last time. Hope was undone, pieces of her missing. Lifetimes of slow awakening all for naught. The world would burn before they ever had another chance like this.

The slow-voiced little thing led her by the hand, out of the room, toward her brother's. "I've heard of you. You're old, like Wally is."

Hope nodded. "Yes."

In the room lay a thin boy, old in frame and face, pale hair almost wet with lifelessness. He seemed to have sunken into the bed, become part of it. A ballerina 'stood awkwardly in the corner, head angled, looking at the ground. She shook mechanically, chin and face vibrating back and forth like a machine with stuck gears, or an old person in her final days. Three great slashes divided her chest-cage diagonally. Her box heart spun, gave a little light.

"This is Nimble," Tub said. "She means everything to me. I . . . I think she's broken inside." The little thing looked up into her face. "She doesn't know me. Would you fix her? I'll do anything if you'll please just fix her."

The ballerina heard them. The jittering stopped and her head lifted.

Hope detached the ring from her vest, slipped it over her finger, felt its feelers slide pleasantly through her flesh and coil around her bones en route to the base of her spine. Her mind lit up with an inventory spanning a century of collection; the discarded sections of hundreds of lives made themselves known to her. Memories, hopes, agonies, associations, aversions, contextual matrices, ghosts, loves. Everything Dorian and Henry had ever saved from every person they had ever changed.

The image of Nimble's face went in through Hope's eyes, met up with her name inside Hope's head, and the ring retrieved all Hope needed to know. In an instant she knew Nimble for the creation she now was, the companion Dorian had remade her as, and the human being she had once been.

With the information and material she now had Hope could give that all back to her, unmake Nimble the ballerina and do a decent approximation of re-creating the original, flesh-and-blood person. But after sifting through the memories and material Hope figured there wasn't much there that any human being would want back. In her mind everything lived: a child's bed covered with roses, a small girl dancing for the moon, Tub floating lazily in his river, and the moment when Nimble learned she had so much to understand about being alive.

"I can fix her," Hope said, waking up. "I can fix everything."

Suni had heard her sobbing as she worked on him. He thought that sometimes she had stopped and held him, hugged him from behind, wept against his back, but he couldn't tell. He couldn't move, couldn't feel a thing.

She had clamped something to his skull and he had been filled with a sudden claustrophobia. He had thought about his life and all that he was losing. He had thought about never seeing his mother again, that he'd never tell her he loved her despite everything; he thought about never again tasting cheesecake, about never *ever* seeing the Louvre. He wondered what university would have been like, had he made it. And just before he had heard the sound of blood splashing as his body began disappearing from the outside in, he wondered what he might have been if he had only survived a little longer.

The very last time Suni had seen Hope she had moved before him, blocking out the city, and did something to the silver thing that hugged the curve of his skull. She had kissed him—one last time—and removed the instrument. And then she had left him there, to watch the lights as her work took hold.

He realized he would never own a dog.

He thought of riding a bike, climbing a mountain, swimming an ocean, giving birth, killing a man, saving a life. He thought of destroying a star, eating a world, the taste of a color and the smell of a sound. He knew the addresses of eons and the road map of the universe.

He knew, suddenly, how easy it was to be somewhere.

He grasped, in its entirety, what it meant to be a part of everything.

He knew, completely and precisely, the purpose for which he had been born.

He was a creator. He was, and had always been, a slave to that drive. A scryer viewing life through the facets of diamond water. A thrall to Muse.

Thrall no more. Master and slave were to become one.

His body fell away.

"I knew it from the instruments," Henry said. "Told me as much, in how they felt, how hot they got, the way they sang. Never felt anger that strong in anything. Knew if you laid a finger on 'em before I made you mine, I'd be dirt. That you'd know what I'd been up to, what I'd been keeping you from."

Walter placed broad, thin hands on the ground by his long head, palms down. "You . . ." He pushed, hard as he could, forearms trembling. "Really thought the day would come . . . when I'd touch my own bones and not know what they were?" He lifted his head enough to look Henry in the eye.

"Hope didn't, did she now? All grown up, possibilities winnowed away, conforming to the laws of the world as she has. Given time I could have turned her around. I could have gotten away from all this. She could have torn everything down. Everything. In a way I'd never be able to."

Walter, lying in the dust, stared at Henry through eyes growing dim. "What about . . . everything you said . . . 'freeing us,' all that . . ." Words became infant storms in the dust. "You wanted to see Heaven torn down? Everything else was just an excuse? That's it?"

Henry didn't react, his voice flat as three AM. "Heaven never did me any favors."

"Fascinating," Felix said, man-formed. He placed a foot between Wally's shoulder blades and the wolfhound collapsed back into the dirt. "But now it is time to give up the goods, yes? Time to give them up to someone who knows how best to use them." Booted foot still pushing down on Wally, pressing the air from his frail lungs, he angled forward, arm extended to withdraw the moonshine blade from Henry's dry old heart.

Delicate fingers—cold and filigreed—took Felix by the wrist of that hand, and someone else told him gently, "Um . . . that's not yours." A short, stubby little thing . . . Felix didn't recognize it. One of Dorian's surviving monstrosities, no doubt. Speaking of which, he recognized the hand that held him as belonging to the ballerina. He looked up, and it was her all right, only with a little too much intelligence behind the eyes.

Ah yes. Things had changed.

Oh dear.

Behind him a third individual wove delicate fingers through Felix's dark hair, tracing pleasurably along his scalp. And then they found purchase.

His head angled back, not too hard, Felix beheld young eyes lit old as its master. Hope leaned a fraction closer, sniffed a morsel of air, leaned back a fraction, and told him: "I know what you're made of."

Her one hand was silver, the other ringed with mercury; her hair as fire of unnatural hue. Eyes beheld him like stars, wet and dark and mythological.

Felix took one last look at the instrument at his fingertips, and smiled apologetically. "I am what I am."

"*You are undone.*"

Walter was flat and dry as paper. His bones were dust and honeycomb. What came next lay waiting.

Hands gently turned him over, feeling like a memory of feeling. Fingers smoothed the hairless skin of his long brow. His head was a roadkill skull. He was close to home now.

"Wake up for me, Walter."

There was music: singing, high and soft.

Wally opened his eyes, beheld her face through a cataract fog. The hand with which she stroked his head was cool and shining. It sang. Her chest was a mass of starlight.

"It's us . . . ," he said. "Look at us."

Hope nodded. "It's us, Walter. We're almost done."

"Good."

"Tub is here. He will tend to you. You need to remain with us just a little while longer."

"All right."

Hope gently lowered Walter's head to the ground, a torn-down veil for a pillow. She got to her feet and walked over to where Henry sat, the Unblade protruding downward from just beneath his sternum, where she had left it.

She got down on her haunches and said his name. Henry lifted his chin from his shoulder and looked her in the eye. "You're here," he murmured. "Wally's not looking so good."

"We'll be fine." As she spoke she could see Henry's condition improving. Being close to the tools again breathed life into him. "I need to take this," she said.

Henry nodded. "Yeah. I guess you do." He took the Unblade in hand, and swiftly pulled—said "ah" like a man settling into a soft bed—and handed it to her. As he did his gloved hand trembled a little.

Hope curled her fingers about the instrument, held it, and settled it among its kin.

Henry looked about the cold, airy place he had called home for so long. "Can I ask you something? I figure you're in a position to know."

"Yes?"

"All that stuff I was told, about God and Samael and all of that. What's the truth of it?"

"Well," Hope began . . . and then thought better of it. Instead she leaned in and said, "Here." Hope raised her silver-taloned hand and made a pistolfinger between them, with the barrel pointed at Henry's head. She lowered her forehead onto the thumb-spike and gently slid her finger in between Henry's eyes. "See for yourself."

Henry didn't struggle or flinch, only closed his eyes.

And all his answers came at once.

The doctor gasped a lifetime's worth, eyes wide—blue—mouth

agog. Breath coming in hard little gasps; tiny, shocked sips. Hands were claws, digging ten trenches to twin points.

Eyes wide on Hope's knuckles before his face, but seeing somewhere else entirely, he slowly relaxed. Shoulders lowered. Breathing resumed.

Hope opened her eyes, slid her forehead from atop her thumb, and removed the 'scope from Henry's mind.

She lowered her hand to her lap and looked at his face.

Henry's mind and sight were still in that other place. Seeing him like this, Hope could almost see the man he must have once been: lean-faced, hard-eyed, and passionate to distraction. This was a good way to leave him. He closed his eyes, held it all for a moment, like praying, then opened them.

"That's pretty good," he said, and left it at that.

"Will you be all right?" Hope said. "You can't go until we do, and Walter doesn't have long."

Henry hitched one corner of his mouth. "You go on now."

Hope said *yes* with her eyes and got to her feet.

She turned back to Walter and Nimble and Tub. In a minute or two her brother would be nothing but bones. She crouched and lifted him effortlessly. The wolf was gone. She was holding a child. "Tub . . ."

The little ogre flexed his fingers around Nimble's.

"It's all right," the ballerina said. "You'd best hurry up."

"It was nice to meet you," Tub said. "Tell Wally I said good luck."

Hope nodded, held her brother tight. So long for this.

And they were gone.

In the moments before Hope left, Henry closed his coat about his legs, got to his feet, and sat himself down on the slab. For the first time in a century he wished he had a drink.

Nimble was there, holding hands with a squat little guy. Henry remembered him from the contexts and imprints and loves he had taken from her decades ago. Couldn't remember his name.

Hope disappeared, carrying her brother, and the speed of Henry's own vanishing surprised even him.

"Hey," he said, barely loud enough to get their attention. Nimble and her friend turned their faces to him. "Listen . . ." The world was fading. His soul rushed to catch its closing eye. "You see her again . . ."

"Yes . . . ?" the little guy said.

"Tell her to shut this place down."

Hope stood in a vaulted circular chamber, beneath a dome of green glass, between wide rows of high bookshelves. It was night. She held Walter close in the seconds he had left, and breathed her last.

The Anxietoscope lunged through her forehead up to the wrist and kept on going. Hope told it to feed on everything, everything it could get, and to not stop. It took her entire being into itself in a second . . . until all that remained was Hope's experience of being consumed, and the 'scope consumed that, until all that remained was Hope's experience of being consumed, and the 'scope consumed that, until all that remained . . .

She and it became both the trawler and the trawled, drawing from her own mind and feeding it back in a never-ending cycle spiraling inward, self-consuming, imploding.

Her body buckled abruptly in on itself, enclosing Walter as she held him close, devouring, twisting like a plastic doll in a bonfire. Hope crashed and spun in on herself, an envelope for her brother and the instruments of angel bone, and in a split moment they had—sister, brother, bones—coiled away to absolutely nothing.

They were gone.

The process didn't stop there.

The dome blows out as books turn to birds, and every moment collides at once.

Tomorrow morning a young man wakes with a sore jaw and finds a limited-edition trading card propped on his bedside table.

Victoria Witherspoon wakes beneath a black-and-silver print of a leopard. Somehow she knows that, in the next room, her son has died. She lies there, pressed down by an impossible weight of grief . . . but feeling it.

Across the world a ballerina sits by a brown river, hands clasped at her waist. In the water a rotund little ogre blows fountains as he drifts slowly counterclockwise downstream.

Lost somewhere in a London cemetery is the grave of a small girl. For the first time in a century and a half, fresh roses have been laid upon it.

There is a many-roomed place that shares a wall with yours. A thin man sits slumped upon a slab of earth, palms up, chin on his chest. He is veiled by slow gossamer. Within his coat, stars no longer shine.

In 1840 a redheaded man and a beautiful woman share an apple on Boston's Smoker's Common.
    When no one is looking, they kiss.

Somewhere beyond time a creature of impossible beauty stands, watching, stroking a glass-eyed leopard upon a bed of tulips.

Through it all she hears the Angel.
    She is all that remains in the world that knows of its existence. Without her, it does not.
    She ensures it sees all she has just seen.
    She ensures it feels all that she has just felt.
    She ensures it knows this has been the last meal it will ever receive.
    Without her it will never be free.

The flesh of her fingers tapers to silver.

Every sound in her new ears forms but one word. The Angel's voice says,

No . . .

She reaches into her own mind and plucks out a single piece of knowledge.

The knowledge that the Angel exists.

Silence.

LATER

*P*EOPLE CHANGE. THE INTERESTING ONES, AT LEAST. YOU start life as one thing, and become something else. Upgrade or downgrade, it's all change—it's all *vital*—and besides . . . up and down is all relative to the angle at which your head's been twisted.

Girls want to be cats, usually. It was when she didn't that she first thought something was different, something had changed. She wants to be something else. Something big, panting, weight on the balls of her feet. Strong enough to penetrate a sternum.

She doesn't want to be a cat. Her coat is empty of starlight and no longer sings. She has silver bones.

She finds a litter of pups in an alleyway. One survivor, lost, pink, blind, and lonely. She feels pity. She takes it and strokes it. Words of comfort, but it mews at her touch. She puts it back amid the cold coils of its siblings, but what she leaves behind has sight and wings and will be able to take care of itself.

Standing here, dressed as she is (with her ragged coat and tangled hair), she is the embodiment of this forgotten, rain-slick laneway. She would appear to any passerby as would the equivalent spirit of any wood, as any sprite, as the embodiment of that place.

In this moment she has the power of immediacy.

In this moment she is God of this one-lane world.

In this moment she is perfect.

ACKNOWLEDGMENTS

Dmetri Kakmi, editor and champion, without whom none of this would have ever been possible.

Sarah Graves, my best friend, my most brilliant critic, and my life's love, for falling to Earth with me and dusting me off afterward. I love you massively.

My parents, Doug and Nardine Rogers, with love.

My fantastic agent, Howard Morhaim, for taking me on.

Tim Mak, editor of the American edition. Thanks for all your work, and for believing in the manuscript.

K. J. Bishop, with much thanks.

Holly Ball, for allowing me to use her song "Playground" in the book.

Patrick O'Duffy, Kate Devitt, Andrew Serong, Jon Swabey, Damien Wise, Haydn Black, and Annette Mattes for invaluable feedback.

Barbara "Barbarella" Welton, for friendship, for the hours of drunken conversation in the gutters and alleys outside Revelations, for the mention that changed everything, for all the feedback, and for being there in more ways than I can list.

Ronald Jones, for never failing to pick up the things I miss or offer something brilliant, and never shying away from reading yet another draft. Thank you.

The other two members of The Basement—Andy MacLean and Peter Noonan—for years of abusive therapy administered in the firm belief that subtlety subx.

Gary Crew, for the First Break.

Suzanne Smith and Erin O'Hara for The Favor.

The Rev. Richard Gracia, for historical advice and mailing me all that coffee.

Rebecca Kearney for kindly taking all those photos at mates rates.

The Drunk Poets Society, Melbourne, for giving me a chance to read some of this stuff to a crowd. *Carpe Vino*.

Brandy Leonard, who's been around from the start and probably knows where all this comes from.

Special thanks to Associate Professor Peter F. J. Ryan, head of rheumatology, Alfred Hospital, Melbourne, for the very kind help regarding coma patients. I hope I've used your information accurately. Any errors are entirely my own.

And—last but definitely not least—Sian Softly, stalwart friend, for loaning me her couch and timesharing her computer while I was in Brisbane, and for always being there when it counts. You're a saint.

CAMERON ROGERS lives in Melbourne. *The Music of Razors* is his first novel.

He's been an itinerant theater student, a stage director, a stand-up comic, a motion-capture model for an elf who needed food badly, and had a question mark instead of a photo in his high school yearbook. He spent three months cutting up vegetables in a stainless-steel cubicle beneath a shopping mall in the company of a defecting Soviet weightlifter, and almost got suckered into working at what turned out to be a yakuza-run all-gay bowling alley in Kyoto. His last Real Job was with the crime management unit of the Queensland Police Service.

He also writes books for children under the pen-name Rowley Monkfish.

He can be contacted via his official website at www.cameron-rogers.com.

ABOUT THE TYPE

This book was set in Electra, a typeface designed for Linotype by W. A. Dwiggins, the renowned type designer (1880–1956). Electra is a fluid typeface, avoiding the contrasts of thick and thin strokes that are prevalent in most modern typefaces.